A FOG FILLED
RELKIN'S MIND . . .

"Come now," the beautiful maiden called to him.

"But I can't, I'm . . ." he began, but in the next moment he couldn't remember exactly what he wanted to say. All he could focus on was the elf maid. She ran from him, then stopped to lean against a tree.

He caught up, stood there breathing hard beside her. She slipped away, her hair glinting under the moonlight. He stumbled forward, feet uncertain. Always she seemed to float just a few feet beyond his grasp. Never had he wanted anything so much.

And then he tripped and fell to his knees. A net dropped over him. He pushed to get back on his feet and the net tightened. He glimpsed a face with overlarge features and bright protruding eyes. Big stocky hands pulled the net tight.

The spell was gone. All thought of the elf maiden vanished. Relkin, awake at last, realized what was happening. He was being abducted by dwarves!

DRAGONS OF WAR

Christopher Rowley

A ROC BOOK

ROC
Published by the Penguin Group
Penguin Books USA Inc., 375 Hudson Street,
New York, New York 10014, U.S.A.
Penguin Books Ltd, 27 Wrights Lane,
London W8 5TZ, England
Penguin Books Australia Ltd, Ringwood,
Victoria, Australia
Penguin Books Canada Ltd, 10 Alcorn Avenue,
Toronto, Ontario, Canada M4V 3B2
Penguin Books (N.Z.) Ltd, 182–190 Wairau Road,
Auckland 10, New Zealand

Penguin Books Ltd, Registered Offices:
Harmondsworth, Middlesex, England
First published by Roc,
an imprint of Dutton Signet,
a division of Penguin Books USA Inc.

First Printing, November, 1994
10 9 8 7 6

To Veronica Chapman
with thanks for her help and advice.

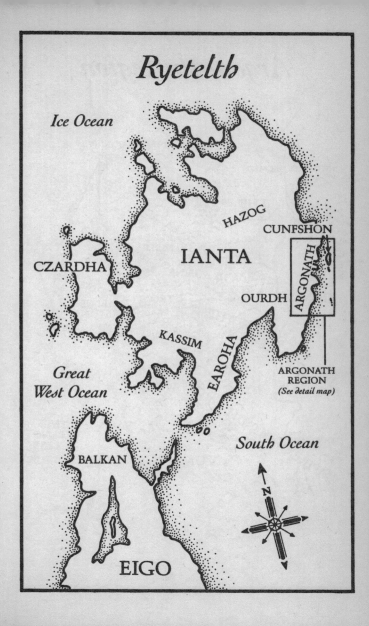

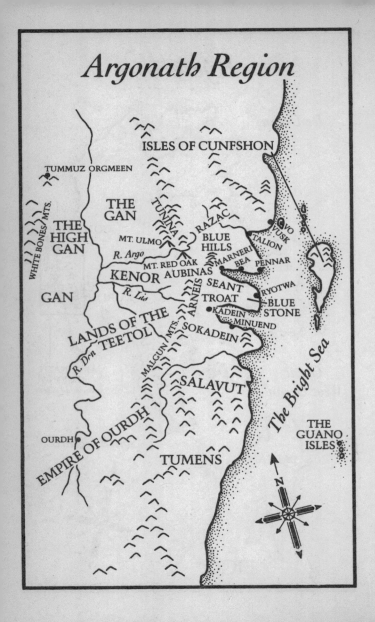

CHAPTER ONE

The sun burned down on the heart of the continent, the ancient land of Padmasa, but there was no warmth in it. Instead a chill wind from the northwest sucked the heat out of the day, leaving the dun-brown hills and withered meadows of lichen as mute testimony to its power. This was a place ruled by winds. A glance at the fantastic shapes carved from the rock pinnacles could tell the traveler that in a second.

Sandstorms blew in from the west, snowstorms came from the north, and desiccating chinooks came down from the mountains to the south. Vegetation of any sort struggled to survive here, and yet this was the center of the greatest power in the world.

Coming over the pass at Kakalon, looking down into the widening valley, the magician Thrembode the New saw the mass of the Square clearly outlined on the dominating, central rise. The jarring straight lines and white stone informed the world that this was the work of men. The smooth-sided walls, two hundred feet high, frowned down like bluffs of pure adamant. The sight chilled the magician and awakened a deep foreboding. This was a place where only wild goats would choose to live, and yet there stood the great slab, one mile on each side, a single vast building thronged by more than a million people, all of them servants of the power that ruled here.

The magician marveled to himself, for he knew that the Square, for all its majesty was but the anteroom to the Halls of Padmasa, which lay deep below, carved into the rock of the craton by an army of slaves, none of whom had survived the ordeal. Indeed, their very bones had been ground into the mortar holding together the stones.

Coming through the pass and into the valley brought Thrembode back into the full force of the wind, which tore at his clothing. He shivered as he fastened his coat all the way up and tightened the belt. It was always cold here, one reason the great ones liked it. The wind shrieked as it honed the rocks into bonelike shapes, eroding the world's flesh and exposing its very vertebrae.

Thrembode thought of the coming ordeal, and would've prayed to the gods if he thought it would give him strength. After what he'd seen through his service to the Masters, however, the magician could no longer believe in gods. Gods would have stopped the Masters, before they became veritable gods themselves. And no thing, no one, could stop them now.

His horse continued down the slope on the great road. Nine of these roads converged here, two hundred feet wide, all running perfectly straight across the valley and up to the Square. Caravans of camels and mules, bearing tribute from half the world to the buried city of the Masters, crowded these roads.

Thrembode approached the East Gate. A long line of slaves trudged ahead of him, Ourdhi men, chained at the neck, driven by the lash of burly imps in the black uniform of Padmasa. Slaves were necessary to every function within the strange city of the Square. It was, indeed, a city like no other in the history of the world Ryetelth, for it was city as ideological fact, with no natural reason for its existence in this cold desert.

On either side, before the gate, stretched row upon row of gibbets. Most were empty, but on a few set close to the road, rotting bodies swayed in the chill wind, a constant reminder that in Padmasa the punishment for most crimes was death. Drawn up by the gate was a regiment of savage-looking imps, armed with scimitars and shields. These imps had the heads of apes, squat manlike bodies and powerful legs. Lurking nearby, he knew, were teams of great, nine-foot-tall trolls, ready to back up the imps in moments if required.

Thrembode was waved through the great gate and into the teeming world of the Square where his pass was stamped as obsequious officials bowed. He was a magician, an Adept and a member of the inner hierarchy. Passed through the security screen, the magician went on down the central internal avenue of the Square.

Above the avenue, the roof rose two hundred feet high and the walls on either side were filled with windows. On the street were shops and storehouses. It was a bustling scene, filled with hundreds of thousands of busy workers, attending to countless menial and clerical tasks. They provided the support structure, even the very feeding, for the real city, which lurked below, far underground. Thrembode's business lay there, in the cold warrens of the Tetralobe.

In the heart of the Square was an empty space open to the sky. In the center were the statues of the Great Ones, the Five. Each was a hundred feet tall and sculpted as a giant of heroic build and noble visage. They dominated the space, ruling it just as they ruled everything in Padmasa.

At the corners of the open space were four distinct towers, each connected to the main structure at every floor by covered corridors that stuck out like ribs joined to a backbone. These were the staircases to the underground city.

Below, down many turns of these stairs, cut into solid rock, lay four distinct labyrinths of passages and caverns, with rooms beyond number. The four labyrinths or lobes were thrust out in a cross on the points of the compass. They were quite separate from one another except for the central hub where they met in the Nexus Halls. The stairs connected the Nexus Halls to the Square and the outside world.

This underground world was the Tetralobe, the heart of the empire of the Masters, an empire of fear, an empire that bestrode Ryetelth and threatened to overwhelm all opposition and bring the entire world under its dominion.

From this place went instructions to a dozen provinces of the power, including such vast fortresses as that of Axoxo in the White Bone Mountains. From here came and went an army of spies and their messengers. From here went messages for men of influence in every land, messages to win favor or demand it. One way or another, the Masters of Padmasa were able to reach any ruler's ear and command his attention.

Thrembode descended the red staircase and climbed down the two hundred steps to the Nexus Hall on the fourth level. His pass was checked by a team of specially bred imps with heads like those of weasels and black, beady, inhuman eyes. They examined him carefully with those eyes, but found nothing to concern them.

He was directed with curt gestures to the exit to the South Lobe, which housed the offices of the Intelligence Apparatus.

He was aware of a fierce scrutiny on all sides, and an underlying field of tension on the psychic plane. With a tremor he realized that his presence on the psychic plane had been noted by those who created the field, Mesomasters in the cells far below in the Deeps. To them he was but a small blip, a young node of powers, infinitesimal compared to the entities below themselves, but they had taken notice of him nonetheless and passed on the news to the greater minds below in the Deeps.

The Deeps, the very name brought an uncontrollable creep of the flesh, a raising of the hairs on his body. In those hidden sepulchres, under dim light, dwelt the Great Ones, and it was there you went if you were to be interviewed. It was an experience no man ever forgot.

On this occasion, however, Thrembode's first interview was with Administrator Gru-Dzek, a tall, hatchet-faced man with grey hair shaved to stubble. He wore the black robe of the Intelligence Apparatus, with purple fringe and a single slash of scarlet to denote rank.

Thrembode was shown a bare, uncomfortable chair, set before a massive desk. Administrator Gru-Dzek took out a scroll, unrolled it, and studied it for a long minute. Then he clapped his hands. The door opened and a mutilated slave, blinded, tongue removed, came in and set up a scribe's equipment at a small table in the corner.

Administrator Gru-Dzek looked up and fixed the magician with pale, unfriendly eyes. He cleared his throat.

"Magician Thrembode, this interview will be recorded in the official record. I must therefore note officially that you are under provisional sentence of termination."

"Termination?" said Thrembode, aghast.

"In the light of your several failures, it was deemed an advisable sentence."

"Several failures?"

"In Kadein, you allowed an entire network to be rolled up by the witches. In Marneri, you bungled a well-prepared assassination attempt. Our choice as heir for the Marneri throne was subsequently killed by the witches. To compound this disaster, you then led a war party of witches directly to Tummuz Orgmeen and allowed them to destroy the Doom there."

Thrembode felt his toes clutch at the soles of his boots.

"Led them? Allowed them," he sputtered. "This is a mistake. This is a grotesque rendering of events."

Administrator Gru-Dzek stared at him coolly.

"Is it not true that the Doom had ordered your arrest?"

"I did my best to warn the Doom, but it would not listen! It had grown contemptuous of all men by then."

"You criticize the fallen Doom?"

"It fell, didn't it? It was flawed."

The administrater's eyes widened. That was a bold statement for the record. It implied criticism of they who had made the Doom.

"In Ourdh last year, you were part of another disaster."

"I must protest. The witches created some sort of counterstroke to the life-giving spell used to invigorate the mud men myrmidons. The Mesomaster Gog Zagozt was perhaps out of his depth in dealing with the witches. I tried to advise him, but he would not listen to me. Of course, I have had considerable experience with them."

"Yes, you have. Perhaps a little too much. You have been scheduled for a detailed inquisition. It must be determined whether they have addled you or turned you traitor."

Thrembode felt his face flush with fury.

"I can reliably inform you that they have not. There is no need for such an inquisition."

Administrator Gru-Dzek smiled thinly. "That is not for you to decide, Magician. I am sure you understand."

Thrembode shrugged, and offered a wan little smile.

"I will be happy to face the inquisition."

The administrater's smile cracked for a moment, then he recovered himself.

"Good. Now, as I was saying, this sentence of termination is provisional. You have an opportunity to keep it that way."

"I am so glad."

"You have a certain knowledge of the cities and the countryside of the Argonath."

"Yes, of course, I have lived in most of the nine cities."

"And so you have been chosen to accompany General Lukash on an expedition."

Thrembode's eyebrows rose. An expedition? With a general?

The administrater made a scarcely perceptible signal, and the door opened again. In came a squat, full-bellied man in the black and maroon military uniform of Padmasa, but bearing a white stripe on the shoulders. His face had the consistency of boiled leather.

Thrembode rose and saluted the general with his palm out, hand thrust out straight in front of him.

"General Lukash," said Administrater Gru-Dzek.

Lukash nodded, but did not return the salute. His features were utterly impassive, walled off within the leathery carapace.

They were all seated.

The administrater began to outline the mission ahead. As he spoke, Thrembode realized with a certain amount of awe that this time the Great Masters intended to throw their full strength against the upstart cities of the eastern coast. Nothing would be left, not one stone atop another, except for the gibbets and the pyramids of skulls.

CHAPTER TWO

It was Summer month in the land of Kenor, the time of flowers. The wild poppies were in bloom along the hedgerows and on the hillsides. A bumper crop of winter wheat had been harvested, and turnips, rye, oats, and barley were ripening in the fields. Fruit growers in every vale were ecstatic about the possibilities of the harvest. In fact, farmers all across Kenor were enjoying one of the best years in a century.

An atmosphere of celebration was evident throughout the province, from the cheerful singing in the fields to the unusually generous sacrifices placed on the altars in the temples to the Great Mother.

And thus, under blue skies and bright sunshine, people gathered from every quarter to the summer games, which this year were being hosted by the Marneri Second Legion at Fort Dalhousie.

The games were already a success. A crowd of nine thousand had packed the stands to watch an unusually strong field compete on the first day of the All-Kenor Archery Championship. In the evening there had been singing and dancing while the craft fair did roaring business along the road from the town to the fort.

Competitors from the other legions in Kenor, plus contingents of troops who'd found a way, by hook or by crook, to get to Dalhousie to support their own, thronged the alleys and avenues of the fort. A lot of beer had been sold, and the afternoon was but getting into its stride. The green outside the fort was gay with colors and loud with the cries of barkers and the general rumble of the crowds.

Over it all came another sound, the distinctive clang of sword on sword, steel whining off steel, accompanied by the rhythmic thwack of heavy shields clashing. Every so often came a thunder of applause. Indeed, while the archery and athletic competitions were very popular, it was the dragon fights that always drew the biggest crowds of all.

One on one, the best of the great dragons were matched against each other with specially dulled blades. They wore heavy armor, padded helmets, and chain mail over their tails. As a result, they were a little slower than normal and less inclined to wield the tail mace.

Still, it was a mighty spectacle, and the crowds always loved to see them fight. Great beasts ten- to twelve-foot-tall, weighing up to five tons, pranced and bounced around each other in the ring with whirling swords and massive shields in play. In truth, the dragons enjoyed it as much as anyone else. Something in the spirit of the wyverns of Argonath was naturally combative. They liked to fight, and they liked to watch the fighting, too.

Of course, this was not like true combat. This was for sport, and under all the armor, the dragons were scarcely visible and seemed sometimes more like mountains of metal plate than actual living things. But the crowds knew the strengths and weaknesses of every champion, and were constantly uttering opinions and questions.

Would Gasholt of the Ryotwa Legion be champion for the second year in a row? What was the status of the strange, wild dragon that served in the Marneri Second Legion? And what about the legendary Bazil Broketail? Ever since his exploits in Tummuz Orgmeen, his reputation had been growing. Could he possibly live up to it? The previous summer, the Marneri Second had been away, in the distant land of Ourdh, and so the broketail dragon had missed the summer games. Now he would be tested by the likes of Gasholt the Great. Aficionados of the games were eagerly anticipating that particular bout.

The afternoon was young, but already the dust flew in the combat rings, of which there were four at this stage. Each was surrounded by a tight circle of wooden bleachers, thrust up far too high in the air and packed with thousands of spectators. Along with the noise and the rising dust came the smell of dragon as the wyverns exercised themselves at combat.

The bouts were relatively brief, ten minutes in all, with a break at the fifth minute. The winner was decided by a panel of six judges, all dragonboys, drawn by lottery. They scored for stroke combinations, touches, falls, and stumbles. Thrusts and slashes to the head were forbidden.

In the second ring waited Bazil of Quosh, known widely as "the broketail" dragon because of the strange angle at which the end of his tail jutted out and away. So different was it that it seemed almost the tail of some other kind of creature. Legend had it that this bizarre tail was the result of witchcraft.

His opponent that day was Burthong of the 33rd Kadein. Burthong was a mighty brasshide, a dragon at the bulkier end of the scale.

Normally a heavyweight brasshide would not be in the sword competitions; they were just too slow. Lean leather-backs, gristles, and hard greens dominated the competition.

Relkin, Bazil's dragonboy, had chortled when he'd read the match lists.

"You're through the first round. They've given you the Kadein brasshide."

Bazil had not been so sanguine himself.

"Burthong? They match me against Burthong?"

"Right," said Relkin. "Burthong, he's a brass, must weigh four tons. You'll take him easily."

Bazil was not so sure.

"This is an unusual dragon, not like most of the heavies. He is said to be pretty quick with the sword."

Relkin couldn't believe his ears, or so he professed.

"You're talking about a brass, Baz. He's twice your weight, or almost, a brass! Big lumbering brute, you'll be dancing around him."

"Fool dragonboy. Brasshides are usually slow, I admit, but this one is different. I have heard all about him. He has a powerful backhand trap, he spins well, and he's sharp with tail mace."

Relkin had suppressed any further comment. It was ridiculous. Why they had even bothered with this matchup, he couldn't imagine.

Now, as he watched Burthong emerge from the opposing dragon door, he noted with misgiving the ease with which the Kadein champion moved his bulk. Burthong drew the dulled, practice blade and made a few smooth moves. The sword whistled through the air. Burthong next worked the kinks out of his tail, slicing the tail mace through the air to make it sing. Despite himself, Relkin was impressed.

"Watch the tail mace," he said to his dragon.

Bazil did not answer, having already noted the facility with the tail weapon displayed by his opponent. He hefted the dulled sword, a clumsy thing, standard legion issue. It had none of the snap, the crackling life that his own blade, Ecator, possessed so fully.

Burthong stood ready. The cornets blew. Bazil stepped forward carefully. The brasshide was huge, half a head taller, and considerably wider than the leatherback.

They circled slowly, swords ready, eyeing each other carefully.

Bazil was about to try a ruse involving a low cut at the legs and a simultaneous strike with the tail mace when Burthong moved instead. Tail mace came around with a shriek, and Baz lifted his shield to deflect it. Burthong's sword was in motion, and Baz parried, only just in time. Burthong's arm was strong, the next blow came quickly. Baz was on the defensive, the Kadein brass lived up to his reputation.

Burthong came on with an overhand while he sought to crack aside Bazil's shield with his own. The shield charge was as strong as any Baz had ever felt; he came off the soles of his huge feet for a moment and then felt himself driven down an inch or two by the power in Burthong's overhand.

He had to do something to get off the defensive or he would be battered to the ground by the bigger, stronger dragon. Bazil spun, whipping his tail mace across Burthong's front, earning himself a yard's clearance when he faced Burthong once again. The brasshide came on, a little ponderously it was true, but still quickly. Bazil shifted sideways and tried a combination, a waist-high cut, an overhand, and then a back overhand. Burthong met him each time and then surged, cracking into his shield and swinging his own overhand and almost getting through for a shoulder score.

Baz evaded, ducked away, and felt Burthong's side trap cut clip the edge of his shield. But for the luck of his trailing shield being there, it would have taken his legs out from under him. Truly this was an unusual brasshide!

Their swords rang out again as Burthong pressed him. Baz could not regain the initiative and was growing desperate, backpedaling around the arena. Again and again Burthong's sword slammed down, and the Marneri dragon could only parry and retreat.

Burthong had a very fluid combination involving alternate side cuts, overhands both forehand and backhand, and a shattering shield blow. Twice Baz was hurled backward by this combo. Now Burthong slipped into it again. This time the leatherback was ready; he stopped the side cut with the shield and trapped it by surging forward and getting inside Burthong's reach. Bazil's tail mace cracked over and rang off the brasshide's helmet, and he shoved the bigger dragon back, getting him off balance. As Burthong scrambled, Baz's sword struck home and scored on the side plates.

Relkin crowed with delight, his fears forgotten. The Kadein brasshide had met his match in a leatherback from Quosh.

A few moments later, the five-minute bell rang. Bazil stomped over to the bench where Relkin gave him some water and whispered advice.

The dragon only half listened. In truth, his head was swimming and his arm was weary. It was a damned good thing he'd scored a full point, because he was sure he would give one up before the end of this bout.

"Go Baz, you've got him, take him now!"

Bazil murmured a mild curse on all dragonboys and their misplaced confidences, and returned to the fray.

It went much as the first half had, Burthong was a mighty opponent and his swordplay was uncommonly quick for any dragon, let alone one as heavy as a brasshide. Bazil spent much of the time on the defensive. He scored again with the tail mace, ringing a half point off the helmet and then took a blow from Burthong's tail mace, which whipped around unexpectedly and caught him on the side of his helmet, almost knocking it off.

Baz stood back for a moment to clear his head, and Burthong charged and struck him so heavy a blow with the shield that the leatherback was knocked right off his feet and fell with a shattering crash to the ground.

He rolled and struggled to regain his feet. Burthong was coming. He got his shield up just in time to ward off the next blow, which would have finished the bout, and swung his sword at knee height, which made Burthong retreat. Baz got to his feet and staggered away backward. Burthong came on.

They clashed. Burthong hissed in his ear.

"This dragon thinks the famous Broketail thought this would be an easy bout."

They spun away, both attempting side traps with the sword, which rapped harmlessly off trailing shields. Their tail maces rang together and then Bazil's strange, broken tail showed its strength, looping over Burthong's and hammering the brasshide on the shoulder and the side of the helmet.

As they spun past again, Bazil snapped his jaws and said, "This dragon know there's no such thing as an easy bout."

Burthong swung a backhand return and then clobbered the leatherback with the edge of his shield. Baz reeled, saw stars for a moment. Burthong struck down, and he only barely deflected the cut and evaded. Burthong came on with a snort of anticipated triumph. Baz fought him off with desperate defensive maneuvers, and then at last Burthong beat aside his sword and struck down and scored a shoulder point.

It was a powerful blow. Baz was hurt, his sword arm felt numb. It was all he could do to keep backing away and defending with the shield and tail mace.

The score was even now with a minute remaining. If they were tied, they would fight an extra time period. Bazil looked forward to such a prospect with dread.

Carefully he moved the shoulder and the arm, but no bones were broken. The numbness was lifting. He released his breath in a long hiss. There was still some fight in this dragon.

They clashed together, belly to belly, then their blades bit into each other with a flash of sparks.

"I think you are tiring, Broketail," said Burthong.

"We'll have to see about that," said Bazil, who detected a hint of wishful thinking in the brasshide's words.

Another series of combinations was played out, and now Baz noticed that mighty Burthong was definitely slowing down. Bazil girded himself for one last effort.

Once more Burthong swung in, went shield to shield, and drove Bazil back. The brasshide gave an exultant hiss and lurched on with sword descending. Baz ducked away, swung back, and scored a definite point on the hip plate.

Burthong gave a grunt of dismay and stared at the leatherback with a mixture of rage and apprehension. Burthong was indeed slowing down. Ten minutes of this was more than even he could maintain.

But he had to keep the initiative, he couldn't allow the

smaller, faster dragon to capture that. So Burthong hurled himself forward once more and swung into a fearsome set of forehand blows, trying to crush the Broketail's guard.

Bazil deflected them easily, and ducked a vicious swipe of the tail mace while his own slipped in and slammed the visor shut on Burthong's helmet.

The Kadein champion gave a cry of rage and renewed his efforts, but now he was getting wild and breathless. Bazil evaded him easily and scored another glancing point off the hip.

The cornets blew to end the bout. Sustained applause rolled around the seat sections.

Bazil and Burthong met in the center. Burthong had a wounded look in his eyes.

"I cannot believe this. I was sure to defeat you, Broketail."

"You fought well Burthong, you are definitely the quickest brass I ever met."

Burthong's pride was partly redeemed.

"It was an honor to fight you, Broketail, though I think I would do better the next time."

Bazil trudged back to Relkin, who was urgently calculating the point totals. It was going to be very close. A lot depended on how much the judges scored for Bazil's fall and roll.

"Should be enough there for a win," muttered Relkin, as Baz took a seat and picked up a pail of water and drained it right off. At that moment he would have had to admit he didn't really care if he'd won or lost. It would only get harder from here on.

Relkin immediately removed the shoulder armor and the pad beneath.

"Nasty blow," he murmured as his skillful fingers explored the bruised area and checked for scale damage.

Other dragons came by to murmur a few words to the Broketail. First was the mighty wild dragon, the formidable Purple Green of Hook Mountain, a behemoth of nearly five tons, bigger than any brasshide but not as bulky. He clasped forearms with Bazil and muttered something in dragon speech. Then came the silky-green freemartin Alsebra, a newcomer to the 109th Marneri Dragons.

"Good swordplay, Broketail, you fenced him well."

"I thank you for that, Alsebra. He was very quick for a brass."

All the while Relkin looked across the ring to the panel of judges who sat in a darkened booth. As Relkin knew, no one from the 109th was on the panel, so he knew he could not expect any automatic bias in their favor.

The decision did not come down quickly, with the crowd on tenterhooks and eerily silent, they all waited while the panel of dragonboys debated the value of certain scores and tabulated point totals again and again.

At last the curtain was drawn, and the decision read aloud. Baz was adjudged the winner, by a mere half point.

Relkin breathed a huge sigh of relief. Five silver pieces were safe. In fact, they would now be ten silver pieces when he caught up with Swane of Revenant. It had been a damned close thing, however. His dragon had been sorely tested.

With a groan, Bazil hauled himself to his feet, and with Relkin in the lead, they headed toward the front gate of Fort Dalhousie. The crowds bustled about them in pursuit of food and ale and seats for the next bout. Here and there citizens came up to see the famous Broketail dragon at close range, something Bazil put up with good-naturedly.

Suddenly Relkin observed an all too-familiar angular figure striding across their path. He came to attention. Bazil too came to a halt as Dragon Leader Turrent came up.

Turrent's dark eyes had a harder glare than normal, and his brow furrowed at the sight of Relkin. The dragon leader had suffered a loss. Had he, perhaps, been betting against the broketail dragon? Against a dragon from his own unit?

There was no love lost between Relkin and Dragon Leader Digal Turrent. Indeed, it was fair to say that there was little love in the whole unit for the dragon leader who had arrived in the early spring and brought to an end the more relaxed rule of Dragoneer Hatlin. Hatlin had been promoted and sent downstream to Fort Kenor with a new dragon squad.

Turrent had been something of a shock to the 109th, which had never suffered a dragon leader before and had grown used to a relaxed attitude to spit and polish. The 109th concentrated on other things, and was not at all relaxed about training and sword practice. Dragonboys concentrated on the health of their charges, which included their mental health, and not on the gloss of their fitments.

Dragon Leader Turrent, on the other hand, was very concerned about the glow of burnished breastplates, helmets, sword hilts, scabbards, and any and all other metal. He was equally concerned with the moral health of his command. He decreed soon after arrival that the 109th drank too much beer: near-beer and ginger beer. He announced that he would enforce the laws against gambling. It was feared that Turrent was a secret member of the puritanical Dianine sect. The 109th had not been a happy squadron for weeks.

"Sir," Relkin saluted. Turrent was one of those officers who insisted on salutes and all formalities.

Turrent returned the salute, but with ill grace.

"So, Dragoneer Relkin, we were very lucky today, I think. Perhaps more sword practice is needed?" There was clear hostility in the dragon leader's voice.

"The Kadein brass was very quick, sir. Fortunately, our leatherback was quicker."

Bazil disliked Turrent so much as anyone and refrained from saying anything. Turrent looked up for a moment, met those big black eyes, and looked away.

"Hmmm, yes, so you say." Turrent stalked off.

Relkin watched him go with misgivings. Turrent played favorites, and Relkin knew he was never going to be one of those. He wondered what it was exactly that Turrent hated about him so much.

All they knew about the dragon leader was that he had lost his own dragon some years before in an accident. He'd seen some action against the Teetol, and had received a combat star that he wore proudly at all times.

Swane said that Turrent was jealous of Bazil's fame as the hero of Tummuz Orgmeen.

Relkin shrugged. This, too, they would survive, somehow. They had to. They had nine years to go before they could take retirement and start new lives in farming.

The front gate loomed up ahead, and they went on into the fort, leaving behind the colorful tents and the boisterous crowds of the festival grounds. Inside the fort were just the familiar lines of whitewashed stone and wood buildings, roofed in slate and thatch, home to the men and dragons of the Marneri Second Legion.

Since their return from the southern Empire of Ourdh last year, the Second Legion had scarcely been out of the place, and of late it had been positively cramped, particularly with Dragon Leader Turrent poking around the whole time with his officious gaze and furious dark eyes.

CHAPTER THREE

It was the hour before midnight, and far from quiet in the Dragon House. From their bunks within their cubicles came the stentorian snores of happy wyverns, asleep on full stomachs and casks of ale.

The dragonboys of the 109th were not asleep, however. They sat up late, polishing breastplates and buckles, hilts and helmets, badges and buttons—all of the dress kit of a battle dragon and dragonboy. There was to be a unit parade the next morning. There had been so many unit parades since the arrival of Dragon Leader Digal Turrent that even the dragonboys had ceased to complain. It was a dreaded but accepted fact of life.

At least the conversation was generally lively, working in a group. They had analyzed exhaustively each of the previous day's bouts and forecast the results of the next.

Now the conversation had moved to the rumor that a strong patrol was going to be sent into the hills of Kohon to scour out a tribe of bandits that had tormented the local folk of Black Fell and High Lake.

"Kohon?" sniffed Swane of Revenant, the biggest and strongest of the boys of the 109th. "I'd rather stay here than tramp about on those hills. Nothing to do, no girls to chase, no beer, no fun at all."

"Come on, Swane," chided Relkin. "We're all getting fort fever stuck in here. Haven't seen the outside world since we got back from Ourdh."

"Don't mention that horrible place to me," said Tomas Black Eye.

Relkin sympathized. Tomas's dragon Cham had only recently returned to active service following the wounds he'd suffered in the Ourdh campaign. Relkin had enough memories of the southern land to last a lifetime, including that of an aristocratic girl who'd given him her love. But beside that sweet memory were the images of war and the horror they'd battled in the pit below the temple of the serpent god in ancient Dzu. They'd seen things that day that would mark them for the rest of their lives. Relkin wasn't planning on returning to the ancient "well-watered land" any time too soon.

"Can't have been all that bad," said Jak, who tended a young brasshide named Rusp. "It seems to me that all you fellows talk about sometimes is what you did there."

"Shut it, Jak," said Swane.

"Yeah," agreed Mono, who along with Relkin was the oldest serving member of the unit. Mono would bear the scars of Ourdh for the rest of his days and so would old Chektor, his heavyweight dragon.

But there were many new faces in the 109th. The casualties in the bitter siege of the great city had been great. Dragons and dragonboys had been slain, maimed, broken, and lost to the legions.

Among the new boys was a slim youth with dark hair and soft brown eyes named Manuel. He was eighteen and something of an outsider with the central group. The rest of them were orphans, but he was military brat who'd grown up both in the city of Marneri itself and in the forts of Kenor. His father had retired from the legions with the rank of commander.

After expressing the desire to join the dragon force, Manuel had received special training for the task of being dragonboy to the great wild dragon, the Purple Green of Hook Mountain, who fought with the 109th because his wings had been damaged beyond repair during his captivity in the evil city of Tummuz Orgmeen.

Being older and educated, Manuel had become the unofficial leader of the new dragonboys.

"You fellows don't like to admit it, but Jak's right. You talk about Ourdh a lot. Personally, I don't blame you." Manuel had a lazy smile that irritated Swane.

"Well said, Manuel," spoke up Bryon, a golden-haired new face from Seant who handled Alsebra the freemartin.

"Right enough," agreed Halm of Ors, who tended Anther, a high-strung, green dragon from Aubinas.

"See?" said Jak.

"Yeah, well, you wasn't there. We saw some hard fighting down there," said Swane.

"I also heard you say that Salpalangum was real easy." Jak knew how to needle Swane.

"Yeah, whenever Swane gets a beer into him, we always hear that one!" Halm chortled.

Relkin spoke up, and that quieted them. They all gave Relkin respect.

"Salpalangum wasn't the worst fight we've been in," he said, "but it sure sickened me. It's bad when men attack dragons like that."

"Damned Ourdhi don't have the wits of an imp," muttered Swane.

"Whatever the nature of their wits, they were brave enough," said Relkin. "Their leadership were the witless ones."

"Well, we're tired of hearing about it," groused Halm.

"I try not to bring it up much myself. But you have to expect it of those of us who were there. It's natural enough."

"Saint Relkin again?" said Swane with a wink at Tomas Black Eye.

"It's true though," said Mono. "Relkin doesn't talk about the past much." Mono was usually Relkin's ally.

"And I'd like to stop fighting about it now," said Relkin with a definitive edge. He changed the subject. "Bryon said he'd heard something definite about Kohon, then we started fighting about last year again. So, what did you hear?"

"General Wegan has picked the 66th to go with the 6th regiment. We're staying here."

"The 66th? They get all the luck," said Mono. "By the breath, but it's tiresome being stuck here all the time. Especially with the dragon leader on our backs. We have drill every day, we have to polish all this metal. At least if we were going to Kohon, he wouldn't have us doing this so much."

"Yeah, Mono's right," agreed Halm of Ors.

"I don't know, Mono," said Jak. "The dragon leader might want us to march and polish at the same time."

"It's enough to make you miss old General Paxion," said Mono.

"Yeah ol' Pax always liked the 109th fighting dragons," said Tomas Black Eye.

"Remember that time he came to the granary in Ourdh city?" said Swane.

"By the grace, here we go again," said someone under his breath.

"Not again, Swane!" said several voices.

"Right, right, by the Mother's own sweat, you fellows get so hot about everything."

"Anyway, stow that noise. How did Bryon get this news? And how come he's the only one with it," said Tomas Black Eye.

"Yeah," said Swane. "How do we know that Bryon got this story right? People from Lucule are famous for being fools."

"And people from Revenant are any different?" scoffed Mono. "Revenant's right in the Vale of Lucule, too."

" 'Course they're different, everybody knows that Revenant people are intelligent and witty and wise. Look at me!"

"Yeah, too bad we have to," said Tomas Black Eye.

"Swane's big, but his mouth is even bigger," said Jak.

"Yeah! You want to try and shut me up, Jak."

Jak was only half Swane's size.

"Come on, Swane, give it a rest. Let Bryon tell us how he heard this," said Relkin.

"Yeah."

All eyes turned on golden-haired Bryon, who seemed bashful all of a sudden. Bryon was secretly a sensitive soul.

"Well, I was, uh, talking with this girl, Sundy. She's a maid for the Wegan family. She told me."

Swane whooped. "You mean you bedded that wench! I'm impressed Bryon. Didn't think you'd ever wet your pecker."

"Don't you speak of Sundy that way Swane," said Bryon with sudden anger, surprising everyone with his vehemence. Bryon never got angry.

"How can you be sure she knows what she's talking about?"

"She's a friend with Wegan's daughter, and she heard her father talking about it with her mother."

There were widened eyes among the dragonboys at this revelation from family life. None of them knew who either of their parents were.

"Just goes to show that some old sayings are true," said Manuel, the exception.

"What's that mean?" said Swane, swiveling to glare at the outsider, who sat slightly apart, polishing the huge helmet casque of the Purple Green.

"You can't keep secrets from the servants, that's what."

"Damn city boy knows everything," grumbled Jak.

"Sounds like that's that," said Relkin with a sigh. "No trip to Kohon for us. I wonder what other patrols he's sending out."

"Up the Argo, of course, we did that one," said Mono. Relkin nodded, he and Mono were the only survivors of the old 109th that set out on that patrol!

"And up to the Dragon Beks. Always gets a few imps and trolls up there after spring," said Tomas. "I don't know how they sneak across, considering the watch that's kept on the Argo country, but they get through somehow."

"I guess we'll have to tie a hope-knot and pray for the best," said Manuel.

They continued their work, dipping into the polish pot with strips of grimy rag, buffing down with sheepskin rollers, making sure every piece of equipment was in perfect order and shining as it was supposed to. Turrent was merciless.

At length they finished, one by one, and crawled away to sleep near their dragons.

CHAPTER FOUR

At dawn, they awoke promptly with the bell and the horns. Dragons were given water and morning feed, and then they paraded for inspection by the dragon leader.

Turrent's mood was dour. He berated Jak mercilessly over a crudely sewn patch on his dragon's harness. He ordered Swane to do fifty push-ups in place when he overheard Swane's whispered comment.

When, at last, he came to Relkin and Bazil, he spent a considerable time going over every piece of kit. He even told Relkin to open his pack, an almost unheard of request. With a grim face Relkin complied, and the dragon leader fished through his things.

Relkin wondered if Turrent was looking for his Legion Star, the great medal he'd won for his part in the fall of Tummuz Orgmeen. Relkin kept the thing in the legion bank, in a locked box.

Turrent pawed around for a while and finished by setting aside Relkin's comb, a souvenir from Ourdh.

"This is a nonregulationary item, Dragoneer. Where is the comb that was given you by the good taxpayers of Marneri? Why are you using this piece of foreign apparatus instead?"

Relkin flushed. The comb had been given him by Miranswa Zudeina, who had given him a lot of other things besides, but mostly an education in the arts of love.

"I lost the other one last year in Ourdh, sir. Due to circumstances beyond my control, we lost several pieces of our kit while we were campaigning."

Turrent did not like references to previous campaigns. Turrent was painfully aware of his own unfortunate shortage of combat experience. He had but a single combat star, and he knew some of these boys had two, three, or even five. He fastened his eyes on Relkin.

"Well now, Dragoneer, you understand that the regulations

exist for a good reason. We cannot allow nonregulationary items to be displayed. We might start with discreet little Ourdhi combs, but we'd end up with no uniforms at all and poor morale."

Relkin had learned that the only way to handle these attacks was to stay calm and not to protest in any way. Protestations only made the dragon leader more excited, more determined to find fault.

"Now I know, and the general knows, indeed the whole world knows what a special dragonboy you are, Dragoneer Relkin, with your Legion Star and all. And, of course, we realize how privileged we are to have you."

Relkin heard a real loathing behind Turrent's words. Relkin kept the coveted Legion Star discreetly hidden. He wore it only for full regimental parades and never for a simple unit parade. Why did the dragon leader hate him so?

"But, Dragoneer Relkin," Turrent was leaning over him breathing into his face. "Despite all that, it does not mean that we want to sit around watching you comb your darling locks with this fanciful nonregulationary comb. Despite all that, Dragoneer Relkin, we want to see you use the proper regulationary item as prescribed."

"Yes, sir," mumbled Relkin.

"What?"

"Yes, sir!"

"So, Dragoneer Relkin, how shall we solve this little problem? Shall I perhaps confiscate this nonregulationary item?"

Relkin steeled himself to show no emotion.

Turrent gazed at him for a few seconds, gauging his response. Finally he sniffed.

"Now, I would confiscate the item, Dragoneer, and thus spare you any agony of decision, but I'm sure you treasure this keepsake, so I want to give you the chance to rectify your error. By next unit parade you will have replaced the item with the proper, regulationary item, which you will obtain from the quartermaster store. Am I understood?"

"Yes, sir, perfectly."

Turrent gave him a brief, triumphant smile. "Right then, Dragoneer, carry on."

Turrent strode past to examine Mono and Chektor. Relkin's eyes followed him with frank hatred.

The parade ended at last, and the dragons ambled back

into the Dragon House. Some were to prepare for combats in
the ring. Others were going to exercise in the yard and practice sword drills.

Bazil Broketail would rest that day, following on the hard
bout of the day before. In the late afternoon he would exercise, doing a few routine movements with weights and
sword at the butts.

Once the dragon was sound asleep, Relkin went to the
north entrance of the river gate. On the second floor was
the legionaries' bank where Relkin kept a small locked box.
He signed the chit for it and opened it with the clever
Cunfshon-made key. Inside were a few papers, a joint will
for himself and the dragon, a bag of gold and silver coins,
his medals, including the lustrous Legion Star, and a few
keepsakes from Tummuz Orgmeen. Here he put the silver-
backed comb that Miranswa had given him. As he did so, he
kissed it and whispered her name.

Then he went down to the quartermaster stores and obtained a regulatory comb, a crude thing of wood, manufactured in Kadein.

Then he brought water and refilled Bazil's water tank and
checked that the dragon still slept.

Sitting there with nothing to do but polish bits of equipment for the next unit parade, he quickly grew bored. After
a while Relkin rose and flung himself out of the Dragon
House. He headed out the gate into the fairgrounds again,
but ignoring the roar of the crowd from the dragon bouts, instead meandered down the road to the town.

At the rear of the Sand Pie Inn, he loitered and was rewarded after a while by the appearance of a girl emptying a
box of ashes from the kitchens.

"Hullo, Dacy," he said, and took the box from her hands.
Her eyes lit up at the sight of him, and she smiled coyly.
"Why, it's my dashing dragoneer, Relkin of the 109th."

"The very same."

He hauled the heavy box over to the ash heap, dumped it
out, then gave it back to her.

"And would my angel of the Sand Pie Inn have a moment
or two to dally with me?"

Dacy was in a playful mood. His hopes rose.

"I might, if I knew who the dashing dragoneer was going
to take to the end-of-games dance. I might very well stay
and dally a moment."

"What a coincidence! I was just going to ask if you would care to go to the dance with me."

Dacy smiled, and leaned over and gave him a quick kiss on the lips.

He reached out to take her hand, but she withdrew it quickly and rolled her eyes.

"But first I need to know if you're old enough for me. How old are you, Relkin?"

He swallowed. Dacy was barely sixteen. This he was sure of. He'd found out by bribing her youngest sibling, a boy of seven who was partial to rock candy. He was older than she by a year, but he was still barely old enough for some strange, irrational reason. He who had lain with Miranswa Zudeina in the Temple of the Goddess Gingo-La. He who had fought in battles up and down the continent, he was unsure about this subject more than anything, and it left him feeling inadequate.

"Seventeen, I think."

"You think?"

"Well, I could be more, maybe even eighteen; it's hard to say."

Her eyebrows had narrowed. "What do you mean?"

"Well," he began, "I don't really know when I was born. I was raised in the orphanage, like all the dragonboys."

She smiled wickedly.

"Well, not quite all, Dragoneer Manuel has a family. Quite distinguished, really."

So Manuel had been playing up to Dacy, too. Relkin was furious, but glad to have the information.

"So will you be coming with me to the dance, then?"

She looked away into the distance.

"Well, perhaps. I'll think about it."

"Go on, say yes, Dacy. I can do all the new dances."

"Mmm, so you say. I'll have to think about it."

Piqued, he stepped down. "Well, in that case, it sounds like I'll have to ask someone else to the dance."

Her eyebrows rose. "You do that and I'll never go anywhere with you again."

"This hardly seems fair."

He never got her response to that because the door opened and a tall lout named Dert Waller lurched out and crashed down the steps. He noted Relkin's uniform.

"Hey, dragonboy, guess what I saw today over at Fresham Landing?"

Relkin did not really want to know. Damn, now Dacy was looking at hulking Dert instead of at her ardent dragoneer. The moment was wasting away.

"Trader there by the name of Dook, he's got a wild dragon he captured up on Mt. Ulmo along with two little ones, a whole damn family. All in cages on the dock. Rare angry beasts they are, I can tell you."

"What's he want with a wild dragon?" Relkin was instinctively hostile to anything involving mistreatment of dragons. A family of dragons? He felt a strong foreboding.

"He's taking them to Ourdh to sell to the circus. Think's he's going to make his fortune."

"By the breath, that's so"—Relkin struggled for words, anger rising in his chest—"so damnably stupid."

"Yeah"—Dert waved a hand and disappeared into the stables—"whatever."

Dacy picked up the ash box and opened the door.

"Darling Dacy, what about the end-of-games dance?"

"I don't know right now. Ask me tomorrow. I'm going to think about it."

She flounced inside, and Relkin was left with the terrible news provided by Dert Waller.

A family of dragons? Captured on Mt. Ulmo. With a sudden flash of realization he knew it could only mean one thing.

He went down to the dockside where a gang of stevedores unloaded a schooner. Sacks of grain were piled on carts and hauled away by teams of mules. The movements were methodical, the scene peaceful. The river Argo, here joined by the tributary river Dally, was half a mile wide, swift and deep. On the far side, the land rose up through pinewoods to the yellow bluffs. The sun dappled the water through the clouds.

A captive wild dragon, most likely a dragoness, and with young. He would have to tell Bazil. He knew what that meant. Relkin had spent two miserable spring leaves sitting in the damp, freezing woods on Mt. Ulmo hoping for the return of his dragon's ladylove, a fiery green dragoness. Once Bazil knew of this captive dragoness, there could only be one course of action.

Turrent, he had to ask Turrent, tell him how important this was. Surely the dragon leader would see the point.

He hastened back up the hill, ignoring the riotous sounds of the festival grounds and went straight to the dragon leader's office.

By that time his initial confidence in this course of action had diminished. Turrent might refuse permission. He might order a watch set to keep Bazil within the fort.

He saw the office door open while he was still twenty-five paces away. The dragon leader came out, followed by a dragonboy. He spun around, walked back to the corner, and slipped out of sight. He was sure that they had not seen him. He went instead to the main gate and tried at the office of General Wegan.

The guard took his name and a slip on which he noted, "My dragon is about to desert."

He waited half an hour in the cold antechamber. Messengers came and left every few minutes. Then the inner door opened and two commanders, Oaks of the 3rd and Sunter of the 8th, came in.

Relkin gave them his crispest salute. Commander Sunter returned it, and pointed him out to Commander Oaks, a tall man with a pointed grey beard and a friendly smile.

"Looks a bit young for a Legion Star," he heard Oaks mutter.

The guard was signaling to him.

"General wants to see you inside."

Wegan had replaced old General Paxion in the spring. He had brought a brisk efficiency to the fort, but the legion had not yet warmed to him. Wegan knew he was replacing a legend. Ol' Pax had taken not only the legion, but an entire expeditionary force and preserved it through the terrible ordeal of the siege of Ourdh.

Wegan also knew that the broketail dragon was a legend in the legion, indeed in the entire army. The hero of Tummuz Orgmeen, he had also been in the final battle in the pits of the dark city of Dzu. Wegan did not want to have trouble with that particular dragon. It would be all over the legions in no time.

Wegan also disliked the thought of captive dragons being sold down in Ourdh. He wished he could do something to stop it officially, but his powers were limited to wyvern dragons, the wingless battle dragons of the legion. He could ask the civil authorities to take action, but he knew they would move too slowly to prevent the trader leaving for Ourdh.

Then he had what seemed like a brilliant idea. If the dragon had a family, then he deserved family leave, which he had never had and was entitled to. The general made out a special order on the spot, signed it, and gave it to Relkin.

"Take whatever transport you can find and get down there. The trader Dook will have to be stopped. I will send an order at once."

Relkin mumbled thanks and then ran to the Dragon House.

CHAPTER FIVE

Inside he found Bazil stirring from sleep, scratching a big leathery ear and yawning every so often.

At Relkin's news, the dragon's big eyes popped and his huge hands came out and seized the dragonboy up around the chest.

"Sometimes dragonboy worth his weight in gold, I think." Then he deposited Relkin high up on top of their closet while he shifted great reptile limbs in a spontaneous jig that shook their cubicle's walls.

Relkin vaulted down, dug out his pack, and began to fill it. The dragon thrust his great sword Ecator in its scabbard, and strapped it over his shoulder. Relkin threw him his helmet. They both seized their waxed-cloth rain capes, and in a few moments were out the door, hurrying to the main gate while Relkin explained that General Wegan had given them a special pass.

They marched down to the dockside, ignoring the sallies of the Kenor folk gathered at the booths. The broketail dragon was well-known in Dalhousie and accepted as a kind of giant mascot.

A woman thrust a bag of pastries into Relkin's hand. A man threw up a bunch of roses. Baz caught it with his tail and a moment later used it to drop the roses into the arms of a dark-haired girl serving at a hot-bun stall. The people at the stall cheered, and the cheer was taken up at intervals all the way down the hill to the town.

They went straight to the dockside and Relkin used the pass from General Wegan to commandeer their passage on the schooner *Starkaor,* which had finished loading with beer from the Dalhousie brewery. The brew was destined for several stops along the river reaches just below Dalhousie. The first of these would be at Fresham Landing.

The schooner unshipped from the dock and clapped on

light sail to get out into the current. She turned her bow downstream and slipped quickly out of Dalhousie harbor and away.

Relkin took himself to a bunk and snoozed, but Bazil stood by the rail on the schooner's bows and stared downstream, willing himself closer to her, the dragoness he had dreamed of for two years now.

There were young! He was a father, of at least two! His heart swelled with pride. To fertilize the eggs of a female dragon while serving in the legions was difficult. Generally, it was the task of those dragons who survived their legion service, or were wounded and mustered out and returned to the villages of Argonath to aid the agricultural effort. Bazil felt the tug of new emotions, feelings of paternity, warm and simultaneously fierce boiled within him.

All afternoon they hurried downstream through the Soda Reach with the purple hills of Strom rising to the south and the endless expanse of the steppe to the north. The river bisected the landscape from here until its junction with the Oon. The change was quite abrupt. On the south were forests of oak, pine, beech, and hemlock. On the north, a straggle of trees limned the river itself, but then this faded out and tall grass prairie began, which went on, flat and unbroken, to the horizon.

By dusk they put in at Fresham Landing, a small town with steep slate roofs rising above narrow cobbled streets strung along the bottom of the river bluffs. Above loomed the mass of Mount Sootberg. The temple bell was calling the faithful to evening service as the *Starkaor* tied up. Relkin had convinced Bazil to wait until he had made the situation clear to Trader Dook. He was afraid that the leatherback would not be able to control himself once he came that close to his beloved wild green dragoness.

Relkin hurried along the Fresham dock, congested with fishing craft of all sizes. Mixed in were a few schooners and brigs from the river trade. Trader Dook's ship was around a curve in the embankment, a brig of sixty tons called *Calice*.

Relkin's inquiries brought a surly, heavyset fellow with a coarse red beard to the gangplank. Trader Dook, he was informed, was across the way at the Hag's Dead Inn.

This establishment, a narrow, three-story building of grey brick, was named for the unfortunate wife of the innkeeper who had never counted a happier day than when his spouse fell out the upstairs window while shouting at the dairymaid and broke her thick neck.

Relkin pushed into the inn's parlor, which held two dozen or more customers, mostly folk of the river trades, at their meat and drink.

Trader Dook, recognizable by his tall green trader's hat, was supping a pint of ale in a booth with two of his crew.

Relkin pulled a chair up to the side of the table and introduced himself. Quickly, carefully, he explained the situation and then sat back.

Trader Dook exchanged a long look with the two hearties on the other side of the booth. He scratched his long nose and exposed grey teeth in a humorless smile.

"Little bleedin' dragonboy come all this way to try and steal our fortune, ain't he, Nert?"

The one addressed as Nert leaned over the table and scowled at Relkin.

"We caught these dragons fair and square. They're ours."

Relkin struggled to keep his temper.

"You don't realize this perhaps, but it is against the laws to keep winged dragons."

"Then I'll clip their bleeding wings right off, won't I?" said Trader Dook. "Get used to it; they're ours, and we're going to take 'em down to Ourdh and sell them. They'll fetch a good price there."

"Heh, damned Ourdhi will eat anything, right, Nert?" the third man said suddenly with a giggle.

"Damn right, Golber," said Nert.

"You're breaking the law."

Trader Dook's powerful hand shot out and seized Relkin by the front of his shirt and pulled him close so the reek of beer filled his nostrils.

"Listen to me real careful, boy. My name is Trader Dook, and I don't care about the damned laws. When this is over, we'll have enough to set up wherever we like. If we can't live in Kenor, we'll live someplace else."

"Look, you don't understand, I'm not alone."

"Shaddup!" snarled Dook.

Relkin was growing tired of this. He shook himself free and stood up.

"You're making a serious mistake."

Dook nodded to the other two, and then all three of them rose and rushed him.

Relkin was taken aback, not expecting violence inside the inn. He shouted for the landlord, but received no more answer than a crowd of faces eager to see a beating. Dook and his boys were famous for it. Relkin spun and ducked and almost made it to the door, but then somebody stuck out a foot and he tripped and went down. By the time he was up again, Dook's long hand closed on his shoulder, and he was pulled back into their reach. Nert held him while Dook and Golber rained down punches. Golber did the body work, and Dook concentrated on the face. Relkin lost consciousness before it was finished. He never felt it when they tossed him out the door, and he landed with a thud in the gutter.

He awoke after perhaps an hour, and groaned aloud as he sat up. His ribs were very sore. Golber was a heavyset fellow and good with his fists.

He put a hand to his face and felt the congealing blood there. Dook had cut him pretty badly. His nose felt like a piece of putty. His lower lip was swollen, the side of his jaw ached.

He got to his feet and staggered back to the schooner. The dragon was gone, impatient at the boy's delay. Relkin prayed that Baz hadn't massacred Dook and his men. They were in the wrong, but they could not be slain for what they'd done. To kill them would mean a court-martial for both of them.

Back on the dockside, he forced himself into a shambling run. It was amazing how many separate pieces of him hurt, but he picked it up as he reached the bend. He had to stop the dragon.

Then, at last, he saw him, a tall figure, standing at the end of the dock staring forlornly out across the water.

The brig *Calice* was gone. While Relkin had lain unconscious in the gutter, Dook and his cronies had unshipped and sailed away. By straining his eyes into the night, Relkin could make out a white sail, already a mile or more downstream.

Bazil was about to hurl himself into the river and try to catch up by swimming when Relkin put himself in front of him.

"No, you'll never catch them, not when they have sail up. We'll have to take another ship."

"Hurry up then, because they're getting away."

Relkin was still staunching the blood flow from his battered nose when he concluded a deal with a captain named

Vlope who owned the sloop *Peralta* and was prepared to sail her on the river at night. For the privilege, Relkin had promised a gold piece, a good chunk of their savings.

The sloop was smaller than the schooner *Starkaor,* and Bazil had to position himself amidships, in the waist. The crew of three worked around him as they set *Peralta*'s sails on the single mast.

Soon they picked up speed. Captain Vlope knew these waters from a lifetime of sailing up and down them. With the intermittent light of the moon, plus the lights on the bluffs and down in the harbors, he could risk putting on speed even at night. The darker than dark mass of the Sootberg soon fell behind them and far ahead the light on Catamount Point rose into view. A careful examination of the reach ahead showed no sail. The *Calice* had already rounded Catamount Point. Trader Dook was wasting no time on his escape, and Dook's own knowledge of these waters was almost as extensive as that of Captain Vlope.

Vlope accepted the challenge. The sloop flew on, lifting occasionally in good gusts and sending up a spray of cold foam from the bows. Catamount Point grew before them and then passed behind. The water now grew choppy as they entered the race where the steep tumbling river Vets came down and joined the Argo. The sloop pitched drunkenly across this section, occasionally her bow picking up and yawing despite everything Vlope's crew could do. Still they made good time. The water was deep throughout this stretch of the river, and now the long Loop Reach was opening up in front of them. Here was an opportunity for the sloop to show her speed.

He scanned the reach ahead. In the murk it was hard to tell, but eventually Vlope spotted a pair of sails far down the reach. The brig?

It seemed likely.

"He has a substantial lead," Vlope said with a wintry grin. "But *Peralta* will show them."

They sped past the little town of Mother Loop, another collection of dark slate roofs, huddled on the southern bank. A handful of yellow lamps lit up the place, and atop the temple shone the Loop Light, a powerful navigation beacon for the whole reach.

Ahead rose the bulk of Grand Bluff. Here there were shallows and danger from grounded trees brought down in the spring floods. Captain Vlope swung the *Peralta* wide, away from the southern shore, and with anxious eyes peering through the dark for the first sign of those treacherous drowned trees, they swept around the bluff and entered the long Randle Reach.

Halfway down the reach, they passed a fishing boat hooking for night eels and learned that they had gained on the brig, but that it was still several miles ahead.

Captain Vlope fell into a sulky silence. Eventually he growled, "Damn that man, he'll be in the islands in the morning light. We'll have to search all day, I bet."

Vlope was prescient. At the end of Randle Reach the Argo was joined by the wide, sluggish Flueli. The river broadened and grew shallow, and the main channel vanished into a network of islands and shallow streams. A ship the size of the *Calice* would have to pick her way carefully here. But pursuers would have to look in a hundred different coves and inlets to be certain that the fugitive was not left behind them.

The dawn came and with it came the famous mists of Flueli, thick clinging vapor that blanketed the river and made progress hazardous.

By mid-morning the mist was lifting, but the *Peralta*'s progress had been slowed to a crawl, and the task ahead was monumental. The brig would have slowed as well, but if Dook simply pushed on to the far side of the islands, he could escape completely while they investigated all the side channels and inlets here. Vlope gambled, and the sloop pressed on, staying with the main channel, seeking to pass through as quickly as possible and close up with the *Calice* if Dook had done the same.

He had not. By mid-afternoon, they were clear of the islands on the western side, and there was no sign of the brig, although several fishing vessels passed by. They had no report of the *Calice* either.

Vlope swung the *Peralta* about and began tacking up river, putting into each side channel as they came to it. Hours passed and still there was no sign of the *Calice*.

"Could be anywhere in these damned islands. It'll take a week to search them all," grumbled Vlope.

The light was beginning to fade and with it Relkin's hopes of ever catching up with Dook, when the sloop skimmed across the outlet of a blocked channel, hidden behind willow thicket. There was no point in putting in there, the water was not deep enough.

Suddenly the dragon gave a grunt.

"Something floating in the water there, look."

Relkin called to Vlope to slow and bring the *Peralta* about until they came abreast of the floating object.

It was the body of Golber, slashed horribly across the throat.

"Golber!" exclaimed Relkin. "One of Dook's men." At the sight of Golber, Relkin felt his sides ache.

Golber floated away, food for fish.

"Up there, in that dead water, I'd say," said Vlope, pointing through the willows to the hidden inlet.

"But how?"

"Entrance on the other side of the island is probably deeper. Brig's anchored just inside, out of sight of the main channel and close enough to be able to run for it if she has to."

"Put me ashore," said Relkin.

Through the gathering dusk, Relkin made his way up the beach and into the tangled thickets of willow and alder that covered the low-lying island. Clouds of mosquitoes arose off the stagnant inlet, and they soon found Relkin's sweating form as he worked his way through the dense thickets. It was an ordeal, but at length he won through to a zone of sand dunes beside the inlet. The water curved away to the north and east, and he followed, splashing through the shallows for a half mile until he rounded the bend and came in sight of a ship. A pair of wan lights at bow and stern gave some illumination. It was undoubtedly the brig. Relkin marked the quarry's position and then returned the way he had come.

Vlope nodded briskly at this confirmation of his suspicions and sent the *Peralta* upstream and around the island until they approached the open mouth of the closed-off inlet.

Bazil and Relkin, stripped to the essentials of dirk and sword, were lowered over the side into the water. Peralta moved away, tacking upstream to await their signal. Bazil rolled over slowly, enjoying the feel of the cold water again. All wyverns loved to swim, an echo of their monstrous forebears.

Relkin, teeth chattering, swam up and climbed astride the dragon's massive shoulders. Now with smooth strokes of the great tail, the dragon headed into the inlet.

CHAPTER SIX

Like some enormous crocodile, Bazil coasted the last twenty yards, scarcely breaking the surface of the water. No alarm came from the ship, and at length they were poised beneath the bow of *Calice*.

Voices could be heard, angry voices raised in argument somewhere aft, but the bow was quiet. Carefully Relkin stood up on Bazil's back, steadied himself, and then leapt for the scroll work of the brig's figurehead, a Snailmaiden with long hair and horns. He landed, got a grip on her horns, and hauled himself up to the rail while ignoring as much as possible the savage stabs of pain from his ribs where Golber's fists had landed.

There was a single figure standing watch on the poop deck. Down below the argument continued. Relkin was able to ascertain that it was coming from the aft hold, where the hatch was open, letting warm yellow lantern light flood up from below. Relkin slithered soundlessly onto the deck between two coiled ropes and crept sternward. The watch made no move. So far, so good.

In fact, the man on watch was the lumpy Nert, who listened with half an ear to the row down below while he grieved for poor old Golber.

The damned cages were just badly designed and poorly made, and that had been Golber's downfall. That and Trader Dook's recklessness. Golber and Nert had been drinking and amusing themselves by spitting at the dragoness. Trader Dook had come by and challenged Golber to get closer so he could literally spit in her eye. Golber, poor old fool, had gone one step too close, and in a movement almost too fast for the human eye to witness, the green dragoness had reached through and slashed his throat and chest with her talons. At least it had been quick. Golber was dead before he hit the floor.

Now, as Relkin listened, they argued. Some of the crew wanted to avenge their loss by killing one of the young dragons. Dook was adamantly opposed. The young dragons were worth a thousand gold pieces apiece to a gourmet club in Ourdh.

Nert was confused. They ought to avenge poor Golber. Part of Nert wanted to kill the dragoness herself, but the other part of him knew that she was worth five thousand gold pieces, and he really didn't want to lose that. On the other hand, what was poor old Golber worth? Was he even worth losing a thousand gold pieces over? It was an ugly decision, one that Nert had decided to leave up to Trader Dook. Sometimes Nert didn't like the world, or even himself.

Taking advantage of the watch's apparent self-absorption, Relkin crept to the edge of the aft hold. The hatch was off. He glimpsed a lantern down below, a circle of men arguing around it. To the other side, he caught a glimpse of the side of a cage and a shadow within.

His blood boiled at that. These blackguards were going to pay. He slipped back to the bow, leaned out, and signaled to the dragon in the water. Bazil started the difficult process of climbing the side of the ship. For a beast weighing two tons, this was not a simple task. Yet he did it quietly enough with the stealth of a top predator at work. His movements, however, sent slight tremors through the ship.

Relkin hugged himself against a sudden night breeze, he was wet through and chilled. His ribs ached, and so did a dozen other sore spots. In a way, he was almost sorry that there would be no opportunity to even the score with Golber. But Golber had paid for his villainy nonetheless. He checked on Bazil again. Not much progress had been made. He relaxed. The traders had noticed nothing, although the *Calice* shifted a little with each mighty heave by the dragon.

He turned back to check on the watch and just caught a glint of something in the air above him. He ducked instinctively and narrowly avoided having his brains dashed out by Nert's heavy belaying pin.

"Why, it's the little dragonrat. You didn't get enough the other night, eh?"

Old Nert wasn't too swift, but he wasn't too slow either. He had been on Dook's ships for ten years now and knew a thing or two. Nobody could crawl around the *Calice* when

Nert was on watch and hope to evade detection for long. At least not if they weighed two tons.

Relkin dodged aside and drew his dirk.

"Oh ho, you draw steel do yer?" Nert lunged and suddenly tried a kick, aiming to tumble the youth. He misjudged the speed of the lad. Relkin had shifted sideways, and the kick sailed through the air, pulling Nert off balance.

Relkin struck in, and Nert was forced to defend himself as that dirk swung from side to side in cutting loops that threatened to lodge into his shoulders or his sides if not deflected with the belaying pin.

Nert took a step back and then another. A cry of anger and then a shriek of fear came from him as Relkin got through and cut his right arm. The belaying pin clattered to the deck.

The scream brought an immediate end to the argument down below. Nert tried to jump backward over a hatchway, but his heel caught on the edge, and he went down with another shriek and a heavy thud.

Feet were thundering on the steps up from the hold. Relkin drifted back to the bow. Where was that dragon?

"In the bows, get him," snarled Nert scrabbling up his belaying pin.

"What is it, Nert?"

Someone held up a lantern. Relkin ducked behind the foremast and stayed in the shadow.

"It's the damned dragonrat!" said Nert pointing with the belaying pin.

"That little rat?"

"He's got a sword, Trader," said Nert.

"I can see that! What did he do to you to make you squeal like a stuck pig?" Dook replied.

"Nert's bleeding, Trader," said Nert in a woe-filled voice.

"Must've got something into old Nert, eh?" chuckled another loutish crew member.

"Shaddup, Fulk," growled Nert.

"Take him," said Dook, gesturing with his cutlass.

The men surged forward, and Relkin fought a desperate struggle in the confines of the bow. He cut one man's hand and knocked aside several slashes aimed at his head. But at last he stumbled over a pile of rope, and somebody caught him with a kick He fell and the end seemed close.

"Tie him up. We'll cook him and feed him to the dragons," said Dook.

Just then the *Calice* gave a heavy lurch under their feet and a huge greenish brown arm and shoulder came over the side, followed by a leg and a tail.

The tail wrapped itself around some rigging up above, and there was a stentorian exhalation of breath. In a moment a full grown battledragon had heaved himself onto the ship's deck, pulling free the dragonsword "Ecator," yard upon yard of gleaming white steel. At the sight of that terrible weapon, the crew drew back with a collective jerk.

Relkin scrambled to his feet.

"Where have you been?" he said.

"It's not easy to climb the side of ship. You should come up with a better plan."

The crew was filtering to the stern, and now Trader Dook alone barred their way.

"You'll not rob me of the dragons," he snarled, and made play with his cutlass.

Bazil hissed and stepped forward quickly while Ecator whistled through the air, sliced through rigging and fretwood, and then sank into the foremast and stuck there.

Dook's eyes lit up with unanticipated triumph, and he thrust forward with the cutlass. His blow was knocked aside by a dirk suddenly interposed. Relkin blocked the way. Dook pulled back his blade, and Relkin hit him in the nose with a left jab. Trader let out a yelp of shocked pain. His stroke went wild. No one had so handled Trader Dook in years.

"Ach!" growled Bazil, putting one leg up on the mast and heaving Ecator free.

Dook had thought better of this. There was blood streaming from his nose. He stepped away and then darted down the steps into the hold.

Bazil and Relkin advanced. The crew retreated and some dove overboard while others climbed high into the rigging. At the steps to the hold, they split up. Relkin pursued Dook while Bazil set to lowering himself over the side of the hold. There was no way a dragon could use the wooden steps leading into the hold.

Relkin jumped the last flight of steps a little incautiously and was almost decapitated as he landed. Fortunately for Relkin, he had tripped as he jumped and landed on his already sore behind while the cutlass zoomed by just overhead and bit deeply into the step.

Relkin squirmed out of the way and felt the breeze from Dook's boot as it traveled past his chin. Frantically he rolled aside and then dove into a pile of straw and wriggled through it until he abruptly collided with the steel bars of a cage.

In front of him looking down was an enormous shape, a dragon's face contorted in rage. A huge green forearm snapped around him.

"No!" he screamed in his best dragon speech. The killing blow did not come. A look of wonder flashed across the dragoness's eyes.

Dook pulled up. The damned boy was right by the cage. He shrugged. He'd leave it to the damned dragoness to finish him. Meanwhile it was time to get on with his emergency plan. The battledragon was still up there, but it sounded like it was climbing down into the hold. There wasn't a moment to lose.

Trader Dook took down the keys from where they hung and opened the cage to the smallest of the young dragons, the green-skinned female. She snarled and crouched and made ready to spring at him until there was a shrieking hiss from the other cage. The dragoness let loose a string of sibilant phrases, and the young dragon crouched back, away from that deadly human steel.

Dook glanced back to the dragoness's cage. The boy was still alive. What was she waiting for? When poor old Golber got close, it was over in less than a second. Damn these reptiles, unnatural beasts, they had no right to be talking in Dook's book.

Dook kept his cutlass in front of him. The little one was the smallest dragon, but she was still as big as he was. He had no doubt that but for the sword, she would have been on him in a flash with those teeth and claws.

"Listen up, dragonrat, you better tell the big fellow to leave me be or else this little one's gonna get it. You understand?"

Relkin stared at Dook with silent rage. The dragoness had released him after a long, terrifying moment. He was not one of the crew, and he was fighting Dook, and so he lived. She pulled back her deadly talons.

"Give it up, Dook. Why don't you just jump for it. We'll let you live, though others wouldn't."

There was a loud scrabbling sound from above and then

an enormous shape fell into the hold with a crash that shook the ship from stem to stern.

A big voice erupted in dragonish curses.

The next moment the dragoness gave a scream of delight and called to Bazil in dragon speech.

Bazil sat up, and a moment later he was at the cage, tearing at the bars.

Relkin had to climb up on his shoulder and yell in his ear to break him out of it.

"Stop it, Baz. The cage is made of steel. I'll get the key!"

At last the dragon stood back. The bars were bent but they could not be broken.

"Boy right, much easier to use a key. Damned human things."

The dragoness, *his* dragoness was there before his eyes.

"You came back, then," he said. "I waited in the spring, two years."

"I came back. I brought your offspring for you to see. That human trapped them and then forced me to get in the cage to stop him from killing them."

"We free you now."

But freedom was not quite won, for Dook had the keys.

"You want to release the bitch-worm, eh?" He waved the keys. "Think again. You get the keys when I'm safely over the side, got it?"

Relkin and Bazil exchanged a long look. There was no way around it, it seemed. Relkin turned back to Dook.

"However you want it, Trader, just leave the little one alone."

Dook shook his head with a bitter laugh.

"By the breath, I will not. This one's coming with me. You get the other two, but this one I will take and sell. Worth at least a couple thousand down in Ourdh."

"Trader, you won't live to see Ourdh, not if you try and take the little one."

"Then she won't live either, got it? You better tell those monsters of yours. They want her to live, they better leave me go."

Relkin edged toward the cage.

Dook gestured with the sword to the small green dragon, then he started kicking her.

"Get out of the cage you stupid thing!" he roared.

The small dragon snapped at him in fury but when he

raised the cutlass, she scuttled to the door. He followed close behind, his sword point in her back.

"Get up the steps!" he barked, and drove her on with more kicks and curses.

Bazil was on the verge of losing control. Relkin could see it in the big dragon eyes. Desperately he hefted his dirk. He'd practiced throwing the thing a hundred thousand times, but never had he had a life at stake on a throw.

Dook had eyes only for the dragon, and he was preparing to thrust home his blade if Bazil moved an inch toward him.

Relkin bent his arm slowly and then tossed the dirk underhand. It flew twenty feet across the hold and sank to the hilt in Trader Dook's throat. The cutlass fell from Dook's nerveless hand. He coughed once, and a moment later his body clattered to the planking.

Relkin ran to the prone figure and felt for a pulse. Dook was dead, no trace of doubt about it. With a groan Relkin retrieved his dirk, lifted the keys, and went back and released the dragoness and the other small dragon.

The dragons were loose, and suddenly there was no room in the hold for a dragonboy, so he took the steps back to the main deck. The crew had mostly abandoned the ship except for a handful way up in the rigging.

"You'll hang for that," snarled someone up above.

"Damned dragonrat, what right have you to come on board with that dragon and kill the good captain."

Relkin spat. "He would have killed the little dragon. You think the big ones would have let any of you live after that? Be thankful for what I did."

"They'll still court-martial you. I know, I was in the legion once."

Looking down on the cavorting dragons, Relkin sighed. Bazil had both the young ones in his arms and was whirling them around in a paroxysm of paternal love. The bitter thing was that the crewmen were right. There would have to be a trial, and at a trial with a human judge and jury, it might not sound as clear-cut and necessary as it had seemed at the moment the dirk had left his hand on that sweet, incredible trajectory.

"Yeah, I know," he said quietly, and folded his arms around his aching ribs.

CHAPTER SEVEN

It was a dismal day. A cheerless rain had been falling since dawn. The courtroom at Fort Dalhousie, where the military tribunal was holding the hearing, was gloomy and grey, although from behind the bar came the mutter of a considerable crowd. The case had attracted a lot of attention in the town. In front of the bar sat officers of the court, the advocates and prosecutors, the administrative staff and the officers of the peace. It was, however, only a court of inquiry, not a court-martial. The tribunal had to be satisfied that the charges were blameworthy before sending the matter to trial.

Relkin sat in the front row, beside his counselor, Advocate Sweeb, a pink-faced twenty-six-year-old, just arrived from the legal mills in Marneri.

Looming above them all was the high bench where sat the three legion commanders who made up the tribunal. These were men of substance, grey-haired, weathered by experience. Their faces were dour enough, but worse by far was the face of the man on the witness seat, Dragon Leader Digal Turrent. Every time he mentioned Relkin or Quosh, his face radiated sorrowful disappointment.

The chief prosecutor was a bullet of a man, a Captain Jenshaw of Sokadein. He was milking Turrent's dislike of Relkin very skillfully.

"And so you would agree, Dragon Leader Turrent, that prior to the day that Dragoneer Relkin left the fort with the dragon, you had never heard a mention of the dragon's, uh, romantic interest in the female dragon that was aboard the brig *Calice*?"

"Never heard about it. Came back to my post and found them both gone. A chit from General Wegan gave them leave, I was told, and nothing to be done about it."

"So, no word to you, their unit commander, and no mention of this, uh, relationship, between the battledragon Bazil of Quosh and this, uh, feral winged dragon."

"None at all."

Prosecutor Jenshaw looked up earnestly to the men of the tribunal.

"May it be noted that the people's prosecutor intends to show that the so-called relationship never existed and was an invention, after the fact, by Dragoneer Relkin."

"Note it," said the center tribune, Commander Vodt.

"Furthermore," said Prosecutor Jenshaw, "it should be noted that we have already shown that Dragoneer Relkin has a tendency to break discipline and to take irregulatory actions, possibly even criminal ones."

Advocate Sweeb was on his feet. "Objection, my lords of the tribunal, no criminal activity has actually been mentioned in these proceedings, other than the crimes charged, namely murder and attempted robbery."

The tribunals looked to one another, eyebrows rose and fell. Commander Vodt nodded slowly.

"Objection overruled. We will allow the statement as it stands."

"But, my lords—"

"But us no buts, Advocate. Carry on, Prosecutor."

"The people's prosecutor has no further questions for the witness."

Relkin sighed. Digal Turrent had done his level best to sink them. They were to be branded as untrustworthy types, ready to slink off at the slightest chance for illicit activities.

Advocate Sweeb advanced to the chair.

"Dragon Leader Turrent, for the record we must ask, how long have you commanded the 109th Marneri Dragon Squadron?"

For the first time, Turrent looked less than completely confident.

"Three months now, although I had a couple of months before that when I was here at Dalhousie but had not yet been assigned to a squadron. I studied the 109th at that time. I knew them well before I ever took command."

"Then you must have noted that Dragoneer Relkin and the dragon Bazil of Quosh have an exceptional record of battle honors."

Turrent shrugged. "Well, they have been in some campaigns."

"Now, Dragon Leader, surely that is an understatement. The dragoneer has five combat stars and three campaign ribbons."

"As to the particular numbers, I could not say."

"And yet you said you had studied the 109th very carefully before you took command."

Turrent shifted uneasily. "I must have forgotten."

"I will refresh your memory, then. They served in the winter campaign against the Teetol. They fought their way across the Gan to Tummuz Orgmeen. They fought in Ourdh last summer and earned more honors there."

Turrent looked as if he had a stomach pain.

"Rather a lot of honors for someone who is barely seventeen, wouldn't you agree?"

Turrent set his mouth in a grim line.

"Suppose so."

"In addition, the dragoneer has one other decoration, the Legion Star, awarded for courage and devotion to duty beyond any requirement. Awarded, I might add, very seldom indeed."

"Yes, Advocate," murmured Turrent.

"So, whereas you have commented quite unfavorably on the characters of both dragoneer Relkin and the battledragon Bazil of Quosh, you admit that they have obviously served the legion very well."

Turrent nodded unwillingly. "Well, I suppose you could draw such an inference."

Sweeb swung back to the tribunes.

"The defense asks the court to note that record of distinguished service and to set it against the charges of insubordination that have been made here by Dragon Leader Turrent."

Vodt nodded. "It will be noted."

The bell on the gate tower rang for the hour. Commander Vodt slammed his hammer to end the hearing for the day. Relkin rose and filed out with Advocate Sweeb at his side, murmuring encouragement.

"General Wegan speaks tomorrow. He will validate your claim."

"If dragons can't testify, then it's my word against the crew of the *Calice*. I'm doomed."

"Dragon testimony will be difficult to present. Dragons are beloved on the battlefield but are not respected in our courts and tribunals. It is a difficult area for many people, they are deeply ambivalent about our great reptilian friends."

"It's all right if we die for them, you mean, but we ain't good enough to have the same rights." Sweeb smiled slightly at the youth's total identification with the dragons.

"Now, Master Relkin, I feel that you are perhaps a little jaundiced in your opinions right now. It's understandable, but . . ."

"But me no buts, Advocate," murmured Relkin.

Relkin knew the way things were, which was one reason he'd been so anxious about the entire venture, from the moment he'd heard the news at the dockside in Dalhousie.

"What did you say?" said Advocate Sweeb sharply, sensing impertinence. Sweeb felt the difference between them very keenly. His soft plump pinkness against the dragonboy's lean, muscled tan for example.

"Look, Advocate, there's folk here that want to hang me over this, and all I was doing was saving the life of my dragon's very own young one, his daughter. So I don't take it well that the court will not recognize either my dragon or his wild mate. Dragons are intelligent, different from us, but intelligent nonetheless. It's ridiculous to say anything else. What other animals in the world can we converse with?"

"Agreed, Dragoneer, agreed, but we have to work around the restrictions, that is what we have to do. Even if a battledragon was allowed to testify that would not solve our greatest problem, for the wild dragon could never be asked to take the witness chair."

They had to pass the sisters of Trader Dook, who crowded to the end of their row and stared at Relkin with bitter eyes, as they did every time the tribunal adjourned.

"You will hang, dragonrat!" said one of them quite distinctly.

Sweeb looked across angrily, but said nothing.

Outside, Relkin noted the pie sellers and water wagons serving the crowd. There was big interest in the case now. Something told him that the tribunal was going to recommend a court-martial. The case provided a handy political test for the political establishment of the Middle Argo towns. The people of the Argo were now numerous enough to feel secure. The country was fast being settled. Why did they need these expensive legions sitting in their midst, eating them out of house and home? Especially those dragons, who could eat a houseful of food in a single sitting!

As a result, there had been a campaign of subtle and not-so-subtle denigration of the legions. The occasional criminal acts committed by legionaries were always played up, along with loud complaints concerning taxation and the cost of the legions. Thus for the legion command, it might be necessary to make an example of Relkin and Bazil to satisfy public opinion, which had become convinced that the famous dragon had gone on a slaughterous berserk and had slain who knew how many honest folk whose bodies had simply not yet been discovered.

The fact that the killing had actually been done by the dragonboy and not the dragon did not matter a whit to the kind of crowd ready to believe these fantasies. There are always those with a sour disposition, eager to avoid responsibility, desperate to evade paying a beek for the common defense. To such folk Trader Dook was already a kind of hero, an honest man trying to make a living in trade, who was set on by a mad dragon and slain aboard his own ship.

The popular imagination could run far on such fuel. Even worse in many ways was the involvement of the green dragoness and the two youngsters.

Wild dragons were the stuff of nightmares, even more terrifying than the troll armies of the great enemy. Such dragons were no longer seen in the land of Kenor, but were rumored to visit the high valleys of Mt. Ulmo and Mt. Snowgirt in Tunina to the north. Such dread creatures were said to be able to eat a whole herd of cattle in a night.

Thus the entire case was cast in a dire light for the popular imagination. There would have to be a court-martial. Relkin gulped. That meant there absolutely had to be dragon testimony, otherwise the trader's sisters would most definitely see him hang before Fundament Day.

He bade Advocate Sweeb good day and returned to the quarters of the 109th. His dragon was waiting in their stall, outwardly calm and dour, but inwardly, Relkin knew, seething with anxiety.

Briefly he described the day in court. The dragon nodded as if all his suspicions had been confirmed.

"So, we are doomed. You will be hanged, and I am to be sent back to Quosh on half rations and made to work in the fields."

Relkin shrugged hopelessly.

"Looks that way, but Advocate Sweeb says we mustn't give up hope."

"We have no hope. I don't want to go back to Quosh and farm."

"Not that bad, you know. You'll get your own dragoness to live with."

The dragon hissed indignantly. "It will not be *my* dragoness. Mine is over the river, hunting in the forests."

Relkin pursed his lips. There was nothing to say. The wild dragoness and the young had chosen not to return to the fort with Bazil. In truth, there was no place for them there. In the current situation, they would be a sore embarrassment to the legion and spur unrest in the town.

The curtain pulled aside, another, even vaster bulk slid into the stall. Suddenly the place was crowded. Relkin climbed up into his cot and got above the massive dragons.

Their visitor was the Purple Green, the largest dragon in the legions and a former wild dragon who had lost the power of flight when his wings had been clipped by the enemy. The Purple Green had once contested with Bazil for the green dragoness herself. Since then he and Bazil had become fast friends.

"I heard that it went badly today," began the great wild one in his usual manner, getting straight to the bad news.

"It did not go well," said Relkin from his cot.

"This means the same thing as badly, right?"

"Right."

"Humans have many words and often turn them inside out. It is hard sometimes for a dragon to understand why." The huge wild one settled himself and exchanged handclasps with Bazil. The dragons spoke together in dragon speech.

Relkin gave a mental shrug. Dragons were utterly confident that they were the superior species. It was better to let them think this way, it made life easier for the poor, overworked dragonboy.

The Purple Green continued to press.

"So now we must consider what to do. We cannot let them hang the boy."

"I suppose not," said Bazil.

For some reason this annoyed Relkin beyond endurance, and he spoke up.

"And what do you think you can do to stop them? What can anyone do? Run off and live wild in the forest?"

"Why not?" said the Purple Green.

They fell silent. Relkin cursed himself for bringing up the idea.

"Because we'll starve. Dragons eat too much to live wild."

"Nonsense," said the Purple Green, "I, the Purple Green of Hook Mountain, lived many years in the wild. I roamed from Dragon Home to Mt. Ulmo, all the length of the northland. I went where I willed, and I ate whatever I found there."

"But that was when you had wings," said Relkin, "and now you fight for the legions and eat legion food because you would have starved to death without them. You think Baz and I can make it as hunters? We haven't hunted since we were youngsters back home in the village."

"We three will go; we will hunt together. I have learned many things while I lived among humans. There are many ways to hunt."

Relkin suppressed his immediate answer. The thought of trying to hunt deer and elk and suchlike with a pair of huge, ground-bound dragons for company was too ludicrous for words.

"And what about Manuel, what does he say?" Manuel had done wonders in his months with the Purple Green. Although there was a certain distance between them, Relkin respected Manuel's skill with the dragon. Relkin had cared for the Purple Green himself and understood how damnably difficult it could be. The wild one's temper was volcanic and easily awoken. Manuel rode out these tantrums with commendable aplomb.

The Purple Green snorted with disdain at the mention of Manuel, however. This surprised Relkin, for he had always thought that the Purple Green liked the new dragonboy. He had always said so, usually on his way to condemning Relkin for some dereliction of duty to dragonish comfort.

"You haven't told Manuel of your plans then?"

"Boy knows nothing. I cannot trust him on this matter."

"Great," muttered Relkin, "we run off to the woods, and I have to take care of both of you."

"You did it before. You did well. I understand that now.

At the time I did not realize. I was ignorant of these matters. You did good job, you can do it again."

Relkin felt his cheeks color.

"You're crazy, I am not going off to the forest to look after the two of you while we starve to death."

"So you want to stay here and be hanged?"

Relkin's anger skidded to a halt. He looked down, unable for the moment to meet inquisitive dragon stares. He knew it was useless to lie, because they would sense it at once. They were uncanny that way, dragons, once they knew you, they knew you through and through, every last weakness.

"Look," he changed the subject in desperation. "I want to get some sleep. Let's talk about this tomorrow. I have to sit in that courtroom all day."

The dragons looked at each other. Tails twitched and big eyes winked. They quietly slipped out of the stall and made their way down to the exercise paddock.

Relkin lay there and tried to sleep. It wasn't easy. The noose was closing in, just as so many had predicted. More than anything he hated the thought of Dragon Leader Turrent being able to watch him hang.

Advocate Sweeb was doing his best, but he wasn't making any progress. Everything would depend on General Wegan's testimony on the next day, and that would come to little more than another character reference. The general had trusted the dragonboy. The problem remained. Without dragon testimony, he could hope for little.

His thought glanced away for a moment to his friends, far off in Marneri and beyond. Lagdalen and her baby, and Hollein Kesepton, who was in his home city for a spell of relief duty and thus could live with Lagdalen and his daughter. How would they receive the news that a certain dragonboy had been hanged for murder at Fort Dalhousie?

And further away, where ever she happened to be, what would the Grey Lady, the witch Lessis, have to say when she was told? If they even informed her, in the scale of things what did the death of one dragonboy in one fort in Kenor matter? And she was a Great Witch with power beyond measure in the empire.

It was all monstrously unfair. Death he had long ago accepted as the risk you took in his line of work. That and hideous maiming. Many dragonboys ended as beggars lacking a limb in the alleys of the ennead cities of the Argonath. He knew he risked such a future. But somehow he had just never imagined that he would die at the end of a rope. It was so ignominious. Death in battle yes, that was possible anytime. He'd envisaged his own death in a thousand ways, but being hanged in front of the regiment as an example to others had never occurred to him. His spirits sank to frigid depths and congealed there.

In this mood he eventually fell asleep and lay there snoring gently, dreaming of monstrous serpents, gods with no names left in human tongue, terrors from beyond the world. Anything but courtrooms and military tribunals.

CHAPTER EIGHT

While Relkin tossed and turned in uneasy sleep, tormented by vague terrors, there were others, far away, who would have understood his dreams only too well and who also faced the uncertain future torn by apprehension, their hearts beset by fear.

Far, far to the east, far beyond even the city of Marneri, hundreds of miles across the sea, where stretched the Isles of Cunfshon, these dream-seers, witches of the highest order of their art, and accidental friends of a dragonboy who seemed destined to hang, were gathering to present their viewpoints to the Imperial Council of the Empire of the Rose. They were aware that they approached a deadly nexus in time, a crucial sticking point, a crisis that would test the very limits of the strength of the empire. They were aware also that the majority of the council were not in agreement with them.

They met alone on the top turret of the Tower of Swallows, which dominated the land around it. Two women of indeterminate age, but vastly dissimilar appearance. The one short, slender, grey-haired and grey-robed, and seemingly utterly indistinguished, a perfectly ordinary woman of about fifty years. The other tall, beautiful, glittering in black and silver garb, her black hair pulled back and gathered behind her head in a net laced with gemstones, her costume decorated with silvered skulls of mice. And yet, while they appeared as mistress and mere servant, they were equals and both more than five hundred years old.

"Sister, it is good to see you in the flesh once more. You seem to be taking to it again," said she of humble appearance.

"Thank you, Lessis. Since my adventures last summer, I have found it necessary to accept your suggestions and attend the council meetings. The threat here on Ryetelth is too great. We approach the great crisis foretold by the mystic long ago."

"As always, Ribela, you are accurate in every detail. But I am afraid that the council is of a timid temperament at this moment. They will not listen to me, I'm afraid. Perhaps I have done a poor job of preparing them for it. I came late to the task; it took me many months to recover my strength."

"You were gravely wounded, my dear."

"And you saved me. I thank you, Sister." Both of them understood the grim irony in Lessis's voice. Both of them had contemplated the blissful escape that death would bring. Their lives had been overlong already.

"The problem is that it comes too soon after the campaign in Ourdh. The losses are still being felt in all the cities."

"And our loss of intelligence from beyond the White Bones continues?"

Lessis shrugged wearily. Verily, the burdens of the world seemed to rest on this one set of narrow shoulders.

"Semelia's disaster continues to wreak havoc for us in that theater. They have taken our network in Axoxo. None of our agents survived. We lost everything in the Tetralobe." She paused and became thoughtful.

"However, we did learn that work had begun on an enormous enlargement of the breeding pens in Axoxo."

"And from Ourdh?"

"Estimates have not changed much in the past month. About twenty thousand women of childbearing age were taken. They have completely disappeared, along with all the cows from the west side of the river Oon. Not a cow to be found for a hundred miles in any direction."

"An enormous breeding program."

"They would have more than one hundred thousand imp by now, perhaps twice that. I cannot guess at the quantity of troll."

"Exactly. The emperor must listen."

"I pray that he will. I am sure that the sight of yourself, attending in person, will concentrate his attention."

"Of course," said the lady in black, the very Queen of Mice, with utmost assurance. "You know, Sister Lessis, that were you to present a more imposing face to the world, you might not have this kind of difficulty so often. Men cannot see beyond the trappings of authority and power. You test them too forcefully."

"Sister Ribela, I take your point. However, I'm just hopeless at such things and must continue as I am."

Ribela nodded, sensing the resolve and strength that lay behind Lessis's outward humility. "I have been saying the same things to you for far too long, Sister. And always I come away knowing I have been bested."

"Sister Ribela, I have nothing of your personal force, and I do not seek it. Perhaps my absence of ambition in those things disturbs you."

Ribela allowed a tiny smile to crack the mask of her face. "Perhaps."

They strolled the tower in silence, communing with the view, organizing their thoughts. Beneath them were arrayed the lesser towers, halls, and walls of Andiquant, a small city purposely built to administer the empire and perched above the waters of the great harbor of Cunfshon. Far across the harbor glittered the lights of the city of Cunfshon itself. The night breeze was cool and helped Lessis to calm her thoughts as she prepared for the council meeting.

After a few minutes, they repaired to the door and began the descent to the council chamber.

There were two capital cities in the Isles of Cunfshon, separated by no more than the tidal passage of the gentle river Susa. On the northern bank lay the ancient city of Cunfshon with its white stone walls and towers. In the harbor reach of the Susa lay a mass of shipping, local craft by the dozen, three-masted ocean ships, luggers, brigs, schooners, and dominating the rest a handful of the white ships of Cunfshon, great three- and four-masted clippers, the fastest ships on all the oceans of Ryetelth.

On the southern side of the river, sitting up on slightly higher ground, stood the second city, the city of Andiquant, the administrative capital of the Empire of the Rose. Walls of dark grey granite topped by mighty towers and outworks betrayed the defensive concerns of the empire. Andiquant had been built as a piece, an administrative capital for the young empire when it had outgrown the institutions of Cunfshon.

The need for defensive strength, even here on the Isle of Cunfshon, was a raw tribute to the great power of the enemy that dominated the continent Ianta. The Masters of Padmasa were that ruling power, and their reach was long and their strength most terrible.

The building of Andiquant, completed in twenty years, had been the second direct challenge to the power in Padmasa. The first had been the founding of the cities of the Argonath. With the strength of the isles behind them, the descendants of the exiles of Veronath the Golden returned to the Argonath littoral and began the reconquest of their ancient land. Success attended their enterprise and eventually even the demon lord, Mach Ingbok, was thrown down and his great place, Dugguth, was taken and destroyed. The Argonath arose to cast a silver-steel light across the mountains where once the gold of Veronath had gleamed. The Ennead cities bloomed and grew apace. Colonies were set in ancient Kenor, now returned to wilderness after centuries of abandonment to savagery. The Empire of the Rose stretched out the hand of friendship to other nations of the world Ryetelth, and with the commercial power of the shipping of Cunfshon behind that friendship, the empire had become well respected in the world.

In recent years the enemy had received two sharp defeats in the eastern region of Ianta. First, in the north, the Doom of Tummuz Orgmeen had fallen. Then in the south, in ancient Ourdh, the Masters had received another sharp check with the destruction of the demon Sephis.

The city of Andiquant knew better than to rejoice overmuch. The power in Padmasa was immeasurably great. The Masters had achieved the status of a high piece upon the sphere board of destiny. In Ourdh, the Sinni had even been forced to intervene from a higher plane to assist in holding them back. Repercussions from such a thing were still echoing through the higher levels of being.

One thing was sure, the Dark Masters would not leave the challenge unmet. A response was certain. It was only a matter of time.

In the lovely blue room halfway up the Tower of Swallows, which rose from the Imperial fortress and dominated the Susa estuary and Cunfshon harbor, the Imperial Council was called to meet.

The full council consisted of the emperor, the heads of the various departments of the Imperial Effort, seven in total, plus two administrators from Andiquant's bureaucracy. Finally an admiral and a general were present on behalf of the fleets and legions.

The current emperor was Pascal Iturgio Densen Asturi, a powerfully built, vigorous man in late-middle years. His hair was streaked with grey, but his beard was still black. His eyes burned with intelligence and passion. He was the seventeenth of the Asturi line, and he was one of the best, as far as the Great Witches were concerned. The Asturi had been remarkable, a stable imperial line over six hundred years. One reason for that stability was the attention paid to it by the Great Witches. Thus were they known as the "gardeners of the Asturi" by those who understood their role. The Emperor Pascal was an example of the very best in the Asturi lineage: active, widely interested in the world, with great powers of concentration and the ability to endure long meetings. The Great Witches had been well pleased with him.

Among the heads of the various departments of the Effort were several of these Great Witches, including Sausann and Valembre, who represented the temple hierarchy, a constant, conservative presence in the affairs of Andiquant. From the Office of Unusual Insight were Lessis of Valmes and Ribela of Defwode, although this last had not attended meetings in human form for more than a century, until the year before when her presence had become essential. These two brought reports from the secret world of spy networks and struggles in other realms of being.

The remaining members of the council were technical advisers. Master Garsk of the Imperial Bureaucracy was invaluable in planning and carrying out any major initiative. Kelfel of the police function was crucial to counterintelligence matters, for the great enemy maintained enormous networks of spies and informers, even on the Isles of Cunfshon.

Then came the military, old Admiral Cranx and General Hektor, now recovered from the poisoning he'd received in Ourdh the previous year.

Cranx had sat on the council for twenty-five years and was coming to the end of his time. Still, behind the white beard and the long white mane of hair there beat a keen intelligence with a wide understanding of the oceans and the shipping upon them.

General Hektor was new to the council, having been

brought to the isles just when his predecessor General Elgore was dying. He would always walk with a limp to remind him of the damage done by a subtle Ourdhi poison. His mind was fully recovered, however, and gave the council an invaluable view of the conditions in Kenor and among the legions.

This was the council, all except for its final member, there was also the mystic, Reshawr, a withered goblin squatting on a tall square stone at the end of the table facing the emperor. Reshawr's eyes were shut. He had not spoken in a decade, but his gentle, wise presence was always there.

Lessis and Ribela were the last to enter the chamber. As they did so, the emperor looked up and forced a smile.

"We are complete then. Please be seated."

"Welcome, Lessis," said Sausann, "Ribela," the heads nodded. Ribela managed a brief, frosty smile. Lessis a warmer one and a word or two with several other members.

When they were seated around the oval table, the emperor began speaking.

"The main issue before us today is the final composition of the trade fleet that will take our ambassadors and our goods to the nations of Czardha."

The emperor was eager to see the great fleet on its way. This expedition had been his dream for many years. It was an ambitious concept, to attempt long-range diplomacy with the nations of Czardha. Both they and the Empire of the Rose were faced with a common enemy, the great power in Padmasa. To be more effective in their resistance to it, it was necessary for them to coordinate their efforts. Pascal had seen the truth of this as a young man, studying the geography and history of the world. Now his dream was close to realization.

"Your Majesty?" It was Petruda of Wolaf, chief administrative officer of the budget and the council representative on the Shipping Committee; a short, heavyset woman, clearly excited by her role in the great expedition to Czardha.

Emperor Pascal nodded for her to speak.

"The Shipping Committee recommends that six white ships will be sent. With the white ships we shall send three frigates. Admiral Cranx has an additional recommendation, I believe."

Eyes switched to the ramrod straight figure of the admiral, who cleared his throat carefully before speaking.

"In the councils of the fleet, it was suggested that we should also send a couple of sloops. The smaller craft are often invaluable in fleet operations, and the cost will be negligible compared to that of sending six white ships."

Bureaucrat Garsk raised his pudgy hand. "For six great ships, we shall have to find crews of two hundred apiece. Twelve hundred full-pay crew for a year, or more. Even getting all the paperwork and interviewing done will take us months."

The emperor chuckled mightily. "Trust the good Garsk to bring us all down to earth at once. Well, my good fellow, you and your clerks shall have to work around the clock, for the fleet must sail by Fundament if they are to make passage of the Cape of Storms before the bad weather begins."

Sausann of the Temple had her hand up.

"May I say something, a word of caution perhaps?"

Again the emperor smiled graciously, "Of course, Sausann, of course."

"May I suggest once more that we consider sending a smaller fleet than this. Six great ships, three frigates plus other smaller vessels. This is a great force that we risk."

"We must take risks to succeed, Sausann," said the emperor.

"This is understood, Your Majesty, but our forces are stretched thin as they are. We cannot afford any great losses."

"Which is one good reason for sending a sufficiently large fleet," the emperor responded. "Admiral, please, your comments again."

Cranx tugged briefly on his white beard.

"Stands to reason, Lady, if we send six white ships with some frigates for ranging around them, then no force in the world can challenge them, or even catch up to them. They will overawe any opposition, and thus more effectively extinguish any hostility before it can be expressed."

Sausann listened. "And still we do risk them, do we not? There may be some quite unknown danger waiting for them. Six great ships could be lost."

Cranx tugged on his beard some more. "Dear Lady, what danger can there be to a well-crewed white ship built in

Cunfshon yards? They can outsail anything else on the ocean."

"A storm, a waterspout, who knows what perils there might be?"

"Dear Lady of the Temple, know you that the white ships have faced and survived every peril of the oceans, and have done so for many years."

"Hear, hear, Admiral, a good point I think," said the emperor.

"And yet ships have been lost," said Sausann stubbornly.

Pascal nodded. "Of course, Sausann, of course, but our ships have plied the oceans of the world for centuries now, and our losses have been few and far between in recent decades."

"Your Majesty." It was Lessis, raising her hand.

"Ah, the Lady in Grey, yes, please tell us your thought." The emperor beheld his greatest ally on the council. Now he could relax and let Lessis sway the conservatives on the council.

However, Lessis's words were a complete surprise, and not only to the emperor.

"For once I must agree with Sausann," she said, and Sausann's eyebrows shot up. "At this moment it may not be the wisest thing to give up the use of six white ships. The voyage to Czardha should be made, of course, but perhaps we must wait another year to send such a large force. Perhaps for now, we should send only a single ship, or a pair of frigates, no more."

The emperor's brows knitted.

"But," he began, "I thought we were all agreed that this year was to be the year?"

"Your Majesty, we in the Office of Unusual Insight have voiced our concern that the great enemy prepares some stroke against us. I know that we have no positive evidence, except the word concerning the enlargement of the breeding pens in Axoxo. However, with that concern in mind, it would be dangerous to weaken in any way our ability to reinforce the Argonath in the event of an emergency in the coming campaign season."

"What are you suggesting though? That all commerce come to a halt? That we hold white ships here in harbor in case they are needed to transport a legion?"

Lessis never employed witchcraft in her dealings with

Emperor Pascal. She knew how sensitized he was to it. If she tried, he would never forgive her and their relationship would be forever changed for the worse. But now she wished that she could, because she feared his resistance. Of course she still refrained, she could not use any spell with an audience of Great Witches and not have them know at once what she did. It was forbidden.

"Your Majesty, we have examined the schedules of the larger white ships, and we are sure there will be sufficient bottoms to carry a legion in an emergency. But not if we send six of them halfway around the world."

"But what of our grand strategy? Now is the time to cement our relations with the nations of Czardha. They are eager for our technologies, our grain, our manufactured goods. With a fleet visit, we can bring them all in at once and form a powerful alliance. With that we can threaten Padmasa from either side of the continent. To send but a couple of ships would be like moving a pawn in timidity, when instead a bishop should be sent surging into the play."

"Indeed, an apt comparison, Your Majesty," said Petruda, who was alarmed at the thought of all her work on organizing the great fleet being destroyed because of some hunch from the Office of Unusual Insight. The Shipping Committee would be devastated.

The emperor compressed his lips, trying not to show obvious anger. He was committed to the great fleet to Czardha. It was his crowning ambition. He saw it as the one sure way to build an alliance that would be able to withstand the strength of Padmasa.

"My friends and advisers, we must consider our strategic goal. An alliance with the Czardhan nations will allow us to strengthen them and to stiffen their resistance to the power that works upon them. They will shut their doors to the enemy.

"We must remember that as they are now, they are in a fundamentally weak position for the coming struggle. They are completely at odds with each other over minor matters, ancestral struggles. But we have already our alliance with Lenkeiseen, we have worked to prepare for this for years. Everything is ripe. Should we not act? Should we not move our bishop?"

"Indeed," said Petruda, "the emperor is absolutely correct. Furthermore, we know that all the major parties in Anson and in the Trucial States are eager to improve trade relations. They have many things that we are interested in. Fine textiles, wine, leather work, many things that they hope to sell to us."

The emperor took over. "While we sell them our excess grain from Kenor, our olive oil from Kadein, and a hundred technologies that they have yet to master. With Cunfshon engineering skills, they will be able to rapidly improve their economies and thus improve their ability to withstand Padmasa." The emperor was alight with the fire of his vision.

"Your Majesty, we of the Office of Unusual Insight concur with your strategy. Our difficulty is that we lack effective intelligence on our enemy's intentions at this moment."

"Your Majesty," said Ribela. They all looked up. Ribela rarely spoke in such council meetings. Usually she agreed with Lessis and she let Lessis do all the talking, but sometimes she had radically different ideas.

"We do have intelligence, of a sort, and it leads me to foreboding. I think that Lessis's interpretation of the current situation is quite probably correct, in which case we must err on the side of caution and preparedness. Consider first, we have no intelligence operation from beyond the White Bones Mountains at this time. Following a disaster for our network of agents in Axoxo last year, we have lost our network in Padmasa as well. We know that the enemy made a massive, intensive counterespionage effort. That is what led to his breakthroughs into our networks. He put out extraordinary effort. Secondly, we had information that the breeding program in Axoxo was to be increased enormously. Third, we know that thousands of women were abducted from Ourdh last year. Fourth, we have nullified his plan for an invasion in concert with the Teetol. We have overthrown the Doom in Tummuz Orgmeen. We have checked his effort in Ourdh. We have hurt him badly."

"And if our fleet proceeds to Czardha, we will hurt him even worse," said the emperor with a smile. "In ten years, we could strengthen the Czardhans to the point where we could imagine coordinating an assault on the enemy."

Sausann and Valembre had been silenced by this unexpected turn. Lessis was on their side for once, and so was the Queen of Mice. Complete solidarity among the witches.

The men would soon start exchanging looks if this went on!

"We have hurt the enemy, Your Majesty, but we have not seriously damaged his ability to make war. We have infuriated him, however. I can inform you that the barriers on the higher planes that surround Padmasa have been more intense than anything I have ever experienced before. They have outdone themselves in this. I sense that they direct their rage against us. This is my fifth concern. Taken altogether, they indicate to me that the Masters prepare a massive stroke against us. We must mobilize to meet it."

"Mobilize?" muttered Sausann. "But that will cost a fortune."

"A fortune, indeed," said Garsk of the Treasury.

"If we disappoint our friends in Czardha, we will be set back for years. The loss of trust," said Pertruda.

Lessis sighed to herself. Of all known governing systems on Ryetelth, the Empire of the Rose was the most effective. A benevolent autocracy, balanced by systems designed to protect the populace and keep them strong in the face of adversity. And yet there were times when even this fine imperial system could not be made to work properly.

"If I may say something," she said. She was not heard.

Ribela raised a hand. Voices fell silent.

"My colleague wishes to speak."

Lessis leveled her grey eyes upon the emperor.

"We must at least convey an official warning to the Argonathi. In particular to Kadein."

"They have been warned," said the emperor. "You asked me to do that six months ago, and it was done. They have taken little heed. They trust their own intelligence, they say. They see no unusual activity along the White Bones."

"But they do not scout beyond the mountains, no one does. We cannot say what the enemy is preparing other than to guess that it will be a great army. We must get them to prepare themselves."

Pascal Iturgio sighed and spread his hands. The complexity of nudging the powerful Kadeini merchant class into accepting the need for war preparations and restrictions on trade as a result was a task that could try the patience of ten good men, and he was just a single emperor, with little practical power over the merchants of Kadein. Kadein had grown so great and powerful that the Kadeini had begun to think of themselves as separate from the empire in some degree. There was talk of independence. Another reason to send the great fleet to Czardha as soon as possible was to ensure that the subsequent trade boom would be overseen from Andiquant and not from Kadein.

"All right," he said with a quiet note of firmness. "I take note of Lessis's concern. It will be investigated. We will press the Kadeini to improve their preparedness. But I will not cancel the great fleet yet. It will not sail for another month anyway, and that gives us a little time to think all these matters through more carefully." He spread his hands over the table palms down.

Lessis bowed her head, as did everyone else. The emperor had given them his decision. Inwardly, Lessis uttered a small prayer of thanks to the Mother.

CHAPTER NINE

The plotters were a diverse group, three dragons and one dragonboy. They gathered in a remote corner of Fort Dalhousie near the southern wall, where firewood was stored and chopped. All was quiet now among the stacked wood. The chopping crew had just finished work and were busy hauling away two cords of split oak and ash, enough to cook the evening meal for the legion and its dragons and keep kettles boiling through the night.

The Purple Green and Bazil had been joined by Vlok, another leatherback, who had been with them through the campaign in Ourdh in the previous year. Vlok had brought his dragonboy. Bazil and the Purple Green were certain that this dragonboy, Swane of Revenant, was the right choice for the task at hand.

"He is bigger than the rest. Bigger than Relkin."

"He is stupid, too," replied the Purple Green.

"Hey," muttered Swane.

"No, my wild friend," said Bazil, "not stupid. No stupid dragonboy lives this long." Swane grinned at this.

"He is, however, foolish. Inclined to jump into things without thinking them through." Swane's grin disappeared.

"Mmm," the Purple Green rubbed his long jaw and considered these words carefully. "Humans are more complex than I ever imagined," he said.

"You are surely correct, since once you thought of men as not much more than food."

"That is true."

Vlok now spoke up for his tender. "Boy Swane is good with pick and clippers, I have no complaints."

Bazil snorted softly but refrained from comment. Both Baz and the Purple Green had had occasion to remark on Vlok's intellectual abilities before.

"So," said the Purple Green, leaning down to face Swane, "you will help us? Vlok has explained what we have to do?"

"Yeah, sure," said Swane. "I know Relkin will probably hate me for a while, but later he'll understand that we're doing this to help him. He'd do it for us if he had to."

Swane was getting a little bright-eyed. He'd come to feel like a brother to Relkin after the campaign in Ourdh and the climactic battle in the pit of the serpent god in ancient Dzu. He, like all the other dragonboys in the 109th, was determined that Relkin should not be hanged.

The dragons conversed among themselves briefly in dragon speech. Bazil and the Purple Green had to explain to Vlok that he could not accompany them. He had a career left in the legions. But the broketail and the wild dragon were done for, unless they saved the boy Relkin.

Vlok had to struggle with all this. He very much wanted to go with them. Being left behind in Fort Dalhousie to face Digal Turrent's wrath paled in comparison to running wild in the forest of Tunina and consorting with wild dragonesses.

Somewhere he had gained the idea that there was more than one dragoness out there in the dark woods across the river Argo. It was a pleasant belief, even if based on no facts at all, and Vlok was loath to let it go. Eventually, however, Bazil succeeded in getting Vlok to accept that he could not come with them, that he had to stay and uphold the honor of the 109th fighting dragons.

At length they turned to Swane, who had been struggling to understand what was going on. Swane's grasp of dragon speech was not as good as that of some dragonboys. Gradually he had come to realize that Vlok was being persuaded to remain behind. Swane felt a shot of relief. Helping Relkin to escape was one thing. Having one's own dragon running off into the woods was another.

Once agreement had been reached, Swane was dispatched to equip himself for the mission and to join them at Bazil and Relkin's stall.

The dragon conspirators waited a moment or two after his departure, followed by that of Vlok.

"The future belongs to the bold, they say," said Bazil.

"Who is they?"

"Some humans."

"Humans are natural chatterboxes. They say many, many

things. Sometimes I wish it were possible to stop their throats and cut off all the talk."

"You not the first dragon to wish this."

"Mmm," the Purple Green scratched himself a moment. "However, on this occasion I think they are right. We must be bold and seize the future."

Bazil chuckled quietly and ignored the wild dragon's look of suspicion.

They lumbered back to the 109th's quarters. As quietly as possible, Bazil and the Purple Green slipped back into Bazil's stall. Relkin, sound asleep, did not stir. Swane came forward with a gag in his hands and a sack over his shoulder.

The dragons carefully reached down, grasped the sleeping boy, and held him still. Relkin awoke to find himself absolutely pinioned by enormous dragon hands. He squirmed and wriggled, but could not free any limbs. A smaller, more dexterous pair of hands now went to work. A gag was forced into his mouth and tightened before he could call for help. Next his wrists and ankles were bound. Then he was unceremoniously lifted and shoved headfirst into a heavy sack. For a moment the sack was left on the floor. Relkin heard the unmistakable sound of the big dragonsword being taken down from its hook and strapped across his dragon's shoulders.

The last thing he saw was the eye of the Purple Green. He knew it was his own dragons who had done this. With some human assistance because they could never have managed the gag or the bonds on their own. Dragon hands were too clumsy for such fine work.

Then he felt the bag lifted and flipped over an immense shoulder, and he knew he was being carried off, abducted into the night by a dragon taken leave of its senses.

He did his best to raise the alarm, but could manage no more than a muffled "moo" into the sackcloth. Then a big hand came down on the sack and squeezed him into silence.

Bazil and the Purple Green, with swords in their scabbards but no shields, timed their exit from the fort carefully. A woodcutting party from the 66th Marneri Dragons was heading out the gate. Military dragons did not wander freely in and out of the fort's gates. Dragons, in fact, only left the fort to exercise or to cut wood or assist the engineers in some task requiring strength and skill.

The woodcutting party consisted of twenty men, marching

at the front, followed by several horse-drawn carts, followed by six dragons. As the dragons went by, Bazil and the Purple Green sauntered into the column behind their friends Oast and Ksodan, who were bringing up the rear.

It was a busy day, with men and dragons going in and out constantly on their way to and from the various competitions and arenas. The guards at the gate were far too busy to take any notice of the fact that an extra pair of dragons had gone out with the woodcutting detail.

Outside the fort, the woodcutting party turned left and went along the high road to Dallybridge, avoiding the town of Dalhousie altogether. The booths and tents of the summer fair were soon behind them.

Bazil quietly bade Oast and Ksodan not to mention the presence of the two dragons from the 109th, and then he and the Purple Green slowed their pace and let the woodcutting party move ahead. They were a league or so south of the fort now, and there were few houses here. They retired into Dingman's wood and made their way in far enough to be out of sight of the fort road. Then they turned and headed northeast, looping around the lee of the bluff on which stood the fort, and heading for the river Argo upstream of Dalhousie.

There was swampy ground and a forest of willows, alders, and rushes that was torture for the two dragons to work through. They had to do it quietly and without recourse to their swords, which would have let them hack their way through very quickly. But flashing dragonswords would be seen from the fort and reported, and so they had to push and wriggle and creep through the boggy parts keeping under the canopy of leaves.

At length they came out upon the shores of the Argo. The river here was almost a mile wide, a hurrying torrent of dark water, freshened by recent rains on Mt. Red Oak and Mt. Snowgirt.

After scouting the river for boats and seeing none, the dragons scrambled down to the water's edge. Here the wyvern waded into the cool current with happy grunts of pleasure. The Purple Green tested the current and squawked.

"It is cold."

"Yes, that is good. This dragon is damned hot after walking through swamp."

"Yes, I suppose so," said the Purple Green, who slowly slid his big bulk into the water, too. In truth, once the shock of the cold water was past, the experience was pleasant. He wondered why he had feared the water in his earlier life. Of course, being a flying dragon he was not a natural swimmer—unlike Bazil, who was at home in the water with almost crocodilian ease—but he had the natural bouyancy of any large animal and all the strength that was needed. Indeed, he'd swum this river twice in the previous spring when he had first struck out on his own and tried to make a life as a ground-bound wild dragon.

Out into the stream they swam until the strong current picked them up and they drifted downstream while they struggled across. At length, they touched ground once more on the other side when they were within sight of the Dalhousie Light.

Quickly they scuttled up the bank and withdrew beneath the eaves of the forest above. They had achieved the first objective. They had escaped from the legion.

CHAPTER TEN

When they had pushed through the thickets more than a mile inland of the river, the two fugitive dragons paused for a breather.

They set down the sack, which showed no signs of life.

"Should we release the boy?" said the Purple Green.

"I was wondering about that myself."

"He will be all right, I hope."

"Seems a bit still."

"Perhaps sleeps. Dragonboys love to sleep."

"Damnably lazy individuals for the most part."

Bazil reached down and ripped open the sack and pulled it away from the prone form of Relkin, who lay utterly still. Bazil reached down and gingerly inserted the tip of his claw under the gag. He pulled up on it sharply, ripped the material, and then carefully tore it away. Still Relkin did not move.

The dragons looked at each other with dismay.

"By the breath of the ancients, he does not move," said the Purple Green.

"By the breath, you are right." Baz nudged Relkin with a foreclaw, a well-tended foreclaw, cut and polished and trimmed and filed. Without a dragonboy, life in the wild would be a lot less comfortable than this particular leatherback was used to.

Relkin remained where he was, seemingly quite lifeless. Bazil used his oddly broken tail tip to prod the boy again. There was still no movement.

"Oh, by the egg, I am afraid," said the Purple Green.

Bazil was, too. Gently, he shook the boy's shoulder with a couple of fingers. Boy seemed slack-jointed, loose, and soft, not at all like the Relkin of old. Baz began to imagine the worst.

"Boy not robust enough for such a trip. Foolish dragons forget that dragonboys are delicate, easily broken."

Bazil felt a sudden wave of sorrow engulf him.

"May the ancient gods forgive me, I have killed him. I did not think it through. The boy is dead."

The Purple Green gave a great groan of woe, and sat down on a log that gave ominously beneath his enormous bulk. Tenderly he poked Relkin in the ribs with a foreclaw. The dragonboy did not spring to life.

"I am very sad. I think I made a stupid mistake. I wanted to help boy. It was wrong to watch him hanged. Boy teach this dragon a great deal. I would not have survived in the legions without him."

Bazil nodded at hearing this confession from the wild dragon. "Quite true," he said.

"Remember how he taught me to use tail sword?"

"Oh, yes," murmured Bazil. That had been a business, how could one ever forget?

"He taught me, and he does not even have a tail. No human has a tail."

"It is one of the great mysteries. How could any race grow so mighty without one?"

They nodded together, this was indeed one of those ineluctable mysteries of life. Here were the humans, with their cities and ships and manufactured things. They were the masters of things in the world, and yet they lacked a tail. For dragons the tail was prehensile, flexible, useful in many ways, almost like having a third hand. It was inconceivable that one would live without one.

For a long time they sat there and stared at the still form stretched out on the ground. Bazil dropped the other sack, which contained the rest of the boy's possessions, his bow, the scabbard for the dirk; the box and pouches that contained his dragon-tending kit.

"Boy will not be needing these things now."

They nodded and fell back into gloomy silence.

"What will we do with his body?" said the Purple Green after a while.

"The humans usually bury their dead in the ground. We will have to dig a hole and plant him."

"By the hot breath of old Glabadza, that is a strange custom."

"I know. They burn dragons, they bury men, even bury dogs and cats."

The dragons had grown immensely solemn now, having accepted the boy's death. Sorrow rode upon their shoulders, they were bowed down with it.

"We will take him to a high place and bury him. His spirit will have a good view for all eternity."

"That is a good idea, where do you suggest?"

"Mt. Ulmo. We will take him to Mt. Ulmo. I know a good place there." A high meadow above the hemlock forests, where Baz had met the Purple Green two years before. The same place where he had come upon the green dragoness, High Wings.

The Purple Green understood at once. "Good, let us take him there."

Bazil picked up the sack and found that he had ripped it almost completely in half. It was now useless for their purpose and an ominous foretaste of the difficulties that would lie ahead for them without a dragonboy.

"Oh, by the breath," he groaned. "We have such clumsy hands for dealing with the human world. All these things that are small and neat and fragile."

"It is true," agreed the Purple Green.

They stood there nodding somberly, completely downcast, drowning in gloom.

They were still standing there a minute later when a voice cut through the air behind them.

"Not a good start for your life in the wild without a dragonboy, I'd say."

Their heads swiveled with an almost audible snap.

The dragonboy was sitting up.

"He lives!" exclaimed the Purple Green.

"No thanks to you." Relkin was still sitting there, breathing, obviously alive.

"Thanks be to the gods of old Dragon Home," said the Purple Green.

"What for? Bringing you two fools into the world? You know, I wasn't dead in the first place."

"What?" The Purple Green was thunderstruck.

"A trick? You tricked us?"

"You deserved it."

The Purple Green exhaled an enormous hiss. His eyes flared dangerously. But Bazil reached down and lifted the boy up and put him on his shoulders before hopping around in the clearing, crushing small trees and bushes while hooting in relief and delight.

"Ha hah, ho ho, boy trick these old dragons pretty damn well. Ho ho ho."

The Purple Green nodded, it was incontrovertibly true. Eventually he too saw the funny side of it and emitted several loud noises that those who knew him understood to be laughter, but otherwise sounded more like a horse being strangled.

The only one who was unhappy with the situation was the dragonboy, wet through, sore at wrist and ankle.

"You damned idiots! Do you understand what you've done? Now we're all under threat of a court-martial for desertion. I was in trouble before, but now I'm done for. Now they'll hang me for sure."

"So we cannot go back," said the Purple Green. He seemed unfazed by the prospect.

"Right," grumbled Relkin. "We starve, and then we freeze if we last long enough. For sure we'll starve in the wintertime."

"No," said the Purple Green. "I have studied this problem. I have a plan to solve it."

"Oh, that's wonderful. How are you planning to cook this plan? I'm told that plans are not very filling food."

"What?" The Purple Green frowned in puzzlement, an expression so like the human that even a wet, angry, frightened dragonboy was forced to smile.

"Look, somebody cut this rope, will you?" He held up his wrists.

Bazil rummaged through the pile of Relkin's things and brought out a sturdy dirk with a blade a foot long. It was hard for a dragon to draw from the sheath and difficult to hold in a huge dragon paw. The leverage to cut the rope was too much for the tail. But by dint of much sweat and concentration, he cut the bonds and freed the dragonboy.

Relkin flexed his arms and wrists a number of times, then snatched the dirk from the dragon and cut the rope at his ankles.

"Let me guess, you got Vlok to persuade Swane to tie me up, right?"

"Yes, something like that."

"We persuade Swane ourselves," said the Purple Green.

"And nobody had enough sense to see that you were dooming us to starve to death in the snow."

"Why need we starve? We two dragons will drive the game, you will kill it with your bow. We brought everything you will need."

"And where are we going to live? When the snows come, I will want to be inside someplace warm, with a fire going."

"No difficulty," said the Purple Green. "We will find a good cave."

Relkin nodded, the great damned things had thought it all out. He was going to be a cave dweller the rest of his days. He would wear skins, and stink of smoke and sweat.

He swallowed and shook his head angrily. Unfortunately, it now appeared that no matter how daft this scheme was, it was going to be his life. He was going to be a ragged, half-starved wildling, living in the northern forests with a pair of eternally cranky dragons.

"Have faith in us," said the Purple Green. "We will be good hunters."

"And we will not be alone," said Bazil.

"What does that mean?"

"We will find High Wings, and my children. We will all live together."

"She will want to return to Dragon Home. She will never agree to live this close to humankind. Besides, dragons don't mate for life."

"We will go north as well."

"Brrr. It's cold up there, eternal snow and ice and all that."

"We are hunters, we will live where the game is."

"Bazil hasn't hunted since he was a sprat. Since we lived in the village."

"You have your bow. We know you are good with it. We will drive the game, you will kill it, or wound it and slow it up enough for us to kill it. I have thought it all out."

Relkin felt something very heavy in his chest. He shrugged and then let out a great groan. There was nothing to be done now. To go back meant a hanging for sure, before the entire legion.

After a while he recovered the circulation in his limbs, and stood up and exercised briefly. It was incredible but true, his old life, the only life he had ever known, was over and done with. From now on he would be renegade. He would never see the cities of the Argonath again. These thoughts depressed him, and he shook his head to try and drive them away.

"We must move on," said the Purple Green, "I am getting hungry; we need to hunt."

Relkin sighed. "And we need to get farther away from the river. The legion will send out search parties for us, and they won't take long to work out where we've gone. They know that your ladylove is living up on Mt. Ulmo right now."

"We go there first, to find her."

There wasn't much alternative.

"Let's move it then. We've got a long way to go."

They set off, heading up the great Argo Valley toward the distant mountains. As they went they kept a sharp eye for anything edible.

After a couple of hours, they found a porcupine. When challenged, it climbed the nearest tree. The dragons eyed it carefully. At the most it promised a couple of mouthfuls, no more. After careful appraisal, they left the porcupine behind as not being worth the effort and continued their march.

Hours passed and they grew hungry. As the sun began to sink into the west, all three were ravenous.

And then at last the Purple Green's sensitive nose caught the scent of meat.

"There is open flesh, blood, not far from here, upwind."

They turned off their trail and headed due north, into an area of bare rock with small pines and oaks clutching to it in the cracks.

Quite suddenly the smell strengthened to the point where even Relkin could detect it. They came over a small ridge and found the source ahead. An elk carcass, torn open and half devoured.

They also came upon the owners of the kill, a pack of six wolves who rose with a snarl at the sight of Relkin and then withdrew to a safe distance when he drew his bow. Then when the two dragons showed themselves, the wolves yipped in surprise and vanished into the short forest.

Relkin and the two dragons were left to inventory the carcass. The wolves contented themselves with staring at them from the safety of the trees.

The wolves had killed the elk that morning and had fed on it all day. The fat had been stripped from it, the liver and choice internal meats had gone first. What was left was the stringy flesh of the lower legs and neck, plus the back and the bones.

Relkin cut himself some ragged strips and built a fire and held them over it on some pointed sticks. While they sputtered and charred, the dragons crunched up the remainder of the elk.

Relkin had a chewy, meal of tough meat. By then it was dark and a cool air was coming off Mt. Ulmo. The dragons, far from sated, laid themselves out to sleep for a few hours. Relkin persuaded them to hack down some boughs with which he fashioned a more or less comfortable mound in which to sleep.

Thus they spent the night. In the morning they awoke, very hungry and set off toward Mt. Ulmo at once.

Before noon, Relkin was able to shoot a rock dove in a canyon above the Argo. He plucked the dove as he walked and roasted it on a little fire when they paused for a rest. He gave the dragons a nibble apiece and ate the breasts himself.

The dragons were starving.

That night they slept hungry, not having come across any game at all.

The next day they continued the slog toward Mt. Ulmo.

In the late afternoon, with hungry dragons fairly groaning from the discomfort in their bellies, they stumbled on a small herd of deer.

The deer spotted them and fled at once in a jumble of white tails, across a meadow and into the trees.

Now it was time to test the Purple Green's theories. The dragons went to the right of the deer and entered the woods while Relkin loaded his bow and hid himself. The dragons were going to work around behind the deer and drive them back to the meadow's edge.

Relkin waited a long time. The deer did not emerge. Eventually two tired and frustrated dragons appeared.

The deer had refused to be driven. They had raced northward each time the dragons tried to get around them and herd them back to the south and the meadow.

Eventually they had distanced the dragons completely and vanished into a thick pine forest that began on the higher slopes a few miles farther up.

Again they slept hungry and awoke hungrier still.

That morning they startled two more small herds of deer, and Relkin spent some time trying to stalk a solitary doe. He got to within a hundred feet of her but before he could shoot, she saw him and fled, bouncing jauntily across a short stretch of brush and disappearing into a patch of birch trees.

For lunch he shot three squirrels. His own he cleaned and roasted. The dragons ate theirs raw, furtively, without looking at each other.

Then, late in the afternoon they had a stroke of luck. A wild boar engaged in rooting for tubers in a clearing took violent exception to Relkin's trespass. The boar charged without pausing to sniff out the scent of dragon. Relkin avoided the brute's charge by swinging up into a little oak tree. The boar proceeded to cut up the tree with his tusks while making a great deal of noise. In his enjoyment of his fury, he failed to notice the dragon that suddenly exploded out of the screen of trees nearby and threw itself at him.

At the last moment the boar realized its peril and turned and fled, escaping the outstretched grasp of the Purple Green and barreling across the clearing and by great good fortune, ran itself right into Bazil's path.

Ecator swept up and down with a great whooshing sound and the boar was cut in twain in a flash, dead before it had any chance to comprehend its doom.

Relkin assembled material for a large fire and roasted the pig while the dragons sat there salivating and staring at the thing.

They ate with enormous grunts of pleasure while Relkin devoured his own along with some summer raspberries he'd found on the margins of a bog.

At length he banked the fire down, and they fell asleep, reasonably content for the first time in their life in the wild.

CHAPTER ELEVEN

Evening's light fell from a clear sky on the white city of Marneri by the shores of the Bright Sea. The bell tolled steadily to bring the faithful for the Temple Service at dusk. Novices in dark blue ran down the marble steps to the entrance of the Novitiate, their bright girlish chatter ringing off the stone walls. On the battlements far above, the guard changed while sergeants barked commands.

In a high apartment of the Tower of Guard, Lagdalen of the Tarcho was ushered into a room with wide windows and a view of the city stretching away to the harbor and the Long Sound beyond it. A white-whiskered, old man, full-bellied under a red velvet robe, rose to greet her.

"Welcome, my child, welcome to my favorite room."

"Thank you, Chamberlain Burly, it is most wonderful. You have the best views of the city from here."

"You honor me, child, but I am chamberlain no longer. That position is held by Axnuld of the Fiduci now."

"Of course, sir, but still I think of you as chamberlain, so long did you serve us all in that capacity."

"Most of the old king's life I served. It wore me out in the end. It is only right that Axnuld should serve the new queen."

"King Sanker was well served by you, sir. I pray daily that the queen will do as well with Lord Axnuld."

"Well, she will have to do her part, too. It is an exacting business being a monarch. She will know that by now, of course."

"She does, my Lord Burly, she does. In truth, she regrets her assumption of the throne every day. Queen Besita is not blessed with an appetite for hard work. To the contrary, in fact, if I may be so bold."

Burly chuckled. The girl was barely twenty, and yet she spoke with an unwonted frankness about the monarch.

Lagdalen was already far more than the girl she appeared to be. She had been inducted into the secret world of the Great Witches. She had served in the most perilous circumstances and seen things that had stripped the childishness away from her early in life.

Burly knew that just a couple of years earlier, Lagdalen had been tossed out of the Novitiate under a cloud. Flighty and irresponsible was the word on her. Now such comments were stilled. There was a sense of gravity to this young woman that spoke of the power of the witches. Already a little had rubbed off on her. Once the witches began their work on her, she started to become like them. At that thought old Burly's chuckle died away in his throat.

"We must remember that Besita has had a difficult life for one such as she," he said. "We are fortunate that they were able to recover her from that web of sorcery in Tummuz Orgmeen." Burly waved a hand. "But you know much more about these things than I. I merely mention it to remind us of our good fortune in having Besita to follow the old king."

"True enough, Lord Burly, although now we face the challenge of getting an heir from the queen. She has avoided the issue to this point."

"She has the choice, Tarquin of Talion is the right age. Brother to the new king there, he would serve well. The blood of Tarquins is hot and strong. Perhaps it would liven up the line of Marneri."

"The queen is not partial to the lord Duke of Talion I fear. She casts her eye to Kadein."

"Ah, she is still enamored of that aristo fop Gellion?"

"I would not dare to say it to anyone but yourself, Lord Burly, but you are correct, painfully correct."

"But she grows in years and must soon choose or forever remain childless."

"It is true, my lord, and we hear discussion of the matter every day."

Burly chuckled, he could well imagine it. How different was the tone in the new reign from that which he had known so well in King Sanker's time.

"But this is not why you have come to me, is it, girl?"

"No, my lord."

"You wish to ask me about the factors of Aubinas." Lagdalen nodded, and her eyes shone with appreciation of his perspicacity.

"Truly your reputation for farsight is well earned, Lord Burly. I do indeed wish to ask your advice in the matter of the grain factors. The queen is torn and quite indecisive. She is under great pressure from the senator from Aubinas. Yet she must allow the judgment to be rendered. The tribunal heard the evidence months ago. The jury handed up a verdict. The man is guilty. He committed piracy and murder. But still the Aubinans demand that he receive the lightest sentence possible."

"And what would that be, pray?"

"Confinement to his own estates; house arrest if you will."

"For how long?"

"For the rest of his life. There is a clause, an ancient one, from the forms of the Vero. He can be imprisoned in his house, and the door can be clapped up and he can be kept there forever or until his death. Once, long ago when the Vero were a simple mountain people, it meant slow death from starvation. The houses of the ancient Vero were not very big. But in the case of Porteous Glaves, the home in question would be a great mansion on a large farming estate. He would live out his days in idle luxury. Clearly, it is a travesty of justice."

Burly nodded calmly. Such travesties occurred. They had to be fought, but not all could be prevented.

"I agree that this would be an abomination. The man, Glaves, was a corn factor in Aubinas. A wealthy man who bought his regiment. He broke under the strain of the campaign in Ourdh and behaved badly. The legions are demanding an end to the practice."

"There is much opposition among the vested interests, particularly in Aubinas."

"The Aubinans can cause trouble."

"Kadein has sworn to stay out of the matter."

"King Neath is a good man. He will stick to his word, I am sure, but they will still be drawn in if the Aubinans switch their grain sales to Kadein. Prices will soar in Marneri."

"Prices will be depressed in Kadein."

"Popular with the common people. And foreknowledge would be most rewarding for those who moved quickly to ship grain back to Marneri."

"Our markets will be disrupted for months."

"And all because of one fat, worthless Aubinan corn merchant that we ought to hang."

"Yes, Lord Burly, exactly so."

"And the queen's Kadeini friends are telling her to hang him. They hope to make a killing in the markets."

"Exactly so, my Lord."

"And the Marneri Council is urging caution. I am sure Fiice and Plesenta want no chaos in the grain markets." Burly nodded to himself for a moment.

"A knotty problem, indeed. Tell me one thing, who are the most prominent among the magnates now trying to put pressure on the queen?"

"Wexenne of Champery, Tafd of Posila, my Lord Burly."

"Ah, of course. Wexenne. The very name of the man bespeaks trouble. A most difficult, insidious fellow for the most part."

Lagdalen nodded her agreement. The Magnate Wexenne always made a point of ignoring Lagdalen completely whenever they chanced to meet in the queen's chamber. Wexenne's voice, at work upon the queen's ear, had become all too familiar in recent weeks.

"Wexenne hopes to profit. Glaves had dreamed of becoming senator. He had built up a strong position for the next election. Now he is ruined. Even if he lives, he will never be able to run for elected office. But he can throw great weight behind someone else. Like Magnate Wexenne. Glaves has wealth and an organization; Wexenne has merely wealth."

"What can be done, Lord Burly?"

"Leave me to think about this problem overnight, child. Return tomorrow at noon, and I will give you an answer. This requires careful contemplation."

Lagdalen thanked the old lord chamberlain at his door and took the stairs down three floors. Then she turned right in the grand corridor and went down to the entrance to her own family's apartments: a series of rooms, large and small that held three generations of the Tarchos of Marneri and their cousins the Dimici, who lived with them.

In the nursery she found her daughter, Laminna, fast asleep in her cradle. Two other cradles were rocking nearby, with Dimici babes born in the past year. The nursemaids, Wessary and Illin, looked up with fond smiles at the sight of Lagdalen.

After a few moments to just look at her baby and then a

quick conversation with Wessie, Lagdalen went on, pausing only to pat little Dur, Wessy's three-year-old boy, on the head at the doorway.

In the salon she found her mother, Lacustra, at work with the cook, planning the menu of a dinner for ten guests that would be held in a week's time. It was to be in honor of Tommaso's twentieth year of service in the Tower of Guard.

"Mother," said Lagdalen with a little curtsy.

"My child, we have not seen you for days. How are you?"

"Well, Mother, perfectly well. But busy, terribly busy."

"And so young. It is a shame. You should be living for your child and your husband. Instead you advise the queen. Barely into your majority, and you advise the queen. Who would've heard of such a thing?"

Who, indeed, thought Lagdalen.

"It was not my choice, Mother. I never asked for this."

"How many times have I heard you say that!" Lacustra turned to the cook. "We will have the puree of turnips I think. The lamb is to be roasted without garlic, and we will want a fresh-mint sauce."

"Cream in the puree, lady?"

"No, Cook, by the goddess's sacred thighs, I swear sometimes you just want to fatten us all up for market. Use a little oil, of course, but no cream; it's too heavy."

"As you wish, lady."

Lacustra suddenly remembered something. "Lagdalen, my dearest, there is a message scroll for you. It came earlier today, from Kenor, I believe."

Lagdalen had been on her way to the great kitchen that served the entire apartment, but she turned on her heel, all thought of lifting a couple of Cook's fine sweet biscuits from the jar temporarily abandoned.

"Where is it, Mother?"

"Ah, now where did I put it? I think it is in the library, on the reader by the window."

Lagdalen swept into the library, which was empty and dark. She lit the lamp and found a short scroll sitting on the reader. It was a military scroll, and as she expected, there was a stamp from Fort Dalhousie. It was the sort of scroll used for short messages, such as those that recalled men to their regiments or announced illnesses and deaths.

It had to be from Relkin. Instinctively she knew that it meant her dragonboy friend was in trouble. She cut the seal, opened it, and found a barely literate message scrawled therein.

It took a couple of takes before she was sure she understood it. To escape a trial for murder and a likely hanging, Relkin had deserted along with two of the legion's best dragons. All three had swum the Argo and headed north into Tunina. She was implored to come to their aid. The message was signed "Swane and Mono. 109th Marneri Dragons."

Lagdalen rolled the scroll shut, and then pushed herself to her feet and headed for the front entrance. Her husband, Captain Hollein Kesepton, would want to hear this news.

CHAPTER TWELVE

The fugitives stumbled through the wet woods of summer, climbing the westernmost foothills of Mt. Ulmo. After two weeks they were gaunt and lean, their muscles hardened by constant travel, their bellies chronically empty.

Indeed, hunting the deer and elk of the mountains of Tunina had proved vastly more difficult than the Purple Green had imagined. Only once, in fact, had Relkin actually brought down a doe, with an arrow through the chest, that killed her instantly as she drank by a stream.

He took a haunch for his supper. The dragons barely stilled their hunger with the rest of her. As always, they awoke hungry to no breakfast.

Once they had come upon the remains of a far larger kill. Great bones cracked, for their marrow littered a clearing. The gnawed skull of a bull aurochs gave them the identity of the victim. The ground was heavily trampled, and many creatures had scavenged the kill that was more than a week old. Still, Bazil was hopeful. It had the feel of dragon kill. Only a flying dragon could attack and devour a mighty aurochs. These wild cattle stood as tall as a man and weighed more than a ton apiece. Something told the broketail dragon that High Wings, his lovely green dragoness, was in the vicinity.

They climbed into the belt of high meadows, where two years before, Bazil and the Purple Green had fought their duel for the dragoness. As they climbed, the Purple Green fell into a morose silence.

Around them the lands of the Argo were visible through breaks in the trees. The river wound sinuously through the highlands to the east, while to the south, the land opened out into the great vale of Dalhousie. There, the Dally and the Tuala met beneath the green eaves of the forest of Valur, a name of antique legend, where once the ancient kings of

Veronath were wont to hunt. In the day, they hunted boars, in the night, women.

The hemlock forest had thinned and been replaced by woods of ash and birch, with mountain beech and hickory and pine. The sun was able to penetrate these woods and the traveling was warm work. But after the stifling cool gloom of the hemlock forest in the lower lands, they were all glad for the sight of the sky.

Shortly before nightfall, Relkin spotted something wheeling high in the sky, far to the east of them, above central Tunina. He gave a great cry and pointed, and the dragons craned their long necks and stared off in that direction.

" 'Tis not she," said the Purple Green, "too small."

There was a silence. Then Bazil spoke up.

"It is Braner, the young male. Mine."

"He flies well for one with wyvern in his parentage."

"Indeed he does. In this he goes far beyond his old sire. Mmmm. I wonder if he swims?"

"Unlikely, they have lived their lives in Dragon Home. The water there is not for swimming; it is all frozen into ice."

The distant dragon spiraled down into the distant forest and was lost in the gloom. The dragons remained frozen in place, their eyes fixed on that distant spot in the gloom where they had last seen the bronze body of Braner.

Relkin busied himself building a fire. He had some wild turnips, a dozen half-ripe, purple tops. He roasted them in the hot coals of the fire. They were bitter but edible, and they were all they had, so he ate several before lying down to sleep. His stomach churned frenziedly as it digested the turnips, but he barely noticed and was quickly asleep.

The dragons now furtively edged over and tried the turnips.

"Disgusting," muttered the Purple Green.

"Exactly my thought. Boy did not say they were good to eat, only that they could be eaten."

"Not by this dragon."

"We find food soon. She is still here."

The dragons sat long into the night, their stomachs tightening, but their hearts set afire by the thought of the dragoness nearby. Warring emotions churned within each great dragon heart.

Only two years before, they had fought for the female.

Now, seasoned by a year in the legion himself, the Purple Green understood the mechanics of Bazil's inevitable victory over him. He, too, knew how to wield a dragonsword now.

"If we were to meet again over the green High Wings, it would not go so easy for you this time, my Broketail friend."

Bazil grunted. "You have gained skill with the dragonsword, my wild friend. And you are very strong." He was diplomatic.

The Purple Green grunted. "I saw you beat Burthong, Broketail. Burthong was too fast for me; he almost as fast as leatherback dragon."

"By the breath of the ancients, that is true."

"But it was not just swordplay that you used. I remember one blow from a fist."

Bazil whistled. "You were trying to bite my neck. I had no choice."

The Purple Green strangled a horse again, a sound that carried in the night air and caused predator and prey alike to raise their heads in wonder on the slope of Mt. Ulmo. Some coyotes caught the scent of the dragons and the roasted turnips, and sat back and howled the news to the world around them.

Wolves in the distant forest of Tunina answered them, first one pack quite close by and then a much larger pack farther away. For a while the howling seemed to echo off the night sky, warning all who could hear, that terrible creatures from the ancient world were abroad in the forests.

At last the howling died away. The winds seethed through the branches, and the moon rose in the west; a crescent, bright silver.

The dragons tossed and turned in unhappy sleep.

Relkin awoke at dawn, stoked up the fire, and cooked the remainder of the little purple-top turnips. They were a disagreeable way to start the day, but they were better than nothing, especially after the semi-starvation of the past several days.

Once more they set off, now trending westward, circling around Mt. Ulmo's crown, heading for the southeastern slopes. As they went, Relkin began to have the feeling that he was being watched. Often he turned around to catch sight of that that observed them, but found nothing. It was an uncanny feeling, and one that would not go away. Briefly he confided to the dragons, and they all kept a careful lookout from then on.

About an hour after noon, they came on the trail of a small group of elk. Relkin estimated three adult females and several smaller animals, yearlings, and fauns.

They diverged, the dragons swinging out to either side, Relkin pressing forward, cautiously, with his bow cocked and ready.

The dragons crept as quietly as possible through the woods on either side of the grazing elk, who had gone out onto a long, narrow meadow that curved around the slope, skirting a pine forest on one side and a birch forest on the other.

The elk worked the center of the meadow. Because the wind was blowing directly down the length of the meadow, they did not sense the dragons lurking on either side.

At length the Purple Green had worked himself close to the margin of the scrubby birch woods. Hidden in a clump of mountain laurel, he was barely a hundred paces from the elk, and they were drifting his way. Anxiously he scanned the woods on the far side. Where was the Broketail? Was he in place? And then came the signal, a single flash from an exposed sword tip. Bazil was on the far side. The wind was blowing across the meadow from left to right; neither dragon was upwind of the elk yet.

The Purple Green knew that the boy would be back at the point where the meadow broke open, in a good spot, waiting to shoot.

All was ready. The Purple Green waited, growing more and more tense by the minute. His belly rumbled within him, reinforcing the need for this kill. Patience was difficult. His pattern of hunting had hardly been the patient kind, when he was a flying predator. He roamed the skies above the northland, and fell on whatever he saw and devoured it. Thus it had always been for dragonkind.

Now he waited, like some enormous cat, his great dark eyes fixed on the elk as they grazed slowly, ever so slowly, toward him. Every so often they would look up, or annoyed by the flies, they would duck their heads to dislodge a tormentor. Still they did not see the peril. The four-ton beast lurking in the mountain laurel was invisible to them, and they were in line against the wind. They were within fifty paces. The Purple Green readied himself.

Then the wind began to shift. He sensed it at once. The mountain laurel shivered, so did the birch trees. Then came another gust, and the elk raised their heads as one. Despair gripped the Purple Green. He was too far. There was no chance of pouncing on one of those fat, luscious elk.

In the old days he would have eaten two or three of them, just by himself. Now he would be incredibly lucky to get in range of any of them. With luck, the boy would get a good shot.

He gave his great hunting cry, launched himself out of concealment, and sprang toward the elk. He bound forward on all four legs, his huge feet digging for purchase in the meadow soil and scattering divots and gravel behind him.

For a moment the elk stared at this terrifying apparition from the ancient era when reptiles ruled the world, long before creatures like elk and lions, bears and men ever strode beneath the sun. Then the elk turned as one and sprang lightly away across the meadow, toward the distant trees. They sprang very swiftly, indeed, and soon distanced the wild drake. However, they did so in the direction of the pine forest on the opposite side of the meadow. The Purple Green gave an exultant roar even as the impetus went out of his charge and his great body began to slow.

The elk bounded on, intending to vanish into the pine trees, in complete ignorance of the trap.

However, for some reason known only to themselves, they began to angle toward a gap between the trees some two hundred paces to the right of Bazil's hiding place. The trap would not work unless he moved, and if he moved the elk would see him too soon. There was nothing to be done about it, Bazil was forced to move, bursting from concealment, Ecator in his hand, and charging at the elk.

The bounding mammals skidded to a halt so abrupt that some of them fell down in their terror. Divots were kicked up from the meadow in the frantic confusion, and they turned to their right and bounded away, down into the open length of the meadow, directly away from where Relkin waited, arrow notched, a groan of frustration dying in his throat.

He stood up and trudged onto the meadow.

"So much for that!" He shouted at the Purple Green, who shot him a defiant, angry look.

Bazil drew up short, slowing to a glum sort of lumber. He

stopped and emitted a groan of disappointment. The Purple Green sank his sword into the ground and squatted down on his immense haunches.

Failure yet again! The three hungry hunters stared mournfully down the length of the meadow at the jaunty tails of the elk as they slowed and began to graze again, feeling quite safe from the strange enemies they had encountered and outrun so easily.

"My fault, I came out too soon." Baz was contrite.

"No, no, you did your best. They broke the wrong way. We are too slow. Maybe I am wrong. We starve to death soon now."

Relkin bit back any remarks. Starving dragons were dangerous after a while. They began to see everything, even dragonboys, as food. Besides, the situation was dire enough without having a dragonboy indulge in sarcasm. He took a deep breath and prepared to head back for his pack, which was still under the trees.

Then a shadow passed swiftly over the sun. There was a tremendous sound, like a gigantic whip being cracked right overhead, and a bolt of astonishing green fury stooped out of the azure and landed square on one of the adult elk. The animal had barely begun to run when it was struck down like a pigeon under a falcon's talons. The dragon's great claws cut down through the elk's neck and chest, breaking her shoulders and cutting her heart in twain.

Relkin felt his eyes bulge in his head. There, standing over the prey was the wild green dragoness, High Wings, who hurled back her head and brayed her hunting cry to strike terror in the woods.

The two battledragons were struck dumb with awe for a moment. Then Bazil emitted a wild, trumpet of welcome, and both great beasts lumbered toward her.

Bazil was ecstatic. "To see you again so soon, my love, it is a wonderful tonic for an old wyvern."

The dragoness was not in a mood for breeding, as she'd explained when they rescued her from the cage on Trader Dook's ship.

"You've lost weight" was the tart reply.

"True," said Bazil, quite besotted.

"I suppose you aren't much good for hunting."

The Purple Green arrived on the scene with his characteristic heavy tread.

"Neither of us is much good at hunting elk. We require larger game."

"The wyvern is right. We have to go to the land of mammoths and bison."

The green dragoness scrutinized the wild drake.

"So, the humans have enslaved even the Purple Green of Hook Mountain," she said scornfully.

The Purple Green's eyes flashed anger, and the scales on his neck stood up dangerously.

"I am no slave. I am free and wild again. We both are. We have left the human world. I want to go to the land of mammoths."

"We are both battledragons now," said Bazil. "You should see this big fellow when he wields a sword. He frightens everyone on the battlefield. Truly, armed with sword, he is the most terrible thing on this world."

"No matter how terrible he is, neither of you are going to reach the land of the mammoths. That is a long flight away. You will starve to death long before you get there."

"We can hunt," said the Purple Green.

"I have watched you hunt," said the dragoness tartly. "I saw you both lumbering around in pursuit of elk. The only elk you will eat is going to be long dead by the time you find it. You will be eaters of carrion, worm-ridden, covered in flies."

"We have a better idea," said Bazil.

Relkin suddenly gave a yip of fright as a small dragon, in a flash of bronze scales buzzed right over his head, wheeled, and pounced at him.

"Braner!" he shouted. "It is I, Relkin, the dragonboy. Remember me?"

Braner settled to the meadow and folded his wings.

"You are not food. You are for talking to, but your dragon speech is strange."

"I could say the same thing about yours. I speak with the wyverns, and I speak with the wyvern tongue."

"You speak it horribly, but you are not food."

"Not food. Dragonboy."

The broketail lumbered up to Braner and swept the small, winged dragon up in a clumsy hug.

"My offspring, the fruit of my egg!"

Braner gave a screech and squirmed free.

Bazil turned back to High Wings. "We have much better

plan. We will live with you and travel to the land of mammoths together."

"Nonsense. We depart for the north in a few days. There is not enough big game in these lands for my taste. It is hard to feed two growing youngsters and myself on just these elk."

"There are other animals."

"Deer and pigs are all I see, if you don't count bears. I hate the taste of bear. I ate too much polar bear when I was young. My mother was very fond of it, and they were easy to hunt."

"But we will travel with you."

"Then we will go north at a snail's pace. Myself and my young will have to go farther, faster, or we will miss the migrations."

"But surely, my love, would you not want me to accompany you?" said Bazil, stunned by her cool indifference to the father of the young.

They were distracted for a moment as the other youngster, Grener, with a skin of green a little lighter than that of her mother, came flying in bearing a young elk in her talons. She droppped the elk, and she and Braner fell on it and began squabbling as they tore at it.

Braner tried to dispossess his sister of her kill. She hissed and lashed at him with front claws. He dodged back and prepared to strike her down.

Their mother sprang between them with a bellow of fury and both backed away. She turned back to Bazil.

"You do not understand the world of dragons. You live in the world of men. I do not need you now. I will not mate for five more years. I brought the young ones to see you to fulfill our nuptial contract; that is good, as it was in the beginning with the ancient gods of Dragon Home. Now it is done. We must go north. You must go back to the world of men."

Bazil and the Purple Green stared at her. Baz swallowed heavily. He felt worse than if he'd just been struck in the head by a troll.

"Five years?" he muttered.

"And I shall not mate with you," she said. "Not that you were not worthy, you proved yourself. But I understand something of the human power with the things they make now. You would kill any other dragon that tried to woo me.

There is nothing in the world you could not kill with those swords."

Relkin nodded. She was perfectly correct.

"And now if you will excuse us, we are hungry and we have to eat."

The green dragoness ripped into the elk she stood over, and tore off half the shoulder and crunched it up.

"Uh, my love, my precious, the mother of my young," said Bazil.

She looked up suspiciously. "What?"

"We are very hungry. The Purple Green and I. We must eat something soon or die."

She resumed her feast.

"Perhaps you could give us a share of what you're eating now?"

Again the look of dark suspicion.

"It isn't very large. And both of you look very hungry."

"Exactly," rumbled the Purple Green, who was salivating at the sight of the elk and barely restraining himself from throwing himself at it.

"Frankly, we are starving to death, my dear, the mother of my descendants."

With a great groan of disgust, the green dragoness ripped off a haunch from the elk with a neat backward and forward movement that snapped tendons and freed it with loud cracks and pops, then she withdrew.

"Take the rest," she said through the shuttered teeth.

They fell upon the carcass, tore it in half, and crunched into it with the fervor of the starving. The sound of the wind soughing through the grass of the meadow was broken only by the sounds of huge carnivores devouring the dead elk. Bones crunched and snapped, huge bellies rumbled as they received the first real food in days.

Relkin knew better than to expect anyone to leave him even a slice of the elk, and so he shouldered his bow and went back to the woods and hunted for a while, shooting a pair of squirrels that he skinned and roasted over a small fire.

The smell of the cooking soon drew the dragons, and by the time he was ready to eat, he had an audience of five great predators, from the huge Purple Green down to Grener, who was only a little larger than Relkin himself.

Relkin ate the squirrels and ignored the pressure in the

eyes of the various dragons. They had just consumed several hundred pounds of meat between them without offering him an ounce. By the old gods, he wasn't about to give up any of these squirrels.

Not a word was spoken, and as the fire died down, they all set themselves to sleep.

CHAPTER THIRTEEN

Relkin awoke at dawn and roused himself, shaking the chill from his limbs and stretching his muscles in the early light. Around him the dragons slumbered, the Purple Green snored loudly. The young dragons nestled near their mother.

He stood up and continued the stretches. Sleeping in the open was nothing new to him, of course, and he knew the wisdom of stretching after waking up cold and stiff. The last thing he needed now was a pulled muscle.

As he arched his back and rotated his arms backward, he felt another presence. He looked up and saw the green dragoness watching him. So intent was her gaze that he almost fell into dragon-freeze. He called a greeting in dragon speech, "Welcome to the day!" But she did not reply. Shortly afterward she turned away from the sleeping huddle of great beasts, cracked her wings open, and took to the air, the wings flapping mightily while she hurled herself from the ground in a single enormous bound. Trees bent over from the force of her wing beats, and within seconds she was far down the meadow and rising steadily into the air.

It was no wonder dragons had such appetites considering the athletic nature of their lives, thought Relkin. Wyverns could not fly, but in the water they became alive in a way that was very different from their manner on land. Their flesh burned when highly active, and they were possessed of a strength beyond anything other than that of mastodons and the very greatest of the rhinoceroses in the land of mammoths. As a result, dragons ate prodigiously. Or at least they preferred to.

The thought of dragon appetites stimulated his own, of course. The squirrels at dinner had been small, youngsters incautious around a bowman. He finished his warm-up, took his bow, and slipped off quickly into the forest.

Moving as quietly as possible, he made his way to the

edge of a narrow valley, covered with hemlocks and pines, with a stream running in the center. Under the mature trees little else grew, and he was able to see a long way beneath the boughs.

He was rewarded with a glimpse of a rabbit and several squirrels. He slipped toward them, fitting an arrow into the slot of his Confshon bow, tightening the spring. Within one hundred paces, he was confident of the rabbit. He needed to get a little closer for the squirrels.

The rabbit detected something when he was still twice that distance away. It stood up and looked around carefully for a full minute and then hopped slowly away into the trees, heading down toward the stream.

He went on carefully. The squirrels were less cautious. They did not notice him until he was well in range.

The bow twanged brightly, and he took his first squirrel. It made no sound as the arrow struck through the neck.

The other squirrels took little notice. He was able to get within range of another. This time his shot was not quite so true, and the animal let out a shriek of pain and alarm, and fell out of the tree.

All the others raced up the trees and hid.

Still Relkin had two squirrels, enough for breakfast. He collected them and turned back to the camp.

The dragons there were only just beginning to wake up. He heard the Purple Green give a heavy groan as he lay down his bow. Relkin gathered together some brush and laid firewood across it. There were still embers from their previous night's fire. Relkin had left a couple of heavy logs smoldering when he went to sleep. Taking these up, he now blew on them to ignite the brush and quickly got a blaze going. It was a matter of minutes to skin and clean the squirrels, skewer them with green wood, and set them over the fire once the pile of brush burned down and gave him a bed of hot coals.

The squirrels soon began to cook nicely, and the smell awoke the sleeping dragons. Grener and Braner were soon drawn to squat down on the far side of the fire and stare at the small bodies, roasting as Relkin turned them over the coals.

"Small food," said Braner with obvious hunger.

"Give me the food," said Grener.

"This is mine," said Relkin. "You eat elk. This is squirrel."

"Very small food," said Braner.

"Give me the food," said Grener.

"No."

"I will take the food."

Relkin stood and drew his dirk. The glitter of the steel gave them pause.

"You will not take this food!"

He felt the other dragons step in behind him.

"What is problem?" said Bazil.

"They want my squirrels, and I'm keeping them."

"The squirrels smell good, they are hungry. They are dragons."

"And I'm hungry, too. They'll eat elk today, or deer or bear or something. These squirrels may be all I'll get."

"That is true."

"I'm glad you see it the same way I do."

Bazil moved around the fire, and Grener and Braner gave way before him.

"You cannot eat the squirrels. They are for the dragonboy. You must hunt. We must all hunt, and we are going to hunt with you."

"How can you hunt if you cannot fly?" said Grener.

"You only have to drive a herd of elk toward us, and we will kill several very quickly. Then we will feast."

Bazil found himself very committed to the idea of feasting. The days and days of hunger and constant travel had set a fire going in his belly like something from the days of ancient Dragon Home.

He doubted that even a herd of elk would satisfy his hunger, augmented by that of the wild one.

Relkin removed the cooked squirrels and began to eat them. Before he'd finished the first, there was a wind roar, and with two giant flaps of vast green wings, the dragoness flew overhead and dropped the carcass of a bull elk onto the green grass of the meadow.

The dragons ran for it. The youngsters flew and arrived first and tore it in half.

Bazil and the Purple Green arrived late and were forced to persuade the youngsters to give up part of the kill.

Neither gave up very easily. There was some growling and snapping of teeth. It was the time of the primal dragon, and Bazil found himself contemplating the ancient wild ways of Dragon Home. He had mated. These were his young. Now he was free of them. They would stay with their mother. He would find other mates and have other young. But he could not live like them, like wild animals.

He would have to content himself with the knowledge that he would live on in their memories. Perhaps they would even tell their own young about their wyvern grandsire. He reflected that this was the way with dragons. He had spent only the briefest time with his own male parent, a great leatherback named Cos, who died when he was very young.

Bazil looked on at the young while they ate their elk. Naturally they had to be chivied to give up meat. They were wild, after all. But Bazil had to admit to himself that he was glad he didn't have to hunt to try and feed them! This idea that they could go out into the forest and hunt for a living was wearing thin. He and the Purple Green could not survive up here alone, and even with Relkin it was very hard.

He ate the foreleg and shoulder of the elk that he had secured from Grener. Braner was still squabbling with the Purple Green over the division of his part of the kill.

Once again the green dragoness appeared, this time flying down with another elk. She landed and ate separately from them, and made no offer of any of her elk, a good-sized animal, to anyone else.

Bazil thought of life in the legion. By this time of the morning, he would have had a huge bowl of hot oatmeal, a dozen toasted wheat cakes, some crispy roast pork or bacon, a dozen scrambled eggs, and several loaves of fresh bread lathered with akh. Ah, for the rich flavors of such food the nuances of toasting and roasting and frying and akh, always akh.

He pushed these memories from his mind, and chewed the stringy elk meat and crunched the hard bones.

Of course, there was the other side to the legion life, the fighting and the risk of death. Bazil was a veteran now of three campaigns, and had seen most of his original companions in the 109th burn on their funeral pyres.

In the legions, a dragon lived well, died in combat, and was burned with honor and glory. Long would they sing of great Kepabar, who fell at Ossur Galan. Or Sorik, who died at Mount Red Oak, or the graceful Nesessitas, who was slain in the arena of Tummuz Orgmeen.

The stringy elk was gone. Bazil's stomach rumbled, demanding more. He rubbed his belly. There was not a sliver of fat left on him. Maybe he really was going to die of starvation.

Relkin had thrown some more brush on the fire and boiled up some water. He pulled out his dragon kit and cleaned swabs and probes. Then he approached Grener.

"You have a rotting wound, let me clean it and help it heal."

The young green dragon eyed him uncertainly. She was instinctively prejudiced against anything human, but the six-inch slash from an elk's sharp horns was increasingly painful and uncomfortable. The entire area around it, and the muscles beneath it, were sore and inflamed.

She said nothing, but drew away from him.

"Come, let me work on it. It will get worse if I don't. A wound like that can even kill you."

"Kill?"

"It is rotted by the invisible small things of the air. They corrupt everything that is not protected by skin. When you cut the skin, you let them in. That is why wounds must always be cleaned and why a dragonboy always cleans his tools in boiling water before he uses them. Boiling water, any extreme heat, will kill the small things of the air."

Grener's eyes were wide-open at all this.

"How do you know this?" she muttered.

"This is the lore of Confshon. It is well-known in the Argonath."

Still she found it impossible to overcome her reluctance, so Relkin signaled to Bazil, who strode up and reasoned with his daughter. At first she resisted, but at last calmed and consented to let Relkin work on the wound. He warned her that there would be discomfort, even pain from the treatment. Carefully he swabbed out the wound. The small dragon, her body not much bigger than Relkin's, let out a piercing hiss that was almost a whistle. Finally he swabbed again, with disinfectant, and the whistle gave way to a menacing growl.

"Easy, easy," he murmured. "The sting tells you that it is working, that is all."

"No like sting. Want to fly away from here."

"Not just yet."

Relkin made a poultice from mashed leaves of Kingswell

with thyme and wild garlic. This he worked around and over the wound, covered it with gauze bandage, and bound it in place.

Grener was unhappy with all of this, even though the pain had ceased.

"Let this bandage stay for two days, no more. Then you can tear it away. The poultice will have done its work by then."

Grener muttered to herself as he turned away and packed his kit. He felt a presence and looked up. The great green dragoness had settled beside him and was examining Grener.

"I have seen this once before, when my dragon with a sword, your Bazil dragon, wrapped the wounds of the Purple Green of Hook Mountain, after they had fought for me."

Relkin was not sure if he had heard this correctly. His mastery of dragon speech was less than complete, and her accent was very different from that of wyverns.

"I have mashed herbs and boiled them and bound them to the wound. Leave for two days, and the wound will heal cleanly."

The dragoness turned back to him with unfriendly eyes.

"I see through your plot. This is how you enslave the wyvern dragons that once lived wild on the coast of Dragon Home."

She saw something in his eyes and nodded in triumph.

"Yes, I have learned much. I met with the oldest dragons of all, the firelords of Muchel. From them, I learned the story of the coastal dragons and the white ships that came and enslaved them."

Relkin shrugged. "In truth, I know little of history. My schooling has been in the arts of war. I have seen so much death and agony, I hate to see any creature of this world suffer needlessly. I have the skill to help dragons, and I use it."

She nodded mirthlessly. "Oh, yes, I am sure you do. You give them regular meals. You take care of their cuts and bruises. You soften their will and rule it with your own. That is the way of men. They are cunning, they have the gift of speech and the power of skilled hands. That is why I hate you and fear you, and will never return to this part of the world."

Relkin, however, was examining a split talon on her right forefoot.

"You know, I could help you with that. I think you know that you need my help."

She pulled her head back. "I? In need of help from a human?"

"That split has gone too far down the claw to heal on its own. In time it will crack all the way to the quick. It will hurt. Then it will corrupt, and it will hurt a lot more. It may even corrupt the entire foot, and you will lose it."

There was a gentle hiss.

"By the breath of the ancients, you are cunning."

"I can work on that talon and prevent it splitting any farther."

She was silent. In truth, she had been worrying about this same exact talon, split initially while she was pouncing on hyraxes on a high mountain ledge. She had a weakness for hyrax, but they were hard to gather. She knew from sad experience just how painful such a split claw could become. She knew of dragons who had been forced to chew off their own feet to prevent the rot climbing the leg and killing them.

"By the first breath of the first firelord, what can you do about such a thing?"

"I will heat the talon and force a hot metal wedge into it so that it will hold together for several months' normal wear, until the talon grows out and the cracked part can be bitten off or left to abrade naturally."

She stared at him for a long time. "I can feel the jaws of your human trap closing on me already." She paused and glared at him. He held his ground refusing dragon-freeze and doing his utmost not to think about the two-ton predatory monster that was staring down at him with all her ferocity.

Finally she spoke. "Do what you can. But be quick, for I would leave this place and these foolish males. You must take them back to the world of humans; they do not belong in the wild."

Relkin heard a heavy tread and looked over his shoulder. Bazil had come up. He leaned over Grener and examined the bandage.

"Good work, as always, boy. As the father of this little darling one, I thank you."

Relkin kept a straight face at this description of the small green hellion. Grener, however, confronted her euphoric paternal parent.

"Why do you always say these things?"

"Why, my beautiful daughter dragon, because they are true."

"That is not enough excuse. Please stop. I know who you are, and I am mildly ashamed. You cannot hunt. You are feeble ground-bound thing, and you must live with the humans."

For a moment Bazil wavered there, smarting from the sting of her words. He made an effort.

"I am ground-bound it is true, but you should see me in the water! And there are compensations to the life with the humans. We were very well fed in the legions."

"That is good, since you are unable to feed yourself."

"Such wonderful children I have. So observant."

"You are crazed."

This tender familial scene was suddenly interrupted by a sudden loud oath from the Purple Green.

"I don't believe it!" growled the great wild one.

"What is it?" said Relkin.

"Boy comes. Manuel."

Relkin craned his neck but could see nothing. Then, far off down the meadow, he saw a moving speck, a dark figure that gradually took shape and form.

It was Manuel, indeed.

Relkin felt a tremor go through him. If Manuel could find them then so could others, so could the legion. They could be pursued and apprehended. They could hang. Or, at least, he would. The dragons would perhaps be given the freedom of the north bank of the Argo and left to starve to death. He, however, would be marched to a gallows with the slow drum, with the whole legion turned out to watch and thereupon hanged by the neck until dead.

He had seen the whole, horrible thing after the relief of Ourdh, when a deserter from the Kadein First Legion had been hanged for raping and murdering on Ourdhi woman.

Manuel was coming fast, and he soon was in range of a hello. He broke into a run for the last hundred paces.

"Hail to you, my friends. I bring you important tidings."

"So," grunted the Purple Green. "I could not leave you behind. You have come to join us."

"I have come to find you. I bring a message that I think you will want to hear."

"Who is message from?"

"Captain Hollein Kesepton."

"The captain?" Relkin's ears pricked up.

"He rode into the fort ten days ago and went to see General Wegan at once. Then they sent for me and told me to find you and give you the message."

"What is the message?"

"The case against Relkin in the matter of Trader Dook will be shifted to the Argonath Court in Marneri. It will be held in the spring, and dragon evidence will be taken and entered into the trial record."

"Dragon evidence!" Relkin hurled himself forward. "They will hear the dragons?"

"They will. It is a promise from on high."

His side of the case was immeasurably strengthened. In Marneri, the jury would also be free of the prejudices of the Kenor folk. He would have a real chance of winning.

Relkin danced around on feet suddenly grown light.

"The lady—our friend Bazil, she does this."

"You have been given absolution for your truancy. No charges will be laid against you for leaving the fort and wandering the forest. However, you must return now. Or you will be charged with desertion and will definitely face trial if you are ever apprehended."

"We can all return?" said Bazil with a nod to indicate the Purple Green.

"All," said Manuel firmly. "That is why they sent me. To try and persuade him."

"He is not in a good mood."

"When was he ever?"

"Good luck," said Relkin with feeling.

"It is better than starvation," replied Manuel, "that has always been the basis of the contract between the legion and the Purple Green."

"Yes, but by the old gods, he will be hard to turn around this time. No one in the world has more pride than the Purple Green of Hook Mountain."

Manuel went across to the Purple Green and unpacked a dragon kit. He took out scrapers and probes and set them ready. The Purple Green gave a snort and turned aside. Manuel spoke softly and reasonably. The Purple Green had sores on his feet, abrasions on the right side of his tail, and a long cut on the left shoulder. The Purple Green had grown used to having these minor annoyances tended and healed by a dragonboy. Manuel spoke soft persuasion. At length the Purple Green surrendered and allowed his dragonboy to attend to his wounds.

While he worked, Manuel spoke gently to the Purple Green, informing him of what had transpired and explaining that he was free to return to the legions.

The Purple Green was hard to move. He lapsed into a moody silence while Manuel worked on his wounds. Then he arose and moved away from them all and arranged himself on an exposed mass of rock.

Manuel let him be.

"He needs to think this all through carefully. I know something of his mind now. His pride and his sense of honor are very strong."

"You read the wild one correctly," said Relkin.

"But he wants to live. Otherwise he would never had consented to serve in the legion in the first place."

"He wants revenge for what they did to him in Tummuz Orgmeen."

"He will come around to it. I have faith in that."

"While he thinks it over, we'd better get Bazil to explain the whole thing to the dragoness."

Bazil accepted this challenge and went over to sit beside the dragoness, who had the young ones curled up on the grass, sleeping, nearby.

Slowly, carefully, Bazil explained the situation. They could go back to the humans. They did not need to starve to death. But they needed to record the dragoness's side of the events surrounding the death of the trader aboard his ship.

"Only the need to fulfill my vow brought me to stay in this region this long. But we have summered now, and I would prefer to leave early and arrive at the migration sites early as well. The caribou will be fat this year. We must leave immediately."

"No, my love, my precious one, the mother of my young, do not say that just yet. We need you. You must go with us to Fort Dalhousie. There you will speak with the humans."

"Fool. How to speak with them when they cannot understand dragon speech and I cannot understand man speech?"

"Dragonboys can speak some dragon speech. Not perfectly, of course, but they can understand well enough. At least some of them, the sharper-witted ones."

"The humans have a great power with speech and its control. I see their designs spread out like sheep beneath my wings. I warn you, the father of these young, you should beware the evil power of the humans."

"They will execute the boy if you do not help us."

She said nothing.

"They will leave us to die here of starvation."

She grumbled. "You deserve no better. Males! I've no need for you now. Nor or five more years, and I won't be coming back to this part of the world to hunt then."

"So you have said, my love, my beauty,"

"Will you stop that, you besotted fool!"

"It is hard. Wyverns mate for life and live together for that period."

"A good reason never to lose your wings. Dragons mate once and never again with that male." She softened. "But these young are good ones. The eggs were large. They fly strong and true. You have been a good mate for me. I am still somewhat surprised by it. I was worried that they would not develop strong wings."

"I am glad to be their father. Still," he continued, "for the boy's sake, I must ask that you come to Dalhousie."

She glanced away to where Relkin stood, watching them.

"He enslaves you. He would enslave me; I can see how they work their magic on you. Always taking care of you. It makes you like young fresh from the egg."

"You overestimate him, I'm afraid. But he is good at dealing with wounds and feet."

"I will think about it. Leave me."

Bazil passed this on to Relkin, who thought about it for a moment and then shrugged and got up and headed down into the birch forest in search of some supper. Farther down there were stands of Red Oak. There would be squirrels available. As he went, he strung his bow and wound its spring. He wandered downslope, through a section cut up by long gullies where small streams had dug into the hillside. Hemlocks choked the streambeads, pines and birch clad the higher ground. Gnats whined through the air. He went on, moving as quietly as he might, eyes alert to the slightest movement.

The forest was strangely quiet. Nothing moved. After a quarter of an hour, he had still seen not a single animal or bird. He began to have the feeling that he was being watched. It was not the first time he had had this feeling, but now suddenly it had returned and become much stronger.

CHAPTER FOURTEEN

Someone or something was moving in the woods around him, but moving so skillfully that he saw and heard nothing. He sensed there were many, and still he could see nothing.

It could not be imps or trolls, neither of which had that degree of woods craft. It could be men. The enemy employed many men whose hearts were turned to darkness. For the reward of wealth and power, they would serve the Masters and do their bidding, no matter how vile. Relkin knew the tribesmen like the Teetol could move through the forest in complete silence.

They were ahead of him and on both sides. For a long moment he crouched quietly, eyes staring into the trees, then he turned and started climbing back up the streambed, moving as silently as possible, jumping from one tumbled rock to the next. Concern was mounting in his heart. He sensed the others out there, keeping pace with him.

His heart sank. It seemed he was leading a pack of Teetol braves straight to his friends. And there was nothing else he could do!

The trees thinned out ahead of him as he scrambled up a clay-covered slope, and at last he broke out onto the meadow and began running full tilt, skipping across tussocks of tall grass and darting around the occasional shrub, anything to put off the aim of the bowmen he felt somewhere behind him.

He came up screeching a warning to the others, who were all standing together watching him.

"No need to run," said Manuel, holding up a hand. "Look! They come."

Relkin turned. A line of slender figures had appeared out of the woods. "Elves," he said in sudden comprehension.

A forest horn went up and was answered by several others. Hundreds of elves, the forest elves of Tunina, clad in soft, grey-green, emerged from the eaves of the woods on both sides of the meadow. They drew forth black bows strung with red-feathered arrows.

"Don't make any sudden movements," said Relkin. "They use poisoned arrows. We're all dead if they start shooting."

The dragons grumbled. Dragoness High Wings gathered the young and prepared to depart with much snarling and growling of horrid threats.

An elf clad in the same grey robes but with fetishes of red and yellow flowers attached to his costume, came forward and called to them in good Verio, albeit with the usual elfish accent.

"In the name of Dodolfin, king of the westmark and Mt. Ulmo. I greet you great beasts of land and air. We have watched your coming with awe and were honored. But we have become concerned at your continued presence.

"Our king, the great Dodolfin, is titular ruler of all this land, from the edge of the Gan to the eastern slopes of Mt. Ulmo, for this is the ancient westmark of Tunina and long have the forest elves lived here.

"Our king has dominion over all the land and the creatures thereon it. But he is a wise king and would not order anything beyond that which nature provides. The animals must live in the forest without hindrance, thus can the elves live in the forest, too, for we live upon the animals.

"Our king must now request that the great beasts of land and air return to their own homelands. Their depredations upon our elk and deer cannot be accepted any further. The elk of Mt. Ulmo are fleeing. The deer are on the verge of panic. There is terror throughout the wood.

"Our king has therefore sent me to give you his commandment. You must go at once from these lands, and if you refuse his just judgment and do not remove yourselves from our lands, we shall slay thee."

A typical example of elf diplomacy, thought Relkin, an all inclusive statement. Not that he wished to argue with it.

Relkin turned to the others. "Well, that does it my friends. We either go back to Dalhousie, or we die. We do not have the strength to march all the way north without hunting the elk and the deer."

"How can they kill us?" said the Purple Green.

"Elves are masters of poison. They will put a hundred arrows into you, and within minutes you will be paralyzed.

Then they will come close with their swords and hew open your throat and take your head."

Relkin turned back to the elf prince.

"We hear the words of the King Dodolfin, and we tend our apologies. We did not know that we committed offense." Relkin briefly outlined the events that had drawn the three dragons to the mountain meadow.

"So you see," he concluded, "we were on the point of leaving anyway, but we will now accelerate our departure. However, it must be said that for all the terror we have caused, we have eaten very little game. We will have to beg permission from you to hunt and eat some more, or we will starve to death before we can leave your lands."

"The dragons have devoured much of our game. I see that two of the dragons are from the Argonath. They are not in our reports. It is the others, the flying dragons, wild drakes from the utter north. They sometimes come to Mt. Ulmo but never for this long. The elk are terrorized. The dragons stoop from the sky like enormous eagles and carry off the largest bulls as if they were rabbits. They have even taken bears and devoured them!"

"The dragons will all leave, be assured of this. The flying ones will depart within a day. The others will go soon after. But I must beg for some food. We are starving to death."

The elf prince had come closer and had dropped his fierce demeanor.

"Now that I understand why you are here, I can perhaps allow this. If the flying dragons leave at once, then the others will be allowed to take elk and deer."

"You know, they're getting tired of elk. Have you any aurochs?"

"I am Prince Edofoon, and I would much rather play the harp and sing songs with you than be forced to slay you, dragonboy. But if you were to kill one of the king's aurochs, then I would have to do just that."

"Oh, well, in that case forget it. We'll eat elk. In fact, we'll eat anything right now."

Now the dragons and dragonboys came together to discuss the situation.

"We cannot stay here. High Wings and the young must leave at once."

"We can go back. There is an offer of clemency." Manuel's use of *we* elicited no response from the dragons.

Baz said nothing. They all looked at the Purple Green. He heaved a vast sigh.

"We go back."

Relkin expelled a deep breath. Bazil spoke up. "Dragonboy will be given fair trial. Not be hanged."

"But the dragoness must go to Dalhousie to give her evidence to the captain," said Manuel.

Bazil turned to the dragoness, High Wings.

"What will it be, my love, my beauty?"

The green dragoness snapped her jaws a moment.

"We will go to Dalhousie. But I will take the boy with me. He will act as go-between. I do not trust the men, ever."

"Take the boy with you . . ." muttered Relkin. "What? You're going to fly there with me?"

"You are smaller than most elk. The human place is not far. A matter of a few dozen wing beats."

"Fly? Like a bird?"

"Like a dragon."

"Fly?"

Relkin was perfectly torn between glee and terror. To see the world as a bird does. And to have nothing beneath his feet but air!

It seemed altogether too soon, but in less than an hour all was ready. The others would stay with the elves in a great camp that night, and they would feast to perpetual amity between elf, dragon, and men. Then they would head back to the Argo and Dalhousie.

The sun was falling into the western sky by this time, and Relkin stood in front of the dragoness. Gingerly she seized him in her foreclaws. The first squeeze was too hard, and he squawked until she relaxed her grip.

Then with a tremendous bound, she hurled herself ten feet into the air; her enormous wings cracked once, twice, and thrice, and she was lifting away. With one more beat she was aloft, and Relkin gazed down in awe as the world fell away and the mountain towered up beside him on his right, cloaked in trees until its very top. The wing beats were fast and regular, and enormous muscles were bunching and releasing above his head. He looked down and gasped, and felt a sudden fear of falling. The meadow was far below now, and his friends were reduced to specks, even the dragons. Then the dragoness turned, and he saw the river Argo and beyond it the great vale of the river Dally, which wound like a silver snake through the dark forest of Dalhousie. The sight was such that in a moment all fear was obliterated and replaced with wonder. He turned his head and saw the line of the mountains, the mighty Malguns, from Snowgirt and Red Oak to Bascoin, Kohon, and distant Livol, ranked like giant guardians of the east, the snow glittering off their crowns.

The grip around his body tightened suddenly, and he looked up and caught the dragoness looking down at him for a moment with one great eye. He realized that she was thinking how easy it would be to get rid of him. She could just open her claws, and he would be lost. He held his breath.

But she looked away again and kept him clutched fast in the enormous grip and flew on across the leagues of forest and vale toward the river Argo.

Relkin gazed south and west and saw in the vast distance, far away, a glitter of fire as the sun shone on the peaks of the White Bones Mountains. Much closer stood the lone cone of Mt. Kenor. In that direction lay the enemy, a rumor of death and terror and great sorcery. Relkin had seen enough of those to understand the enemy's power.

His gaze returned to the south where the vale of the Dally narrowed up against the plateau of Kohon. To the west of Kohon lay the basin around Lake Tuala. Relkin dreamed of owning a farm someday, and he had heard that the Tuala basin had excellent soil.

And now they were above the river Argo, and the dragoness turned and flew downstream, her wings carrying them closer to Dalhousie with every powerful beat.

CHAPTER FIFTEEN

Into the glorious light of late afternoon the dragoness flew, her mighty wings crackling every so often as she soared above the river. When they were still several leagues distant, Relkin caught a glimpse of Fort Dalhousie on its hilltop, and he let out a whoop of exhilaration. What a return this would be! His legend would be set in stone forever after this. The truant, the deserter, who came back in the talons of a flying dragon.

The dragoness circled over the town, and below him Relkin saw panic break out. Horses bolted. Carts were overturned. People stared upward with open mouths. He heard distant screams and saw people running this way and that, and then the town was behind him and they were swooping low over the fort.

Cornets were blowing, screaming into the evening air. Men appeared from tents and buildings, and then began running. The dragoness swung right, passing just above the top of the tower gate. Relkin fancied he saw General Wegan himself staring, openmouthed, from a high window at this apparition. Then the tower was gone, and he was speeding just above the walls and back across the serried tents and buildings of the fort to the parade ground, where with a sickening suddenness the dragoness dropped to the ground. She landed hard, and released him quite suddenly, so that he found himself running to keep his feet, and unable to run fast enough, he tumbled and went head over heels in a forward fall.

He came back onto his feet in a moment, still breathing hard, amazed by the power and speed of flight. Such things he had seen that were not given to any other man in the history of the world. To soar above the land of Kenor with the mighty Malgun Mountains as a rampart to the east and the flat vastness of the Gan spreading out in the northwest. Such things he had seen! The world could never seem the same.

The dragoness was waiting with her wings still unfolded, her body crouched, ready to spring at once into the air again if the approaching men should threaten her with arrow or spear.

A crowd of men, with dragons shouldering through from the north avenue, was pouring out onto the parade ground. The cornets were still screaming the alarm from the tower tops and officers were barking orders, but the great mass of the men merely came forward with awed expressions and complete silence. These were men used to dragons. They trained, they marched, and they fought alongside dragons, but the monstrous beasts they fought with did not fly! And to see something this huge, with wings that seemed to fill the sky above the fort, was in some way a fulfillment of the myth, the very promise of dragons. The winged dragons were the ultimate dragons, the greatest wild predators of the world. Few men had ever been lucky enough to see one and survive to tell the tale.

And here was one, unloading a dragonboy right on the parade ground. Now she stood there before them, her great wings flapping slowly, her lean, muscular body covered in green scales, her mouth glittering with terrible teeth, and they were mesmerized by the sight. No man raised a weapon, and even the cornets on the towers had stopped their calls.

Dragonboys elbowed forward and cautiously approached. A familiar loud voice rang out.

"Well, I'll be damned for a fisherman, it's our friend from Quosh." Swane of Revenant was the first to reach him. Then came the rest of the boys from the 109th in a leaping, hugging crowd.

"Ol' Turrent'll be feeling sick after this!"

"He was gloating until the captain came."

"The whole army is talking about it."

"You'll never live this one down Quoshite!"

Relkin was hoisted onto their shoulders and carried away up the avenue.

To questions from officers, they called that they were taking him to General Wegan and thus no one ordered them to stop. Right to the entrance to the tower gate they brought him and set him down.

Soldiers at the gate drew back. The general himself appeared among them. His face was flushed, his mouth set in a grim line. His voice shook with suppressed anger.

"I do not care to see this man brought to me as if he was some conquering hero. He is charged with desertion as well as murder. By rights he should be in chains. It is not fit for him to be treated thus."

General Wegan glared at the dragonboys of the 109th. They hung their heads but said nothing, disagreeing completely with every word.

"As for you Dragoneer Relkin, I will see you inside. At once."

"What about the dragoness?" said someone.

Wegan turned, almost said something, then checked himself and changed his mind. In a quiet voice he said, "Feed her. I'm sure she'll be hungry."

Dragonboys raced off to fulfill this command, not daring to speak until they were well out of earshot of the tower gate, whereupon they declared that Relkin was no deserter and certainly no murderer. They all knew that now that dragon's evidence was to be heard, the case against Relkin could not succeed. Their shouts and bursts of song carried away to the parade ground.

Meanwhile Relkin faced General Wegan across his desk. Wegan was furious.

"If it was up to me, boy, you'd face desertion charges this evening and the end of the rope tomorrow. What you think you're playing at coming in like this, I don't know. But it won't get you any soft treatment from me! You've started a panic in the town and upset the rhythms of my fort. This kind of grandstanding would be bad enough from an officer, but from a dragonboy, it's more than I intend to put up with."

Relkin tried to swallow but found it hard.

"Well," snapped the general, "what have you to say for yourself?"

Relkin tried to speak, failed, and tried again.

"Come along, speak, man!" General Wegan scowled.

At last he found his voice. "Begging your pardon, General, but I was not in control of the dragoness. She flew where she wanted to fly. I'm sorry for any damage caused in the town, but it was not my decision to fly that way. I think she wanted to terrify everyone. These kind of dragons, they like to terrify everything else that lives."

"But what were you doing flying here at all? Who gave permission?"

"Uhh, no one, sir. When we got the message from the captain, we had to persuade the dragoness to give a deposition. She agreed, but she refused to wait for us to make our way back to the fort by land. She wants to leave these parts for the north. The game migrations are about to begin. So we agreed that this would be the quickest way to get her deposition to Captain Kesepton. We thought that would be the best thing to do, sir."

Wegan stared hard at the youth. This one was special, they said, a real survivor. Yet there had been murder charges. Of course the charges stung the worse because Wegan felt responsible. He had made a hasty decision to allow the youth and the dragon to go in pursuit of the Trader Dook. He had never expected them to kill him. The political damage to the general in the Argo towns was serious. And then this deserter had pulled strings to have his case moved to Marneri. Had brought down the great hero Captain Kesepton to plead for him in person. In person! Wegan wished he had friends like that. And now this bit of grandstanding! It wouldn't go down well in the town. It meant even more political damage. He took a deep breath. He reflected. Still, all in all, his anger was perhaps a shade unjustified. he stuck out his lower lip for a moment. His first duty was to the men and the dragons and to the dragonboys. All this could hardly be bad for morale now could it?

Wegan's attitude softened. "So this wasn't just a show-off for the crowd?"

"Not at all, sir. I was petrified the whole way. If you knew the dragoness, you'd be petrified, too."

"What do you mean? Is she dangerous? Should she be excluded from the fort? Will she attack the horses?"

"Only if there's nothing else to eat. She says she dislikes the flavor of horse and much prefers aurochs and elk." Relkin lied quickly. Dragons loved horseflesh, raw or roasted, anyway you chose.

"Elk? Auroch?" Wegan raised his eyebrows. "Well, considering how wyverns like to eat, we must recognize that the appetites of such a beast must be tremendous."

Relkin nodded with complete, honest agreement.

"Yes, sir, they are."

Wegan stood up and paced around the room, reconsidering. Then he spoke to an orderly.

"Send for Captain Kesepton. I want to see him here, at once."

A few minutes later Hollein Kesepton came in and saluted crisply. He did not even glance at Relkin, and Relkin kept his own eyes averted.

"Well, Captain, my fort is in an uproar, and we have a very hungry extra dragon to feed. That said, it does seem that your plan is working, more swiftly than we had ever imagined."

Kesepton said nothing.

"Now, Captain, I want you to accompany this young rascal and take the necessary deposition from the dragoness that's sitting out there on the parade ground."

"Yes, sir," said Kesepton. "The translator will be Dragoneer Feregold from the 66th Dragons."

"Old Feregold, eh? Well, he's the best they say."

"Yes, sir."

"When it's done, I want that monster removed. She's to have no more than one feast upon our stores."

"Yes, sir."

"And this dragonboy is to be turned over to his dragon leader, who no doubt has a long list of punishment rosters to discuss with him."

A few moments later Relkin was hurrying across the camp beside the captain. "Captain, I want to thank you for what you've done."

Kesepton flashed him a warning glance.

"You're still going to stand trial. You killed a man, Relkin."

"I had no choice. He would have killed one of the dragons."

"You will be asking a jury of men and women to weigh a human life in the balance with that of a wild dragon."

"But they will hear the evidence of the dragons! That will mean it will not be simply my word for it. Dragons would not lie."

"We will hope that the jury of good folk in Marneri will see it that way. Many would not."

"Perhaps that is because they know little of dragons, even though they depend on them for their very lives. You and I both know what would happen to all our cities if we had no dragons with which to face the enemy."

Kesepton nodded and hardened his face. It was true, and the folk of the Argonath cities had almost forgotten their peril and the need for the heroic cooperation provided by the wyverns.

The translator, Feregold, was waiting for them, having been called even before Kesepton went to see Wegan. Now he fell in behind them, and they all turned in at the administrative tent, where a scribe was summoned along with scrolls and pen. Then a column, Relkin and Kesepton at the head, then the scribe and Feregold, and then the two men bringing chair and desk, made its way across to where the dragoness was feasting on a side of beef, raw, pulled from the butcher's cool room.

She looked up and licked the blood from her chops.

"Who is this?" she said in suspicion with breath that was redolent of blood.

"This is my friend," said Relkin, "our friend, Captain Kesepton. Bazil told you about him."

"Yes, so he did."

"Welcome to Fort Dalhousie," said Hollein Kesepton, and Relkin translated for him.

Then Feregold stood forward and introduced himself. His dragon speech was the best in the legion, and the dragoness was both surprised and pleased at this development.

Feregold explained his role, and the shape and form of the deposition. The dragoness was astonished by the concept of writing down her words, witnessing them, and using them months later in a far-off city as a weapon in a struggle conducted solely with words. This glimpse into the unholy complexities of the affairs of men unsettled her. She resolved anew that never would she return to the places of men.

Then, to Relkin's surprise, she consented at once and became most cooperative. At his look of astonishment, she commented, "Only the ancient gods know what those two fools will get up to with my children while I'm gone. I want to go back tonight."

"Then you shall," said Feregold, "for this matter need not take long at all."

The scribe sat down at the desk and began to write as Kesepton paced up and down and framed the questions, doing his best to keep things simple. The dragoness, to his surprise, responded with a clear impression of the events. The scribe's pen scratched, and Relkin felt a weight lifting away from his shoulders. With the dragoness's evidence, which essentially confirmed his own story, he would at least stand a chance in court.

It took less than an hour to complete the task, to check the writing, and to read it back to the dragoness and make a few corrections. Then the text was witnessed by Captain Kesepton and Feregold, and rolled up by the scribe.

The dragoness immediately went back to her beef, which she devoured with considerable gusto.

When she had finished, Relkin went to say farewell.

"This meat was good, as good as the young aurochs. I would like more of this meat."

"I don't think General Wegan will allow that."

"Then maybe I will eat your General Wegan."

Relkin wisely refrained from commenting on this suggestion.

"Farewell, High Wings of Tundra Lake. I hope the young of the broketail dragon grow strong and true. I thank you for not killing me when you might have."

She looked at him with a sudden fierce glare.

"I take my young and go north. Never will I return to the land of humans. I see now how your power is derived. You wield authority of complexity set upon complexity. No dragon can think in such tiny patterns. It hurts my mind to even contemplate them."

The setting sun had gone down in a ball of fire in the west. Watch fires were lit on the towers.

"Good-bye, boy, live long. Take care of the Bazil dragon. He has a good heart."

With those words she tensed and sprang into the air while her wings beat down and sent a wind whistling through the camp upending tables, tearing out tent pegs, and sending Relkin scurrying for cover.

When he looked up he saw her, an immense dark shape beating away across the town and heading upriver. The sun caught her scales, and she gleamed like a great emerald in the sky.

With a sigh and a shrug, Relkin turned away from the fantastic to the mundane and made his way to the quarters of the 109th Marneri Dragons and his inevitable interview with Dragon Leader Turrent.

CHAPTER SIXTEEN

Three weeks later, Relkin was summoned once more to General Wegan's office.

The dragons and Manuel had returned a few days previously. Both dragons were on heavy labor details, and Relkin had kitchen, slops, and garbage details. Dragon Leader Turrent had become a constant presence in his life, hectoring, peering over his shoulder, and ordering fresh punishment details.

General Wegan told Relkin that he had decided to send the 109th to Kohon for the fall campaign against the Cralls a bandit clan of the Kohon Hills that had been raiding into the fertile fields around High Lake. Wegan had decided to double the dragon force for the mission. The Cralls had slain twelve men and abducted their women from a hamlet near Wachau. The Cralls must be taught a lesson they would never forget. Cralls would be taken and tried and hanged for all to see.

"There are questions in your mind, Dragoneer. You may ask them."

"Well, sir, I suppose I should ask why you are telling me this?"

"Because, Dragoneer, I have made this decision with you and your dragon in mind. I want you both somewhere where you'll be too busy to get into any more trouble, and I don't want to have to put you behind bars.

"And if you should die in battle over the winter, then I'll be saving the legion from an embarrassing trial. And I will also be helping to defuse the political controversy here. This killing has been used by certain interests to demand cuts in the contribution to the legion budget by the provinces of Kenor."

Relkin's eyes widened.

"I see you hadn't thought of that. Well, boy, wake up to

the truth of the world. The people of the Middle Argo have been spared war for many years. Recent events in Tummuz Orgmeen have reduced their concerns even further." Wegan smiled a wintry smile.

"That was then and this is now, and the good folk of the valley see a chance to reduce their taxes. The folk of Kenor came here to escape the cost of taxation in the East."

"I understand, sir."

"Yes, you're a sharp one, I knew you would. And if you should survive, as I rather expect you will, then in the spring we will send you to Marneri for trial."

Relkin said nothing.

"And now you can have the pleasure of informing your friends of these orders. Tell Dragon Leader Turrent he is to report to me. Dismissed."

The next day was a feast day in honor of the founding of the Kenor colonies. The fort was thrown open, and stalls and tents set up in the open spaces.

Relkin was late joining the festivities since he had a mountain of chores to finish for Turrent, but at length he completed them and made his way down to the bonfire and the colored tents.

He found a group of dragonboys, Swane and Tomas in their midst, swaggering away from the apple shy.

"Hey, Relkin, guess what," called Tomas.

"Ol' Swane scored three hits, won a ticket to the fortune-teller for all of us, come along."

"Oh, that's all right, I thought I'd just get some fried fish."

"We'll all get fried fish later, first we get our fortunes told, for free. Come on Quoshite, it's on old Swane." Swane took his arm, and Relkin allowed himself to be pulled along.

The fortune-teller was a most impressive old man whose name Mumplepeezer the Great appeared on a signboard in gold and scarlet lettering outside his red-and-white-striped tent. Mumplepeezer had a long white beard, a purple conical hat covered in magical signs picked out in gold and silver, and a black velvet robe. He sat hunched over a small red table on which sat a great glass globe that glowed faintly within.

"Come in, boys, welcome to Mumplepeezer's realm. Sit thee down and pay attention. Who wants their fortune told first?"

Swane pushed forward. "I won the apple shy, so I gets to go first."

The fortune-teller opened a long narrow box and produced a set of ivory sticks.

"Now, be still in that seat young man and compose yourself. Let us have no giggling, no fidgeting, for these things can throw off the all-seeing eye of Mumplepeezer and corrupt the view of the future."

He passed one hand over the glass and mumbled a phrase or two. The glass dimmed, then brightened.

He threw the sticks into the box and examined them carefully.

"It seems that your romantic nature will soon be rewarded. You will meet a young woman who will be the answer to your dreams. Make sure to treat her politely and generously, however, for she will be of noble blood."

Swane chortled, "Hear that, lads, I'm gonna find me a girl from the nobility and retire to her father's castle."

The face of the fortune-teller was uneasy, however. He stirred the sticks with a long finger.

"Curious, very curious." He shrugged. "It must be a randomizing element, sometimes these things creep in. Now, let's not be boisterous, boys, who is next?"

Tomas Black Eye took the seat. Once more the hand waved over the crystal ball, and the ivory rune sticks were thrown into the box.

The fortune-teller's eyebrows shot up, and his mouth tightened into a line.

"Well, now," he said, giving Tomas a searching look. "It is possible that you will live to a ripe old age, marry a handsome woman, and have seven children by her."

"All right," said Tomas happily, not believing but not wanting to disbelieve either.

"But there is a matter of destiny. I have thrown it again, the Indicator. Not as strongly as the first case but still it is there. The seven stick is in the House of War and also the House of Destiny. You will face a great trial, and you may not survive to enjoy the rest of your fortune."

"Ho ho! A great trial, sounds like you've got the wrong dragonboy, sir." Swane pushed Relkin forward. "Do Relkin next, he's the one who faces a trial."

The others all laughed.

Mumplepeezer eyed him carefully as he sat there. The

aged hand passed over the ball of glass, the other hand tossed the sticks.

There was a sharp intake of breath. Hurriedly the sticks were taken up and thrown again.

"Mother preserve us!" said Mumplepeezer. He stared at Relkin with something like awe in his old, washed-out grey eyes.

"War, a great battle is foretold. Your destiny lies on that battlefield."

"Of course," Relkin replied, feeling uncomfortable with the old man's stare. "Nothing surprising about that, we're dragonboys."

But the fortune-teller was not finished. "No, you don't understand. For each of you I have thrown the Seven on Seven, the Indicator, which signifies great events in the offing. Then there was the Hanged Man and the Cat O'er the Moon for the first and the second, which signified that the wheels of destiny are in motion. N

Mumplepeezer's withered old face and the ivory rune sticks clattering in their box.

at the fry were greasy and watery. Swane's bragging and ordered was flat and unappealing. Swane's bragging and silly jokes fell as flat as the beer, and Relkin left them quite early, turned himself in, and lay in his cot. Sleep claimed him then, and he slipped away into dreams marked by

spoke again. "Well, I understand ... sons. You dislike the human form."

Irene and Lessis smiled together. Ribela made no response at first, although the dark eyes perhaps sparkled momentarily and a gleam or two came from the fringe of silver mouse skulls along the hem of her gown. Then at last she spoke, in a deceptively mild voice.

"Sisters, we all contribute to our great effort in our individual ways." The silver skulls of mice twinkled.

They nodded. Ribela's fight was carried on in dimensions

beyond normal human understanding. Neither Lessis nor Irene could match the powers of the Queen of Mice in those areas.

"So. What news do we have?"

Lessis turned to Irene slightly. "Sister Ocean has disturbing news from Czardha."

Ribela's black eyes riveted on the Queen of Oceans.

"I got the word last night. Trader put in from the Bakan. One of our sources in Czardha had word that mammoths had been captured and bred in captivity by Padmasa. Quite recently, with the entire operation kept extremely secret. Our source found out only because two men who had hunted the mammoths for Padmasa had fled the hand of the Masters and sought new lives in westernmost Czardha."

"How many mammoths?"

"At least one hundred. Several herds were destroyed to capture at least one hundred cows, plus a dozen bulls."

"They are trying to create a new class of troll."

"Perhaps. Although with this kind of thing, their ingenuity is endless. Irene suggested they might create sea monsters, creatures that would attack shipping."

Lessis and Ribela exchanged tiny smiles. Irene's pale blue eyes grew hard for a moment. The Queen of Oceans had a tendency to exaggerate the importance of her realm.

"That would be a menace to all our trade," murmured Ribela politely.

"Which faces menace enough as you know," said Irene. "The pirates of the Great Straits are growing worse each year. We must do something."

"We shall, Sister, we shall," said Lessis.

"But? I detect a tremor here. What has happened?"

"Nay, Sister Oceans, it has not happened yet. But a terrible blow is due to fall on us soon. In the Hazog, they brew something new and utterly monstrous to throw against us."

"Why have we not heard of this before?"

"Bah," sniffed Ribela, "there has been a catastrophe. Tell Irene the truth."

Lessis smiled with an effort. In truth, this was painful for her. These had been her people, her networks.

"Our network at Axoxo was penetrated. We lost everything. Later they tracked down poor Semelia in Padmasa. We are virtually blind and deaf when it comes to Padmasa now."

Irene was stunned by this news. "We have no agent in the Tetralobe?"

"Everything is gone there. The Masters move in complete intelligence security, if they but knew it."

"So a great blow is coming. Raised from the abducted women of Ourdh?" Despite her blind spots, Irene had a quick mind.

"Naturally."

"What does the emperor say?"

"He will 'prepare our response.' He is constrained by political needs. The cost of the mission to Ourdh was enormous. There is growing resistance to the cost of maintaining our legions at the current fighting strength."

Irene did not hesitate, a trait that had always endeared her to Lessis. "What can I do to help matters?"

"If only all the Sisters responded as does our Queen of Oceans," murmured Ribela, who knew of Lessis's fondness for Irene.

"The Queen of Mice has always set a firm example for us all," replied Irene calmly.

Once again the mouse skulls seemed to twinkle.

"Still, the goodwill of all our sea folk will be vital during the coming storm." Lessis's voice deepened with concern.

Irene's pale blue orbs gazed long into the grey eyes of the Grey Sister.

"Yes, Sister Ocean," said Lessis. "Unless I am greatly mistaken, this storm will test the limits of our strength."

Ribela's facial mask cracked ever so slightly to allow a smile. "And when was the Queen of Birds ever mistaken?"

Lessis turned to Ribela.

"I'm afraid that someone has had to make decisions," said Lessis. "Usually I've been the only one of us to be here."

"Sausann?"

"Is preoccupied. She enters the mystic."

"May the Mother protect her," said Irene, kissing her nails in prayer.

"May the Mother protect us all. I fear that Lessis is absolutely correct. There is a new barrier erected on the higher planes to protect Padmasa. We cannot get in. I suspect that they are screening this great blow that they prepare."

"What is to be done, then?" said Irene.

"We must have more and better intelligence. What you have brought us is invaluable. We know that our enemy prepares some dread stroke for the battlefield. We suspect he readies an enormous host. We have the emperor's agreement. We can prepare. But we need more if we are to anticipate the enemy's blow."

"I will go to the Argonath at once," said Lessis. "Perhaps I must try to enter Axoxo myself."

"Ever and again you risk yourself. Did you not learn anything from Tummuz Orgmeen?"

Lessis smiled. "I learned that faintness of heart brings no rewards."

"This will be a great risk, Sister."

"We have no choice, Sister. You said so yourself. We must have better intelligence. There is really only one way to get it, and there is no time to train someone else."

Ribela sighed. It was true enough. Time was pressing urgent.

"I will leave for the Argonath shortly. Sister Irene will rouse the hearts of our sea folk, and the Queen of Mice will renew her watch upon the astral planes."

"Others can keep that watch. I deem it more important that I spend time at council and with the emperor."

"I thank you, Sister. With your strength behind him, the emperor will hew to the correct path, I am sure."

"The trick will be to make him accept our analysis of the situation. He is a scion of a good line, but he is a man. He finds it hard to take advice that conflicts with his own beliefs."

"Which is why I must go to the Argonath once more."

"And there to Axoxo? Like a moth to the dark flame."

Lessis smiled. "Sister Ribela is in a mood for humor this night."

Irene smiled, too. "I agree, Sister, never have I seen her in such spirits."

Ribela's annoyance flickered again. They teased her, they always did.

"I might even joust with the mystic," she said, and went along with their mood. Lessis said she bristled too quickly. Dignity had become too important to her. All right, she would be as frivolous as anyone.

CHAPTER EIGHTEEN

Three hundred men, one hundred horses, twenty dragonboys, and twenty battledragons made up the expeditionary force to the Kohon Hills. A flotilla of schooners, sloops, and flat-bottomed river brigs had been assembled to ferry them up the navigable rivers Dally, Tuala, and Darkmon, a distance of around one hundred leagues.

The dragon squadrons were the 66th and 109th Marneri. The cavalry century was from the Talion Light Horse and the infantry centuries were the 322s (Third Century, Second Regiment, Second Legion Marneri) and the 182s (first Century, Eighth Regiment, Second Legion Marneri). In overall command was Captain Rorker Eads, twenty-eight, with almost nine years service in the legion: a tall, sandy-haired man with a determined expression most of the time. A seasoned officer in every respect, he'd had four campaigns against the Teetol and had seen combat against raiding parties of imp and troll in every summer.

On the third day out, slowly beating upstream on the broad, sluggish Dally, they passed prosperous farms with red barns, white houses, and orchards decorating the hillsides. This was the legendary Valose, land of fruit and vine. Here they grew the hardy Hopsrung grape, from which came the famous white wines of Lodover and Chanay.

Aboard the river schooner *Alba,* the 109th Dragons lazed, and even dragonboys had an easy time of it. *Alba* was a good ship and easy to manage, her crew old and efficient. There was little for dragonboys to do except feed and water the dragons. Their kit was immaculate, of course. Months of the rule of Digal Turrent had brought about that much, at least.

The dragon leader ordered exercise sessions for everyone in the early morning, and then again in the afternoon. The dragons exercised alone, since Captain Noonce would not have more than one of the great beasts moving around at a time. As it was, he prayed for the timbers of his old but graceful vessel every time the Purple Green moved. Turrent had vowed to keep everyone in the unit "lively," however, so exercise for the dragonboys continued at full tilt.

The only thing that disturbed Relkin's dislike of Turrent was the fact that the dragon leader took part in all the exercise sessions himself, leading them in push-ups and sit-ups, running on the spot, and various calisthenic exercises. Everything else about the dragon leader was a sheer pain. Being cooped up with him aboard a small vessel like the *Alba* was close to hell.

There were midday "parades," more like inspections, carried out every day. But the 109th's equipment was already spotless, and it wasn't being used.

Then there were spot inspections, when Turrent would tear open their packs and search for contraband. And there were impromptu work details, scrubbing the aft decks for instance, something that pleased Captain Noonce considerably since he and his elderly sailors had let the old boat get a little crusty. But even with Turrent in command, there were many hours for just sitting around, watching the world go by.

Relkin still had plenty of extra work, of course. Turrent had made it plain that it would take an "eternity" before he would relax his grip on Relkin of Quosh. Relkin peeled turnips, carried slops, and drew water for much of every day.

The others helped him out, surreptitiously, for Turrent was fierce with anyone caught doing it. But there was a general dislike of the dragon leader and a genuine respect for the Quoshite. He was a legend in the legion, and more importantly, he was their legend and they were proud of him. Sure he was a bit taciturn, but they knew him as a steady comrade and a good fighter to have behind your back.

And so buckets of water were furtively carried in to the dragons whenever Turrent wasn't looking. And Swane and Tomas, usually with Mono, too, would gather outside the galley while Relkin peeled turnips and mashed garlic for the akh. While they talked, their knives worked on the turnips and garlic, and with three or four to do it, the work was soon done.

In the afternoons they played desultory games of mungo and double-sevens with the dice. Swane usually bet too heavily and was starting to pile up debts. The new boy Bryon was showing great skill at mungo and was clearly ahead. Tomas Black Eye possessed fabulous luck in streaks, but bet incautiously and rarely broke even. Relkin was usually uninterested in the games. He was just not in the mood. The experiences of the past weeks had affected him strangely.

Often he thought back to the wonder of that flight from Mt. Ulmo to Dalhousie. The vast open spaces of the sky and the land below, and soaring across it effortlessly.

At times he looked at the great Purple Green and wondered how the former wild dragon had ever been able to accept the life of the ground-bound.

Knowing in tiny part just what the great wild drake had lost had made Relkin empathize with the Purple Green. He'd also realized anew how important the support of Bazil had been for the wild dragon. Nothing but such support would have held the Purple Green within the traces of the legion life.

At other times Relkin thought about how close he had come to being lost himself, condemned to a life as a wild vagabond, living from his bow, trying to keep two dragons alive in the forest. Life had been kicked over and sent spinning like a milking stool ever since the dragoness High Wings had been captured by Trader Dook.

As a consequence, he was feeling very serious and grave. Life was real and life was earnest, and the goal was not the grave, or so said some prayer he half remembered concerning the god Caymo.

Bazil, too, seemed subdued. Humbled for a while following the disastrous folly of the recent past. Bazil knew that his exemplary legion record was now besmirched. There was a mark of instability there that would never be erased. Still, they had come through it in the end, and he and Relkin were yet together, man and giant beast, blood brothers across the gulf between wyvern and human being.

Bazil was also mourning the great love of his life. She was gone and would not return, or so she said. But he had the memories now of his progeny, of strong, darting Braner and graceful Grener. They were beautiful and so young. And there were also moments when he was quietly grateful that he would have nothing whatsoever to do with them for the rest of their lives. Wild dragons possessed such uncertain tempers!

And so the third day passed in the manner of the first two. Relkin sat by himself as much as possible and brooded on the passing riverbank.

Swane finally won a few rounds at mungo, and his exultant whoops started an argument. The game broke up early as a result, and after everyone had taken water to their dragons, they found themselves lurking by the ship's rail amidships.

The conversation turned to the Cralls, the bandit clan in the Kohons that they were due to chasten.

"How much trouble can they be?" said Swane. "I'm sick of everyone worrying about them. They get on a battlefield with us, and they're done for. We'll have to bury them. Remember Salpalangum? Without dragons they can't fight us."

But some of the younger boys weren't reassured.

"Salpalangum was different. These Cralls are cavalry skirmishers and kidnappers. They fight with treachery and bribes and booby traps. They aren't going to take the field against us."

"Well, in that case we'll take their homes and burn 'em along with everything they own. Either that or they'll have to carry it all with them and that will slow them down and then we'll have them."

"Swane's always too confident."

"Yeah, too right. It's always Salpalangum this and Salpalangum that."

Relkin sighed. They were back to this again.

"I don't see old Chektor chasing down no cavalry, nor Vlok, either," said Jak.

Relkin turned away from the others. It was all speculation. Quite likely the bandits would simply decamp for a season or two once they knew that there was a punitive mission in the territory. He leaned over the side and gazed at the landscape. He noticed that things had changed. The afternoon light was deepening, and a few languid clouds were blowing south and west of them. The farms were dwindling rapidly, and soon they petered out completely. Forest took over the banks of both sides of the river.

"Where are we?" said Swane.

"This is the forest of Valur."

"The haunted wood."

The character of the country changed entirely. Dark forest

primeval, dominated by immense oaks, beeches, elms, and occasional giant willows, took over and hugged down close to the riverside.

Gradually the forest grew denser and denser, and soon they moved along in a hush broken only by occasional bird-calls, and once by the howl of a wolf somewhere to the west.

In the late afternoon when the light was filtered green through the multitude of leaves, they glimpsed the ruins of the ancient fane of the Nolgar. These were the gods of old when the early tribes of the Vero, the Ota, the Abbad, and the Shanti came down from the mountains and assumed the lordship of this land.

From the Nolgar arose the old Donoi gods, which held sway until the rise of the worship of the Great Mother on the Isles of Cunfshon. These were gods with wild ways and hab-its both cruel and capricious. Asgah, the ancient god of war, symbol for the first dynasty Veronath kings, held a rose stem in his mouth from which blood ran. Jolly old Caymo, lord of wine, song, and the pleasures of the flesh, was known by his horns and swine's tail and big red nose.

Now the fane was desolate, tended only by a few mystics of the older religion. The roofs had long fallen in, leaving but the stone walls of the buildings, along with shattered statues and crumbling stone-flagged plazas. Pylons carved with strange runes jutted above the trees. A long wall was just visible, straggled with the roots of the trees that now grew atop it. Through it all was a brooding spirit of silence and darkness.

However, the desolation was not total. At night the woods were filled with pixies and danger. Elves hunted the deer, and when the full moon rose, the shees were dancing to the high pipe and fiddle. Human travelers made haste to be well away from these woods lest they become bewitched by the music and wander away into the trees and be lost forever. Many unfortunates had lost their lives in Valur woods this way.

Some authorities claimed that such poor souls eventually perished of starvation, dazed, lost in some dark glade deep within the wood, their minds undone, never to recover.

Others told an even darker tale of elves gathering the be-dazzled and selling them as slaves to a hidden realm of dwarves, survivors of the ancient times, who worked them to death in the fabled mines of Veronath. The mines, once the source of half the gold in the world, had long been lost, their location swallowed up in the first Dark Age following the fall of Veronath. And yet there were many legends that linked the mines to the ancient wild forest, and thus a steady stream of wanderers and adventurers entered it in search of golden riches. Few ever returned, and those that did were often crazed and spoke of dancing endlessly to the music of the elves in their shees beneath the moon. Furthermore, no gold mines had ever been discovered and no nuggets ever brought to the outside world.

There had been those solid folk with no belief in the magical realm who had dared to colonize the ancient forest. They had failed. The land was weird, haunted by the ghosts of ancient Veronath. Farmers' luck always ran bad. A malevolent spirit took control of draught animals. Placid oxen suddenly turned and gored their masters. Donkeys became implacably fierce. Crops failed. Rabbits multiplied in their corn. People grew hungry and desperate.

Though the colonists gave up, the river traffic continued to pass through, for the land of Kenor was knit together by its navigable rivers. Travelers on land tended to go around the forest and to travel by day when doing so.

The dragonboys were quieted by the ruins. Even Swane forgot to compare them to the great ziggurats of Ourdh. Indeed, these ruins were not on such a grand scale, but there was a spirit brooding in this place. It was oppressive to the dragonboys and to the men. Only the dragons were oblivious.

Alba continued her stately progress, and at length the ruins fell far behind and left them with the world of trees and water. When darkness fell, the fleet put about and dropped anchor in a well-known cove behind a point that jutted out into the river.

The moon rose a little later. It was close to full, and above the great trees seemed ancient and golden and somehow closer to the world, as if they had been snatched back to an earlier age. The sky was crystal clear, and a few stars in the southern sky were visible still. The forest was dark and almost silent. Little gleams of pink and yellow spoke of the passage of pixies through the haunted woods.

Captain Eads ordered a doubling of the watch throughout the fleet. He was most concerned about men going overboard, bewitched by some phantasm. The reputation of Valur was well-known.

Evening meals were cooked up and afterward some of the men, who'd had a little whiskey tucked away, started singing the Kenor song and "La Lilly La Loo." They kept it up for a few minutes, but the forest seemed to grow more oppressive with each verse. At length they fell silent, the songs stuttering out aboard each ship in turn.

Relkin felt restless and stayed on deck, leaning over the side and gazing off into the forest. Once he thought he saw a distant light, hard and bright, not the little blurs of the pixies but something much more substantial. Another time he heard a short snatch of music, just a few bars, pipes and fiddles, far away. Then the darkness and the silence were resumed, until the moon broke through the shadows and cast her light across the ship.

His thoughts came back to himself and his situation in life. He was seventeen, in his third year of active service. One more and he and Baz would be eligible for a year's duty in the home city.

Seven more and they would be finishing up their legion careers. They would be entitled to forty acres apiece of good, level land. The Soil Survey wizard Ton Akalon had told him all about Tuala. It was just opening up now, but even in seven years, there would still be good land available. It was a wide basin, cloaked in oak and beech forest. Small towns had sprung up around Lake Tuala. In time he would visit those towns, perhaps live close to one.

In the meantime, he had seven years to put in as dragoneer in the 109th Marneri Dragons. Seven years to survive. Seven years to try and keep his dragon alive.

His service in the legion had shown him with brutal clarity how high mortality rates among dragons could be. There was a tendency to rely on the dragons and to place them at risk. They enjoyed battle, or so it seemed. But the toll was heavy. Bazil and Chektor were all that remained of the old crew, the original 109th.

His thoughts came back, as they did so often, to his own dragon, the amazing Broketail. In truth, Relkin knew he owed everything to the big leatherback. Toppling the Doom in Tummuz Orgmeen was enough to build a legend on, but then in the dread city of Dzu, Relkin had seen Bazil in the greatest battle of his life against the serpent god itself. And between himself and the dragon there existed a bond so strong that he didn't think either could live without the other.

An amazing dragon, who wielded his huge blade with the skill of the best swordsmen in the legion. A two-ton monster who could dance and pirouette through a sword fight with lethal grace that was sometimes almost human.

There was a lump in Relkin's throat. He was seventeen and still felt somewhat awkward and unfinished. He was growing again, putting on another inch in height and thickening in the chest and the arms. His beard was thick enough now to require a daily shave to satisfy Digal Turrent, who held beards on dragonboys to be irregulationary.

Relkin sighed. All they had to do was survive and stay together. Him and that two-ton sword wielding monster. They would retire together and make a great team for creating a farm on the land they'd be alotted. They'd get horses for the routine labor, of course, but for cutting wood and clearing land nothing could match a battledragon.

He smiled to himself. And eventually they'd both have to get mates. There would be a woman in his life again.

A sudden warm breeze came off the river, sparking memories of other rivers, when he had spent warm riverside nights with Miranswa Zudeina, lying on the warm marble casement of the fane of the Goddess Gingo-La. Effortlessly he could recall her body, her warmth, but it was not to be his, ever again. She was a lady of wealth, now that her inheritance had been secured and her aunt Elekwa had been sent down from the great city to live under guard on her own estate. Miranswa, was a lady in high society and expected to represent her family at the functions of the social round in Ourdh. It was out of the question for her to wed such a "wild oat" as an orphan boy from Quosh. Nor would she leave her southern home for the uncertain life of a soldier's wife in Kenor. And so they parted after a single summer together, those blissful months after the siege of Ourdh.

And this summer? This summer he would be in the Kohon Hills, in pursuit of a vicious clan of bandits. It didn't portend to be nearly as enjoyable. Relkin had a morbid fear of booby traps. Their first campaign in the winter against the Teetol had shown him how deadly such things could be. It was a nerve-wracking business taking dragons through an area with traps and pits and snares. Dragons weren't good at picking up the traces. Dragonboys had to study the ground the whole time.

He was quite lost in thought when he heard a small sound at his elbow, and he looked up and found himself gazing into the eyes of the most beautiful young maiden he had ever seen. They were large, green eyes, long-lashed, slanted slightly above a face of exquisite, slender beauty.

He drew in a long deep breath and was captivated. She arched her back and smiled at him in a way that spoke of hidden passions and carnal delight. A simple, one-piece costume made of deer hide was all she wore. It left little to his imagination. She was beautiful, a perfect nymph of the forest.

Now she was gazing into his eyes. Was it yearning he saw there? Amazement gave way to joy in his heart.

And still he shook his head. What was this? Where had she come from? Who was she? The questions pumped in his brain.

At last he noticed that she was wet. She had been swimming in the dark river at night.

"Who are you?" he said.

She smiled, giggled, and pointed to the river.

"Swim," she said quite clearly.

"You do understand me," he said.

"Swim," she repeated.

"I can't do that right now," he said.

She slipped back over the rail with the grace of a gymnast and clung on the outside of the rail, feet planted against the side of the ship.

"Come, now," she said.

Something heavy was pressing down his eyelids. A fog filled his thoughts almost as if he'd drunk one beer too many.

"But I can't, I'm . . ." he began, but in the next moment he couldn't remember exactly what he wanted to say.

His foot was up on the rail, and he was plunging down into the river, striking with a splash and going under and arching up and rising, spouting, glad to be alive.

The guard had seen him, shouts went up on the ship, but they seemed to be taking place in a far-off world, hidden away behind a membrane.

All he could focus on was the elf maiden, now swimming away with backward looks every so often. She raised a leg, and a spray of drops gleamed in the moon. Playfully she dove beneath the surface and vanished. He looked below but could not find her. And then she swam past him and pinched him as she went.

Aroused, he accelerated in pursuit and had almost caught up when he grounded. She was ahead of him and climbed out and ran up the bank and beneath the trees with a giggle as she went.

The shouts behind him were increasing, and several lamps had been lowered over the side, but he didn't pay them any attention. Ahead was only the slender girl, running from him, stopping to lean against a tree.

He caught up, stood there breathing hard beside her.

She stretched herself out against the tree.

"Put your hands on me," she said, or at least that's what it seemed she said. He stumbled forward, feet uncertain. She slipped away behind the tree, her hair glinting under the moonlight.

The shouts behind him were getting fainter as he ran. Always she seemed to float just a few feet beyond his grasp. Never had he wanted anything so much.

And then he tripped and fell to his knees and felt a net fall over him. He pushed up to get back on his feet, and the net was tightened. He glimpsed a face with overlarge features and bright protruding eyes. Big stocky hands were pulling the net tight. Relkin tried to get to his feet. A heavy boot kicked his legs out from under him.

On the ground again he noted that there were two of them. Dwarves! Short, knobby, heavyset dwarves, just as they were described in the ancient legends.

The spell was gone. All thought of the little elf maiden vanished. Relkin, awake at last, realized what was happening. He was in the process of being abducted by dwarves. The legends were true!

He struggled furiously and yelled for help at the top of his lungs.

The boots thudded on his body in response until he stopped. Ropes were tied around him, a gag was shoved in his mouth.

The mines, the legendary mines of Valur, that was where he would finish his life working as a slave until death released him.

It could not be. The future was in Tuala, on their farm with a wife and children and another life.

But there was no way to even move a muscle now. The dwarves had trussed him tight. Now they slung him from a pole and with one ahead and one behind, carried him on their shoulders away into the forest.

CHAPTER NINETEEN

The journey through the forest lasted no more than an hour before the dwarves halted in a grove of large, heavy-limbed oaks. One of them whistled, and in response there came a plangent tone. The dwarf moved a stone, pulled up a large brass ring, and opened a trapdoor covering a set of steps leading down into the dark.

Through the trap they carried Relkin, still swinging in the net beneath the pole. As they went, they whistled a little tune together, and Relkin's heart sank to its lowest level yet. He wondered if he would ever return to the surface again.

They went on down a long corridor past walls carved with bas-reliefs depicting ancient scenes from dwarvish history. A pair of enormous double doors gave way to a large rectangular room filled with opulent furnishings. The walls were resplendent with tapestries in brilliant color. Sculptures of a dozen schools of dwarf sculpture crowded the corners, everything from the ultra-baroque of Veronath to the stark, horrifying shapes of the Tummuz Orgmeen school.

This was journey's end. The dwarves dumped Relkin unceremoniously on the floor. From chairs that were virtually thrones, two dwarves, resplendent in robes of purple and scarlet velvet, arose with cries of delight.

Relkin lay perfectly still, conscious of the heavy boots on his captors' feet.

The high dwarves stepped down to look him over. Enormous pieces of jewelry, stones glittering from heavy chains of gold, hung from their necks. Emeralds sparkled in their earlobes, rubies and diamonds glittered on every finger.

The tongue of the dwarves was unknown to Relkin, but then the very existence still of dwarves in the world had been but an old legend until very recently to him. Now the dwarves haggled over his body, for in their language, as in any other, the intonations of bargaining were the same.

It was a spirited debate. Each side indulged in lengthy perorations with many gestures toward the prone dragonboy. There were gasps and flutters of the hands, there were groans and cries of pain, disgust, woe, the whole panoply of the bargainer's emotional palette. This was haggling of a fine art, way beyond the efforts of mere dragonboys. Relkin actually found himself carried away by the performances. It was an amazing experience to be haggled over like this, as a thing, an object, a piece of property.

There was a sudden, rude interruption. There came a mighty rap on the doors. The dwarves fell silent with a hiss. The silence stretched out into several seconds.

The doors were suddenly attacked with great energy until they burst open and a small crowd of nimble forest elves, clad in green homespun burst in. In their hands they had bows with arrows drawn. With them came a draft of warmer air, redolent of the nighttime forest. Behind them, the last to enter, was the elf maiden. She stepped to the front and addressed the high elves. There was no doubting what she had come for, payment.

The robed dwarves stepped back with loud barks of indignation. The elf maiden repeated her claim.

The argument grew hot.

At one point Relkin and the maiden happened to look in each other's eyes. To his disappointment, even horror, there was no feeling for him there whatsoever. He had been nothing to her except a piece of prey, like a deer to the huntsman. For some reason this thought made him ill. He laid his head on the floor and shut his eyes. Still the dwarves, all four of them, would hear nothing of the elf maiden's remonstrances. Whatever it was that she sought, they would not give it up.

Relkin never saw the first blow, but quite suddenly the forest elves attacked the dwarves. His two captors wielded clubs and boots with vigor. The high dwarves drew swords from behind their thrones. Steel rang beneath the dwarf lords' ceiling.

The dwarves were driven back with oaths and curses. Suddenly two elves bent over him and cut free his wrists and ankles.

Relkin scrambled to get to his feet, but his legs wobbled under him and he fell to one knee, which proved fortuitous for a dwarf had just then aimed a blow at his head with a club. It missed and pulled the dwarf off balance, whereupon he tripped and fell with a bloodcurdling string of oaths.

Relkin seized the chance. Staggering back to his feet, he had the dwarf's club in his hands and hammered its owner hard amidships with it. The dwarf doubled up on the ground. Relkin gave out a whoop. It felt good to dish out a little of what he'd been served by these dwarves.

Something brushed the back of his head, and he put up a hand by instinct and caught a noose of deer hide that was being dropped over his head by one of the elves.

Relkin snarled with anger, jerked the elf off his feet and kneed him hard in the belly. Swinging the club wildly before him, he dove for a narrow doorway to one side of the room. This gave onto a dark little corridor with a sour smell. An elf got in his way, and he bowled him over and trod on him. An arrow bounced off the wall, then he was through the doorway and into the dark, narrow passageway. Shrieks of dwarfish rage resonated in the main chamber.

He turned to his right and ran toward a dim light, a guttering candle, set beside a narrow door. He pulled the brass door handle and to his relief, the door swung open easily.

A larger corridor greeted him with cleaner air and no smell. He turned right, blundered into another door, and found himself in what seemed to be an empty apartment, dimly illuminated by a series of foot-wide squares of a phosphorescent glass set into the walls and ceilings.

There were many large, spacious rooms, empty but for dust and an occasional piece of furniture, abandoned long ago. Behind him came the sounds of pursuit. Elf and dwarf had come to terms it seemed, having realized that without Relkin they had nothing to fight over.

He went through a dozen of these huge, empty rooms leaving a trail of footprints through the dust until he came at length to a locked door. He looked around for some other way out but found nothing except a hatch set down low in one wall. He examined it by touch and found a handle that he pulled hard on. Nothing happened. He put his foot up to the wall and heaved as hard as he might. There was a little give but not much. He tried again, heaving on it until he thought his arms would come out of their sockets. His foot slipped and he sat down hard, and accidentally pulled down on the handle. A catch gave way, and the door slid sideways on hidden rollers.

Beyond was a dumbwaiter in a narrow, vertical shaft. The pursuit was getting close. There was no choice. He climbed into the dumbwaiter and pulled the hatch shut.

The dumbwaiter immediately dropped precipitously down the shaft and crashed to the floor twelve feet below. Relkin rolled clear and came up with a thud against a heavy table.

Slowly he got back to his feet. His head was ringing from the impact. It was dark, but not pitch-dark. There was a dim light coming from somewhere to his left. After a while his eyes adjusted and he saw more tables, and along a wall a series of tubs and sinks.

He was in a large kitchen, unused for an age. He moved toward the light, found a huge door half off its hinges, the wood rotting away at the bottom. Beyond the kitchen was a maze of cellars and storerooms, pantries, and more kitchens, each one with a dumbwaiter to the rooms above.

All were empty.

At length he came out upon a landing. This was the source of the light that came from somewhere above. He slipped quickly down the stairs, farther into the darkness below.

The air in the shaft was cool and smelled of stone. How deep it went into the world was unknown to Relkin. But if it took him farther away from the dwarves and elves, that was all he asked.

CHAPTER TWENTY

The call came two and a half months after his arrival in the Tetralobe. An interval that Thrembode the Magician had filled by earnest study in the library, broken by bouts of the inquisition.

It seemed almost miraculous to him now, but he had survived the inquisition virtually unscathed. They had hardly even tortured him. Just a slight roasting of his left hand and some needlework under the fingernails of the right. He was healing quite quickly, and in the library he had been able to examine a number of rare and important works, including the Negek Deem, one of the high-level praktika of the great magic.

For the last few weeks he had lived in a luxurious private cell, eight feet by eight, equipped with a pallet of straw and a blanket. Such blankets were marks of privilege. He had tickets for two meals a day from the Nexus Hall kitchens, though the meals were monotonous. Each consisted of boiled rice, boiled cabbage, and a sauce derived from unidentifiable meat and beans. There was just enough to keep a man going. One would never grow fat while dining on the Masters' board in the Tetralobe.

And so the days had passed in active inquiry. All the while, however, a low, rising fear had grown in his heart. Around him, in the library, in the cavernous feeding hall, there were hundreds of other grey-faced men, like himself, waiting to be seen. Gaunt men of indeterminate age and hopeless eyes. None spoke to any other, especially not in public. At the refectory, they ate their cabbage and gruel in silence, and then returned to their cells. It was possible to wait for years in this way.

Thrembode did not want to waste his life like this. Though the material in the library was useful and he had learned a couple of new spells, still he would rather be on his way, back to the warmer, lusher lands of the East or

West. He had need of a woman, but dared not frequent one of the brothels in the square; not when he was under scrutiny.

To keep him occupied there had been the business with General Lukash. He needed to meet with Lukash, to study Lukash, to come to understand the general. The problem had been that General Lukash would never honor any appointments. Lukash had shown him nothing but enormous disrespect, and Thrembode was infuriated already by the thick-necked, bullet-headed general. Lukash was a Teetol half-breed risen from the ranks in Axoxo. The Doom there had seen good qualities in Lukash, and he had risen far. Then he had been sent to Padmasa and had performed well in command of an army in Kassim. Lukash was also said to have been involved in the great secret program that was going on beneath the Tetralobe. This made him every bit as important as he evidently believed himself to be.

Even in the rumor mad world of the Tetralobe, there was no actual knowledge of what exactly the secret was, only that it was huge, and was taking place in a special complex, dug out below the Tetralobe itself over a period of two and a half years. No one, at pain of their lives, had been allowed into the section since. Only imps and a handful of Mesomasters had ever gone in. The imps had all been of the new breed, the ones with overlarge heads.

Lukash was involved somehow in this business, that was all Thrembode could discover. Even Administrator Gru-Dzek could find out little. Lukash had nothing but contempt for everyone, or so it seemed to the disgruntled administrator. Thrembode was relieved to discover that Administrator Gru-Dzek was getting the same treatment he was.

Still, there was the worry that his part in the upcoming war would be a disaster unless he could somehow establish a better relationship with Lukash. He had to at least meet with the man once or twice. How much did Lukash know about the Argonath? Had he ever been there? Did he speak Verio? There were many questions for which he had no answers. And so the magician had been forced to keep trying, leaving message after message with the general's office despite the humiliation of never receiving a reply.

As the days had lengthened into weeks and finally to months, Thrembode had felt a strange, quiet despair enter in and settle across his heart.

He was a fellow of the bright world of the cities. All the great cities of the world, that was where he was at home, from Ourdh to Lenkeiseen, from Kassim to Kadein, places with light and color and life. He was not meant for life here in the grim Tetralobe.

Worst of all, he could not indulge his passion for women, not here in Padmasa where it was regarded as a weakness and nothing more. He practiced absolute continence, aware of the unseen but constant scrutiny. *They* watched him now.

Yet there were times when it was a torture, and he felt a terrible sexual heat come over him. He had to struggle with himself to keep it from overwhelming his mind and sending him running to the brothels in the Square.

And so he remained, after nine weeks of this, rotting away in a tiny cell, always cold, always hungry, always watched, and always waiting. he began to wonder how long he could stand it.

And then, quite suddenly, there came the break. One grey cold morning like any other, he returned to his cell from the refectory and found two of the strange, megacephalic imps waiting for him. Their tunics and breeches were of a glistening black material that looked almost like skin. Their heads were enormous, bigger than a man's, but the faces were tiny, squeezed together in a look that was perfectly ratlike with pointed noses jutting out above projecting teeth in over-crowded jaws. They were hard to look at for very long.

"Where have you been?" said one of them in a thin, reedy voice.

"I have been at the refectory, eating."

"You had permission?"

"Yes."

"From whom did you obtain this permission to be absent from your cell?"

Thrembode's brow furrowed. He was not about to be interrogated by a pair of imps!

"Who are you?" he said.

They stared at him a moment, their eyes blinking.

"We have been sent to summon you. You are wanted for questioning."

There was a small red insignia on the right breast of their black tunics. He saw the mark of the Five, a pentad of red circles.

"To the Deeps?"

"You talk too much," said the first imp.

"Indeed, perhaps I do. I have waited a long while for this privilege."

In truth, Thrembode would have preferred not to enter the Deeps ever again.

"Come," they said as they turned and walked away together. Thrembode hesitated. They looked back.

"Come, you are wanted, now!"

There was no escape. Despite his naked dislike of the creatures, he followed.

They kept up a brisk pace and passed quickly through several large halls, filled with lines of petitioners, waiting to see administrators. At last they pushed through a pair of huge wooden doors into an anteroom guarded by a dozen large men who wore black armor and carried shield, sword, and spear.

Above the next pair of doors was a gallery cut from the rock where sat the monitors, a row of strangely mutated imps with overlarge eyes and ears.

Thrembode felt those strange eyes upon him and knew those ears were straining for the slightest whisper he might make. He composed himself with the utmost decorum and strode on behind the megacephalic imps.

Beyond the doors lay a vast open space clouded in darkness. Somewhere far below tolled a giant bell. In the center of the floor gaped the great Shaft that lead to the Deeps. The Shaft was three hundred feet across and smooth-sided. It went down into dim red-lit darkness.

An immense system of spars and wheels overhung the Shaft on one side. Here were lifts and chains that descended deep into the depths. Equipment was piled to one side, and a great gang of slave eunuchs was strapped to the cables. A boxy carriage was waiting.

More guards in black armor stood by, including a lurking troll in the darkness by the wall of equipment. Thrembode shuddered at the sight. He'd always had a loathing of the things, man-eaters all. He wondered what they fed it. Unfortunate worn-out slaves most likely.

Once he and the megacephals were in the elevator coach, the door closed, a whiplash cracked, and the cage began to descend into the darkness of the Shaft.

The descent continued for several minutes and at length broke out into another even more enormous dark space.

Points of red light glimmered far away in the immensity. Thrembode shivered and observed his breath frosting in the air. The temperature had dropped many degrees. There came a bright flash of light from below, and the great bell tolled once more.

This was the Prime Abyss.

He glanced out the window of the coach. The megacephals glared at him, but he ignored them. The distant lights were as much as a mile away, he estimated. The Prime Abyss was an ancient volcanic magma chamber, drained long ago and frozen ever since.

The coach came to rest beside a rickety wooden platform supported on stilt legs more than a hundred feet high. It was a temporary structure. There was no railing, nothing but this narrow wooden platform that jutted out into the empty dark. On the platform waited a group of megacephalic imps. One of them pointed.

As Thrembode turned in the indicated direction, he saw that the darkness here was anything but empty.

Floating in the dark about a hundred paces away, slightly above the level of the rickety platform, was a great black sphere. Flashes of light blasted the space around it every second or so. The bell tolled loud enough to make one's ears ring.

He gazed upon the Five, the very Doom Masters themselves, at work upon another of their creations.

A thirty-foot-wide sphere of black marble hung there, a steel collar around its middle connected to a dozen heavy chains that rose to the top of the Shaft. Floating around this mass were five forms, humanlike but hidden in shadow. Every so often a flash of red light would come from one of them, and a beam would lance down into the black stone and illuminate a small section of it for a moment. At the same time there would be a fierce hiss, then the ringing sound as if a bell had been struck with a hammer.

Thrembode gazed in awe. This was the pinnacle of his world. These were the Masters. They worked the stone with their mighty magic and knotted it full of a dark mentality, a being of pure intellect and no physical form, trapped inside the rock, a slave to their will.

The shadows moved, the rock rang the tune of creation. All their energy was directed at the huge block of stone, but still there was enough radiating outward into the space to make Thrembode shiver. The strength of these energies was enormous. Such power they had! Nothing on this world could match them, certainly not the gaggle of hags at work in the eastern cities. Soon they would be strong enough to control the entire world.

He waited on the end of the ramp proudly inflated, his hands clasped behind his back. He stood close to the edge. After a while he realized he was listening to a kind of seething rustling going on below him, a constant sound.

He turned to one of the megacephals and inquired as to its cause.

"Cockroaches, four feet deep. They eat everything that falls to them."

After that Thrembode stood back from the edge and tried to tune out the hideous sound of a billion insects down below.

Then with a thin wail, a body went past, tossed from the heights, a worn-out slave.

After the impact, the seething grew intense.

Suddenly the field strength around the nascent Doom shrank and faded. Thrembode looked up at once.

The Great Ones approached him, floating on pure psychic power. Now he could actually see them, glittering things, covered in horn. Their eyes were now scarlet slits set in bulging crystalline orbs. Whorls of horn had grown up and out from their cheekbones and the temporal lobe. Thrembode felt his sense of awe overcome the terror.

"This is the second time you have stood before us, Magician Thrembode," said one of them, he could not tell which.

"Yes, Masters, I am privileged."

"You have been very busy in the East, Magician. In Kadein, in Tummuz Orgmeen, in Marneri, and most recently in Ourdh, a series of catastrophes."

Thrembode bit back any response.

"In Kadein we lost an excellent network of agents, I believe."

Thrembode kept absolutely silent. The seething went on undisturbed beneath him.

"And we lost a Doom in Tummuz Orgmeen. A fine Doom, one of our best."

"Except that we understand that a certain magician expressed criticism of the fine Doom that we had wrought."

"This magician said that the Doom was 'flawed,' did he not?"

Thrembode felt his mouth go dry.

"Something's caught his tongue."

Thrembode struggled for a moment to speak and at last regained control of his tongue.

"I am most sorry to have given offense. I did not mean to suggest that there was anything wrong with your work. I was frustrated by my inability to make the Doom understand our peril. It did not understand how troublesome the hags can be."

"Nonsense." This was said very fiercely.

Thrembode gulped, took a deep breath.

"I meant no criticism. I beg your pardons for my stupid remarks. I am an unworthy critic."

There was a long silence.

"This is true, and we have many complaints against you. However, we have put aside the charges. We have a mission for you."

"You have a good knowledge of the language and customs of the so-called Argonath cities."

"And you have spent time in the hinterlands there."

"That is why you have been chosen to advise General Lukash."

He looked down, oppressed by the pitiless stares of all five of them. He was but a gnat, a flickering thing of impulses compared to them. He struggled for the courage to speak, knowing that it was vital.

"But, Masters, there is a difficulty." He couldn't believe he was saying it, but he was.

"Difficulty?" A note of incredulity.

"General Lukash refuses to meet with me. I have had no contact with him. I cannot advise unless I can speak to him."

There was a long, ominous silence.

"Lukash will meet with you, Magician Thrembode. You will advise him." There was a dreadful finality in the words.

CHAPTER TWENTY-ONE

Dragon vision was acute in the darkness, the legacy of aeons of predation. In the forest of Valur, this was proving to be a useful trait.

Bazil moved again, closer, easing his bulk through the trees and then freezing behind a massive pine.

Up ahead the eerie light continued to shine from elfin lamps while the high whistling music went on unabated. Forest elves disported themselves on the shee, and they were too busy with the fun to notice the two-ton monster that crept upon them.

Once more he slid forward, stepping on a rotten branch that broke, but not very loudly. He froze. The music went on. He peered between the branches of two small pines and finally saw them at their dancing.

High and fey they were, leaping on pointed toe beneath the moon. The musicians, six of them, played flutes and whistles, tambourines and small snare drums. The dancers, perhaps two score, perhaps more, formed a circle in the glade. The music was elastic, lively, guaranteed to set the heels of anyone to bouncing, except for dragons, who were impervious to most magic in the world. While Bazil watched, the elves danced, spinning, twirling, and even tumbling. Some of them were spectacular tumblers, doing double back flips at the end of every turn of the reel. Hand-to-hand and toe-to-toe, they flew through complex motions and fancy steps.

Among them was a fellow with a regal bearing, clad in a costume of finely worked deer skin dyed a brilliant scarlet. He seemed a leader of some sort, someone who might have information.

Baz measured the distance to the fellow. Once out of concealment, he would have fifty feet to cover. He gathered himself. If anyone could tell him what had happened to

Relkin, it would be an elf. They knew everything that happened in their woods.

High flew the dancers, back flips, spins, and all. Away sang the music, away to the Mountains of Lorn and the ancient days of yore. Suddenly the pine trees shook as Bazil lurched out of concealment and sprang among the circle.

There was a moment of incredulity. The dancers stopped, mid-whirl, on point, hands high and then with a collective shriek of dismay and bewilderment, they broke and ran like mice scattering from a barn cat.

The one clad in scarlet ran toward the forest with the acceleration of an athlete. Bazil altered course and sprang after him, gathering himself for a great leap.

He sprang, the elf darted sideways, and Bazil missed him. He tried to halt his momentum, but he'd jumped too hard and he lost his footing and fell and rolled into a thorn thicket.

When he'd extricated himself at last, there wasn't an elf in sight. With a groan, he started forward.

He'd been out in the woods for hours. Everyone else had long since returned to the *Alba.* The rest of the fleet had gone on. The *Alba* could only wait a few more hours.

But the boy was lost, bewitched, bedazzled, something had overcome his wits and he had absconded. Bazil had heard the tales concerning elf abductions and the dwarf slavers who lived below the ground. These were not the civilized elves he knew from the Argonath cities, with their sophisticated elf quarters. These were forest elves of Valur, with all its antique glories and hidden magic.

What was certain was that if he didn't find the damned boy, he was going to be without a dragonboy. He hated sharing. He'd had to share Relkin with the Purple Green for a few months and that had been rough. Now it would be even worse.

He chided himself for thinking this way. He had had Relkin since he was no more than a child. They had grown up together. They were each other's family. The dragoness hardly counted as family, since she was pursuing caribou and grizzly bears in the far north. Baz couldn't leave the dragonboy behind, he had to find him even if it was a damned nuisance to be out here, ripped up by thorns, hot and bothered, utterly lost, even bewildered.

He stumbled on through the forest, not knowing what he

was looking for. In the glades he would look up to the moon, so bright, so pitiless. He cocked his ears but heard nothing, except once the cough of an elk in the distance.

Then while negotiating a thicket of small trees, he heard another sound, something that froze him in place. Someone was cursing at high volume. Loud vituperation in a high-pitched voice. The emotion was unmistakable, even if the language was unknown.

There was a moment's silence and then another outburst, the same elfin voice, a female voice.

Bazil moved in its direction, across a slope covered in laurel and box elder. It was impossible to be completely silent, but it didn't seem to matter. The female elf voice continued to vent loud criticisms. As he got closer, he could hear other voices, deeper than the elf's, shouting things back. They were muffled, however, and he knew they were shouting from within a structure, or a cave.

He pressed on and came over the top of the slope and saw an elf maiden in simple garb, leaning over the edge of a hidden passage. She screamed a few more choice insults and then turned away. Bazil saw a head come up from the ground and yell something after her in a tongue that he did not recognize. The head spat, then an arm came up, and pulled shut the trapdoor.

Bazil was on the scene moments later. There was no visible sign of any door. All he could see was bare ground with a rock half buried in it. For a moment the dragon was nonplussed. Then he shook himself from neck to tail. This was magic of course, and magic of a high order. He studied the ground. Clearly it was a puzzle of some kind. He wished Relkin was there. Dragonboys were so much better at this kind of thing than dragons.

He focused on the rock, about the size and smoothness of a dragon's egg. Cautiously, he reached down and touched it. It felt very smooth to the touch. He pushed at it with a finger. Nothing happened. He stood back and studied it. It was too smooth to be anything but part of the spell. There was something unreal about it. He tried it again. On a hunch he curled his big hand around it and squeezed.

Immediately it changed beneath his hand, shifting shape and becoming a big brass ring attached to a bolt sunk into the ground.

He pulled on the ring and a patch of ground six feet by

four came up smoothly on invisible hinges. A set of steps led down into the dark.

He knew he was never going to catch that elf girl in the night forest. Perhaps he could get some answers to his questions down those steps. Someone lived down there, that much was evident.

CHAPTER TWENTY-TWO

Relkin ran lightly down the steps into the deeper darkness of the lower levels. Here the landings gave out onto immense halls, all empty and silent, replete with the dust of the ages. He had no light and thus did not realize that he ran beneath ceilings encrusted with gemstones and inlaid with gold. He noticed mirrors but did not know they were made of solid silver.

He heard the pursuit far above. Loud voices bellowed in the language of the dwarves. They were coming down after him, there were lanterns flickering in the stairwell.

He'd gone down twelve levels, and the last staircase had been several times as long as the first. Now the stairs ended, leaving him on a vast floor of stone carpeted in dust and the bones of unknown animals. In the light from the descending lanterns, he saw that there were tracks in the dust, quite recent. The skull of a dog lay nearby. He picked it up. Even in the dim light he could tell that it had been gnawed.

He set his jaw and headed through a wide entanceway into a space of immense dimensions, a ceremonial hall. Any sound he made seemed to echo back to him in the stillness. From far above he heard a triumphant dwarvish bellow.

He could just make out the dim outline of the far end of the hall. There was another double entrance. The doors had been broken down and lay shattered just inside the hall. Relkin picked his way through the rotten wood and went on into a second hall. There was a sour smell in here, something like unwashed socks. Now the light was so dim he could make out no far end or even the ceiling. The lack of light was going to make it difficult to go on too far in this underground city. What he needed to find was another staircase, some means of returning to the upper levels. Either that or a lantern.

He padded across the dust-strewn floor with a slow-growing sense of unease and awe at the scale of this room. It was bigger than the other one, bigger than even the Temple in Marneri.

He noticed that the sour odor was getting stronger. Something about it made the hair on his neck rise. He glanced over his shoulder and almost jumped out of his skin.

Lurching along just behind him was a pale manlike creature, covered in white hair, with red eyes sunk in cavernous sockets. It gathered itself to spring on him.

Relkin yelled in fright and jigged sideways, and the thing blundered by with arms outspread. He felt fingers brush past his face.

His heart pounding from surprise and fright Relkin danced backwards, away from the thing.

That smell came again, but stronger than ever. He looked back and saw another pair of similar creatures. Beyond them were others. With a sickening realization, he understood.

"Lurkers," he whispered. The legendary inhabitants of all the deep, dark places of the world. Lurkers! Misshapen things with long forearms and knuckles that brushed the ground. They were said by some to be the ancestral parents of the race of trolls. They ate whatever came into their cold, quiet realm. Now they lurched after him, grunting in anticipation of the feast to come.

He had no weapons, nothing to fight them with. They looked very strong, but they were slower than a man. He darted away from one pair as they came close and jinked past another one and went on until he reached a wall. He turned back to the dim light emanating from the distant stairwell. He started to run that way and then stopped. To go back there was to turn right into the dwarves. He couldn't go back. He had to go on. He turned and sped along the wall through the dark. He outpaced the lurkers and reached the remains of the doors at the far end of the great hall. These fragments of timber were still in place. They had been broken off at the ground, however, to allow the lurkers to pass through as they pleased.

The space beyond was totally dark. Relkin's nostrils twitched in time. That sour smell again, they were in there, waiting for him to blunder into their arms.

He backed away. The smell grew stronger, they were coming through the door for him.

With a cry of despair, he turned and ran back the way he had come. Lurkers were waiting for him.

It was like some nightmarish game, except that he was the ball and if they tackled him, they would eat him. The lurkers converged toward him, trying to herd him to the wall.

He couldn't allow that. There were ten of them at least, they'd catch him for sure if they cornered him. He braked, cut back, and spun away from one that dove in at him at knee level.

Another swung up an arm. He kicked it in the chest, felt the lurker give way, and then he sprang past, just evading the creature's grip. He ran for the end of their line, his breath coming harsh now as he accelerated to his limit.

He distanced them, and curved back to the door. He was faster than the lurkers, that was all he needed. But a few were still closer to the door, and they converged there quickly. He sprinted, pushing himself harder than he'd ever run before and slipped the grasping hands of the closest. He actually felt a hand slide down his back and almost grab hold of his belt before he was through and into the first chamber.

Thankfully, there were no more of them ahead, and he slowed a little and ran for the distant staircase. Better the dwarves than the lurkers any day. He muttered a prayer to old Caymo and wondered when the old god was going to take notice that his servant Relkin was in a terrible plight.

He left the hall and almost bounded into a small group of waiting lurkers. He ducked a hand, felt another grab his shirt, but tore free and spun around. A hand struck him in the face, and he swung and connected with a roundhouse left that hurt his fist. He stumbled, almost fell, and then was past them.

There was nothing to do but to run for it. There were more of the things emerging from another doorway. The lowest level was infested with them. His hand hurt, he cradled it in the other as he ran. They were right behind him, bowling along like apes on all four limbs.

He was trapped between the worst and the second worst possibilities in life—to be devoured by the lurkers or to be enslaved by the dwarves.

He reminded himself that while there was life, there was hope. He wondered if old Caymo was ever going to step in.

He wondered if he shouldn't try an appeal to the Great Mother.

He reached the stairs and sprang up them, two at a time.

The lurkers were on the stairs a moment later, and they sprang up them three at a time and soon began to gain on him. He looked back and received yet another fright as he saw how close they were.

The lanterns were still far above as the dwarves searched, level by level.

The lurkers were virtually designed for climbing stairs, perhaps the grim secret of their success. Once something came down into their world, it could never escape. Now they were snatching at his heels, even as he picked up the pace to take the steps three at a time.

His legs were tiring. Exhaustion was near. He gave a despairing cry and tried to redouble his efforts. He leaped the steps, three or four at a time, just matching the lurkers behind him.

But his despairing cry had set off a chorus from a few levels above. Lanterns were shining down. Voices bellowed in triumph. He ran the stairs, legs extending prodigiously in front and behind. He ran to the dwarves.

At the landings he increased his lead by a few steps, on the stairs the lurkers pulled back his head. Level by level they gained.

The dwarves could not be far now, he called out again. And then a lurker caught his heel. He lost his balance and stumbled. They were on him in the next moment. His breath was knocked out of him, they piled on and they lifted him and started to tear him apart limb from limb. He screamed and fought them but they were far too strong for him.

His scream brought an answering chorus of cries from just above, and the dwarves, with steel in their hands, slew a couple of the lurkers and the rest fled screaming in rage and frustration.

Relkin lay huddled on the steps for a long moment, struggling just to breathe. His arms felt as if they'd almost been torn from their sockets, which was true enough.

Rough dwarfish hands reached down and lifted him up. Someone cuffed him across the back of the head. He took a deep breath. He was struck again and cursed roundly by several of the others.

He spun and kicked the dwarf behind him in the stomach.

It doubled up with a gasp, and he turned to try and escape them and get past on the upward side. He almost got there, but a club swung and struck him on the side of the head, and he was unconscious before he even hit the stone steps.

CHAPTER TWENTY-THREE

With his head throbbing, Relkin awoke to the sound of a noisy clatter, as if any empty barrel were being run over cobbles. He opened his eyes, and cautiously raised a hand to the injured area. There was a swelling along the top of his cheekbone. Struggling to sit up, he probed at the swelling and moved his jaws. There was stiffness, but not the lancing pain of a broken bone. His ear was tender and crusted with blood.

He lay on a pile of straw in what seemed to be a broken-down stall, in a stables. The walls gaped open, slats were missing, and he could see through to the other stalls. There were lamps, curiously ornate in design, hanging from corner posts at either end of a wooden wall about eighty feet long. A wheel was set against the wall. Piles of rope lay neatly coiled farther on.

He sat up fully, and immediately lay down again as a wall of nausea threatened to overwhelm him. He took several deep breaths. Someone ran past the stall in which he lay. He glanced up, saw a dwarf carrying a heavy sack, shuffling as fast as he could.

More dwarves ran past, shouting back at someone behind them. Suddenly there was the clangor of a bell farther away.

Then Relkin discovered that he was chained by one ankle to a ring sunk in the ground. Idly, he tugged at it. It was not loose in any way. A massive padlock secured the chain.

Another wave of sickness passed through him. Gritting his teeth, he rode it out.

He tried to remember where he'd been before this. It didn't come easily.

His speculations ceased as two dwarves, clad in brown, burst into the stable and pulled him to his feet. They jabbered to each other as one used a large key to open the lock.

Then they pulled him out of the stall and pushed him ahead of them. He stumbled out into a wide passage.

Other dwarves came by, a family group, two plump adults and four plump children. Behind them came three slaves, men of uncertain age bowed under chests and heavy sacks. They were virtually naked and covered in the scars left by the whip.

Relkin shivered. The dwarves pushed him along with curses. The dwarf family hurried on ahead. The painfully thin slaves staggering behind them. This would be his life, too, if he didn't find some way out of this.

No obvious escape presented itself, however, as he emerged in another even broader place, where dwarves climbed into rickshas while their chests and sacks were piled behind them. Then the slaves got between the staves of the rickshas and began to pull. The dwarves screamed abusively to urge the slaves on, and most plied a whip in much the same manner one would upon a horse or donkey.

In the most beautifully made ricksha, an open carriage with fretwork in pale wood and gold inlay, sat the two regal-looking dwarves Relkin had been brought to before.

They clapped their hands and barked harsh commands to the two lower-class dwarves who were hustling Relkin along. They pushed him between the staves and chained his wrists to the handles. Then they removed the ankle chain.

To his astonishment, both lower-class dwarves climbed onto the back of the ricksha and sat down on a backboard. He was supposed to haul four of them, plus heavy chests filled with their possessions!

The regal dwarves yelled at him suddenly in Verio. The one in the purple velvet robes took up a long coachman's whip.

"Slave, pull, pull hard, pull now or else whip!"

They did speak Verio!

"You cannot do this to me. You have no right!" Relkin felt the anger surge in him. When the legion found out about this, they'd sack this place and burn it out.

"Silence. You are slave. Pull, pull hard or else whip!"

"I will not. Damn you, I am a free man, I am not a slave!"

Both dwarves screamed in sudden fury.

Relkin remembered the ricksha men in ancient Ourdh. Was this to be his fate? Virtually a draft animal, consigned to pulling a carriage through the underground realm of the dwarves for ten or twenty years until he was too worn-out to be of any further use?

The dwarf in the purple suddenly struck him with the whip, a stinging sensation leapt across his shoulder.

He screamed at them in rage and stood in his tracks. He resolved that he would not pull the cart. He would not be their slave. He would not allow this to happen to him.

The whip cracked down upon his back, and he jumped with the sting. Again it came, and then again. There was blood running down his neck.

He would not do this! He was resolved. Even if they beat him to death, he would never haul four fat dwarves around like a beast of burden.

The dwarves were shouting, the whip was being applied freely now. Relkin felt blood trickling down his back. He sighed somewhere deep inside. It seemed the damned dwarves were just going to beat him to death then and there. His acquaintance with dwarves had been very brief, for which he was heartily glad. He fell to his knees, his hands above him, still locked in place. The dwarves screamed invectives and kept the lashes raining down on him. If they wanted to kill him, they would. There was nothing he could do now.

Dimly, he wondered why old Caymo had never intervened. Perhaps old Caymo hadn't heard the prayers of his worshiper. Perhaps, Relkin concluded sadly, old Caymo didn't exist anymore. The days of the dancing god of pleasure and commerce had truly ended long ago. Either that or Relkin was just so bad at worship and prayer that Caymo had never heard him. He wondered if the Great Mother would accept him into Heaven after all.

There was a sudden tremendous noise, and the dwarves all shrieked in unison. A great light flashed about them for a moment and then faded. Relkin became aware of a kind of golden glow coming from his right.

The whip had stopped. The dwarves were silent. Relkin stared, shook his head, and stared again, unsure whether to believe his eyes.

The elf maid was back, but now as a prisoner, caught between two other figures who looked as if they had stepped right out of ancient legend.

By their golden armor, their stern beautiful faces rimmed with silver curls, he knew that they were elf lords. Their helmets were of an antique design with small silver wings jutting forth above the ears. At their waists they wore swords, and in their right hands they bore heavy spears tipped with steel.

The elf maiden pointed to the dwarves and made a long, loud complaint. The moment she finished, the dwarves erupted with loud protestations of their own.

The elf lords listened for quite a while to the dwarves, who seemed capable of continuing their complaints forever. Then the elves suddenly raised their spears and gave a loud cry in unison.

To Relkin's amazement, the dwarves fell silent.

The elf lords spoke, and not in the tongue of the dwarves but in the ancient tongue of their kind, the mother language of all languages, and Relkin understood them quite clearly and was amazed further.

"In the first part," they began, "it is found that the young man will not be yours. He is to be freed at once."

Relkin heard and felt his heart beat more strongly in his chest. This was going in the right direction. The dwarves gave a low moan of disappointment.

"Furthermore, know ye that this man is marked by the Sinni. Ye may not interfere with his destiny."

The dwarves fell silent.

"In the second part, in the matter of the complaint by the maiden Debeneni, it is found that you did cheat her of the payment due her."

The dwarves hissed.

"In the third part, in the matter of the Law of the King of the Forest, Dethelgolin the Great, you are found guilty of unlicensed slave taking."

The dwarves were pale, trembling, but remained silent.

"Free him," the golden elves pointed to Relkin.

One of the low dwarves climbed down and sullenly freed Relkin from the staves.

Relkin measured the fellow's chin.

"Do not strike the dwarf!" said the golden ones.

Relkin put a hand to his throat, pointed to the dwarves, made the sign of the evil eye, and backed away.

The dwarf nearest him raised his knife with a snarl. The golden glow grew momentarily much brighter, and the two elves hefted their spears. The dwarf fell back with an oath and retreated to the rear of the carriage. Relkin stood beside the elves.

Close up the golden elves were distinctly unhuman. Their ears were pointed, delicate with long lobes. Their eyes were aslant and larger than those of any man. They betrayed no emotion whatsoever when they gazed upon him with those golden irises.

Relkin muttered some thanks. He exchanged glances with the elf maiden, but he detected no human emotion there, either. Then she looked away and did not look back.

"Your destiny does not lie here," said one of them.

He stared for a moment. "Then where does it lie?" he said.

"There is a rose garden in the land of Arneis. You will stand in that garden."

"A rose garden in Arneis," repeated Relkin, and he shivered, for he recalled the words of the fortune-teller in Dalhousie. Some calamity lay ahead of him, that seemed pretty damned certain.

"The ways of destiny are the province of the Sinni. This is from their insight."

He looked up. The Sinni? Were they watching?

"Why do you look up?"

"Are the Sinni here?"

"No. Why should they be? We are here."

"Well, yes, but—"

"Come. There is work to be done, and then you must rejoin your comrades."

Relkin gestured to the four dwarves.

"What about them? Are they to go unpunished?"

"They are to be punished."

"How?"

"Watch."

Relkin turned back and saw that the dwarves were sitting still, as if frozen. They didn't even seem to be breathing.

"What has happened?"

"They will not move for one hundred years."

"One hundred years?"

The elven lords had turned and were going up the passage.

The urge was irresistible. He took two steps and tweaked the nose of the dwarf in purple robes.

"Leave the dwarves alone!" said the golden ones.

"Where are we going?"

"We must calm the dragon."

"Dragon?"

"There is a great dragon loose in the city of the dwarves. Its raises havoc."

"By the breath, let me guess."

"It is your dragon, Relkin of Quosh."

"Where is he?"

"We must hurry. The dwarves are an endangered species. We try to conserve their numbers. The dragon is about to slaughter them."

"Where?"

"Come, we will take you."

He gestured to the elf maiden, who walked between the elves.

"Why did she aid them?"

"They promised her fine jewels. She is young and head-strong. She will go with us to the Chancery of the King of the Forest to be judged. You need not concern yourself with retribution."

The one on the right, who had perhaps the firmest chin and the smallest nose, came close to him, reached out, and attached a golden chain to Relkin's belt.

"What's that for?" Relkin caught it up in his hand. It was smoother than silk, about five feet long. The elf tugged on it and pulled Relkin toward him. The elf maiden had been freed and sent on her way. She did not look back. Relkin stood between the elf lords.

"Run," they said.

"Where?"

"Run."

"I'm still getting over my last run, don't expect too much."

"Run."

He began to run. He felt dreadfully weak, his head throbbed with every step. The elves ran alongside him with a smooth, seemingly effortless stride. They hardly seemed to breathe. Then Relkin noticed that all three of them were accelerating as a unit, as if bound together by invisible threads. They were speeding now far more quickly than a man could run, as fast as the fastest horse, now faster than that. He continued to run, to stagger along, but they hurtled through the dimly lit passageways of the underground city at an increasingly rapid rate until Relkin's eyes bulged as they zipped around corners and darted through crevices.

Their journey took less than a minute, and then they emerged in the gate chamber inside the Gate of Madrubab. Relkin saw at once that the situation was explosive.

It was a big place, big enough for a battledragon to wield a sword with full effectiveness. The dragon stood in the open gate. A tremendous mass of dwarves and dwarf carriages pulled by dogs, slaves and small ponies, was crammed in the chamber from wall to wall, hemmed in by the dragon and the gleaming steel of Ecator.

These dwarves had been in flight from the invasion of the dragon, but he had caught up to them here at the gate, where they were locked in a tangle of carts and carriages, sedans and rickshas.

Some clambered from their conveyances and prepared to run for it. Bazil snarled and roared, "Where is the dragonboy?"

Dwarves ran.

Ecator came whistling down and chopped through a small white coach. The pony bolted away with the front part. Bazil strode through the wreckage, turning over carriages, pushing others out of the way. Ecator rose high.

Relkin and the elves were in front of him the next moment.

"I'm here, Baz, here!"

The dragon stopped in mid-swing. A half dozen terrified dwarves were saved from death.

"Boy!" he roared. Then he returned his gaze to the two elves who flanked the boy.

"Who are these?"

"These are, well, I don't know their names, Baz, but they've been very helpful, shall we say."

"Boy looks like he is barely alive. They were not helpful soon enough."

Relkin put a hand up to his battered ear. "Right," then his eyes filled with concern as he saw the tattered condition of his dragon's hide.

"What in the name of the old gods has happened to you?" he said.

Bazil chuffed, "I ran into thorns in the forest. Elf difficult to catch."

"Oh ho, you were out catching elves while elves were out catching me. We've had quite a night of it."

Bazil's concern grew when he saw Relkin's back now cut to shreds.

"Boy will have a convict's back," he said grimly.

The elf lords spoke up.

"You must return now to your comrades. Come, we will show you the way." The elves led them out of the Gate of Madrubab and onto the forest way. The golden chain was withdrawn. The elves raised their hands.

"Farewell, dragonboy. We leave you now."

"Wait, there is more I would like to know. The Sinni, why are they involved?"

"That is not for us to know."

"What are they, then? Can you tell me at least that much?"

"High Lords, risen in the dawn time. Always they have guarded Ryetelth."

"We must go now, dragonboy. Return to your comrades. They come."

"Wait, tell me your names. I must know to whom I owe my life."

"We are Althis and Sternwal. If ever you are in need of assistance in the forest of the King under the Tree, you need only call out our names."

They turned and began running and soon disappeared, moving at tremendous speed, taking their golden glow with them.

Relkin exhaled and took a long breath. The dragon was a massive reassuring presence in the dark. They walked down a wide pathway through the trees, which at length came out upon the riverside. In the mid-distance, they spied the lights of the *Alba*.

The water was cold, but the dragon bore him up on his broad back, and the shock of the cold brought new life back to him. He turned and looked back to the forest of Valur. The world had been revealed to him as a stranger place than he had ever imagined.

"A rose garden in Arneis," he mumbled. The Sinni were interested in him. It was an unnerving thought.

CHAPTER TWENTY-FOUR

Back aboard the *Alba,* Relkin endured the ire of Dragon
Leader Turrent and the ribbing from the dragonboys. Mono,
who was the best hand with a needle, sewed up his back.
While he did so, he pestered him with questions about his
frolics with the elf maid.

Relkin had his teeth gritted and his eyes screwed tight
during the procedure but at length he managed a grin.

"Couldn't stop myself, Mono, Relkin the great lover and
all that."

Bazil, sitting beside them, emitted a huge chuckle. "Elf
understand this boy's obsession with fertilizing the eggs,
that's what."

The chuckle died away, and the dragon eyes sparkled dangerously. "But better for dwarves that I never meet them.
They never steal dragonboy or anyone else ever again."

When Relkin awoke, it was to return to the life of punishment details and empty hours in which to ponder the future.

Arneis was a lush province on the other side of the
Malgun mountains, near Kadein. It was famous for red
wines. Why he should go there to fulfill his destiny was a
mystery.

Then there was the matter of the Sinni. What did those
strange beings want with him? He recalled the eerie shapes
that had hung in the air over him in the pit at Dzu and shivered.

He recalled the dark witch Ribela's words, "Upon the
sphere board of destiny lie all the pieces, child. There is a
piece for each one of us, even you, and the smallest piece
can play a vital role in the affairs of worlds."

He resolved to write to the Lady Lessis. Under the fort's
patient teacher, who taught a mixed class of legionaries and
farm boys their letters, he had worked hard through the winter to master reading and improve his writing. Lessis had

told him to write to her, and he would. Perhaps she could answer some of the many, many questions pounding in his brain.

He scrubbed. He peeled. He lathered. He polished. The days went by, and the *Alba* made her slow but steady way up the river against the gentle current.

Relkin's back healed, and the purple bruise above his cheekbone slowly turned brown and faded away.

At last they reached the Darkmon Break where the river dropped a thousand feet in the space of half a mile. They debarked and marched up the Imperial road to the top. As they went, they passed the grain chutes built by the Imperial engineers. These chutes were one of the wonders of Kenor. Sacks of grain slid smoothly down the chutes on their way to the docks at the head of navigation down below.

In fact, there were seven separate lengths of chute, and at each break in the system, there were teams of laborers who maneuvered the grain into the next chute downward. All in all the chutes were a perfect example of the Imperial engineering philosophy at its best.

At the top of the break, they stood on the upper reach of the river, a wild place completely different from the placid lower reach. From here on they marched.

Later that day they passed a dredging crew busy canalizing the upper stream. Three great dragons, old brasshides, sat on the bank, eating an enormous lunch. A dozen men, twice that many horses, and lots of equipment made up the background. In the channel, half buried in the water, was their dredger with its steel-tipped scoop set on cross-braced beams a foot thick.

These older dragons and the 109th exchanged friendly greetings mixed with cheerful dragonish insults while they marched past.

When they were past the dredgers, the dragons of the 109th fell into a spirited discussion of the possibilities of such a working life. Dragons in retirement were given the choice of farming in Kenor, taking up work in the Engineering Corps or going home to the village of their birth.

"Engineer dragons, they have a good life," said Anther, the green from Aubinas.

"Get paid well, eat all they want," said his dragonboy Halm of Ors.

"Have to dig like that, every day?" said the Purple Green.

"They build bridges, too. It's really a big part of the Imperial Effort."

"I would consider it," said the Purple Green. "Better than having to grow plants to survive."

"But the farmer owns his land, dragons have property rights, too," said Bazil.

"I do not trust such things. When all this land is fully settled, will the men still let dragons keep theirs?"

"The empire will always honor the dragons," said Halm of Ors.

"But the empire may not survive forever," said Alsebra, the green freemartin from Aubinas. "Men have ruled themselves in many different ways. Only the empire has proved a friend to dragonkind."

The other dragons looked at Alsebra and blinked heavily as they adjusted. The freemartin was formidably well-informed and, they feared, more intelligent than any of them. She was also very good with her dragonsword, "Undaunt!" All the dragons in the 109th had been both intimidated by her and attracted to her since her arrival. Except for the Broketail that is, whose heart's desire flew the great northern skies, haunting the herds on the migration routes.

"Alsebra not have to worry. Empire last longer than any dragon here."

"But someday, Broketail, someday there will be many, many humans here, and then they will not want dragons to live among them. You know how it is in the cities."

"Dragons well treated in Marneri."

"Yes, but not all the time. I think you've had your own bad experiences."

Bazil nodded, there had been his first job, working for the Lord of Borgan county in Blue Stone province. His first experience of trolls had come from that encounter.

"True, but farmer can grow rich growing grain for the empire. Grow rich and hire men and horses to work for one. Dragon not have to work anymore."

"Now that sounds better to me," rumbled big Chektor, the old brasshide.

"But the engineer dragon gets to travel. You go all over the empire. Build bridges in Kadein. Dredge river in Kenor," said Anther.

"Aha, green one wants to travel," said Vlok. "Take advice from this dragon, don't travel."

"Vlok is well traveled?" said Alsebra.

"Vlok has seen the world."

"So then, why not travel?"

"It's uncomfortable. On ships you are all cooped up like some big chicken."

They all laughed at that.

"That Vlok, he should have wings," said Alsebra.

This brought mirth from the Purple Green.

"By the fire of Glabadza that would be a bad idea!" he roared.

Also on the road they met wagon trains hauled by teams of giant horses.

"Biggest horses I ever seen," said little Jak.

"They're Imperial drafts," said Manuel.

"Imperial?" said Swane. "You sure about that?"

"Sure, look at them. Those white manes and tails on the greys, that's a sign they're Imperial draft bred."

"All Kohon is famous for horses," said Bryon. "Wheat and horses, that's what they say."

"And they take the very biggest for the Imperial draft."

"What do they taste like?" said the Purple Green innocently from behind them. The dragonboys all howled at him in disgust.

"Bah," grumbled the Purple Green, who occasionally licked his chops when he contemplated the smooth, rolling haunches of the Imperial draft horses, "dragonboys just haven't eaten horse before. I show you how to eat it."

They shuddered and bade him be silent.

The next day they marched into Kohon Town in the early morning. The town was already bustling on the commercial streets and the mouthwatering smell of hot bread and frying bacon came from cookshacks along the dockside. And yet, as they marched, they noticed that something was amiss.

Kohon Town had grown up beneath the steep cliffs of the Kelderberg, and the streets wound up the slope through residential neighborhoods of fine houses, built of wood, brick, and wattle. There was an air to the place that spoke of success. The town was the natural governing center of the growing province that it formed the gateway to.

To the east and south, the High Lake stretched out, more

than ten miles across. To the north lay the bountiful plains of Kohon, and to the west stood the dark face of Black Fell.

Relkin sized up the fell quickly.

"Going to be hard work chasing bandits over that."

They headed for the fort built above the town. While marching through the town streets, they noticed that outside of the commercial district the town was eerily quiet. Everyone they saw wore nothing except black clothing. This reminded Swane, of course, of the folk of Ourdh, many of whom also wore black. There was also an abundance of high-crowned black hats with wide round rims that shadowed the face.

"Notice something else?" said Jak.

"They've shut down all the beer halls," said Relkin.

"So they have," said Swane in a tone of horrified amazement.

"Every inn?"

"Seems like."

"Where's that old Caymo now?" grumbled Swane.

On the road above the town, they passed neat houses with thick stone walls and heavy thatching. Winters here were short, but fierce, in part because of the elevation. From the windows they caught glimpses of children's faces, rapt with awe as they gazed on the marching men, and then the dragons.

The fort was small, tiny after Dalhousie, normally it was home to a detachment of cavalry, rarely more than sixty strong. Now tents were erected across the former parade ground, and dragon huts went up. Soon the place seemed crowded.

Captain Eads came around soon after they were settled in. He wore a troubled expression.

"I understand how tight a fit this is right now for everyone," he said, "but very soon we'll be starting patrols and that will ease things here considerably."

Even as that thought was sinking in, however, his tone became grim.

"I'm afraid I have some bad news for you all. While we're here in Kohon Town, we'll be drinking water only. There will be no leave, and no one will be allowed in the town except on duty. This is not my doing, I hasten to assure you. It's a demand from the town elders."

His audience was thunderstruck. The legions drank beer

as a matter of course every day, man, dragon, and dragonboy. Drunkenness was frowned on and was rare, but everyone got their beer every day, and no one missed it more than dragons.

Captain Eads could see the question in every eye. "I'll explain. For the last year now, the town has been run by a Dianine sect. For those of you who haven't heard of them, the Dianines are, shall we say, fond of prohibitions. They frown on frivolity of any kind. They have banned all alcoholic drinks. In fact, they have banned a great number of things. Such as dancing, garlic, and newspapers. I think you will agree that a town without beer and dancing is not a town worth visiting anyway. We are not welcome in the town. We will not go to the town. Understood?"

Ead's face was a rare color at that moment. He was plainly angered by this development. The damned townsfolk did of course want, nay demand, that the men and the dragons climb the mountains and slay the Cralls, but they did not want them on their streets. Rorker Eads would have happily turned his force around and gone back downstream. He didn't care what the Cralls did to the damned place, if this was how they were.

Afterward Relkin walked out just ahead of a group of indignant troopers who were angrily discussing the Dianines.

"They're fanatics, I tell you. We have them in Vo right now. They want all the girls to wear black, all the time."

"This is going to be a miserable spell of duty."

One of the troopers noticed him.

"Hey there, Relkin, what will the dragons think of this, then?"

"We starved 'em in Ourdh, and we just got by. I mean, they didn't eat anyone, but it came close. They're going to get cranky and mean. They love their beer. I wouldn't want to be on the wrong end of a dragonsword anytime soon."

"Let's just hope we get an early patrol. Be better off out in the woods than stuck here. If the dragons get all nervy, you can be sure the horses are going to sense it, and then we're going to have trouble ourselves."

Relkin agreed. Far better to be out there on patrol than in this cramped little fort with no beer supply. He sighed inwardly, life could get very difficult here.

CHAPTER TWENTY-FIVE

Angered by their treatment by the puritanical town elders of Kohon, Captain Eads's force took to the hill campaign with a will. The losers were the Cralls. Men and dragons marched back and forth across the fells while the troopers performed prodigies, and within a month they had smashed the Crall power forever.

One by one the Crall fortresses were reduced and destroyed. An abundance of stolen property, including the treasure chest of Bleuse Crall himself, the Crall's chieftain, was recovered and returned to its owners or sent downstream to Fort Dalhousie.

The Cralls laid snares and dug pits and set ambushes, but they inflicted few casualties. The dragonboys and the men of the 322s and 182s were too sharp-eyed and quick-witted for them.

On one occasion only, the Cralls attempted to give battle. Within ten minutes they had lost one hundred men, and their power was shattered. The lesson was driven home. Against disciplined, well-trained Argonath legionaries, stiffened by dragon forces, any attacker risked all.

On the last day of the month, Bleuse Crall himself was captured at Hanging Crag and brought down to Kohon Town. After a legion trial at the fort he was found guilty of the murder of more than four hundred people. The list of crimes took more than an hour to read out. Bleuse Crall was hanged at sunset the very same day.

Thereafter, life in the fort became quiet and boring.

In honor of their success, the high elders of the Dianine sect had decreed a redoubling of their vigilance against sin of all kinds.

Shoes were to be replaced by clogs. All spices were banned along with garlic. Fruits were only to be eaten cooked. No books were to be read other than the Book of the

Dian. No music of any kind was to be played after nightfall. It went on and on. For many offenses, there were now whippings and stonings ordered.

Occasionally horrid screams floated up from the town in the afternoon when the punishments were held. In the fort they looked at one another, rolled their eyes, and shrugged.

There was little to do but work on improving the fort and keeping fit. Turrent became obsessional about their kit, which gleamed even more than it had before. They all joked that if they were to parade with the rest of the legion, no one would see them because of the shine on their brass and steel.

One day Relkin and little Jak were summoned by Turrent and given the job of going into the town to fetch up some bales of hides that were to be stretched for shield repairs. In addition, they were to pick up six cartons of steel nails sent up from Dalhousie at the request of the fort's engineer.

Relkin and Jak were put in charge of a huge mule with wicked-looking, yellow teeth and eyes filled with malicious calculation. The mule was nicknamed Snapper, and he soon showed them why when he nipped Jak on the rump in an unwary moment.

When Jak finished howling, he whacked the mule a few times with a piece of planking but the mule merely shook its head, snorted, and then emitted a series of honks indicating amused contempt.

Relkin took the piece of board away from Jak.

"C'mon, Jak, let's get on with it. Keep back of him and watch his feet. He's ornery as a nest of hornets."

They went on down the street into the somber town. As they passed the shuttered windows and silent alleys, Relkin became uneasy.

"Turrent would just love it if we got in trouble."

"Well, we're going to be careful, then."

"Just keep your hands to yourself, and don't make any faces, either."

"Yeah, and you stay out of trouble, too. I haven't been in any real trouble yet. Not like some."

Relkin was tempted to cuff the younger boy, but refrained. It was true enough, after all.

"Yeah?" he said with a sneer. "Then how come you're here with me?"

"I just can't polish metal bright enough for him. He always complains about ol' Rusp's joboquin clasps. I just don't know how to get 'em shined up like you do."

"You got to get a second pair, Jak. They detach easily enough. You keep that second pair shined, and you put 'em on for inspections. That's the only time he expects to see them shining."

Jak was amazed. He'd missed this trick somehow when he was coming up.

The town was eerily quiet. The view out over the lake was breathtaking down toward the lakefront. The lake shimmered under the sun, lost somewhere between blue and white in haze. Distant hills glittered. Relkin's spirits soared despite the unease he felt.

Then as they passed the central plaza, they saw where everyone was. A crowd was gathered to watch public chastisement. Men wearing tall black hats stood on a platform where a man and a woman were bound naked over the stocks. At a command, two men stepped forward with rods that now rose and fell upon the unhappy lovers. Their cries echoed off the Kelderberg. Relkin averted his gaze and nudged the mule onward. Little Jak stuck his fingers in his ears to block out the sounds. A man in black clothing frowned at him from a doorway. Relkin frowned back, forgetting his injunction about not making faces.

Moving on, they passed a shuttered inn, the door nailed up, the sign torn from its chains. Three dour-faced men in somber clothing stared at them on the street. After watching the dragonboys go past, these men muttered prayers. Their prayers were harsh ones, filled with condemnations of the unholy and the wicked who knew not the Dian.

Surreptitiously, both Relkin and Jak made the sign of the evil eye back at the men, and Relkin whispered a curse he'd learned in Ourdh concerning each man's parentage and his descendants unto the third generation.

They reached the dock without incident and got in line at the warehouse. Here there were a few people from outside the town, tight-lipped drovers and mule skinners in from the farmlands.

There were four loading docks, and they had to ask at each for the shipment they had come for. Neither shipment had been set out. Their inquiries brought out another pair of dour-faced men in black cloaks who examined their credentials and questioned them closely.

It soon became apparent that these men had heard about Bleuse Crall's treasure chest. Relkin marveled at the speed with which such news could travel. These men asked many questions, but kept returning to the treasure. Had the dragonboys seen it? Could they describe it?

Before Relkin could stop him, little Jak blurted out,

"Sure enough. It's a chest of gold and silver coin. We found it in a wagon at Hanging Crag."

Relkin stamped on Jak's foot.

"Ow."

Jak shot him an injured look and then realized what he'd done.

"Oh, by the breath, I'm sorry Relkin."

The Dianines murmured together.

"Excuse me," said Relkin. "The hides? Can we start loading. We'd like to get back to the fort."

The warehouse men looked up. "It will be a few minutes. It will have to be located."

"Well, hurry it up, will you?"

The men ignored him. Then they went back inside and left him and Jak standing there with Snapper.

They waited by the dock but although loads were put out for others, crates of tea, sacks of kalut, even bales of hides, none was put out for them.

Relkin was feeling hungry enough to faint, so he left Jak in charge of the mule and went down to a street-side cook-shop that served the dock area. There he bought hot bread lathered with sesame sauce.

Outside the cookshop, he paused by the dockside to wolf down the bread and sauce. Looking out across the lake with the hills beyond it dappled with sunlight, he was struck once again by the beauty of the place. If only all the people here weren't so strange. Even the Cralls were easier to understand than these religious fanatics. Relkin would be glad to get back to Fort Dalhousie. The atmosphere in Kohon Town was oppressive.

A boatman was sitting nearby drinking a cup of kalut.

"So dragonboy," he said, "how do you like the land of Kohon?"

The sound of the public beating came back to Relkin. The boatman wasn't wearing the funereal garb of the Dianines, so he didn't hold back.

"I'd have to say I don't care for it much."

"Hah! Well, that's honest enough." The man looked over his shoulder. "But you want to be careful what you say around here, the Dianines don't care for such honesty in strangers."

"They seem to be obsessed with rules and punishments. We hear the sounds all the time up in the fort."

The sailor leaned forward and lowered his voice.

"Maybe that's because most people here are terrified, and they're only going along with the fixations of an all-powerful minority."

"I still don't understand how things got this way. Don't these people worship the Great Mother like everyone else?"

"As to that, I couldn't really tell you. They worship the Dian, right? That's their way of seeing the Mother. The folks in black hats say it's the only form that's real and the only one they'll worship. I thought the Mother was in all things, everywhere. Anyway, it wasn't always like this. The town was a good place to visit up until three years ago. That's when they managed to get one of their own elected as mayor. This merchant called Emser had converted to their beliefs, but he kept it from everyone, even his own wife. Then when he was elected, he started putting them in charge. They terrified everyone with arrests and public floggings."

The sailor paused and finished his cup of kalut.

" 'Course, there was a need for the town to get a little more civilized. It used to get a little too wild here on market days. Those farm boys out there in Kohon don't see another soul for days until they get to town. Once they'd had a skinful of beer, they'd go wild. The jail was always full of them for days after."

Relkin raised an eyebrow.

"You mean it's not full anymore?"

"The stocks and whip are a lot cheaper. And stoning people in the stocks is about the only fun left in the town. Other than watching floggings."

"That's their idea of fun?"

"They put the lash to boys and girls who steal a kiss after prayers, and they all spend a lot of time just praying, especially the young."

"Don't they sing in the temple anymore?"

"Only the priests of the Dian sing. Everyone else just prays."

Relkin shivered at the thought. Nothing bored him more than organized prayer. Then he caught himself wondering if the old gods were really still alive, and if they ever thought about a dragonboy who called on them every so often but never prayed much. He shook his head to dispel the unwelcome thoughts that came on the heels of this reflection.

"Tell me about Portage Town," he said, gesturing out across the lake.

The sailor laughed. "Now that's what Kohon used to be like. It's a good town, if you ask me."

"How about these Dian people, are they there, too?"

"Wouldn't dare show their noses in Portage Town. Now don't get me wrong, the folk there are worshipful, but of the Mother and in Her Place. Like everyone else in the Argonath." The sailor grew indignant. "But they know that there's more to life than just praying and standing around watching another whipping."

Suddenly a shadow fell over them. Relkin looked up into the grim visage of a tall man in the black cloak of the Dianines. Several others, with tall conical hats, stood behind him.

"Uh-oh," said the sailor getting to his feet.

A long arm reached out, and a bony hand clapped onto Relkin's shoulder.

"What is this? Idle youth! Sitting about gossiping about your betters! Talking about religious matters without a license. Defaming the Dian! Loitering with intent to do mischief!"

"No, sir, not at all. I'm just taking my lunch. I've got a mule and a load of hides, over there in the warehouse, and I'm taking them to the . . ."

"Silence!" The man had a nose that was comically large, red, and protuberant.

"I'm taking them back to the fort right away," said Relkin with determination, getting to his feet.

"Nonsense, you're going up before the judge, you and this rogue here."

"Rogue?" said the sailor backing away at once.

"We overheard you," said one of the other men in black.

"Defamed the Dian, I heard it," said another.

"He'll get the lash and a week in the stocks."

"And the boy?"

"The lash for certain. He may be too young to take a week in the stocks."

"I told you I think that age limit has to go. Everyone, no matter how young should take their turn in the stocks if they stray from the path of the Dian."

"Wait a moment!" Relkin was incensed. "You can't do that without a military tribunal. You have to send to Captain Eads up in the fort."

"Trying to tell me my business, are you?" snarled the man with the big red nose. "We'll decide what the law says and who we need to ask about it." He snapped his fingers.

"Take them away!"

The sailor bent down and threw a stone that knocked away a conical hat. The men cried out in rage. Relkin dodged a clumsy grab, darted left and right, and tore across the street and ran into the warehouse.

The mule stood there alone. Little Jak was gone.

A slack-jawed fellow standing on a line for sacks of wheat leaned over and whispered.

"They arrested your little friend. Said he defamed the Dian and took him away."

"How long ago?"

"Just a minute or two. You'd better get out of here."

Relkin looked back to the door of the warehouse.

"Thanks," he said, and he took the reins on Snapper and led him out to the street.

Relkin was only just in time. A posse of five Dianines was hurrying forward to seize him. Relkin pointed Snapper in their direction and then jabbed the cantankerous mule in the haunch with his dirk.

Snapper lurched forward with a harsh bray and lashed out with his hind hooves. Relkin had ducked and was already sprinting away in the opposite direction, straight up the hill toward the fort.

Old Snapper was not one to pass up an opportunity to avenge himself on human beings, and the Dianines were forced to scatter in front of his hooves and teeth, giving Relkin a precious twenty-yard lead on the pursuit.

CHAPTER TWENTY-SIX

Sitting in the stocks outside the courthouse, Jak tried to be brave while he waited for his sentence to be carried out. He was due to be lashed within the hour.

Three little boys and a girl who was rather older came by in a tight little group. They were clad in black like everyone else. They stood in front of him in a solemn little line.

"You will have to be stoned to death," said one of the little boys.

"The stone sellers will have a big day," said the girl.

"Why is that, Ferina?" said the boy that had spoken first.

"Because this is a dragonboy, Kerik. Dragonboys are notorious thieves."

The boys all stared at him with fierce little eyes.

"Thieves are bad people."

"Who must be killed."

"We will help them stone you."

Jak mumbled that he hadn't stolen anything. That he wasn't even charged with stealing, but only with having blasphemed against the Dian.

"You're lying. I bet you are a thief," said the girl, who already had the thin-lipped look of the adult Dianines.

"Look, I'm not from your town, I'm a dragoneer. I serve the empire."

"We know that, silly," said the girl, "but all the men in the fort are thieves. That's what my father says."

Jak protested that the so-called thieves had just ended the menace of Bleuse Crall.

"So what?" said one of the boys.

"So, doesn't that rate a little gratitude?"

"There can be no gratitude to those who do not follow the Dian, thus it is written," said the boy with a peculiar blank-eyed stare.

"Where is this written? I have never heard of this before."

"It is written in the Great Book of Dian. If you have not heard of it, then you must be a sinful person," said the girl, staring at him with angry eyes.

"You people don't make sense." Jak's head was swimming. He felt terribly alone and afraid, and angry, too.

"Only the word of the Dian can be listened to. Come, boys." The girl pulled her smaller companions away from him. With many backward looks, they went on across the square and out of sight.

Soon after that, the judges and the men known as "the Instruments of the Dian" came out. Two burly men, they seized up the boy from the stocks and prepared him for flogging.

A crowd was quickly gathering, and a man with an immense red nose took charge of the proceedings.

"Now, fellow servants of the Dian, we must once again contemplate the works of evil. Wherever callow youth be allowed its head, it will demand license. Freedom for such youth will cause abuse! The Dian demands discipline!

"Again and again, we see the mark of laxness and the evil of covetousness among the unfaithful who visit our holy town. Again and again we are called upon to mete out the justice of the discipline of the Dian."

"Use discipline!" shouted the crowd.

"Here we have an example of the worst sort, a drunkard, a thief."

"Use discipline. Stone him to death."

"Nay, brethren, he shall not be stoned to death. He is too young for that. He shall merely be flogged and kept in the jail. There he will be given the chance to repent and accept the Dian in his heart. If he does not repent, then he shall be flogged again. If he still resists the truth, then the stone sellers will be sent out."

"Shall anyone be stoned to death today?" cried a disappointed voice.

"Why do you ask, pray?"

"The stone sellers are waiting. The people itch to purge themselves of the wicked."

"Then we shall stone to death the sailor."

A whistle brought several men into the street carrying boxes filled with smooth, polished stones that they began selling to the crowd.

The judge expelled his breath with a hiss.

'This is military mutiny. You will all hang."

More cornets were blowing, and a dozen riders came surging into the plaza at a gallop. They pulled up in front of the stocks where the dragons loomed over the judge and the Dianine elders.

Captain Eads sat the saddle with an expression of cold anger on his face.

"Judge Penbar, I don't know what you were thinking of doing, but you have no legal right to punish anyone under my command. You may arrest them, but at that point you must communicate to me that you have done so and on what charges they have been detained. All the men, boys, and dragons under my command are ruled by military discipline, and that is only conducted through the legion courts. I hope you understand me."

Rorker Eads was famous in his generation of officers for his fierce temper. He was obviously very close to losing it.

The judge of the Dianines would not budge.

"This is an outrage, Captain. You will be cashiered for this! I will see you hanged, sir!"

Eads looked dangerously close to drawing steel on the judge. Troop Leader Croel let his horse loose a moment to nudge the captain's and distract him a moment. With a great effort, Eads pulled himself back from the brink.

"You, sir," he snapped, "are a fanatic and a murderer. Watch what you do, because there will be military discipline imposed here, and then you will find youself on the chair before real judges."

"How dare you!" roared the judge. The other chief Dianines turned purple with rage.

Eads spurred past and drew up beside the broketail dragon's imposing bulk.

"Dragoneer Relkin, you are making a habit of getting into trouble. This must stop. Return to the fort. This evening, you will report to my office. I will want a full explanation for this, do you understand?"

Relkin nodded, "Yes, sir." Before Eads turned away, though, Relkin spoke up again.

"Sir, request opportunity to speak, sir!"

"Speak, Dragoneer!"

"There was a sailor who was arrested with us. He did

nothing wrong, no crime, except to sit on the dock and talk to me while I ate my lunch. That's not justice, sir!"

"Indeed, not as I understand it."

Eads's face grew thunderous again.

"What are the charges against this sailor?" he demanded from the judge.

"He has blasphemed against the Dian. He was overheard by a true believer who reported the crime."

"What did he say exactly?"

The judge turned to the elders behind him.

"He claimed that the Dian was only an aspect of the Cunfshon goddess."

"Well," said Eads, "isn't that the truth of the matter?"

"Most recent exegesis has shown that this is not the truth. The Dian is a perfection, an elemental that rises beyond such matters as gender and duality."

Eads cocked an eyebrow.

"I think you better take that up with the witches, Judge, not with me. As far as I'm concerned, the sailor's perfectly correct. What was his punishment to be?"

"Ah," said the judge. "He had been found guilty of the foulest crime, and so he was sentenced to stoning."

Eads rocked back in the saddle. "You were going to stone a man to death for saying what virtually any reasonable person would agree with?"

"Our recent exegesis has shown that beyond any doubt, stoning is the best response to such wickedness."

"Silence. You have come perilously close to committing murder under the laws of Kenor. By the authority vested in me by the legion command in Dalhousie, I will override this sentence."

Captain Eads turned to Lieutenant Grass of the Talion light horse.

"Free the sailor; bring him to the fort to testify."

Eads swung his hand over his head.

"We will now return to the fort. There will be no destruction of property, no further hostilities. Am I understood?"

Ten pairs of big dragon eyes looked to him. They were still aroused and quite eager to level this town where there was no beer and where someone had dared to threaten a dragonboy for no good reason. Jaws clacked, but discipline retained its hold and after a long moment they turned about and started away, dragonboys bouncing along beside them.

CHAPTER TWENTY-SEVEN

The sun was sinking behind Black Fell by the time the res-
cue party marched back into the little fort. The dragons were
generally elated and went back to their stalls with much
cheerful banter and mock aggression.

Captain Eads went to his office at once to compose a message for General Wegan in Dalhousie and had it sent immediately, the rider thundering out at a gallop for the Darkmon
Breaks.

A deputation from the town merchants arrived some moments later to lodge a vehement protest. They demanded that
the "escaped prisoners" be returned to the justice of the
town and its chosen judicial officials.

Eads listened to them for a while and then silenced them
by producing a copy of the *Laws of the Land of Kenor*. To
cap it off, he brought out a dog-eared copy of the *Legion
Manual of Control and Discipline*.

"As you gentlemen are well aware, the Laws of the Land
do not give township judges powers of life and death except
in cases of murder, and even then there must be a fair trial."

"This is Kohon Town, Captain," they replied.

"If you like I'll get out the *Weal of Confshon*. You show
me in the texts where it says a man should be stoned to
death for saying what the sailor said about the Dian."

They fell silent. Eads tapped the dog-eared tome in front
of him.

"Legion manual don't allow me to execute a man except
in cases of murder in the course of mutiny."

He drummed his fingers on the top of his desk.

"So, gentlemen, when I consider the actions of religious
fanatics who would ignore the laws of the land, go beyond
the *Weal of Confshon*, and ask me to do something not in the
legion manual, then I think I will look forward to the court-

martial and to the full investigation of the administration of justice in the town of Kohon that is sure to follow it."

The merchants looked at one another. They were plainly not satisfied with this, but they found Captain Rorker Eads impervious to any further complaints.

In the dragon quarters, Dragon Leader Turrent summoned Relkin and Jak. He greeted them with a mirthless smile.

"So, Dragoneer Relkin, you are returned to us safe and sound."

"Yes, sir."

"Stand to attention when I address you, Dragoneer!"

Relkin stiffened, so did Jak.

"Yes, sir." Relkin wanted to groan aloud. Turrent was going to use this as another excuse to load him down with details. He would spend the rest of his life scrubbing cook pots and hauling wood and water.

"Once again, Dragoneer Relkin, you have been the center of attention."

Turrent flicked a glance down to Jak.

"And now you have taken to leading our younger members astray. This time we almost lost young Jak here, who came close to being flogged to death. Am I right, young Jak?"

Jak gulped, swallowed. "I don't know, Dragon Leader Sir!"

"Well, I do. Dismissed, Dragoneer Jak. Be ready for full-kit inspection by evening horn."

Jak stared stupidly at Turrent.

"Did you hear me, boy? I said dismissed. Now get out of here!"

"Yes, sir." Jak scurried away. Turrent turned back to Relkin.

"Dragoneer Relkin, why is it that you are always at the center of disaster?"

Relkin remained silent.

"Now, Dragoneer, as I have explained to you before this, I do not want a dragoneer in my unit who is always courting danger! I want a steady dragoneer who does his job and keeps his head down! Is that understood?"

"Yes, sir."

"I do believe, Dragoneer, that the Mother has not quite made up her mind about you. She wants to slap you down, I think, but She takes pity on you for being so young and so promising. But what She won't do I will. You are a disgrace! You can't seem to do the slightest thing without getting the whole army involved. Now I don't think this problem is caused by a lack of intelligence. I know that you are as sharp as they come. So I can only assume that the problem is a lack of diligence, of concentration, of willpower! Now, if it was a matter of intelligence, then I would throw up my hands. That is something that only the Mother can change. But if it is only a matter of motivation, well this is something I can cure. Oh yes, Master Relkin, I can, and I will; so help me I will."

At length Relkin was released. There was a mountain of work to do and with a grim sense of doom barely averted, he returned to it. After the evening meal, he went to Captain Eads's office. Eads was cool but not unfriendly.

"You have been living an exciting life, Dragoneer. Too exciting. I'm sure Dragon Leader Turrent has conveyed this view to you."

"Yes, sir."

"Tell me what happened."

Relkin repeated the tale. When he'd finished, Eads looked down at a scroll in his hands. He made no comment. Relkin began to grow nervous.

Finally Eads looked up.

"Your account squares with that of the sailor."

Eads was looking at him with intent blue eyes.

"Something is going on here, Dragoneer Relkin. What can it be? Are you accursed? I heard that you just about single-handedly destroyed the Temple of Gingo-La on her isle in Ourdh. Has she put a curse on you?"

Relkin had wondered about this, but he recalled Lady Ribela's contemptuous sniff when he'd asked her about the possibility of a curse from Gingo-La.

"It was not I who did the damage, sir, it was the dragon. And I was told by someone who knows much of the lore of goddesses that there was nothing to fear from that particular one."

Eads chuckled. "Well, someone seems to have it in for you. You must be more careful. You are the only dragonboy in history to win the Legion Star. I don't want my command to be remembered as the one in which you were lost!"

Eads was smiling, but his gaze was still fastened intently on Relkin.

"Yes, sir, I'm sorry, sir, I don't know what's happening, either. I seem to be on a run of pretty bad luck. I mean, anyone could have been sent to fetch the hides. It just happened to be me."

"Yes, well, we shall have to try and stay out of such scrapes from now on. Am I understood?"

"Yes, sir."

Eads was on the point of dismissing him when there was a sudden shout outside and below. Then came a commotion. Boots were thumping on the wooden sidewalk. Voices were shouting in the distance.

There was a sudden knock at the door.

"Enter," said Eads.

A flustered-looking Sub-lieutenant Apteno came in.

"Sir, the beacon on the Kelderberg has been lit. We can see it clearly."

Someone came running up behind Apteno, the broad figure of Sergeant Quertin.

"Captain Eads Sir!" said the sergeant, crashing to attention in the doorway.

"At ease, Sergeant, what is it?"

"Beacons are lit from the Kelderberg to Keshon Heights, from Keshon down to the breaks. With the telescope we can see beacons lit on the Beks in Tuala."

"Thank you, Sergeant. What do you think it means?"

"War, sir."

"It is, indeed. I wonder what is going on."

Captain Eads arose. Relkin was dismissed and ran at once to the high tower and climbed until he could see the beacon lit atop the Kelderberg on the northwest face. Then across the river and farther down, he glimpsed another distant fire, the beacon on the Keshon Heights

"War!" yelled someone down below. Distant shouting came from the town.

Something big was in the air, the world was turning on this moment. Relkin felt a shiver run down his spine as a cool breeze blew down from the Kelderberg. War, it was a terribly familiar sound to a dragonboy from the peaceful village of Quosh.

CHAPTER TWENTY-EIGHT

The news sprang eastward across the Empire of the Rose. War! The great enemy in the West had finally launched its stroke. Havoc and terror rode like storm clouds at the front of a vast army that marched out of the Gan and drew upon the western marches of Kenor. On a front forty miles wide it came, snakelike columns of squat imp soldiery, stiffened with nine-foot-tall trolls and controlled by thousands of men: fell men with dark eyes who served the power in Padmasa. In front and on the flanks rolled a great cloud of nomad cavalry.

War! The beacons were lit on the high points, leaping from mountain to hill to mountain to seashore. In the north it went from the great volcanic cone of Mt. Kenor to the Tuala Hills and Dalhousie and then on to the Upper Argo and Mount Red Oak. In the south it went from Fort Teot and then up the river Lis from hill to hill until it was picked up by the soldiers high up on the south col of Mt. Livol, overlooking the High Pass.

Then from the mountains the message flashed to Razac and the Blue Hills, to Arneis and Par Navon, and thus at last to the watchers in the Tower of Guard in Marneri, the High Tower at Castle Point in Kadein, or any of the other fortresses of the Argonath. War was coming!

The cities convulsed.

Following the beacons came messenger birds, pigeons bred in Cunfshon, doughty, relentless fliers. Within two more days, every city and major town in the Argonath had the news.

When the news reached the great cities of the Argonath, the ports of Talion, Vo, Vusk, Marneri, Bea, Pennar, Ryotwa, Minuend and great Kadein, there were further explosions of activity. Witches instructed trained herring gulls and fastened message loops to their feet. The gulls rose and set out at once, across the Bright Sea to the Isles of Cunfshon, the motherland of the Argonath, the nerve center of the Empire of the Rose.

The winds were favorable to the flight of gulls, and the messages began arriving in Cunfshon an hour after breakfast the next morning.

At once the beacon was lit on the Tower of Swallows above the city of Andiquant, and it sped on across the isles as the ancient watch towers of Defwode, Nusaf, Par Convon, Wick, Byrn, and Exsaf lit their fires. Even the distant, small isles of Ilf and Alaf were reached by noon with word passing from ship to fishing boat to ship until it was in Alaf harbor as the bell began tolling midday in the temple tower.

Great War was begun, an assault against the western edge of the empire.

And everywhere that that message came, flashing and flickering, the empire responded. Long laid was the planning against this day.

In this was revealed that remarkable quality of the Empire of the Rose that had enabled it to survive and prosper throughout the long wars. For now, even before the enemy's great blow could actually land, the empire was at work upon the response.

Throughout the western parts of Kenor, the women were setting out in boats and on horseback, heading east away from the danger of capture by the enemy. Men mustered to their volunteer units, while in the forts the legionaries prepared for a siege. It had long been expected, everyone had work to do to prepare, and all went about it with grim efficiency. Steel was sharpened, arrows were fletched by the hundred thousand, minds and spirits were prepared for the coming ordeal.

In Andiquant there was a tremendous stir, as was to be expected from the purposely built Imperial capital.

Immediately, the Great Witches convened, reviewing the situation with the emperor in a private meeting. The rest of the Imperial Council waited outside, nursing injured dignity and growing anxiety as the minutes mounted. Within the locked star chamber, the Emperor Pascal rubbed his knuckles to relieve tension. He muttered in self-reproach. The news had shaken him.

"Our storm crow was telling us to beware, but we would

not. That is what I recall, Lady Sausann. The Grey Lady told us to fear this and to act on that fear, and we did not."

"Yes, Your Majesty," said an ashen-faced Sausann. She had willfully blinded herself to this possibility. It was she who had organized the opposition to Lessis. Now she tasted real fear.

Emperor Pascal Iturgio saw a catastrophe looming.

"I was so determined to open our mission to Csardha, I was blinded by it."

The cool magisterial tone of the Queen of Mice broke in on these self-recriminations. "Your Majesty need not torment himself. He was not the only one to discount the news brought us by Lessis." Ribela stepped forward to the great table.

The map of western Argonath was unrolled across it.

Pascal Iturgio strode up, laid his hands on the table, and leaned across. His eyes met those of the witches.

The emperor groaned softly. "My fault, it is my fault. You are but advisers."

They did not meet his eyes. All had failed him, and he had failed himself in this matter. All except Lessis, and she was not present, having sailed to Marneri weeks before.

It was an uncomfortable moment for them all.

"What are the latest-known dispositions, Your Majesty?" said Ribela, examining the lands of the far west. She sounded indifferent to the shame around her.

The emperor shook himself into life. His voice grew louder and firmer. Some vestige of the Imperial force reasserted itself.

"There is a suspicion that the enemy host is actually breaking in two. But there are so many Baguti cavalry surrounding the marching columns that we lack precise intelligence. We can only guess at their intentions. Fortunately, we have long planned for such contingencies."

He placed markers on the map.

"Here is what we expect. The enemy will strike at Forts Kenor and Teot simultaneously. Since each is held by a single legion, they will be forced to remain inside the fortifications and accept a siege."

He pointed to a place on the river Oon just south of the solitary cone of Mt. Kenor.

"Here at Cudbern's shoals, we expect the northern force to cross."

He gestured farther south.

"The force to be sent against Fort Teot would likely cross here, just above the junction of the Oon and the Lis.

"Once the forts are invested, then large forces of imp and troll will be freed to march upriver, pillaging and destroying as they go."

"The womenfolk," breathed Sausann. "What of they?"

"They will be evacuated well ahead of the onrush. Already I would expect a great tidal wave of refugees is proceeding up the valleys."

Ribela looked up now with her dark eyes.

"What will be our response on the ground."

The emperor shrugged, "This is a question for General Hektor. I can only answer in generalities."

"Your Majesty, generalities would suit me perfectly well. I would not ask for more from you. General Hektor will speak to us presently, but I for one need to catch hold of the very basics. As you know, I have not given much thought to such things in recent time."

Not in the past century at least, thought Pascal Iturgio. He had never seen the Queen of Mice until she had suddenly begun appearing in the flesh a year ago, during the Ourdh crisis. He had spoken with her, sensed her on the astral plane many times since childhood, but never had he seen her. It was sometimes oddly frightening to deal with these women, these creatures, who had lived centuries before one was born and would go on living centuries after one was dead and in the ground.

"Lady, I can do that at least. Should they capture either of the forts, then they will strengthen that side of their assault force and move it upstream. We will seek to block them with the legions at Dalhousie and Fort Picon. However, we will be much outnumbered and will sooner or later have to fall back. In the meantime, we will raise an army in the Argonath, five to seven legions in strength, reinforced from Cunfshon, and move it to confront the enemy wherever he concentrates."

"And this will give us enough time?"

"We believe we can get two legions from Cunfshon to Kadein within a month and from Kadein to the High Pass within ten days more. If we can concentrate several legions at either the pass or in the Upper Argo country, we can hold back the enemy's thrust. Then we will mobilize our full strength and bring it to bear. Eventually, we will take the battle to him and drive the invaders back across the Oon."

"There will be enormous damage done in the meantime."

"Inevitable."

Ribela had her chin resting on her right hand.

"Your Majesty, have there been any recent reports concerning trolls in the enemy force? Any unusual trolls?"

"All I have heard is that there are a great many trolls. Perhaps a thousand all told."

"How can our forces in either valley stand against that many?" said Irene.

"We will slow them up with traps and pits. The bowmen of Kenor will seek their eyes. Our dragon squadrons will attack where necessary."

"We will hold them up, but we will not stop them."

"We cannot hope to stop such huge armies with single legions. Even with the volunteers, we will simply be too few in numbers to do more than slow them and harass them."

"But there have been no reports of unusual trolls?"

"No, Lady, not yet at least. You refer to the mammoth question that Irene brought before us?"

'Yes, Your Majesty. Lessis has been seeking information on this matter, but when last I heard from her, she had not yet discovered anything concrete."

"She is in Marneri again?"

"She is, Your Majesty."

Sausann was white-faced now.

"If they can seize the High Pass, then there will be nothing to stop them crossing into Arneis. They might even reach Kadein."

A silence fell on the witches. Sausann was panicking.

"Everything we have built up over these last three centuries will be laid waste. Everything will die."

"We shall hold them at the pass, good Lady Sausann."

"What force do we keep there now?"

The emperor spread his hands. "I am not sure, General Hektor mentioned the recent economy drive when I spoke to him. There is perhaps a company, perhaps less."

"They cannot hold the pass against such huge numbers of the enemy."

"Of course not. They will be reinforced."

"May the Mother preserve us, I feel so afraid." Sausann pressed her hands together.

"Do not fear, Sausann, our forces are already in motion. I heard from Marneri that Captain Hollein Kesepton left for the High Pass this morning with thirty riders."

"Thirty? That hardly seems enough."

"The forerunners of several hundreds more. And there will be some from Kadein and Minuend as well. The High Pass will be held."

"Captain Kesepton did you say? I know only the general."

"The captain is old Kesepton's grandson, I believe. He has already established a strong reputation in the legions. He was one of the heroes of Tummuz Orgmeen, for instance."

Sausann shuddered at the thought of that evil city. The emperor had not finished, however.

"And we must remember that he served alongside the Lady Ribela herself in the final struggle in Ourdh. In the pit with the monster."

Sausann looked to the Queen of Mice. Gentle Sausann had never understood Ribela. She could not conceive of fighting anyone, of actually taking up a sword to smite them.

"I see," she said, and looked down again. Soon she would leave all this, it was time for gentle Sausann to enter the mystic. This war threatened an end to all her work, or so it seemed.

The emperor turned to Irene, Queen of Oceans.

"How is the news being taken in Kadein? I have had little word from there."

"It so happens, Your Majesty, that I received a message from the Witch Ina, who serves in the harbor at Kadein. She says that panic reigns among the wealthy classes. Some private guardsmen tried to seize control of the white ship *Cloudsride* in the harbor. *Cloudsride*'s crew repulsed them with some loss. Every berth leaving the city is taken. They are boarding up the great houses and hurrying south."

"The king?"

"King Neath is with his High Council. He has sent word that Kadein will muster a full legion within one month. He promises a second within another month. The second will be of reserves and veterans."

"The emperor turned back to Ribela.

"Have we heard from Lessis?"

"We have, Your Majesty. I am going to join her in Marneri."

The emperor was puzzled.

"What means this?"

"We have a terrible need of better intelligence. Our Office has failed us all in this matter. We suffered a disaster last year and consequently failed to pinpoint when this attack would come. Lessis has a plan to improve our situation."

The emperor nodded, understanding.

"Once again she will risk herself for our cause. And yourself, Lady? Will you be at risk? Both of you are very valuable to our cause. Please be careful."

"I believe Audacity is the Lady Lessis's middle name, Your Majesty."

"Then I must rely on you to temper her impetuosity, for the good of the empire, Lady."

"I will try, Your Majesty."

CHAPTER TWENTY-NINE

The white city of Marneri glowed ghostly in the light of the waxing moon. Through the city's streets the deeper quiet of the night was settling. Only the lights of a few inns that served the late night trade still showed on the main thoroughfares. On the city walls the guard was changing. The bell for middle night was ringing from the Temple. If you were close enough, you could hear the Sisters in the Temple begin the singing for the service to greet the new day.

Inside the Tower of Guard, the massive fortification on the highest ground in the city, the families of officials and legion officers were abed and asleep. The guard was changed atop the tower with the customary barks of command and the crash of men in heavy sandals coming to attention, but none of this disturbed the sleep of those who were as used to this as they were to the rising of the sun in the mornings.

To the routine inquiry as to the state of things, the outgoing sergeant muttered something about the chamber on the uppermost floor that only the witches used. The place where people materialized out of thin air, or as the troops said, "where three go in and four come out."

Great magic was underway. The chamber was rarely used, and the soldiers attached great significance to the event. It was a visible sign of the witch power, the secret strength of the empire. The outgoing guards listened carefully as they passed the solid oak door of the chamber. Those who were sensitive to it felt the hair on their arms and necks rise as strange, fantastic fears and fancies popped into their minds, but they heard nothing from within the black door. On they went, feet tapping nervously down the stone steps into the lower floors, whispering together, infused with strange emotions of pride, suspicion, and fear of the weird.

In the chamber of the Black Mirror surrounding a tall

stone stood three women in a circle. Two wore the grey robes of the witch, the third the more sumptuous mantle and gown of the priory. The witches were Lessis of Valmes, slightly built, utterly ordinary in appearance and Fi-Ice of Marneri, dark-eyed, raven-haired, and statuesque of appearance and profile. The third was the Abbess Plesenta, a plump lady on the verge of retirement after a long career in the service of the Mother.

Both witches were calm and composed as the spell was said. Lessis and Fi-Ice brought great power to the spell, and the abbess was there only to form the triune and to make the responses.

With a powerful crackling sound, like a giant's frying pan being plunged in water, the mirror opened above the stone, a window into the dark subworld of chaos.

The abbess swallowed with difficulty. Her recent experiences around the Black Mirror had not been pleasant. Indeed, on one occasion just a couple of years before, they had come within a hairbreadth of losing Lessis to a Thingweight. In fact, the monster might even have seized all of them. Plesenta included. She shuddered every time she thought of being seized up by one of the dread rulers of the dark chaotic ether.

The mirror sizzled. Waves pulsed through the grey and white ocean of motes. Jumbled, quaking shapes suddenly flew past and sounds like the hiss of hot metal broke across the constant rumbling of the surf of chaos. Suddenly a fat red spark leapt from the empty non-surface of the mirror and broke with a sharp crack in the room. A smell of ozone followed.

Plesenta shivered. Sometimes she wished that she had never been chosen to be trained in the knowledge of the Black Mirror. Indeed, as her time for retirement drew closer, these desires grew stronger.

But something stiffened in her heart. She was the Abbess of the Marneri Priory. She would not flinch. She would do her duty. She had volunteered, long ago, for service to the Office of Unusual Insight and had been accepted. She had always been proud of this service. She would not disgrace herself by flagging now. Plesenta was no Lessis, no Queen of Birds, but she also served the empire in the secret world and knew some of its mysteries.

The ether surged in the mirror. Looking in was like falling

through tumbling masses of cloud. But if the onlooker's attention hovered too long on any single point, pseudo-vortices would appear at once, shifting in contrary directions, sickeningly swift, capable of producing intense nausea. Plesenta shifted her view from here to there and kept her grip firm on the hands of the others.

How long, she wondered. How long would they stand here, trembling on the brink of death? The ether boiled, waves seethed in the grey-white backwash. Plesenta felt the sweat trickling freely down her sides. Her under arms were damp.

And then, very suddenly, there was a tiny dot in the midst of the mirror. It was stable, unmoving in the midst of fluid chaos. Lessis murmured softly, "She comes."

Plesenta's mouth had gone dry. Now was the time of the greatest danger, for as the traveler drew closer to the Black Mirror in Marneri, so would she draw the great predators after her.

Half a minute went by. The dot had scarcely increased in size. The ether of chaos raged and buzzed. Another red spark leapt from the mirror, arched into the air, and exploded with a pop above their heads.

Still there was no sign of the curtain of energies that would mark the presence of a Thingweight. Plesenta looked briefly to Fi-Ice, but the witch had her eyes closed, concentrating on her sensing spell. Plesenta had no such spell, and clung on between the two witches, praying for a safe journey's end.

And then suddenly the dot resolved into a tiny figure, and this form grew swiftly until they could see the witch, her black robe fluttering around her in the winds of the chaotic ether as she flew through the surf of vortices.

A moment later, she stepped forth from the mirror as if from a hidden room and stood there in front of them on the stone. The witches raised their arms and broke the spell. The mirror snapped out of existence, and the witch stepped down to join them.

Ribela, the Queen of Mice, stood there, clad as always in her black velvet garb with the decoration of silver mouse skulls.

"Welcome, Sister," said Lessis with palms pressed together and a tiny nod.

"Thank you, Lessis, and my thanks to both the Sisters of

Marneri. Your mirror was well placed and strong. I had no trouble homing to it."

The abbess was moved to dare a comment.

"A smooth journey, for once."

"Indeed, Abbess, not at all like my last visit to this tower."

"The abbess is the most steady of all response givers," said Lessis. Along with the words came a subtle spell that the abbess was unaware of, but suddenly she felt suffused with pride in her achievements and of her service at the Black Mirror.

"I thank you, Lady," she said.

"Quite all right, Abbess, quite all right." Lessis patted her hand for a momet, and then she and Ribela passed out the door held open by Fi-Ice. Outside they paused for a moment as Plesenta pulled out the great key and locked the massive door, top and bottom. Then they strode down the passageway to the central landing. Together they made their way down two flights of stairs until the Great Witches halted and bade good night to Plesenta and Fi-Ice.

All was quiet and few lights were showing in the Tower of Guard, except in the sparsely furnished suite of rooms on a high floor, where Lessis stayed when she visited Marneri.

Lessis and Ribela spoke together in the hidden tongue of cats, a language familiar to both their animal personae.

Then came a knock on the door. Lessis opened it cautiously. A young man wearing the worn, green and grey uniform of a frontier Ranger entered.

"Ribela, this is Ranger Hawthorn. He rode here from Fort Teot."

"Nine days, Lady. 'Tis a record."

"Not even the Talion horse can equal it." Lessis sounded absurdly proud. Ribela was less impressed. In nine days a man had ridden a distance a little farther than that she had just traversed in three minutes.

Lessis felt Ribela's derision and smiled sadly.

"Ranger Hawthorn was on the fringes of the enemy army for five days before he rode here from Fort Teot."

Ribela's attention quickened noticeably.

"Indeed?" she said.

"Yes, Lady. I was out on the breaks, not far from the Oon, where the Gan grass is still high. The land is flat, one can see a great distance with a good glass."

The Ranger, his face brimming with honest achievement, patted the telescope case he wore over his shoulder.

"And what did you see, Ranger Hawthorn?"

"First thing I saw was a mob of Baguti cavalry. They had the death's head on their flags. I do not know this tribe."

" 'Tis Hazogi," said Lessis, "from the cold lands."

"Aye, I had thought it possible. They were very numerous but they were never closer to me than about a mile, and they did not see me or my horse in the tall grass."

"What else?"

"I waited, perhaps an hour, and then I saw long lines of banners coming from the west. Imps, Lady, tens of thousands of them. So many they seemed to cover the earth. I was forced to keep retreating to the east while I made observations. However, I soon spotted lines of troll, about three miles from my position."

"What kind of trolls?"

"Tall albinos, some very heavyset blue-blacks, and others that were unfamiliar to me, covered in brown fur."

"How many?"

"Hundreds. I counted one line and reached thirty nine."

"What else did you see?"

"Just as I was about to retreat, I took a last look around. The nearest imp regiment was about a half mile away. Then I saw them. Another line, quite a distance away, maybe four miles. But my glass is a good one, a Spitzberg from Cunfshon."

"I am sure it is, young man. What did you see?" Ribela was impatient, a fairly common event.

"Giants, my lady, giants they was."

"What do you mean?"

"Well, at first I thought they was trolls. I thought the grass was shorter there, for it only came up to their knees, but then I saw the flowers of braxberry bushes, and they only came up to their knees as well. Braxberry don't flower unless it's five feet high, Lady. These things were three times that height."

"Giants," murmured Ribela.

"At least fifteen, sixteen feet high, Lady. I watched them for as long as I dared, and then snuck away while the imps were but a couple of hundred yards distant. I retreated about two miles and watched again. But I only glimpsed them one more time, and then I had to break away when a division of the Baguti cavalry came patrolling along the front. I rode all day and the next night, and came to the shoals above the Lis. I changed horses at the fort there and rode directly to Fort Teot, which I reached at sundown the following day."

"You have done very well, Ranger Hawthorn," said Ribela at last.

Hawthorn seemed to swell with pride. Lessis turned to Ribela.

"A pigeon brought us the word at once. I asked the Ranger to come on to Marneri for a detailed interrogation. He has given us a great deal of good information while undergoing extensive questioning. He has put up with it all marvelously."

"My duty, Lady. I understand the need for it. It's hard to remember everything without it. And it'll be over soon, I think."

Lessis thanked the young man and then sent him down to the refectory with a note requesting that he be fed and given a warm bed.

After he had gone, Lessis and Ribela sat across from each other at a square table of heavyset appearance that betrayed its age and unfashionability.

"Giants then," Lessis said grimly. "As we feared."

"A weapon to break our battle lines and overcome even our dragon force."

"If our battle lines can be broken, then our armies would be finished. We would be overwhelmed by the enemy's numbers."

"They have tried to keep this weapon hidden from us, and they have almost succeeded."

Ribela unrolled a map of Kenor across the table.

"The emperor believes the enemy will divide his forces soon. A force will go north to mask Fort Kenor."

"Having questioned these young Rangers," replied Lessis, "I have to say that I think the enemy is actually dividing his forces in three. Another smaller force is being sent south. The central force is still very great, however. Our estimates run to one hundred thousand imp, a thousand troll. Tens of thousands of cavalry."

Ribela understood at once.

"One force marches to assault Fort Picon."

"This frees their central force from having to deal with that legion, coming to reinforce either Teot or Fort Redor. It leaves us with only the half legion or less stationed at Fort Redor."

"Not enough to do anything to stop such a host."

"What can we do?" Ribela was suddenly at a loss.

Lessis pointed down at the southeast corner of Kenor.

"The High Pass, that is where they are throwing their weight. I think we may not be able to hold them there. The force they bring is overwhelming. And they will cross the Malguns and come down into Arneis. That is where I think the last battle will be fought."

"Last battle?"

"If we lose this battle, we will never win another. All our available strength will be on that field, perhaps thirty thousand legionaries, plus every dragon we can muster. We need to know more, much more about our enemy's plans, and about these giants. Can we perhaps combat them the way you did the mud men at Ourdh?"

"Mud men would never be able to make the march. They last only for a single moon. I am inclined to accept the mammoth information that Irene brought us."

"We need to know more."

Ribela looked up. The Grey Lady looked back at her frankly. "I have a plan."

"I rather thought you might have," said Ribela.

"We cannot penetrate Padmasa on the astral plane if I understand you correctly."

"No, we cannot," said Ribela.

"We have no one left inside the Tetralobe. We shall have to penetrate it ourselves."

Ribela's eyes widened. "You jest, Sister. No matter how we disguise ourselves, we would be detected if we tried to enter."

"Not necessarily, Sister Ribela. If we underwent the spell of full animancy, we could go in inhuman guise that would never be suspected.

Ribela blanched. "I a mouse?"

"And I a sparrow. Or a wren. The smaller the better."

"To actually be physically within the confines of the Tetralobe. Why it would be monstrously clever." Ribela turned to Lessis with an open look of admiration. Then doubt returned.

"A good concept, but how are we going to get a mouse and a bird all the way to Padmasa? If we set off at once, I think we will arrive within about forty years. A mouse can only go so far."

Lessis nodded happily.

"They will ride on the shoulders of a great eagle. A third will join us in the spell and be cast into an eagle. The eagle can cover such a distance in a matter of days. With luck, we can return with useful intelligence before the enemy even reaches the High Pass."

"I see," Ribela nodded.

"But to practice animancy upon a third party, that will take skill, indeed."

"We know the party well. She is brave enough to quench into an eagle's fierce, narrow mind."

"You speak of young Lagdalen. But what of her motherhood? Should we risk her in such fashion?"

"I am afraid we have no other choice. Fi-Ice is a Mistress of Animals, but she is too old, too strongly set in her ways. Lagdalen has the heart for this, and she is young. This will be a brief service. We will be gone for only a week or two. It will not be like her service in Ourdh."

"Could you not take the eagle?"

"I could, but I am sure we will need both mouse and bird to investigate within the Tetralobe. And we might even wish to enter the Deeps, and there I think a bird will be invaluable."

"The Deeps of Padmasa, I have only ever glimpsed them from afar in the astral plane. Never did I think to tread there!"

They stood up and were about to part when Ribela remembered something, "One moment, Sister, there was a letter for you, delivered in Andiquant, not official business."

"Oh?"

Ribela fished out a small envelope, instantly recognizable as a military mailer. " 'Twas posted in Fort Dalhousie."

Lessis slit it open with her thumbnail and glanced within. Her face broke into a wide smile, "By the breath! Sometimes She moves in curious ways."

"Yes?"

"It's from a certain dragonboy that we both know very well. He has some questions for me."

CHAPTER THIRTY

The throne room in the city of Marneri was a brighter place in the reign of Queen Besita than it had been during that of her sire King Sanker. The dowdy wall hangings and heavy brocaded drapes had been removed, and the walls had been freshly painted white and pale blue. The drapes were modest, in a contrasting dark blue, and new carpets of white Marneri wool covered the floor.

The courtiers in the room had changed as well. There were a few holdouts from the old regime, but most of Sanker's cronies had gone home to their estates to mourn their king and prepare themselves for their own deaths. Besita was surrounded by a younger crowd, with many more women among them. The spirit had changed, becoming lighter and more cheerful.

One thing had not been changed, however, and that was the throne itself, the ancient seat "Pellaras," with its rigid, straight back and uncomfortable arms. Carved in black teak, it was plain and exceedingly heavy, an heirloom of ancient Pellin from the golden age of Veronath. During the Dark Ages, it had been conveyed to Cunfshon and stored in a warehouse. Then at last, on the re-assumption of civilization and the founding of the Ennead cities of the Argonath, it had been brought back, as uncomfortable as it had ever been.

Most of the kings and queens of Marneri had managed to suffer the throne stoically. Besita, however, was not made of such stern stuff. She had had the thing cushioned, but the straight back and the rigid sidearms were still hideously uncomfortable no matter how you slouched or squirmed.

Meanwhile, the tedious business of the Aubinan Magnate Porteous Glaves went on and on.

"Really, this case has taken up an inordinate amount of time lately. Why cannot it be disposed of?"

Lord Axnuld, the new chamberlain, turned his infuriatingly condescending smile upon her.

"Your Highness, the case is complex. There are conflicting testimonies."

Behind the throne, Lagdalen winced. As First Lady in Waiting, Lagdalen spent many hours sitting, in a comfortable little upholstered chair that was tucked away just out of sight behind the Pellaras throne. Lagdalen had heard the testimony. There was little conflict, in fact. Glaves was guilty by every account except his own.

He was, however, enormously wealthy and influential in the grain traders' association of Aubinas.

"In that case, why is it not being resolved in the courts, where it belongs. I have enough to do as suzerain for the empire in this city without adjudicating a criminal case."

"It is a ticklish situation, Your Highness." Axnuld had moved close to her side and was leaning over, to whisper in her ear.

"The Aubinans, madame, are threatening the grain market again. We could face a major dislocation if they carry out their threat to ship their grain to Kadein."

"Oh, my." Besita sat back and rubbed her chin. It seemed that almost anything one did threatened some disaster or other. Now she had to listen to all this drivel once again or risk famine in the streets.

The Magnates of Aubinas came forward and bent the knee in formal fashion. One of them, a large, full-bodied man in a suit of sparkling yellow satin with much lace about the throat, stepped forward with a scroll in his hands.

"The Honorable Faltus Wexenne," murmured Axnuld, "landlord of Champery."

"Your Highness, may I address the court?" The man in the yellow satin suit had a surprisingly heavy voice.

"You may address us, Wexenne."

Wexenne then launched into a long screed in which he pled once more for a cessation to the criminal case against poor Porteous Glaves of Aubinas. A commander in the legion with a record of proven heroism, Glaves had captured a banner in the battle of Salpalangum and sent it home to raise the morale of the city. He now faced vicious charges placed by jealous men of lesser stature who sought to bring him down with their calumnies and lies.

It was true, of course, that he had been aboard the white

ship *Nutbrown*. But that was because he had been forced to take over the ship from her near-mutinous crew so he could take the ship to do battle with the fell enemy in Dzu. He was on his way to slay the demon there when he was ambushed by mutinous dragonboys and dragons alas, and taken captive. Then, these unjust charges had been laid, and he had spent months in confinement.

This was too much for the counsel for the prosecution, Lord Burly of Sidinth, who had been chamberlain for the old king.

"Your Highness!" he said, rising to his feet and raising an arm.

"I cannot sit still while listening to this pack of lies. Wexenne is turning the case on its head. There is testimony from a dozen sources, and all is agreed on the man's guilt. Except for his own fabricated story, he has no defense."

Axnuld intervened smoothly,

"Your Highness, I must rule the Lord Burly out of order. Wexenne has the right to continue speaking by the protocols of the throne room."

"Yes, of course, Lord Chamberlain." The protocols were a wonderful old fallback. To Rodro Burly, she snapped, "I would think that you, Burly of Sidinth, would know that such outbursts are impermissible in the throne room of Marneri. You will be silent until Wexenne has completed his remarks, or you will be removed from our presence."

Burly bent the knee and shuffled back into the line of dark-robed men and women who stood by the rear wall of the room. Wexenne continued his oration with a shrug.

"As I was saying, Your Highness, before I was so wrongly interrupted, the gentle Porteous Glaves of Aubinas begs pardon of Your Highness and a cessation of the relentless prosecution that has dogged him since the end of the Ourdh campaign. The case is a travesty, a mockery of your majestic justice."

At last Wexenne gave up the right to speak. Rodro Burly of Sidinth took his place and hammered away at the salient points, that the testimony in the military trial had been entirely set against Glaves's story. That even his claim of capturing a banner single-handed at the Battle of Salpalangum was suspect, with others claiming the enemy flag for their own. That, in point of obvious fact, the whole thing was a tissue of lies put out by a wealthy man who was trying to buy his way out of the justice he so richly deserved.

At length Besita raised her scepter.

"Honestly, it is enough to make one's head throb. Why does this awful case keep coming back to me? Really, my Lord Chamberlain, it is most vexing. We order a recess. We will return for a further audience this afternoon."

Besita got to her feet and hurried back behind the throne even before the assembled grain factors, courtiers, and functionaries could bend the knee; something that would never have happened under the Old king, who knew how to conduct these matters with proper ceremony.

Besita meanwhile had retreated into her private chamber, where she flung herself down on a couch with a groan.

Her ladies-in-waiting, Lagdalen of the Tarcho, Pessila of the Clamoth, and Kuellen of the Brusta, hurried in to revive her spirits. Pessila brought a cup of hot tomato broth. Kuellen of the Brusta brought toasted tea cakes with honey, a favorite of the queen's. Lagdalen massaged the queen's aching shoulders and neck. The queen was feeling very much put upon by her life.

"That damnable throne is the most uncomfortable seat in the entire world. It's no wonder that my father was in such a dire mood the whole time."

Lagdalen kneaded the knots in the shoulder muscles. The queen was upset to the point of tears.

"Oh, my dears, you are such a comfort to me, only the Mother knows, but really it is all getting to be too painful too bear. All day I sit there and listen to these awful men go on and on with their complaints and their greedy desires. If it isn't the grain factors then it's the builders, or even worse it's the ladies from the Temple. And to think I have to go back in there for another afternoon with the Aubinan merchants. Sometimes I wish . . ." she sobbed, as all three of the ladies-in-waiting looked to each other and rolled their eyes, how many times had they heard that sob? "I wish I were still a princess. Oh, why did my brother have to die like that? I was quite happy. I had my place. I had my little duties, and I had lots of time to pursue my other interests." More sobs followed.

She lurched up for a moment and shouted. "And I didn't have to sit on that horrid lump of wood all day!"

Lagdalen waited until the queen had settled back on the

couch and was sipping her tomato broth. Then she spoke, recalling Lessis's words on how to cajole a sulky monarch.

"Your Highness, you really are not powerless in the matter. You don't have to let them get away with sending this case back to you again. It's cowardice on the part of the judges. You can simply order the judgment served and a sentence handed down. Send it back to the court. That will stop the Aubinans' attempt to overturn the justice of the Marneri Court."

"Oh, that would be wonderful, child, and then the Aubinans will start shipping their harvest straight to Kadein. They ship from Sequila anyway, we have no direct control as we might if they shipped through Marneri. And if they ship their harvest to Kadein's market, then our grain prices are going to go sky high. We need the Aubinas grain to stabilize things, especially with war coming. We'll have panic, then hoarding, and then food riots."

Lagdalen kept her eyes down as she replied.

"Your Highness is correct, the Aubinan grain merchants might do such a thing; but even they might find it hard to justify to the people of Aubinas, especially under conditions of war. Our very existence is threatened, and the Aubinans cannot put aside their petty resistance to justice?"

Besita glared at Lagdalen.

"And now you will lecture me, Lagdalen? Such sauce and stuff do I get from you. You lecture me, you always do, and I know who eggs you on to it!"

There was a silence. Pessila and Kuellen looked to the floor. They all knew that Lagdalen was not just a lady-in-waiting to the Queen of Marneri. She was, in fact, representative of the Grey Lady, Lessis of Valmes. Lagdalen was not yet twenty, but already she was involved in the Secret World, in which agents and spies moved behind veils of mystery. Pessila had heard from her father that Lagdalen now belonged to the Office of Unusual Insight. This was the most shadowy of the Offices of the Empire and the most fascinating to outsiders. But Lagdalen would never speak about her service, except in Ourdh, where she had spent many weeks before, during and after the siege. Lagdalen preferred to talk about her baby, Laminna, now sixteen months old and tottering about. Laminna had pulled a chair down on top of herself, and Lagdalen had nearly died from fright, but the child was unharmed. Sometimes they seemed to be made of rubber. Pessila and Kuellen both had elder sisters with young children. They had heard more than enough about babies. They wanted to hear about the horrors of Tummuz Orgmeen, and the great magics performed by the witches. She had assisted Ribela the Great, the seeress, the Queen of Mice herself. What had that been like? But no, nothing of this could they learn.

Besita surrendered to the inevitable. She would have to endure a scene and the lasting enmity of the grain merchants in Marneri's most prosperous province.

"I should do what the Lord Axnuld tells me, I should stall and avoid any disruption to the markets, but"—she shrugged, the girls looked at her with eyes shiny and bright—"I must keep faith with our legions." She sighed and fluttered her hands at the ladies-in-waiting. "Leave me now, my dears, I would rest a while in private."

Lagdalen and the others went out, past the guards, and stood a moment on the landing. The great staircase of the Tower of Guard was always busy.

Pessila and Kuellen had barely had time to congratulate her on her success in stiffening the queen's resolve, when a messenger, a girl in the plain blue smock of the novice, appeared in front of them.

"I have a message for the Lady Lagdalen of the Tarcho. Is she within?"

"Better than that girl, she is right here," giggled Kuellen.

"I am Lagdalen, what is it?"

The girl was suspicious. "You hardly seem old enough."

"Appearances can be deceptive. If you have a message for Lagdalen of the Tarcho, then give it me. If not, then be on your way."

The novice compressed her lips. "Oh, very well, here it is, from way upstairs, one of them, if you know what I mean."

Lagdalen opened the sealed letter with a flutter in her heart. She did know, all too well, what it meant.

"I must go, please give my apologies to the queen."

"Of course, Sister," said Pessila with a knowing look to Kuellen. Together they watched Lagdalen disappear, heading up the staircase to the higher levels of the great tower.

CHAPTER THIRTY-ONE

Lagdalen climbed high inside the tower, passing the floor where her parents lived, in the ancestral Tarcho apartments, and on, to high floors she had never visited until her introduction to Lessis of Valmes almost three years before. That event had changed her life forever.

There was a row of doors, each made of dark brown wood with a brass number on the front. She knocked at the third, which swung open on its own, without human assistance. She stepped in, and it closed behind her. Lagdalen was used to such things.

Wearing a plain grey linen suit, Lessis was waiting at a small table with a white ceramic pot of Ourdhi kalut in front of her. From the aroma, Lagdalen could tell the kalut was of high quality. She'd learned a lot about kalut during her time in Ourdh.

Lagdalen understood at once. The Queen of Mice would be present as well. Something important was in the works. Lagdalen knew that the seeress, Ribela of Defwode, was very particular about kalut while ordinarily Lessis drank very indifferent stuff, weak tea, cold water, the juice of a lemon once a day.

"How goes the queen?" said Lessis, after they had discussed baby Laminna's growing use of language.

"She has decided to fight the Aubinans at last. She will send the case of Commander Glaves back to the court and demand that judgment be given and a sentence handed down."

Lessis nodded gravely. It was a serious case, and one that could have a powerful negative effect on legion morale. The purchase of commissions by wealthy men had become a source of intense controversy. Lessis's instincts were against it.

"The queen complained, I suppose, when you stiffened her spine."

Lagdalen blushed. "I am clumsy with her sometimes, but I am much better than I used to be."

Lessis smiled. "You have become quite the guileful creature, my dear. You will be a Great Witch someday, I'm prepared to wager on it."

There was a short silence. Lagdalen knew she was about to be asked to undertake some onerous task. She braced herself. Her thoughts flew away to her husband, Captain Kesepton, now riding for the High Pass. For the umpteenth time that day, she prayed for his safety.

"My dearest Lagdalen, you understand the gravity of our situation, I think. We face a terrible test." Lessis leaned forward and hunched her narrow shoulders.

"I must ask of you a great sacrifice, to aid the effort of our Office in this moment of crisis."

Lagdalen looked the witch in the eye, with a sinking feeling in the pit of her stomach. Was there no end to their demands?

She cast her eyes down for a moment. She'd missed Laminna's babyhood the previous summer. What would it be this time?

Lessis's glance flicked to the inner door that opened and admitted the Lady Ribela.

The Queen of Mice was clad in her perennial black velvet garb, the hems decorated with silver mouse skulls. Her face was the perfect mask it had been for centuries.

"Lagdalen my dear, it is good to see you again." Ribela did the unheard of and reached out and squeezed Lagdalen's hand for a moment before she sat down.

"You have made kalut, Sister?" she said in feigned surprise. Indeed, her nostrils had told her that there was some hot kalut while she had still been outside the door.

Lessis looked down at the pot, she had quite forgotten it.

"Yes, or, well, no, I make terrible kalut, but I have obtained some from our friend Narsha."

"It will not stay warm unless we perform prodigies on the magical plane. Perhaps we should drink it while it is hot."

"Of course, of course," Lessis poured the thick, aromatic beverage, and they sipped in silence for a moment.

Lessis turned to Lagdalen again.

"The problem, my dear, is that we lack any source of intelligence from Padmasa. We are blind, and we cannot anticipate our enemy's moves except in the most general terms. This blow is the strongest our enemy has ever launched against us. We must get some clear idea of his intentions if we are to be able to defeat him."

Lagdalen's concern grew and darkened. This attack from the enemy sounded more threatening than she had previously understood.

"We are blind. And so we must attempt something rather daring. We must infiltrate the very center of the enemy's power. We must enter the darkness of the heart of Padmasa. We must go into the Tetralobe, and then to the Deeps."

The very idea brought a chill to Lagdalen's bones. Tummuz Orgmeen had been one thing, the fortress of a Doom, but the Tetralobe of Padmasa? The lair of the Masters themselves? How could anyone enter that freezing nadir and hope to evade capture?

Lessis, however, seemed oddly cheerful about the matter.

"You are wondering how we might enter that dreadful place and ever hope to reemerge. Naturally, we will not be entering it in human guise."

Lagdalen breathed a deep internal sigh of relief. So, they wanted her to help them with some great magic. That was all right, Lagdalen would gladly serve. She would do whatever had to be done while the witches rode the chaotic ether in the astral mode.

Ribela set down her cup. She made a tiny gesture, and Lessis ceded to her.

"Unfortunately, dear, we will not be able to attack from the astral plane. We cannot get through on the higher modes of perception. The Masters have developed great barriers there. They have become very strong."

Lagdalen was left groping. "But if you cannot use magic, and you cannot get inside, then how will you do this?"

Lessis smiled gently. "We will go in with physical bodies, but we will not go as human beings. We will make our entrance in more humble, miniature guise."

Lagdalen's eyes widened.

"Animancy?"

Lessis nodded.

"Yes, my dear, it will require great power to achieve success, but it will be done."

Lagdalen heard the certainty in Lessis's voice. Lagdalen

knew that of all witches, these two were the greatest practitioners of the art of animantic magic. Verily were they known as the Queens of Mice and Birds.

"In such small forms, it will be easy for us to enter the Tetralobe unobserved and to explore, We will be too insignificant for the Masters to notice."

"However, there is a problem," said Ribela.

Lagdalen had seen it already.

"You have to get to Padmasa in human form and then change."

"No, my dear, we intend to complete our transformations here and travel there in nonhuman form. Which means we will require some means of transport, since I will be a very small bird and Ribela will be a mouse."

"How? What?" The dread in her heart changed direction dramatically. She felt her heart thud in her chest.

"No!" They wanted her soul? For that?

"We would ask only that you assume control of an eagle for a few days. Just enough to fly us there and to bring us back after our mission."

Animancy? She would be removed from her own body and placed in the mind of an eagle, another creature, a wild, predatory bird? What of her child? Her darling Laminna.

"Will I be able to return? I mean, will I stay an eagle?" The eyes of both witches sparkled momentarily.

"The effect will only last a few days," said Lessis. "Just enough to get us there and back. It will be arduous, child, but it can be done and it is our only hope."

"Yes, I see," said Lagdalen with heavy heart.

"There is no one else we can ask for this service," Lessis said softly. "You have the heart and the spirit and the intelligence, and you have worked with both of us in the past and understand more about our work than any stranger could."

Lagdalen sighed. Lessis sighed. Lagdalen sighed again.

"Once again, we must ask you to sacrifice your motherhood for the sake of the empire."

Lagdalen felt Ribela's eyes hard upon her and managed to prevent herself from being unforgivably weak in the presence of the Queen of Mice.

"There is a terrible peril, child. We must sacrifice ourselves if need be at this time. Our cause is greater than any individual life."

Lagdalen looked to Ribela, and found words.

"I had only heard that there was war in the West and that the enemy was going to attack Fort Teot."

"The truth of the situation is being kept quiet lest it spark general panic. As it is, there was panic in Kadein. Riots over seats on coaches and berths aboard ships. The enemy brings more than one hundred thousand to bear upon us."

"But how could they breed so many?"

"They abducted thousands of women from Ourdh during the dark days a year ago. Those women have been used to produce this horde of fell imps."

"It is possible that they will overwhelm our forces in Kenor and reach the coast by winter."

Lagdalen shivered. The thought of the prosperous home provinces with their towns and farms and villages being overrun by a horde of vicious, man-killing imps was too terrible to contemplate.

"They have to be stopped," said Lagdalen. There would be no future for Laminna unless they were.

"Yes, my Lagdalen, you are right."

She realized the trap had shut close around her.

"I will do whatever is needed," she heard herself say.

CHAPTER THIRTY-TWO

New orders flew up to Kohon Town on the wings of Imperial carrier pigeons. Captain Eads was to immediately pull his force out of Kohon Town and head back to Dalhousie. The Second Marneri Legion was being dispatched at once to reinforce the legion in Fort Kenor.

Eads had anticipated such orders. Within the hour the first units were loading onto barges. By the end of the day, the whole force had embarked and was being hauled down to the top of the breaks at Keshon. Behind them they left a sullen town, quite suddenly emptied of soldiers, except for a small detachment in the fort.

Down below the Darkmon Breaks, they waited briefly for a river ship to take them off. While they were waiting to board, they cast longing eyes at the taverns nearby. It had literally been a month since any one of them, man, boy, or dragon had tasted the slightest drop of ale. But, alas, more orders had arrived and were waiting for Captain Eads. He was enjoined to make all haste. The crisis on the frontier had grown sharper. The legion had already left Dalhousie and hurried down the Argo to reinforce Fort Kenor. Eads was to follow, all the way to Fort Kenor, at once.

They embarked at once therefore, with no time for the taverns. On the riverboat *Floz,* they were tightly packed. It was a smaller ship than *Alba.* There was some grumbling. Tension was rife. Two fights broke out among the legionaries in the first hour.

Captain Eads had foreseen this, however, and had managed to purchase a dozen casks of fine ale from the Blue Pelican while the force was embarking. That evening, as they headed downstream on the broad, gentle Darkmon, Eads ordered the issuing of a couple of rounds of ale. He and the other officers joined the men in the singing and the early roistering, then withdrew to their own quarters at the rear, leaving the men to the bawdy verses of the old songs when they came around again.

The grumbles died away. Praise for Captain Eads was universal, and talk turned to the future instead. A major war was in prospect. Now they would be tested as soldiers as they had never been tested before.

In the meantime they returned to the pattern of the previous voyage, except that now they were going downstream, which was easier and faster. Several days went past during which the old *Floz* was virtually taken apart and rebuilt by the dragonboys and men under the urgings of sergeants and dragon leaders.

Soon they were on the outskirts of the haunted forest of Valur once more. As promised, Relkin was going to remain below the entire time they were within the margins of the fell wood. But before they had more than entered the forest reach of the river, a small, swift sailing vessel hailed them from the opposite direction and very shortly Captain Eads had a new set of orders from Dalhousie.

As he read them, Eads's face became grim and set. He called in his officers and told the captain of the *Floz* to turn his ship around and return at once to Brok's Town at the head of the Darkmon.

The captain was stunned. But he gave the orders at once, and the *Floz* was brought about, headed around, and set to tacking upstream on a light but favorable wind.

Eads explained to his officers, and they to the men. The situation had grown complex and very dangerous. The enemy's assault had long been prepared. Fort Teot had been masked by a force estimated at forty thousand. Armies of thirty thousand imps had attacked Forts Kenor and Picon and prevented any aid from going to Teot. In the meantime, while Teot was besieged, a huge force, perhaps one hundred thousand strong, was proceeding up the River Lis.

Eads was ordered to take his force back upriver, cross the Grand Portage at High Lake, and then to work down the river Bur to the Lis. There he would receive new orders and be told to either head for Fort Redor or the High Pass. They were to make all possible speed.

Dragon Leader Turrent called the 109th together and told them what he had just learned from the captain. When he'd finished, the dragonboys went back and told the dragons.

The great wyverns took the news solemnly but philosophically. Whichever direction they went, they were due to get in some fighting. That much was certain.

The dragonboys perceived rather more than this. Everyone knew that there was but half a legion, likely less, stationed at Fort Redor. Since the establishment of Fort Picon and the pacification of the northern Teetol, Redor and the central Lis valley had been a peaceful region.

Half a legion, some Kenor militia, plus themselves, would be set against a host of tens of thousands of imp, hundreds of troll, thousands of riders.

Later the boys sat together on deck and discussed war in quiet voices. The younger boys were unsure about the future, both frightened by the gravity of the situation and also exhilarated at the thought of finally seeing battle, real battle for the first time.

The older boys had seen plenty of fighting and they were quiet, sensing that the odds were suicidal.

Swane groused, as usual, but this time with a willing audience.

"Silly generals, they send us all the way up the river, then all they way down, and then all the way back up again. If they'd worked it out right the first time, we'd be down the Grand Portage by now."

"We'll be there soon enough."

"Dragons won't like it."

"Hard on the feet. Rough country down that side, I've heard."

"It will be rough all the way down the Bur. It's a wilderness over there. There's rapids forty miles long below the Feutoborg Forest."

Little Jak's eyes were luminous. In his relatively short life, he'd never been in true wilderness. Never been anywhere except Marneri and Fort Dalhousie.

"We're going to see real fighting," he said brightly to cover up his nervousness.

"Yeah, little one," growled Swane, "and it won't be no picnic, either, no beer and skittles."

"More like trolls and cavalry with dragon lance," agreed Tomas Black Eye.

Jak nodded, abashed but still looking forward to the shock of battle with a part of himself that was as yet unbloodied by the world. The fight with the Cralls had been easy enough, though everyone had said it would be hard.

"So how do you feel about it, Relkin?" said Manuel.

Relkin had been silent so far.

"I don't know, scared, I suppose. But the 109th has been in tight spots before. We'll come through."

" 'Course we will," barked Swane. " 'Course. Silly bugger Manuel."

"Shut it, Swane," said Manuel.

"Oh, yeah, and who's going to make me? You? Think not Manuel."

"Please, Swane," said Relkin.

Swane grumbled but kept it to himself.

"I've always dreamed of the day I'd see real combat, with the dragon," said Halm of Ors. "You know, doing what we've trained for all our lives. But now I suddenly see another side."

"You saw combat against the Cralls, didn't Anther make the most kills?"

"The Cralls were easy meat, we all know that."

"This isn't going to be easy," said Bryon. "We're probably all going to die."

He said this with such a straightforward seriousness that it left them all silent. Swane raised his head, was going to speak, but felt the silence and dropped it again.

"Better go see to that old dragon," said Mono, getting to his feet and heading for the hatchway.

The *Floz* returned them to the breaks, which they climbed once more while cargoes of wheat slid downhill in the Imperial chutes.

In Kohon Town, they found the elders busy hanging half a dozen members of the cult who'd been caught eating food with salt on the third day of the week.

They transshipped to lake craft and set sail that same evening. Behind them the lights of Kohon Town dwindled. Above rose the crescent moon. The stars glittered in the west.

Far to the east, across the mountains, the same stars glittered above the Tower of Guard in Marneri. Inside the tower, in a room on a high floor, great magic proceeded by the light of a fire of reeds in the grate. The blinds were drawn tight, and the heat in the room caused trickles of sweat to run down the invisible faces of three women.

Lessis chanted with a poet's passion. The blood from

Lagdalen's arm hissed on the amulet, still glowing from the fire.

A wave of nausea rose in her gorge. Lagdalen fought it down. It was a side effect of the toxic mixture they had all three imbibed from Ribela's flask.

The mixture, derived from red toadstools, Rumeric seeds, and crushed Dixanth beetles, had a foul taste and an extraordinary effect on the mind.

The amulet seemed to spin before Lagdalen's eyes. She felt the magic power at work. The very warp and woof of the world was in play. Lightness welled in her chest, as if a balloon were inflating there. She imagined herself floating away, legs pointing down, mouth open in a soundless shriek. She giggled inwardly and then caught a flicker from the eye of the presence hovering at the side of the spell making, Ribela. Lagdalen brought her attention back to the work in hand. The nausea had subsided, for which she was thankful. The amulet glowed and seemed to spin. The motion was unpleasant, there was a tension gripping her stomach, tightening her diaphragm until it was hard to breathe.

Lessis made some peremptory gestures. Ribela threw a handful of twigs and herbs, bound in a yellow silk thread, into the fire where it exploded with a white flash that startled Lagdalen and left her mouth gaping in surprise.

For a moment the torrent of words ceased. They approached the climax. Lessis had warned that it would be very difficult.

Ribela held a beaker to her lips.

"Blood?"

"The blood of one eagle, the blood of the eagle ye shall be," said Lessis. "The blood of a wulfeagle, a white-tipped sky ruler from the mountains, an old friend of mine."

Lagdalen steeled herself not to taste and drank some of the dark blood. Ribela cast the rest onto the amulet where it smoked and stank atop the dried crust of Lagdalen's blood.

Without any need for a summons, the door opened, and one of the acolytes of the Temple came in carrying a standing perch, atop which sat a wild eagle with a small bandage wrapped about its left leg. Lessis went up to the bird and brought it down to the fire on her arm. The immense talons could have crushed her arm like a twig, but they did not. The eagle was subdued, with a glazed look to its eyes.

Ribela began chanting now while Lessis put her hand over

the bird's head, shielding its eyes and moving close to Lagdalen.

Lagdalen stared at the bird, so strangely passive. She knew that it was lost in some all-encompassing web of sorcery cast by Lessis, the Queen of Birds.

"Cuica, warden of the sky, is his name," said Lessis. "You will see so much with his eyes, my Lagdalen."

"I am ready."

The acolyte positioned the perch beside Lagdalen, and Lessis returned the bird to it. She then took up a little leather pouch connected to a strap that she fastened around the eagle's neck.

Now Lessis and Ribela thrust forward their right arms. Lessis gave Lagdalen the knife. The hallucinogenic poison gave her another heave of nausea, but she fought it down. Struggling to concentrate, she slashed each of them across the forearm. Blood welled and ran down their pale skin. With a hiss, the witch blood joined the other bloods already dried upon the amulet.

The chant resumed, and Ribela completed the motions. Herbs burned in the fire, and within the smoke there ignited a flare of bright red light, like lightning in a distant cloud.

Lagdalen stared into the eyes of the eagle, which stared back with an utter glossy blankness.

And then with a peculiar wrenching effect, she saw herself staring back at her as if from a mirror held close up to her face. Every pore, every wrinkle was visible to her from vision far more acute than anything she had ever known. A feather was out of place on the inside of the right wing. The cut on her heel tingled slightly. She ducked her head, without understanding how or why, and preened the feather.

There was a strong desire in her to lift away, to soar, to put a great distance between herself and this place. Her wings beat a few times.

A whistle intruded, a soft pulsed whistle. She looked around. Lessis was whistling, Lessis's eyes were staring in at her, peering in like portholes in a dark firmament.

"You must control him, Lagdalen, almost like riding a horse. It seems very strange now, but you will adjust. You will feel what he feels, just as you will see what he sees. As I mentioned, you will get used to it."

And now Lagdalen realized fully that it was done. For better or worse, her mind was now fixed within the eagle's.

Her body continued to sit cross-legged on the mat, eyes closed and breath coming in regular, disciplined fashion, but she no longer inhabited it with her mind. From now on it would be watered and fed by the acolytes. As long as she lived, that was. If the eagle died, so would she. On the other hand, if someone were to destroy her body, she would live on in the mind of the eagle, for a while. At length, however, several years perhaps, she would fade and be lost forever. Lagdalen was familiar with the legends concerning animancy and the practice of werewolfing. Now she herself had taken part in this most forbidden of the great magics.

Now the truly bizarre began to become the normal. Long afterward, she would still question what she thought she had seen at this point.

A small cage was set on the table. A mouse opened the cage door from within and emerged and sat still on the table. A small bird, a wren, flew in and settled on the table and hopped around the mouse, pecking at microscopic items in the dust.

Lessis and Ribela carried on with the many complex motions of the spell. First Ribela, then Lessis, cast bundles of herbs into the fire and leaned over and inhaled some of the thick, evil-smelling smoke that resulted.

With cheeks distended and eyes bulging, they turned back to the table and blew the smoke over the little animals, which became as still as stones.

Ribela sank into a lotus posture beside Lagdalen. Then Lessis, too, sank down and sat while she finished the final declamations.

A great flash of red light lit up the room. Lagdalen's eagle eyes blinked against it.

Somewhere on the interior high plane, a peal of thunder began that went on and on as if the very world would crack apart and fall to flinders. Slowly it died away.

The mouse and the bird became animated once more. The wren flew up and circled the eagle before landing on its shoulder.

Lagdalen became aware that the mouse was climbing up her leg. She had to fight hard against the instinctive desire to lean over and rend it in half. It climbed, crawling on her. Cuica was disturbed. The great wings rose.

Lagdalen exerted herself, urging calm on her great flying steed. The wings were folded again. The mouse climbed into the leather cup while the small bird perched on the edge of the cup. They were ready for departure.

The door of the room was opened. Two women came in. After quickly inspecting the three human forms, sitting silently, eyes blank, chests moving in and out in slow, steady respiration, the women pulled back the blind and opened the window.

The eagle flapped to the windowsill and then launched itself. Lagdalen felt momentary panic as the bird left the side of the tower. Suddenly she was floating on air, high over the ground. But the great wings beat with tremendous force and within a few seconds she was rising, circling the Tower of Guard once and then soaring above the town, out toward the Long Sound and the western shore.

CHAPTER THIRTY-THREE

The eastern half of Kenor was split north from south by the Kohon Scarp, a land feature two hundred miles in length with a long gentle slope to the north and a swift, sharp scarp slope to the south. The Kohon Hills and High Lake lay on the very crest of the scarp.

To the south of the lake, past the town of Portage, deep gulleys scoured the land where swift, seasonal streams thundered after storms. Farther on, they coagulated into the beginnings of the river Bur, which tumbled in a foaming torrent down a gorge before bending eastward and opening out into the Feutoborg Reach.

Captain Eads's small punitive force had to make its way down the Bur Valley, using the river where possible. To this end they built some square-ended boats, called "scows," and purchased some fifteen-man canoes. Each scow was built to take two dragons and two dragonboys, and to be portable around rapids.

As a consequence of its uselessness for river traffic, the country around the river was still virtual wilderness. Resettlement of Kenor had proceeded apace in the lands to the west and south, but along the Bur there were only occasional towns and fishing hamlets. Fur trappers were still the most common folk in the woods. You could go for days and not see a soul.

Indeed, not since the high days of Veronath had people dwelled here in any numbers. Even then there had been no cities in the region. So far, not even the engineering corps of the legions had found a way to make the Bur usable for river traffic.

The dragons were required to learn how to control the flat-bottomed, clumsy scows with oversized paddles that boasted blades four feet across. The dragons were not enthusiastic about this work, nor were they very adept at guiding the scows through the shallow, fast-flowing channels of the river.

The Talion Light Horse were accompanying them, but at a distance, riding overland, down the valley toward Widfields where the Kalens River emptied into the Bur.

By day they worked their way down steep canyons, on crystal-clear water running over a bed of boulders. Scrub oak and dwarf pine were all that managed to struggle out of the bare rock. The clear river waters were home to many fish, and they glimpsed enormous trout every so often. At night they hauled their craft out of the water and camped on shore under the stars.

The weather was clear and warm. Sitting around the fires with their evening meal and the river rushing past under the stars, it was easy to forget that they were heading to war and were not on some quiet patrol.

The dragonboys agreed that they had a problem. The dragons were not likely to learn how to paddle and steer at the same time. After a fairly young age, it became difficult to teach anything to a dragon. The dragon mind did not remain elastic, capable of accepting new things, new systems of thought, throughout a lifetime, but instead hardened at an age of six or seven years. Dragons were quick learners before then, however, and soon mastered the art of wielding the dragonsword.

The scows were not sturdy enough to stand up to collisions with the rocks in the river. Several halts were made every day to repair one scow or another. The Purple Green was particularly difficult at first.

On the third day, however, the dragons all got the hang of it, almost at once. It was uncanny. First to achieve proficiency was Alsebra, the green freemartin. Then came old Chektor and Cham. Then Vlok and the Broketail, and then all the others, Rusp and Anthe, even the Purple Green at last, discovered how to steer a boat.

The dragonboys exchanged looks of amazement. The dragons said nothing. The dragons were unusually quiet that evening at the campfire on the shore.

It turned out that the dragons in the other squadron, the 66th Marneri Dragons, had also learned how to paddle and steer that day.

There was plenty of driftwood for fires. They boiled legion noodles and doused them with oil, salt, and garlic.

They drank the ration of beer, a pint per man and a gallon per dragon and unrolled their blankets in short order. All went as usual until the dragons in both squadrons gathered for a short conversation. Dragonboys were pointedly shooed away out of earshot.

The dragonboys gathered on their own on a massive flat-topped boulder sitting in the shallows of the river.

Swane ascribed the dragons' behavior to the ancient pact between the old gods and the dragon lords. As fire god of the ancient Vero, Vesco, maker of lava, had been much concerned with dragons, as they were his heraldic beasts. When the dragons of the northland were attacked by frost trolls, Vesco had taken up his great hammer and gone to their aid. In the resultant battle, Vesco hammered the frost trolls and created snow. However, in the process a vital piece of Vesco was lost in Dragon Home. According to ancient lore, that part missing was his penis. Vesco's servants rode out across the world and searched everywhere, but could not find it until at last they came to Dragon Home where they found the god's lost member. Vesco rewarded the dragons with the gift of speech and the gift of shared thinking.

Relkin chuckled. Swane knew all the stories about the old gods, especially the rude ones.

"You, Swane, are a blasphemer, now shut it," said Halm of Ors, who came from a very religious family.

Swane bristled, but before he could offer a retort, Manuel spoke up. They were always surprised by these odd, occasional sorties from the usually silent Manuel, and when they came, everyone listened respectfully.

"At the Institute of Dragon Affairs in Cunfshon, they believe the dragons achieve a collective consciousness every now and then. It is a response to great stress."

Manuel was the odd one out, the academy student. He knew a lot of things about the dragons that the other boys did not.

"Well, that may be," said Relkin, "and maybe even old Vesco is responsible. I don't see why not, but the dragons were all just as surprised by it as we were."

"You ever seen anything like it, Relkin?" said Swane.

"Dragons learn things in mysterious ways. We've all seen them suddenly pick up a sword trick after they'd been shown it a thousand times and never got it right. Then all of a sudden they've got it, and they never make a mistake with it again."

"No half measures with the big ones," said little Jak.

Swane broke in excitedly.

"You remember when we was going down to Ourdh. That time we went through the swamp, and you couldn't sleep with all the frogs croaking. But the dragons went really weird. They all went to the rail and just listened. They didn't say anything."

"Dragon ain't human is all it is, Swane," said Relkin.

"I know that, you Quoshite. But you sort of forget it sometimes. And then they show you something, and you really remember it."

Some of them laughed at that.

"It's something to do with life in the sea, that's what we were told at the academy," said Manuel, the educated dragonboy.

"They go crazy when they see the ocean."

"Whether they're crazy or not, it's going to make the rest of this river trip a lot easier."

"Thought I was going to go crazy yesterday myself," said Bryon. "Alsebra was impossible, just downright vicious."

"Maybe we'll get to Fort Redor in time," said little Jak.

"Now, why did you go and say that?" groused Swane. "Now I'm never going to sleep."

They all felt the same shiver of apprehension. What lay ahead seemed dark and shapeless, filled with threatening thunder. An ominous cloud that hung across the horizon. A cloud filled with nine-foot-tall trolls, armed with swords and hammers.

Yet despite Swane's words, he did sleep, after a few minutes lying in his blankets on hard ground. They all did, too exhausted not to.

They breakfasted brutally early. Captain Eads knew the situation was very grave. Fort Redor might fall, or simply be masked by another besieging force while the main enemy army continued up the valley. The obvious target was the High Pass. He had determined to turn east when he reached the Lis. That would mean paddling upstream, hard work, but on the gentle Lis it was possible, especially in summer when the water was low and the flow much reduced. The important thing was to get to the High Pass.

The boats were on the water an hour later and with newly

proficient dragons, they made much better time than they had before.

Still, it would take days more to get down the Bur, which stretched more than two hundred miles ahead of them. The easiest length of the upper river was the reach alongside the Feutoborg Forest. Here they glided quickly across smooth water past a dark, gloomy forest of ancient oak and beech.

Relkin had had enough of weird forests. He was anxious for them to leave the ancient wood behind, and only relaxed when at the end of the afternoon the little town of Grettons appeared on the east side of the river. They drew in and beached their canoes and scows on a broad strip of sand.

This tidy village of four streets and twenty stone houses with thatched roofs also held an ancient fane to the Great Mother, a small temple of beautiful proportion. It had remained hidden to all but her worshipers during the long night of the Dark Ages. The foul agents of the demon lords never suspected that the fane of the Hidden Mother lay here, at the gateway to the Feutoborg Forest. The fane was still kept up by a group of young witches, volunteers from Bea and Kadein.

Eads directed the men to set their tents along the shore just past the end of the town. The cooks began a boil up and sent into the town for bread and ale and fresh vegetables.

Stretched out along the sand beside the little town, they ate their fill. The sun sank way out on a western reach of the river. It was warm, full summer, and the weather had remained sunny and mild.

The townsfolk were hospitable, and there were several rounds of a good ale made by one Bosun Chesnew, who'd retired to this quiet spot after a life in the legions.

Bosun Chesnew was, in fact, happy to sit down with them and hear stories of north Kenor, Dalhousie, and the Argo country. He was also the bearer of news. Since the beginning of the invasion, they'd seen folk passing down the river, hoping to get to the High Pass and out of Kenor. Then a few days before, they'd started seeing a few riders coming the other way, up the old road to the Lis and then going on into the Feutoborg Forest. These folk were convinced that the enemy horde was actually close to falling upon the valley of the Bur at any moment. Chesnew had heard from another traveler, an Ugoli trader no bigger than an elf, that Fort

Redor had fallen already and all its defenders had been slaughtered. Fort Teot was still holding, however.

The enemy army was said to be moving in an endless series of columns up the river road in Livolda. Enemy forces were also moving through the country on the other side of the river, in Picon and Gueva. Despite being set way up the river Bur, the folk of Grettons were getting anxious. You couldn't buy a donkey around the town for love or money.

Eads called Captains Senshon, Deft, and Retiner together. Retiner was for staying in Grettons for fresh orders. Deft and Senshon were for pushing on south in the hope of getting to the junction with the Lis in time to turn upstream toward the High Pass.

It was time for a commander's judgment. Eads would have to decide and take responsibility. They might also have to face the fact that the enemy could reach the confluence of the Bur and the Lis before they could, in which case they would have wasted time and effort to no purpose.

Such a possibility also raised the question of what they might do in such a case. Eads understood all this.

"We're in a race to get to the High Pass, gentlemen, and that's where the battle will be fought. We will need every man, every dragon that we can get there to hold the pass.

"The quickest way to the High Pass is by following the rivers."

"So we're to press on regardless?" said Captain Retiner of the Talion Light Horse.

"That is my decision, Captain."

"Yes, sir." It was obvious that Retiner disagreed, but he refrained from insubordination. Eads paused a moment.

"If we find that we're too late, then we'll turn around, but for now we will go south. We have to accept the possibility that we may be too late. However, we cannot pass up any opportunity to reach the High Pass."

The captains returned to their units and passed the word. They would be going on in the morning, south, toward the enemy, toward the High Pass.

In the last hour of twilight, Relkin found himself with a very rare moment with nothing to do. Dragon leader Turrent was busy going over poor Jak's kit, which had fallen into "disrepair," according to the booming voice of the dragon leader. Relkin slipped away and walked through the little town. There were girls everywhere, including girls his own age who cast him big eyes and enticing smiles.

Behind the girls, however, loomed their homes, and on the porches sat their fathers and brothers, heavyset men for the most part with truculent expressions.

Relkin wandered onto a path that wound through groves of moon-dappled trees, eventually bringing him to a clearing with a small temple built of white stone. It was sixty feet long and perhaps half that wide, and at the front stood four pillars of exquisite size and balance. Worn steps, made of marble that glowed whitely in the moonlight, led up to the fane.

He took the steps easily, drawn by the beauty of the place, but then stood, hesitant, at the entrance. The doors were thrown open, and inside were lit a few candles and a lamp in the center of the ceiling. By their light he saw a single room, a floor of polished white marble and walls of light grey sandstone on which the classic short prayers to the Great Mother had been carved. There was a simple altar, a dark stone on which to burn offerings. Relkin thought he had never seen such a bare temple, with so little in the way of decoration or comforts.

Overcoming his uneasiness, he slipped in and slunk along one wall, his fingers pressing against the carvings as he went. It had been a long time since he'd attended a service in a temple. He recalled the many long evenings he'd spent in the temple in Quosh.

He sensed someone watching him and looked back to find a young woman, clad in an austere smock of plain grey homespun and soft doeskin slippers, standing by the entrance. She came closer. He knew at once that she was a witch, probably the guardian of the place. Relkin had seen enough witches in his young life to know one instantly. They were always surrounded by an aura, a field of expectancy and energy.

"If I can help you at all, I will," she said in ritual greeting, and put her palms together and bowed.

"Thank you, Sister." He hesitated. She looked as if she was but twenty-five or thirty years, but she might as easily be ten times that. He knew the Lady Lessis, for instance, to be older than the very cities of Argonath.

For once he was tongue-tied, uncertain about everything. There were so many things he wanted to say. But was this the right place to say them? If there was a Great Mother who watched over them all, then he was sure he had offended her mightily with his prayers to the old gods. How was he to say what he needed to say without offending this witch?

He felt that great events were in motion, and that they somehow concerned him, but they were all taking place on a plane beyond his understanding. It was as if he heard voices, distorted by distance, and was sure they were talking about him, but he could not understand them no matter how he tried.

"I sense a troubled spirit within the fane," said the witch. She wore her pale gold hair in braids, with a silver headband across her brow. She was of stocky build with fleshy arms and a round, cheerful face.

"Let me help you," she said.

"I don't know how anyone can help, lady. I thought that if I wrote the Grey Lady Lessis that she might be able to sort it out for me, but who knows if I'll ever get an answer from her before I peg out in the next big fight."

The witch Dassney blinked and stared hard at the youth. He did say the Grey Lady Lessis? Who was this boy who so casually tossed that name around?

"No one can help unless you want them to."

"It's like this," he shrugged. "How do I find out if the Mother is angry with me, so angry that I can never win her favor in this life again? I feel accursed. Amend that. I am accursed. Everything has gone wrong for me for months."

"Have you taken a life?"

"Well, yes, of course."

The young witch's eyebrows rose involuntarily.

"Did this happen recently?"

"Yes."

"Has it happened before?"

"Yes."

The young witch shook her head and looked sharply at him. He wore a uniform, red and blue cap, jacket, breeches and boots, he wore a sword and a long knife. He was in the legion. She breathed a little more easily.

"How did you come to take this life?"

"In battle, with the Cralls on Black Fell. They attacked, and we killed them."

"In battle? But you are so young."

"I am a dragonboy."

"Ah, of course. How obtuse of me. And so you have been in battle, and you killed a man. You think that because the Mother does not countenance killing, she will no longer give you her favor."

"No, not at all."

"No?" Witch Dassney's forehead creased in surprise.

"Well," he said, gesturing, "we fight for the peace of the Great Mother, don't we? I've always been taught that. I've seen fighting all up and down the land, and I've killed more men and things that ain't men but can fight like 'em, than I can remember. And I've nearly been killed by them on a few occasions. I could say that I've seen all the killing I ever want to see. But it's all been done for the Argonath. Well"—he checked himself—"all but for Trader Dook, but that was different."

"Such taking of life can be defended as necessary to preserving the peace of the Mother in Kenor. You can be sure of the Mother's forgiveness. You fought in Her service, after all."

She stared at him with a peculiarly penetrating gaze, and again he was reminded of the Great Witches.

"But you may have unjust and unnecessary life taking on your conscience. For that you may have to pray for forgiveness, and it may be withheld."

His lip curled. Who was to say what was unjust? When you parried an imp's sword and ripped his guts with your dirk in the hot press while steel rang all around you, where were such concepts as justice and injustice? Things moved too quickly at such moments. One slew or was slain.

"But it was necessary, Sister. But that's not why She doesn't care for me. It's because of the old gods. See, I think they still live on, although they're not as strong as they used to be."

Dassney shook her head in wonderment. The old gods was it? A worshiper of the older deities of the Vero peoples? This youth with so many lives taken by his sword was worried about the old gods?

"What is your name, Dragoneer?"

"Relkin of Quosh, Dragoneer First Class, 109th Marneri Dragons. Attached to the Eighth Regiment, Second Marneri Legion."

"And so, why do you think the Mother has withdrawn her favor from you?"

"I don't know if I believe in her. The old gods feel more real because they belong to the world. They breathe and eat and make love and fight one another. Old Caymo with his wine and dice. And Asgah of the sword, I think he watches over my dragon. There was a time when we were hard-pressed on Mt. Red Oak. Asgah heard our plea and came to our aid. He rolled the stone on the trolls."

Sister Dassney took a breath.

"The Mother is simpler than any god or goddess, child. Her word is kindness."

"I know, I fight for Her peace. An end to unjust violence and unchecked greed. I learned all that in school. But since I left my village, I've seen nothing but chaos and a lot of killing. I'm not eighteen years, and I've seen battles, sieges, everything. How can there be a Great Mother and so much killing and horror in the world?"

The young witch smiled and came close to him.

"Perhaps it is a long and arduous job, purging the world of its horrors. There are a great many of them, and they've been going on for a long time. The Great Mother's work is scarcely begun."

"But we're told the world was made by the Great Mother. If She made the world, then why didn't she make it without the horror and the killing? Why does it have to be so cruel?"

"Do you ask this question of the old gods?"

"Well, no, the old gods, they're sort of like ordinary folk. They're capricious. Sometimes they're cruel. Caymo carries that knife to cut your throat if you gamble away your inheritance. They're part of the world, that's why I understand them. They're not sitting apart from it, criticizing it and setting an impossible standard for everyone."

"Well, Dragoneer Relkin, you can be sure that unless you take life unnecessarily in their name, the Great Mother will not frown upon you. She accepts the need for the old gods. They bring some dash and color to the world that believes in them. But as you said, the Great Mother holds to a higher standard than they do. She carries no knife to sever the hopeless gambler's life. She embodies the infinite and the eternal."

Relkin heard but struggled with acceptance.

"It's hard," he said quietly.

"I know, but that is the way of the good things in the world. The evil comes easily, the truly worthwhile is hard."

Relkin shrugged. "I suppose so."

And with that she excused herself and left him. Once again the fane was empty but for himself. He sighed. The fane was very beautiful like this, so simple and undecorated. It was just unfortunate. There were no easy answers.

He left the temple and made his way back on the moonlit path to the camp. His dragon was sitting on his haunches watching the sky. The dragon star, red Razulgeb, rode high in the zenith.

"Welcome back," said Bazil.

"I didn't think you'd still be awake."

"Red star is high. We are all awake."

Relkin glanced around himself. It was true. The other dragons were all sitting up, their eyes fixed on the heavens.

"So did dragonboy learn anything at the temple?"

"Yes," he said, and slipped into his blankets. Already the fatigue in his bones was willing him to sleep.

"What was that?"

"There are no answers, Bazil, that's what."

CHAPTER THIRTY-FOUR

Between Kenor and the lands of the Argonath there were but two routes through the long chain of the Malgun Mountains. One was the break occupied by the river Argo, which ran between Mt. Red Oak and Mt. Ulmo. The other lay to the south and was known as the High Pass.

Here was a gap less than a mile wide and more than a mile high, bending between Mt. Livol and mighty Mt. Malgun to the south. Grey rock lay bare to the sky. Only a few goats survived in the mists. To the human eye, the strongest impression was of sheer desolation. The wind keened over the bare rocks and whistled through the gulleys.

The Empire of the Rose had built a level road, forty feet wide, to traverse the pass. It was interrupted solely by the gates of Fort Roland. The rectangular fort cut the pass in two with its fortifications facing west.

In the cool light of morning, Captain Hollein Keseptom stood on the battlements above the gate. To the west the view was blocked by low clouds, which turned the pass into a funnel running into a wall of mist.

Out of the mist, packed on the road, came an endless procession of refugees, thousands upon thousands of women, children, the elderly, the lame, and the frightened. There were herds of cattle and sheep, teams of horses, wagons by the hundred, and even a few luxurious coaches pulled by teams of six or even eight fine horses. All were driven by the same overpowering urge, to pass through the great gate of Roland and reach the safety of the lands of the Argonath. But Hollein knew that that safety was illusory, for what came behind the refugees was a great devouring beast that was treading up the Lis Valley and would go over the mountains and devour the cities of the Argonath unless it could be stopped right here. And to stop that monstrous threat, there were but a few hundred men including himself.

He turned at the sound of someone climbing the stairs in the turret and saw a familiar, grim visage emerge from the pool of darkness. Lieutenant Liepol Duxe came to attention and saluted.

"At ease, Lieutenant," said Hollein. Duxe had taken promotion at last, making the jump between the ranks and the officer class.

"I didn't think I'd see you again so soon, Captain." Duxe showed that familiar wintry smile.

" 'Tis our fate it seems. I search for some pattern, some sign of the Mother's hand in all this."

"You will not find it. This war is the mark of more vigorous players. Our enemy grows mightier each time we cut him down."

"You were not a defeatist, before, I doubt that you are now." Liepol Duxe grinned. He was tall, sandy-haired where Kesepton was dark, and wore his beard at medium length but clipped neat and square. Older than Kesepton, he had risen from the ranks and carried a hefty chip on his shoulder toward officers. He had served with distinction in the campaign against the Doom of Tummuz Orgmeen.

"You are correct, Captain."

"Can we do it?"

"Can we get rid of him? Yes, sir."

"No, can we hold them? Long enough for reinforcements to reach us."

Duxe looked along the walls. They were well built and well sited. With a few hundred men you could hold off an army. But what was coming against them was, by all accounts, a host of legendary proportions.

"I honestly doubt it, sir. But we will try. Every man here, except one."

Kesepton looked away, down to the road. A wagon loaded with children, dozens of them packed in tight, went rumbling into the gate. The children started singing the Kenor song, their voices high and shrill. The men inside the gate roared with laughter and joined in on the chorus.

"You know we heard from Fort Redor. The enemy was five days just marching his columns past the fort."

"Redor will fall, Captain." Duxe expressed this with gloomy certainty. "But Teot will not fall. I served three years in Teot. 'Tis the strongest fort in Kenor and has the deepest well."

"You're right, Lieutenant. Unless they can breach the walls, which I doubt, Teot will stand to the very last. They have a spell of adamant wrought deep upon those walls by the witches."

Duxe shrugged. "As to spells, don't ask Liepol Duxe about that! But the enemy will have spellsayers, too. Yet Teot's walls are hard to come to since they stand on the bluff. You can only come against the place by going straight up at the gates, and they are very strong."

"The approach to the gates is a death trap. No, I think the enemy will not waste his resources trying to take Teot. But the men and dragons inside Redor are doomed, I fear."

"I wish we had them here. It seems such a terrible waste."

"And we have no dragons. Nothing to put against their trolls."

"Trolls are poor climbers."

"That is our only consolation. But they will surely bring a ram and break the gate."

Duxe smiled his wintry grin again. "I have heard, Captain, that the gates of Roland have a mighty spell on them. I would expect the walls to give way before the gates."

Hollein shook his head. "My friend, we shall have to face the trolls before this is over. You know what comes against us."

Duxe shrugged. "All that is only half our problem. The other half, I'm sure you know."

Hollein Kesepton grimaced, "Commander Hodwint."

"A bought commission, Captain. You may have run into this problem before."

Kesepton pursed his lips. Indeed he had, having suffered the consequences during the siege of Ourdh.

"I had breakfast with the commander."

Duxe grinned without mirth. "He don't know what to do, foul himself running or foul himself standing still. The man's a coward and a fool."

Kesepton had to agree. Hodwint was an aristo from Kadein. He had some huge family estate in the Minuend country. He'd bought a commission as commander so as to earn the right to wear legion armor and uniform for his family portrait.

His idea of service in the legions had been to spend a riotous few months in Kadein lurching from tavern to brothel. After some wild late-night run-in with the guard, General

Pekel had concluded that the safest place for the boisterous fool was up at the High Pass.

Hodwint would have resigned his commission at once if he hadn't faced ruinous financial penalties. He had tried to use his influence at the court of King Neath to overturn Pekel's order, but without success. At length he had been left high and dry in the barren surroundings of Fort Roland.

Now, faced with an onrushing horde out of some painting of the lower levels of Hell, Commander Hodwint was toying with ordering a general retreat from the High Pass.

As he had informed Hollein Kesepton at breakfast, the only truly safe place now was Cunfshon itself. He was obsessed, he said, with getting himself across to the isles as soon as possible.

The Masters would never subdue Cunfshon, not unless they could win control of the seas, and the sailing folk of Cunfshon were the greatest mariners in the world and had raised the arts of shipbuilding and sailing, and fighting at sea, to the highest levels ever known on Ryetelth.

Commander Hodwint had been very emphatic on this last point. Fortunately, the Hodwints had ancestral lands in Cunfshon and still owned several estates. The Cunfshon side of the family was perhaps backward and narrow-minded, they had roots in Defwode, but they would take in their Argonathi kin. It was better to be a guest at the fireside in Defwode than ground to dust beneath the heel of the dark enemy of Padmasa. That was the stark choice that Commander Hodwint saw and confided to Captain Kesepton.

Duxe took Kesepton's silence for agreement.

"I've discussed it with the sergeants, sir, and they agree. It all depends on you, sir, since you are the senior officer present. Obviously we must be united on it."

"We will be. Of course it means a court-martial if we survive."

"Not much likelihood of that, Captain."

Hollein grimaced, "At least that's one thing we won't have to worry about then, right?"

"Right, sir."

Duxe left to organize the proceedings. Hollein stayed on the battlements to pull together his thoughts.

There really was no choice. Hodwint was a treacherous fool, and would destroy their chances of holding the enemy back at the High Pass. But to break legion discipline and confine the commander would be mutiny, and the high command had always taken a very dim view of mutiny. He might not hang for it, but his career would be effectively destroyed.

He shrugged to himself and stared down at the refugees passing below, into the great gate of Roland. He consoled himself with the thought that Lagdalen and the babe were safe in Marneri. Even if all else failed, the white city on the Long Sound would stand. They would be safe. For a moment he closed his eyes and prayed for the preservation of his little daughter, and his lovely wife. When he opened them, he glanced upward and he caught sight of an eagle soaring down the pass, heading into Kenor and watched it vanish into the wall of cloud.

Lieutenant Duxe was back. Hollein wasn't sure that Liepol Duxe was any easier to deal with as an officer than he'd been as a sergeant, but he was glad the man had taken the examinations at last and moved up. He had been wasting his talents as a sergeant.

Behind Duxe were the sergeants of the small garrison.

"Sergeants Hack, Dulu, and Epwort, sir."

Hollein saluted. "Good morning, gentlemen. You understand the likelihood of a court-martial for all of us in the event that we live through the coming battle. You also know that we have to do this, for we must hold this pass."

They all agreed. The men were behind them.

Hollein marched at once to Commander Hodwint's office in the tower gate. Commander Hodwint looked up in surprise from a large meal of sausages and wheat cakes that he was washing down with a flagon of ale.

"What the hell is this, Captain? Since when do you barge in here without getting permission?"

Kesepton saluted but refused to meet Hodwint's eyes.

"Begging your pardon, sir, but I am forced to inform you that as of this moment, you are no longer in command of this fort."

Hodwint virtually choked and spat shreds of sausage across the table.

"Furthermore," continued Hollein in an implacable tone of voice, "you are to be confined to your quarters. With the backing of the men and the junior officers, I am taking command so that we may present as durable a defense of this position as we can possibly manage."

Hodwint leapt to his feet. "Mutiny! I'll see you hanged, you insolent puppy!"

"You will be released when the engagement is over, and you will be free to do whatever you want then. We all expect a court-martial. However, since you intend a general retreat from this fort, I was left with no choice. I will send to Kadein for fresh orders at once."

"General Pekel will have you strung up on summary judgment."

"Sir, I doubt that. General Pekel will understand why I have to do this. We have to hold this pass. We cannot retreat."

Hodwint stared at him. "You're mad. We have to get out of here today; they're coming, they'll be here soon."

"Sir, please go to your quarters. It would make things easier for all of us."

Hodwint sputtered and screamed and had to be rousted out and dragged away by the sergeants.

Kesepton and Duxe toured the fortifications and made careful preparations. They still had some time. They would make the most of it.

CHAPTER THIRTY-FIVE

The river Bur lived up to its reputation for difficulty. The weather broke the day after they left Grettons, and a heavy rain began in the afternoon. A fierce wind cut up the surface of the river and tore at the dragon boats threatening to spin them around. Eads ordered a halt, and they turned to the shore.

On the way, Rusp and Jak's boat foundered tossing them into the stream. Rusp was a big-bellied brass and he swam well, but Jak would have been swept away if Manuel and the Purple Green hadn't been right behind. Manuel dove in and fished out the gasping, younger boy while the Purple Green kept the boat steady with huge strokes of his paddle.

On shore, they scavenged for scraps of dry wood and started the cook fires while the tents went up. At last a wet and weary band of soldiers ate a half-cooked meal and went to sleep.

It rained most of the night and finally stopped around dawn. The river had risen to a flood of dirty brown water that was clearly beyond their powers to navigate.

They spent the day drying out. To keep them busy, Eads ordered them to make charcoal to resupply the cooks. Parties scoured the surrounding forest for deadwood, which was brought in and heaped in the sun. Dragonboys turned the wood, drying it out before splitting it and then stacking it in three great piles on the beach. Fires were lit, and around the fires were wet stacks of wood which were left to slowly smolder into charcoal. All night they kept the fires going, busy work for dragonboys and men, working in shifts and cleaning off with dips in the river.

Meanwhile, the smith and the best carpenters were building a new boat for Rusp and Jak. For this they had to work with green wood right out of the forest, but they caulked it

with good tar and secured it with iron nails, giving some
hope of it lasting for the journey down the river.

By the following morning the river had subsided considerably, and a party of dragons swam out to the spot where
the boat had sunk and searched the bottom. At length they
found Rusp's great sword "Doceras" about a quarter mile
downstream where the torrent had tumbled it. Rusp had been
on tenterhooks all night, and was enormously relieved to
have the sword back in his hands.

They set out again in the late afternoon and continued as
far as the hamlet of Widfields just below the confluence of
the Bur and its tributary stream the Kalens. The folk at
Widfields, having heard rumors of enemy columns actually
coming up the Bur Valley were preparing to flee north to
High Lake.

Eads was nonplussed. By his calculations, the enemy
could not have passed Fort Redor and even reached the
mouth of the Bur by this time.

They passed an anxious night there, and in the morning
carried out a portage of the five-mile-long rapids known as
the "Lion's Roar." It began to rain again that day, and this
made the portage, which was difficult in good conditions,
quite horrendous. There were patches of mud along the way
that turned into a near liquid after the first few men and
dragons had dragged their boats through it. The last few
were wading through the stuff knee-deep.

Below the Lion's Roar they halted, wet and exhausted.
Eads saw the condition of the men and ordered the cook fires
lit. Now the fresh charcoal came in handy, for the woods
around them were soaked and there was little usable fuel.

With everything wet, including the tents, their second
night under the rain was much less enjoyable than the first.
In the end they slept, however, ignoring damp blankets and
cold feet.

By morning, the rain tapered off and left a rising mist on
the river to greet them.

Relkin rose early despite having awakened several times
in the night. He smelled kalut brewing at the cook fire and
headed in that direction at once.

During the night the cooks and their assistants had put up
a rough-hewn structure of fallen limbs and hewn uprights to
enclose the cooking pits and now this small space was
crammed with men, eager to get warm while they drank

some hot kalut. Relkin waited in line for the chance to fill a pan. A nudge at his elbow announced the presence of Swane and Tomas.

"Messenger canoe came in early this morning, up from Lake Bur," said Swane.

"Went in with Captain Eads, hasn't come out since."

Relkin frowned. "How do you know, you been watching all night?"

"We did it by turns. They're still in there. It must be important."

Relkin grabbed a sack of hot bread and a pot of akh for the dragon, then took a pan of fresh brewed kalut and returned to the tent.

The dragon, who had just returned from the river dripping wet ate while Relkin packed their gear. Together they dismantled their tent and stowed it in their boat, which they pushed down to the waterline, ready to be off when the order came.

The other dragons soon joined them, forming a neat line. A little farther down were the 66th, also ready. Dragon leader Turrent came by to inspect and could find nothing to berate Relkin about, although he searched long and hard. But Relkin had dried all their belongings by the fire the night before, turning them again and again through the night hours to ensure an even dryness. There was nothing for a sour-faced dragon leader to complain about.

The sun shone, and they relaxed. The dragons sat or went out into the river to cool themselves, leaving their swords in the boats. They waited for the order to set off.

It did not come. Instead Captain Eads appeared, accompanied by a slight fellow in a grey uniform with a back pack and a wide-brimmed hat of cowhide.

Eads had a spyglass out and used it to peer way down the river.

Bazil had returned from a brief dip and was steaming in the sun. Suddenly he nudged Relkin.

"Look, boy, see that man? It is our friend from ship on the Argo, last year, before we went to the land in the south."

"Ton Akalon?"

Relkin looked again. So it was.

Eads put down the glass, spoke to the smaller man beside him, then turned and gave orders to Sergeant Quertin, who was standing at the ready.

Within a few moments they were told to stand down in their positions and to remain at ease.

Eads and his officers disappeared back into the captain's tent. The little man in the big brown hat strolled along the river's edge and approached the dragon boats.

He was carefully studying the new one, built overnight for Rusp while talking with young Jak, when Relkin slipped up behind him.

"And hello to you, Sir Ton," said Relkin.

The little man spun around.

"Well, well," he cried, "Dragoneer Relkin. We meet again."

Ton Akalon, soil surveyor from the Isle of Cunfshon, had changed somewhat in the course of the year since they had first met aboard the riverboat *Tench* on the Middle Argo. He had broadened some and grown very tanned and a little weather-beaten.

Ton Akalon clapped Relkin on the shoulders.

"And you have grown, Dragoneer. I hardly recognize the boy I saw last year."

He caught sight of the dragon, who was standing quietly by, resting his weight on the hilt of his great sword.

"And greeting to you, Sir Bazil the Broketail. I have heard your legend now. I am honored."

Bazil's oddly bent tail twitched slightly.

"Hail to you, Ton Akalon of Cunfshon. Why do we see you here?"

"I have been in every corner of Kenor since last I saw you, Sir Bazil. From the good soils of Tuala to the light calcareae of the Esk Valley, I have examined them all. In the end my survey took me to Bur Lake. There are some worthwhile soils there, even in the midst of the Bur River wilderness."

He sighed. "And thus I came to scout ahead of the folk who are fleeing up this way, and I find you here. So we meet again in strange circumstances." His face grew grave. "Alas, it is a fell time, and I wouldst that it could be different, but the enemy has unleashed his great blow against us. Long have we awaited it, it is said. But not enough preparation was made."

"We are going downriver to try and get to the High Pass," said Relkin. "Captain Eads thinks we'll be needed there."

Ton Akalon shook his head. "Can't be done, my friends.

The enemy is way ahead of you. They burnt the settlements at Bur Lake two days ago. If you look downriver now, you will see the refugees struggling toward us. The enemy is close behind, nipping at their heels, trying to capture women."

Relkin stared at him. "That close?"

"There has been a terrible disaster in the valley of the Lis. Fort Redor fell, did you know that?"

"We heard a rumor. I did not credit it possible."

"The enemy has many new and terrible weapons. Apparently Redor was too undermanned to withstand them. Following that disaster, the enemy began to catch up on the rear ranks of the refugees from the Teot and Don lands. Butchery most terrible took place. Imps broiled many prisoners alive and fed them to the trolls. The river ran red with blood, it is said."

Relkin was staggered.

"Enemy cavalry seized the mouth of the Bur several days ago. They had ridden nonstop from the sack of Redor. There was a panic up the river and most of the population left their homes at once. This saved a lot of lives, for the next day it rained and the river became impassable. The enemy cavalry almost caught up while the refugees were trapped by the floodwaters. I was in the settlements at Bur Lake. We were working on soil profiles of the basin around the lake. It will be good land." He paused and sucked in a breath. "If we can ever win it back."

"We will, we have to," said Relkin determinedly.

There was a shout from Swane, who had been sitting up in a tree. Chektor stood up in the shallows and craned his head.

"Someone comes. Many boats."

Within five minutes, an armada of small boats was in view, dozens of them, of all types, from canoes to a large river yacht.

Voices began bellowing orders.

CHAPTER THIRTY-SIX

The refugees streamed past for an hour in hundreds of canoes, scows, even fragile-looking lake punts. Among the people huddled aboard, Relkin saw many women. The sight chilled him. He knew the enemy would make a great effort to capture fertile women. The folk of Bur Lake had been lulled into complacency by their location in the backwoods. Now their women folk were in terrible danger, for in the hands of the enemy they would be marched westward to serve as breeding slaves in the dungeons of Axoxo.

According to Ton Akalon, there were upwards of five thousand imps, a hundred trolls, and perhaps five hundred cavalry coming up the valley in pursuit.

The leaders of the Bur Lake folk came ashore to meet Captain Eads and discuss strategies. Later they were joined by a Captain Whiteart of the Kohon Yeomanry and by Bowchief Starter from the Bur Lake bowmen. Their forces, about 350 strong, were providing a buffer of sorts between the refugees and the pursuit. At the most they could slow the enemy with occasional ambushes and sniping.

Soon word was passed down through Sergeant Quertin. A party of perhaps five hundred Baguti cavalry was approaching on a forest track that ran parallel to the river. It would run down to the river about two miles farther northeast at Gemma's ford. They would have to march on narrow hunting trails through rough country to reach it.

Eads had decided to march inland at once and set an ambush. If he could catch them on a track through dense forest, then he could do serious damage while they were bunched up and unable to maneuver.

The main enemy force of imps and trolls was much farther back, and Bowchief Starter was confident that they would not come close for hours.

In the coming campaign, Eads knew that he had to reduce

the enemy's cavalry advantage. He had a century of Talionese Light Horse, superb cavalry of course, but the Baguti tribesmen of the steppes were virtually born in the saddle, and there were five times as many of them. Still, Bowchief Starter had given Eads great news. There was a perfect ambush point at the ford.

Orders went out, and the men fell in. The 109th Dragons formed up for the march and took their place in the line. Eads sent them forward, with guides from the local bowmen, on a narrow country path through the woods. He himself rode ahead with a party of scouts to investigate the ambush site personally.

The way was cut up by gulleys and short rushing streams, well fed by recent rain and quite arduous to cross, especially if one was carrying equipment. The dragons enjoyed the streams, but everyone else simply got soaked and miserable. Nor was there time for any break in the pace. On better ground they virtually ran. Time was vital.

Along the way, detachments of the Kohon Yeomanry began to join them out of the woods. The yeomen were mostly retired legionaries, and they came well armed, with swords, shields, and spears. Most wore their old legion helmets, and many had breastplate and greaves.

The 109th Dragons kept up the pace, although the Purple Green complained mightily about having to march so quickly. At one stream, where the water was jetting downslope between the boulders, Relkin lost his footing and almost fell into the raging torrent. Manuel, fortunately, was right beside him on the rock. He got hold of Relkin's sleeve and hauled him upright once more.

The broketail dragon ran well. He was fit and hale, and ready for battle. He did not concern himself with odds. He felt Captain Eads was trustworthy and competent. Like most dragons, he didn't dwell too much on the ominous future, as long as the red star did not ride above the moon.

They covered the two miles in less than half an hour and arrived to find a handful of armed farmers, under the command of farmer Besson, holding the ford.

Captain Eads and his party had crossed and were up on the other side.

The ford was situated at a point where the river had cut down through some gravel-packed hills. The stream was deep but narrow, except at this ford where it broadened out across a shallow bar. On the far side loomed bluffs, set back a hundred yards from the river. A dense thicket of oak, hornbeam, and hemlock covered the ground. The trail ran on into this forest and vanished. However, Relkin could see a rider at the top of the bluffs, signaling to Captain Senshon of the 3rd Century, Second Regiment, Second Legion, the 322s, who was in command.

The armed farmers gave them a cheer as they lumbered across the ford and plunged into the gloom beneath the thicket. The path turned sharply leftward and went along upstream for perhaps a hundred paces before it curved rightward and climbed steeply up the side of the bluffs, where they were angled away from the stream for a space. As they climbed they had a steep, barren slope above on their left and an equally abrupt drop on their right, down into the thicket on the stream plain.

At the top they were met by Captain Eads, who directed them to their places for the coming ambush. Eads planned to take advantage of the Baguti's confidence that they had gone around the flank of the retreating force of Kenor bowmen, which had caused many casualties farther downstream. They were riding hard, trying to get ahead of the fleeing fleet of boats. They had a short, simple screen of scouts out in front. They weren't expecting any trouble. They were eager to seize women for which their masters would pay a heavy bounty.

The site was bisected by a wide gulley, bubbling with a dirty brown stream. The gulley split the bluff and ran down into the thicket, choked with debris, branches, driftwood, even tree trunks. Dragon Leader Turrent ordered the 109th to get down into the gulley and conceal themselves.

Dragonboys accompanied their charges. The dragons quite happily splashed in the foaming tide of rainwater.

Relkin urged Bazil to hunker down between two rounded boulders. The water ran by on either side. Relkin dug in the bank of the gulley with his dirk and his hands, and threw the soil over the dragon and rubbed it in.

Swane had completely hidden Vlok under a downed pine tree. The same tree concealed Alsebra and Byron. The Purple Green was concealed in a wallow under a hanging rock. In fact, the dragons seemed to have disappeared into the ground, so well were they concealed.

All around them now, Eads was placing his force. Kenor

bowmen were hidden on the slope above the path, ready to pour down fire on the enemy once they were packed on the climbing pathway. These were men who knew how to fade into the landscape. They lived by hunting in the wild woods. Now they vanished into cover.

The 66th Dragons had been sent upstream to hide themselves in a dense patch of hemlocks by the riverside. The river there was passable for dragons. Their mission was to cross unseen and to come down and close off the ford behind the enemy cavalry, bottling them up in the ambush.

The Talion Light Horse had been sent a mile or more down the road, hidden in a grove of birch trees. They were to provide the "clapper" on the bottle.

The two hundred legionaries, along with eighty Kohon Yeomen, were set back in the dense thickets on either side of the path, ready to join the Light Horse in the assault on the head of the enemy column.

The 109th were to wait for the signal and then to advance down the gulley, through the thicket and to throw themselves on the horsemen who would be bunched up on the path along the riverside.

Eads himself had found a vantage point up in a massive beech tree that grew on a prominence set back one hundred yards from the position of the 66th by the bank of the river. From his perch he could see the ford and the point where the path gained the top of the bluffs. Everything depended on timing and near-perfect execution of movements. Tension began to build.

Suddenly there were movements on the far side of the river. Several small, dusky men riding swift, well-fed horses, came cantering down to the stream. For a moment they paused and scanned the scene. There were signs on the ground that a considerable party had recently crossed the river. The scouts turned back and called out in triumph. Refugees were close, there would be women. Soon they would be rich!

The scouts plunged over the ford and rode on through the dense thicket. They climbed the steep path to the summit and paused there to make a cursory inspection of the surroundings. They did not take the trouble to ride off on either side very far into the thickets, just to be safe. They were too concerned with being among the first to catch up to the fleeing women.

One of them was told to ride down and report. He complained loudly, but went. The others turned and spurred their horses up the road. They saw nothing of the bowmen, nor of the soldiers hidden back in the thicket. They never even considered looking in the gulley down below.

Now further halloas went up from the scouts at the ford. Within moments, the van of the Baguti column appeared and then they came, five hundred men with greased black hair coiled in pigtails, greased beards, and mustaches, and big floppy hats of rawhide, the best light cavalry in the world. They trotted across the ford and then went confidently up the sloping path to the top of the bluff.

Eads had already sent his first messenger, riding just ahead of the enemy's scouts, up the road to the waiting Talion Light Horse. Now another messenger was dispatched to set the 66th Dragons in motion.

The first contact would come between the enemy scouts, now rushing heedlessly ahead up the road, and the charging Talionese.

When he heard the first sound of alarm from up the path, shrill screams and then a piercing alarm whistle from the Baguti, Eads gave the order for the attack.

Shrill blasts of the legion cornets suddenly resounded through the woods. The Kenor bowmen rose and opened fire on the Baguti right beneath their feet. The Bagutis reacted with rage and momentary confusion. Some pulled out their own horn bows and began to reply, others tried to press on to reach the top and get out of the confinement of the narrow path suspended over the thickets below.

And in the thickets the 109th Dragons were on the move, scrambling down the gulley and then forcing their way through the dwarf trees with their huge swords at the ready. Dragonboys danced along behind them, doing their best to keep up and not get crushed in the charge.

Now a couple of the Baguti scouts came flying down the road, whistling in alarm.

At the top of the path up the bluff the Baguti horsemen were just starting to open out their position but they never completed the maneuver, for in the next moment the Talion Light Horse came thundering down the path and pitched straight into them with sabers aloft. The impetus of their charge carried them and the van of the Baguti column back down the steeply inclined path, and bottled the enemy up there in a knot of confusion while sabers and scimitars rang off each other and men tumbled from their saddles with black fletched Kenor arrows sticking up from their bodies.

At this point, the 109th Dragons broke through the thickets on the flat and fell on the horsemen who were bunched up on the path by the riverside. Dragonswords sang and wove a tracery of death in this fight in which all the advantages seemed to accrue to the dragons and dragonboys.

More cornets had started blowing and now the legionaries and yeomen came over the crest and joined the fray on the narrow path, pulling Baguti from their saddles and killing them on the ground.

The final stroke came with the sudden appearance of the 66th Dragons, who burst out of the woods on the far side of the stream, splashed across, and fell on the rear of the Baguti, near the ford.

It had all happened in the space of a minute with near-perfect execution of the plan. In his perch in the tree, Captain Rorker Eads let out a wild whoop, climbed down, and leapt into the saddle. He hadn't dreamed the whole complex plan could work so well. But by the time he reached the scene, the fight was over. The Baguti were fierce but not foolish. After the initial clash they flowed back downhill, and finding dragons holding the ford amid the bodies of men and horses, went straight into the river and swam their horses across below the ford.

Still, they'd taken dreadful punishment. Nearly a hundred Baguti corpses were pulled out and piled up by the ford. Eads could be certain that at least as many had taken wounds and sprains. The enemy's cavalry advantage still existed, but it had been reduced. Furthermore, Eads was sure the Baguti would be far more cautious in the future. That would slow their pursuit of the settlers from Bur Lake.

Best of all from Eads's point of view, his own casualties had been light, six dead, a dozen wounded. The dragons were virtually unscathed except for an arrow here and there. The Purple Green had taken a slashing wound on one enormous leg, and Alsebra had a stab wound in her right forearm, but neither would be put out of action. Arrows rarely penetrated all the way through a dragon's thick hide.

Eads ordered the piled-up Baguti bodies set afire. Brush was pulled out, piled up high, and set aflame. Then they threw the bodies onto the flames and left a huge smoldering funeral pyre by the side of the ford.

They rode up the path and went on upriver into the country of the Kalens Valley.

CHAPTER THIRTY-SEVEN

They marched upriver singing the Kenor song, their hearts uplifted by their victory. At the bottom of the Lion's Roar, they came upon the rear guard of the refugees. All the way up the rapids the refugees were stretched out, struggling with bags and children. Possessions, prized until this moment of truth, when they had to be carried on their owner's backs, were discarded all along the way. Their boats likewise were abandoned at the bottom of the rapids.

From here on they would have to march, men, women, and children, in a desperate race for the Malgun Mountains, which lay more than a hundred miles to the east.

Eads had been in deep conversation with Bowchief Starter, who knew the land well, having hunted along the Kalens in his youth. Eads needed a place where he could make a stand. They had to buy some time to allow the refugee column to get a good start.

The Talion scouts reported that the Baguti had regrouped and were approaching at a cautious distance of two miles. They had a heavy screen of pickets out in front. The Talion scouts had had several run-ins with them.

Eads's nightmare was of being harried through open country by the Baguti, unable to stop and take a stand because of the overwhelming power coming up behind them. With only a few hundred men and dragons, he could not give battle in the open field to an enemy with one hundred trolls and thousands of imps. He would have to fight a skillful, tactical campaign.

Eads consoled himself with the thought that at the least the sharp little clash at the ford had taught the Baguti a degree of caution.

Bowchief Starter knew of two good places, the first just at the head of the Lion's Roar where the river cut through the hard Kalenstone conglomerate. The valley narrowed to a tight little notch, with precipitous cliffs of Kalenstone to either side and no good place to cross and get on the flanks of the defenders for fifteen miles either north or south.

Eads's hopes had risen instantly on hearing of this final detail. On the way through the rapids he had noted the defensibility of the spot. Now he was reassured that they could hold the place and not be flanked. He sent orders for everyone to pick up the pace, and he set the sergeants and lieutenants to keep the men moving quickly. He also ordered some of the best canoes to be carried up. He had an idea that they would be very useful during the march up the Kalens river valley. The second good place for a stand was in the marshes of Dern's Bend where the river broke into a hundred confusing little channels. Canoes would be useful in such a place.

Eads felt a tight, hard determination in his chest. He was a self-made man, risen from the slums. He had received no favors on his way to a captaincy, but had won it on the merits. Most of his combat career had been spent against the Teetol, so he naturally thought of traps and snares, the stock-in-trade of that kind of war. Now he vowed to show the enemy every trick he could muster. The odds against them were heavy. Outnumbered ten to one all told, and five to one in trolls to dragons, with a slow-moving refugee train to protect, by all rights they should soon be overwhelmed. Eads would not make it easy for them, this he swore.

Even while climbing the Lion's Roar, the men kept singing the Kenor song. There was jubilant spirit among them. Nobody could defeat well-organized legion soldiers, backed by dragons and cavalry.

Among the dragons and dragonboys there was a special elation, the sense of shared success in the first fight for the renewed 109th Marneri. In truth the 66th were just as bouyed up. They had all hammered the Baguti in the fight by the ford. A few minutes of such fighting created an immense bond between dragons and consequently between dragonboys. They willingly put their shoulders behind the loads being lugged up the rapids. They whistled and sang as they helped push and carry the refugees through the mud and across the bare slippery rocks. Everyone was singing.

Happiest of all, perhaps, was Dragon Leader Turrent. He had faced down his fear of enemy cavalry, and had overcome it and fought as well as anyone. He was half certain that it had been his sword thrust that had taken down one

Baguti chieftain. In the confusion, the whirling dance of men, horses, and dragons, he hadn't seen the man fall since he'd been too busy ducking Alsebra's great blade as it whirred over him. Swords of all sizes glittered and rang, the enemy screamed as they were cut down, wounded horses screamed as well. Blood and vomit and the stench of guts, the fight had been terrifying, and yet he had responded with his own savagery, plus the skill of years of training. And the dragons had been magnificent! He'd never seen a whole squadron in action like that, ten dragons, swords whirling as they cut into the Baguti, sundering men, horses, everything in their path.

He had fought with these dragons and dragonboys, sharing in the peril and the victory. He had seen them fight, all the boys had fought well, wielding their rapid-fire Cunfshon crossbows with deadly accuracy. Even little Jak had shown himself to be a demon on the battlefield, ducking along beside the great hulk of Rusp, covering the rear and the flanks.

Turrent was bonded to them now, and they to him. Even though he would keep them on their toes, he would never feel the same about them when he surveyed their improper kit and unshined metal.

If Turrent was the happiest among them, it was little Jak who had the greatest play of emotions after the brief little fight on the riverbank.

Jak had killed his first man that day, his arrow taking a Baguti in the throat. It had been his third arrow of the engagement. He had watched the man topple, then ducked a scimitar aimed at his head, and scampered sideways to stay clear of Rusp's right foot. The sword had whistled overhead, and the Baguti had paid for his proximity to the dragon. Then Jak stood over the man he'd killed and found the sight both elating, and somehow sickening. In death the Baguti man seemed much the same as any man. He could even have been Jak's unknown father, except that Jak was sure his father was no steppe nomad. But equally certain was the fact that the dead nomad had been someone's son and maybe someone's father. Only now he lay dead on the field with Jak's arrow in his throat.

And it had been about that moment that the fight had ended. The nomads bellied into the water. Escape from those terrible dragon blades was all they could think of. Jak would remember the moment all his life.

Relkin had been nearby and had seen the shine of victory in the younger boy's eyes. Relkin was only a few years older, but already he had lost that shine.

Still, it had been a complete victory, and Relkin shouted with the rest of them. On the surface he was with them. Underneath he seethed with anxiety about the mysteries of destiny and Arneis, which seemed to be where they were bound to go. And at last, there was a disgust with the leavings of war, the twisted, crumpled forms, the viscera, the sundered limbs and scattered heads. Relkin felt strongly that men should never be placed in a position where they must fight dragons.

And yet it was a victory, and Relkin knew they would need many victories in the days to come if they were to live to see the lands of the Argonath on the far side of the mountains.

They climbed the Lion's Roar, and at the top they began fortifying the narrow gap where the river plunged through a jagged cut in the hard dark stone. It was a natural gate. On either side were cliffs, cut from the same hard Kalenstone.

They felled what trees they could find a little farther upstream and floated them down to the beginning of the rapids, where the dragons took turns fishing them out. The trunks and branches were then twisted and woven together into a dense, difficult barrier.

Meanwhile, the Kenor bowmen were at fletcher, and with them were those dragonboys who didn't have wounded dragons to tend.

Bazil had come through the scrap by the ford almost without injury. A horse had kicked him on the breastplate, and an arrow had found a chink in the joboquin, but had not penetrated the hide. Relkin had immediately extracted the arrow and cleaned the wound with Old Sugustus. The dragon felt nothing, and he always complained of the sting of Sugustus disinfectant, so Relkin knew the wound was trivial.

Relkin made arrows with the rest of the dragonboys while the dragon enjoyed himself standing up to the waist in fast-moving water and grabbing the small oak trees that were being floated down from the woodcutting parties.

Other dragons, and most of the men, including farmers from Bur Lake, were hard at work adding new material to the barrier, which was now continuous across the gap on the southern side. In form, it was a monstrous tangle of tree limbs, rocks, and brush. On the northern side there were still some gaps, but they were in the process of being plugged. The Purple Green and Chektor were moving some rocks into position to buttress the barrier on that side.

Eads and Bowchief Starter surveyed all this with some satisfaction. The enemy was coming on, but slowly. The Talion scouts reported some Baguti down at the bottom of the Lion's Roar, but the main column was still a few miles back. They would not face serious attack until the morning. There was plenty of time for Eads to fortify this place so that his five hundred could hold it against thousands.

The enemy would have to flank him, marching many miles in either direction to find a reasonable route up the Kalenstone cliffs. And that would buy time for the long column of refugees, tramping up the Kalens on the south bank. He had armed as many of the women and old men as he could. From Widfield they'd taken all the field implements, scythes, rakes, forks. None would go easily into the horror of captivity in the breeding pens, but they had to keep ahead of the oncoming enemy army.

Eads passed the smithy and nodded approvingly. They were fashioning spearheads from pots and pans abandoned by the refugees along the path by the rapids. Nearby, men were splitting and sawing spear shafts out of some of the better oak trees they'd found. When they were cut, they were rolled in hot ashes and heated over a fire to harden the wood. They were then fitted to the spearheads and finally placed aside for inspection. With one hundred trolls or more to fight, they would need a great many spears. His dragons would be outnumbered, so the men would have to help in dispatching trolls. Men with spears could do the job, though it was risky.

Both Eads and his men knew that they would have to take such risks. The enemy would not present them with any more easy victories. The enemy knew that they had dragons. The enemy also knew that they had more than enough trolls to overwhelm them.

All through the night, the scene at the notch above the Lion's Roar was alive with activity. Behind the wall of woven oak limbs, they built platforms for archers. In front of it, where possible, they dug a ditch.

Men collected rocks for the dragons to throw. A dragon

could serve as a crude sort of catapult, hurling rocks as heavy as a man over this sort of barrier.

Eads met with his officers and the leaders of the refugee column, just as the moon was rising above the trees. The night was clear, the stars bright and hard. The river roared in the chasm below their position and threw up a mist in that direction.

Captains Senshon, Deft, and Retiner stood to one side with Dragon leader Turrent, Sergeant Quertin, and Bowchief Starter behind them. Opposing them in a looser group were the refugee leaders, landed gentry for the most part, self-elected leaders. From Bur Lake there were Farmer Besson, a red-faced man of fifty years and massive countenance, plus the obstreperous Tursturan Genver, who owned a large estate near South Bur Lake. From Upper Lake, twice as far away, there was Hopper Reabody, a small, wiry man, nearly bald, who favored a suit of green leather and boots in an old-fashioned, knee-high mode.

Eads laid out his plan, turning to Bowchief Starter for occasional details concerning the terrain of the Kalens Valley. The refugees were to march straight up the south side of the river where the best paths existed. Thirty Talion troopers would go with them to provide a covering cavalry screen. Other than that, they would have to defend themselves if the Baguti caught up.

"But that is terrible, you would leave us naked to the enemy!" shouted Tursturan Genver.

"I can spare you no more than the thirty Talionese. I may even have to call them back in case of a real emergency. I will need every man to hold the enemy here for a few days."

Genver huffed and puffed.

"But your mission is to ensure our protection, sir!"

"Which I can best do by holding the enemy here for perhaps three days. If we can win three days here, then I think we can certainly beat them to the mountains."

Genver and Reabody were visibly unconvinced. Eads pressed. "Your people can be eighty or ninety miles east of here by then." They blanched. His tone grew firmer. "You must push them. We have sent messages ahead to the farms of Midvale and Wattel, and there will be some food from them, but for now everyone must march on empty stomachs and not let up.

"Once they winkle us out of this position, we shall have

to fall back up the river. This will not be easy in the face of their superior numbers. We will need every man we've got to hold them off while we do this. We will then delay them in the woods, but not for long. There are no easily fortified positions there. Our next good chance of a blockade will come at Dern's Bend, in the swamps."

"Ah yes," blustered Genver, "the swamps. You want us to make our way through the center of the swamps using nothing but a trader's trail."

"We have a guide who knows the swamps well. The enemy will not be so blessed. Furthermore, he will still have to deal with our forces, and we will slow him considerably in the swamps."

"I have heard many evil things of the swamps. They are said to be haunted by dwarves and monsters from out of the mists of time." Hopper Reabody had a thin voice almost permanently raised in complaint.

"Such creatures would be well-advised to remain in the mists. I saw the good folk from Bur Lake go marching away with scythes and forks over their shoulders. They looked fierce enough to take a place in the battle line."

This upset Farmer Besson. "My women folk are not bred for fighting like common men!"

"That may well be, Citizen, but I expect they'll fight rather than surrender to the enemy."

"I do not understand why we didn't go up the Bur Valley to High Lake."

"We did not go that way, Citizen, because my men and dragons will be needed on the other side of those mountains. There will be a great battle over there, I believe."

"What?" Genver purpled. "Are you suggesting there will be warfare in the Argonath?"

"How strong is our force at the High Pass? How ready can they be when the onslaught comes? I am neither optimist nor pessimist, but I am a professional soldier. I must plan for all eventualities, even the very worst."

Genver, Reabody, and Besson wore a look of mutual shock and remained unusually mute.

Eads seized the opportunity.

"Well, gentlemen, I hope we will be reunited once more within the week. I expect to see you on the shore of Lake Wattel. Captain Retiner has detailed thirty troopers to go with you."

Farmer Besson was confused, however. "I don't understand where all this is leading."

"I thought it was obvious, sir. We head for the Kohon
Pass. It's our only sure way through the mountains now."

"But the High Pass?"

"Will be under attack, good Farmer Besson. If there are
five thousand imps pursuing us here, think of how many
there will be marching up the Lis."

Besson swallowed heavily. He had heard the stories concerning the size of the enemy host.

"But how can we cross there? It's too high," said Genver.

"It is high, but not impassable. It is long and arduous, but
if it is a choice between that and death, I am confident which
one we will choose."

" 'Tis forty miles through snow and bare rock. We will
lose many of the older folk."

Eads was nodding, his features grew somber.

"We will lose many of them all along the march. In truth,
gentlemen, you delayed your departure by much too long.
You could have been to the High Pass by now."

Tursturan Genver spluttered.

"The Bur, we should go up the Bur to High Lake."

"There are as many portages on the Bur as there are on
the Kalens, actually more. There is no safety at High Lake,
and with more than a thousand women in our party, we can
be certain this enemy army will never give up."

"We can cross the lake and go down to Dalhousie on the
Argo."

"Gentlemen, my men and dragons will be needed in
Arneis. We go for the Kohon Pass."

"You can't be serious. You're suggesting that the enemy
will take the High Pass!" Tursturan Genver refused to believe it.

"Let us hope it does not happen, but I must work with that
eventuality in mind."

At length the refugee leaders left, and were rowed upriver
in the canoes that had been carried up the Lion's Roar.

CHAPTER THIRTY-EIGHT

The next day was one of slow-building tension. Baguti cavalry were seen some ways down the Lion's Roar in the morning. By mid-afternoon, Talion scouts reported heavy masses of imp moving up the trail toward them. Among them were squads of tall, monstrous trolls.

The dragons peered over the barrier, long necks craning, eyes straining to glimpse these great brutes.

The trolls came into view, immense things like bears crossed with men. Over their shoulders they carried great axes and shields.

"Not so big, after all," sniffed Vlok.

"How long do they have to be cooked to make them edible?" said the Purple Green, who was always seeking some variety in the monotonous, though ample, legion diet. The other dragons rumbled with amusement.

Eads had set out small ambush parties of bowmen, and by late afternoon the men and dragons at the barricade could hear, one after the other, a small fracas taking place at each ambush site.

The bowmen came drifting back shortly thereafter. Soon the last few scouts came in. The word was that the enemy were massed not more than two hundred yards down the path, where it ran through a jumble of huge boulders, pieces of the Kalenstone that had been broken off and pushed downslope by the river's erosive power.

They waited. Eads ordered kalut brewed and distributed. He and the other captains moved around the position, crossing the river by canoe, showing themselves to the men, working to keep up morale.

Everyone knew what to do. Everyone knew what to expect. The tension built anyway. They knew they were enormously outnumbered and on their own. Still the enemy held off. Men began to think that they might be spared the battle that day. A few murmured prayers of thanks to the Great Mother. The sun declined in the west toward the distant Kontok Hills. Flocks of waterfowl came winging by, heading east. The men watched them with envious eyes.

And then with a ringing blast it came. A hundred horns blared, and the enemy's drums thundered. Up the steep paths came a swarm of squat, hideous imps, made huge by the light of the setting sun behind them. Their war cry, shrill and piercing, rang off the crags. Their black banners bore the red hand of Axoxo.

With them were squads of skilled bowmen in the black uniform of Padmasa. Now arrows were whistling over the barricade and even coming through it where the branches were few.

The defenders held their fire, waiting for the order. Men spat, chewed their lips, and made bitter little jokes.

Beyond the imps came trolls, nine feet high, enormous axes over their shoulders. They came in squads of ten, one after the other. The horns screamed. The drums hammered.

"Fire!" came the order at last, and the bowmen and the dragonboys rose and sent a volley of shafts into the advancing horde. Imps fell along the line, but were scarcely noticed by the onrushing mass. More arrows flew among them. And now the dragons set forward and seized boulders from the piles that had been collected. With massive grunts of effort, they sent these heavy rocks flying over the barricade and down among the onrushing imps. Shrieks of terror and brief screams came from the throats of the imp mass as the rocks fell among them. But paradoxically it only caused the imps to hurry their feet. They came to the barricade and scrambled up like a tide of human crabs to go shield to shield with the defenders.

Bazil, Vlok, and the Purple Green were set to defend a V-shaped salient on the south side of the river, where the barricade thrust forward to encompass a projecting finger of higher ground made by a slab of Kalenstone. Bazil was set on the point, with Relkin behind him. Vlok and Swane were to the left, the Purple Green with Manuel was to the right. Each dragon was spaced twenty to thirty feet from the next to allow room for the wielding of the dragonswords.

Set between each dragon, crouched down and waiting, were pairs and trios of men from the 322. They were armed with heavy spears in addition to their swords and rectangular shields.

Set back from the line as a mobile reserve were the Kohon Yeomen, forty or so on either bank of the stream. These were older men, ex-legionaries, for the most part. They had families and farms in Kenor. They were fighting for their homes, but they would lack some of the staying power of active legionaries.

In addition, the Talion horsemen were busy out on the south flank, maneuvering to keep the Baguti in view. The nomad cavalry was riding for the south passage over the Kalenstone. The Talion Light Horse would have to block them if they could.

On the flanks were small squads of horsemen and Kenor bowmen. Infiltrating parties of imps that scaled the cliffs were intercepted and broken up and hurled off the cliff face.

But now the imps came close to the top of the barrier, and the men and the dragons stepped up to meet them. Digal Turrent leapt to his feet blowing the cornet. The first imps to reach the top came face-to-face quite suddenly with ten-foot-tall dragon forms, looming over them, huge shields bearing the flower of Marneri, terrible great swords screaming down.

Screams of "Gazak!" rang from impish throats and were then cut off in the sounds of steel and war. The scream of "Gazaki" went up all the way back down the line, huge filthy dragons there were, with terrible swords for slaying the imp. But still they came on, their stomachs filled with the black drink, their brutish hearts racing and their savage minds filled only with the urge to kill.

The dragonswords rose and fell, and imps were scattered, sundered, hurled away in fragments.

The fighting at the salient over the kalenstone was fierce from the beginning.

A dozen imps rushed up the barricade and converged on Bazil's position at the point. Ecator flashed in a long forehand sweep. An imp's head flew away like a shuttlecock at rackets. Others flattened themselves and came on crawling like beasts.

Relkin kept up a swift, steady fire, and here and there his shafts struck through imp armor and roused a shriek. Still they came on.

Bazil made smooth, continuous strokes with the great

sword, forehands followed by backhands. Each time he sundered one or more imps from their lives. Arrows rang off his helmet and stuck impotently in the joboquin. One struck him in the forehead but bounced off the thick bone, leaving just a jarring pain and a cut that spattered hot dragon blood across the rocks.

For a moment his stroke went wide and ended weakly, cutting down into the trunk of a small oak tree, piled into the barricade.

An imp cut inside his shield. It tried to stab him in the thigh, and he was forced to give a step back, but this also let him bring the tail mace to play. His famous broken tail cracked, and the mace struck down upon the imp's helmet with a flash of sparks; the imp toppled.

The sight of the dragon's blood had raised concern in Relkin's eyes. The dragon clacked his jaws together.

"Just a nick, already healing."

More imps were coming over the top of the barricade, and Relkin was forced to engage with a swart creature wearing a black pot helmet with a spike in the top. The imp wielded a short, heavy sword with some rude skill.

Relkin met the imp's sword with his own and held him. The imp snarled something in its harsh tongue and spat at him. Their swords rang off each other again and again. Then with a sly maneuver, the imp came in close and forced Relkin back, shield to shield. Although several inches shorter than Relkin, the imp was horribly strong, and Relkin was forced out of his chosen position.

Another imp was to his right. He caught this foe's sword on his shield, but it was a heavy blow and he was driven almost to his knees.

Freed of Relkin's attentions, the first imp had turned inside and was hacking at Bazil's right hamstring.

The dragon jerked his shield back to cover, but that let an imp in front of him get inside. A sword cut upward to stab the dragon through the gizzards and by a miracle was deflected by the studs on the joboquin. The imp got no second chance, for Bazil smote him with the hilt of Ecator the next second and then tore him in half with his hind feet.

Meanwhile Relkin feinted and dodged and took advantage of luck when the imp on his right lost its footing for a moment. Relkin sprang close and brought his sword down on the imp's shoulder. The sword buried itself in the flesh and dark blood gushed forth. The imp gave a shriek, dropped to one knee, reached up and seized hold of Relkin's boot, and jerked him off his feet.

One powerful imp hand seized him by the throat. The creature rolled on top of him, even though his sword was still embedded in its shoulder. Blood poured down on him as the imp crushed his windpipe. He was too strong and heavy to throw off.

Relkin scrabbled for his dirk and found it. With a prayer to ancient Asgah, god of war, he stabbed upward, aiming for a space below the vest of mail worn by the imp. On the second try he struck home, and the dirk entered below the rib cage and went deep. With a groan, the imp lost its grip, subsided, and fell away.

Relkin was already scrambling to his feet, only just in time to evade another sword blow. Now, however, he was without a sword for his own was still buried in the dead imp at his feet. The foe laughed insanely and came on with its own blade whirling above its head. And was stopped by a spear lancing in from the left, taking the imp in the side, just above the hip. One of the men of the 322s was there, foot on the imp's chest, heaving the spear free.

"I thank you," said Relkin.

"'Tweren't nothing you wouldn't do for me," said the soldier, now with his spear up and in the face of the next imp on the barricade.

Relkin wasted no time in retrieving his own sword and getting back into his position on the barricade. Another imp was upon him. Their swords rang on each other. Relkin's arm was starting to turn numb, and the fight was just begun.

And then the dragon's tail mace came down and caught the imp in the middle of the back. The imp was flung to his knees, and Relkin's sword was deep in his neck the next moment.

Bazil swung Ecator in another back-and-forth combination, and two more imps were bisected and scattered in a shower of viscera.

And then the battle rage faded for the moment as the imps fell back. More horns were blaring. Other imps were coming through the mass of those retreating, and with them came trolls.

The dragons hissed to themselves. The trolls came on and clumsily stepped up onto the barricade. This made them unhappy. They much disliked the loss of contact with the ground. Trolls had notoriously poor balance. One, in fact, toppled over and rolled back down and knocked over two more who fell into several others, causing chaos for a moment in front of the Purple Green and Alsebra. The dragons seized up boulders and hurled them down on the fallen trolls.

Dragon mirth was short-lived, however. There were too many trolls for that, and they kept coming, urged on by the blaring horns and thundering drums. Still complaining and promising to eat pesky imps for supper, the trolls climbed. Around their feet like hounds around hunters came packs of imps, and among these were men, the officers who ran the imps, men in the black of Padmasa.

One of these vaulted over the top of the barricade on the heels of four imps. Ecator flashed and cut down two of the imps. Relkin put an arrow into another and then ducked behind a branch of oak as a black arrow sang past his head. The enemy skirmisher leapt for him, sword in hand.

Relkin met him sword on sword, but the man was twice his size and heaved him backward right off the barricade. Relkin landed, staggered, and recovered, then got his sword up in time to meet the enemy's. He deflected a killing thrust and used a low slice to force the fellow to lift his feet. Relkin's shield struck inside the other's and he got a thrust home between mail and hauberk. He saw the man's face go pale, then he was down and Relkin was pulling his sword free.

He looked up and saw a great troll, easily nine and a half feet high go shield to shield with the Broketail. The troll wielded an immense ax, which the dragon met with his shield.

Ecator swung, and the troll raised his shield to block the anticipated blow, but instead Bazil shoved forward with his own shield and brought the tail mace over with a whistling crack to ring off the troll's heavy iron helmet.

The troll staggered backward and came in perfect range for Ecator, whistling across and sinking deep into the troll's torso, which collapsed at once.

More trolls were there, one was swinging the great ax, Bazil dodged aside, but still felt some of the ax blow ringing off his right greave. His shield absorbed another blow, from his left. Ecator struck back, both trolls were knocked sideways. An imp ran in, Relkin's arrow missed, and it tried to get Bazil's hamstring. Relkin flung himself on it, heaved back the misshapen head, and cut its throat with his sword.

There was a huge shriek of rage and pain on their right, and Relkin saw the Purple Green lift a troll up bodily overhead and throw it straight into two more of its fellows who were climbing over the crest of the barricade.

Bazil deflected more clumsy blows with the giant axes, but then one troll got a full two-handed swing, and Bazil's shield was hewn through, above the arm grips. The shield was held fast by the ax stuck into it, more trolls were coming. Bazil unshipped the shield and swung Ecator with both hands. The great sword clove through the troll's shield.

Now they were even. The troll came again and they grappled, hand to hand. The troll kicked Bazil in the stomach and tried to bite his muzzle. The dragon kicked back, then gave a heave and flung the troll aside, knocking down a pair of imps like ninepins.

Two men from the 322s were positioned perfectly, their spears thrust upward, and buried themselves in the troll's vitals. It gave a hoarse scream and died, black blood gushing from its mouth. The imps were just getting to their feet when it fell on them crushing them into the torn and shattered oak trees of the barricade.

The horns were blaring again, the light was dimming, the sun was down behind the hills.

The trolls and imps were pulling back, ebbing away from the barricade. It was over; they had survived the first attack.

CHAPTER THIRTY-NINE

The next day dawned with lowering clouds that opened within the hour and poured forth a cold, constant deluge that lasted almost the entire day.

The enemy mounted a few probing attacks, but with so much water, so much mud, and the barricade already proven to be a tough nut to crack, he did not engage with full force.

For once, the men and dragonboys did not complain about the rain, even though it soaked through everything and made it impossible to keep more than a single fire going for the cooks. As long as it rained, the enemy would hold off, and they would regain their strength.

When the rain finally ceased in the late afternoon, they stood to at once and waited anxiously for the expected attack. It did not come. The enemy had given up on that day altogether. All night they heard the sounds of hammering and constant motion from lower down the Lion's Roar. Great fires blazed down there, which caused some wonderment since all the woods were sopping wet. The next morning dawned brightly and soon brought on the first assault. The enemy had built crude shelters to protect their archers, and these were brought forward until they were positioned just beyond the range of a dragon throw. Bazil and Chektor tried to hurl smaller rocks, the size of a man's head, at them but fell short. The enemy archers set up a constant ranging fire that made the barricade a dangerous, difficult place to stand. To show one's head above the edge of the tangled mass of broken oak limbs and trunks was to draw an arrow in an instant. The range was too great for the little Cunfshon bows of the dragonboys, but the Kenor bowmen dueled with the enemy archers, their heavy composite bows snapping loudly as they drove their projectiles off and away.

Soon the enemy attacked with full force. Mixed parties of imp and troll, driven on by the men in the black uniform of

Padmasa surged up to the barricade, climbed on the torn and tattered oak limbs, and engaged the dragons and men behind it. Attack after attack shattered there and fell back. Twelve trolls were slain and a hundred imps. Not one dragon was killed and only a few suffered wounds.

The enemy paused for three hours and tried again in the waning daylight, as on the first day. Still he could not break the line. Despite the overwhelming advantage in numbers, the defense was adamant.

For a third night, they slept by the barricade. The enemy worked ceaselessly down below.

Captain Eads had several rafts built earlier. Now as the surgeons finished with the wounded men, they were loaded aboard the rafts and hauled upstream by local farmers' plow horses.

Among the dragons there were a lot of cuts, abrasions, and bruises, but only a few serious wounds. Two dragons were disabled: Tenebrak of the 109th and Ninu of the 66th. Of the pair, Tenebrak was the more serious case. A troll ax had hacked deep into his side, breaking ribs, opening the body cavity. The surgeons had stitched him back together and poured medicinal honey into the wound to dry out any deep infection. The use of sugar in this kind of deep wound was a popular remedy in the Empire of the Rose. Old Sugustus was applied to the surface tissues, and then the wounds were bandaged. Finally Tenebrak was loaded onto a raft and sent upstream. Ninu had a broken right forelimb and some serious slashes from imp swords. Ninu was a hard green, a breed with a legendary disdain for pain. The surgeons, with the aid of the strongest men in the unit, set the immense broken bone, treated his wounds with disinfectant, and set him to marching upriver on the trail.

That night the skies clouded over, and a merciful downpour began two hours before dawn. The enemy would be slow to attack in such conditions. The sun rose as a dim grey light lost behind heavy clouds.

Captain Eads was roused from his tent by the arrival of Captain Retiner of the Talion Horse. They conferred over a cup of kalut, and then Eads ordered the retreat.

They had finally been flanked. A party of perhaps a thousand imps, with Baguti cavalry and trolls, had climbed the Kalenstone scarp some ten miles to the south and was advancing on them slowly. They were being held up by the rain and mud and the Talion Light Horse.

Eads sent out the bowmen and some of the yeomanry to help the Talion Light Horse while the rest of the men rose, ate cold porridge with strong, hot kalut, and set out eastward, moving as quietly as possible.

A few miles farther upriver, there was the last usable ford for forty miles. The trail on the south side of the river was much the better one. On the north, there were a series of sharp gulleys and steep-sided little hillocks, which went on for miles.

At the barricades, they left behind a handful of skirmishers who kept the fires going and sniped at the enemy in their shelters down below.

This was enough to keep the enemy from pressing things for several hours, and it was not until almost noon that he discovered the truth and sent up a full-scale assault. The skirmishers slipped away upriver on foot and by canoe, and with them went the last of the Talion Light Horse and the bowmen, who had been harassing the Baguti cavalry.

The rain eased up in the afternoon and settled into a constant thin drizzle. Now it became a footrace through a waterlogged world of mud and steaming vegetation.

Eads's men had a good lead, and the Talion Light Horse had done a brilliant job of delaying the Baguti. The Talions were tiring, however. Eads had already recalled the thirty men from the guard on the refugee column, rotating out thirty others who were the most exhausted, wounded, and in need of a rest.

The Baguti were still probing cautiously, but Eads knew they would change soon, because now they could range ahead of his force, outflanking them to the south. Still the nature of that country, a tangled, wild woodland of oak, beech, and hemlock, would slow them some. He kept most of the Kenor men out on the flank, working with the Talions to set up small, deadly ambushes of Baguti outriders.

The main mass of the enemy marched straight up the south side of the river behind them, confident that in time he would catch them and crush them in the open with his vastly superior numbers.

From a canoe, Eads had personally measured the enemy's speed of march with his long glass. He reckoned the enemy to be marching a little slower than his own men, about twice as quickly as the refugee column, now about sixty miles ahead of them, negotiating the beginnings of the marshes.

There the Kalen's main channel swung wide in a flat bend, and there were many smaller channels and cut-off ox-bow lakes, lost among a wilderness of marsh.

There they would turn and make another stand, guerrilla style.

CHAPTER FORTY

The marshland was a wilderness of another kind where purple-headed reeds, ten feet high, formed the world. The wind made ripples in the sea of stems, flashing bright sparkles from sunlit leaves. Below the purple was mud, narrow river channels and winding trails. It was a good terrain for guerrilla war.

Four dragons, four boys, Dragon Leader Turrent, and twenty men from the 322s crouched in ambush in the reeds overlooking a trail. Coming toward them slowly was a party of Baguti, riding in single file on the narrow trail. Gnats whined about them and occasionally bit. Dragons were impervious to mere gnats but the dragonboys and the men were not, and there was much slapping and quiet cursing.

Bazil hefted his shield and felt reassured by its familiar mass. The boy had done well, getting the shield repaired even under the chaotic conditions of the retreat. Without the shield he'd felt nervous, almost unnatural. It had come to be almost a part of him.

It was another example of the power in the things men made, things that changed one's life and became so important that one could hardly live without them. The Purple Green sneered at Bazil's dependence, but Bazil could see the wild dragon slowly but surely growing addicted to the power of the sword and the shield.

And now the shield was good again, perhaps not perfect, the repair had been hurried, but he was confident it would turn aside spears and lances and even troll axes. With a good shield and with Ecator in his hand, the broketail dragon was ready for anything.

Relkin returned, after reconnoitering the trail to their left, ahead of the Baguti. He reported to Turrent and then joined his dragon.

"It's all clear to our left. We just hit them hard and turn up the trail to get away."

"Good."

Bazil craned his neck and was afforded a view across the reeds. Close by, to the right, they came to an end by the river's edge. There, invisible beneath the reeds, lay the trail.

He felt a nudge in his side. It was the Purple Green.

"Broken-tailed friend, have you considered my idea?"

"Concerning the Baguti horses?"

"Of course. We will take one, only one, and roast it. The men can have all the others that we capture."

"The men will not allow it."

"The men will not? Who are they, Gods? We are free dragons. We fight for these men, and we need to eat something interesting once in a while. Horse makes good eating, and I want to try it this human way, burning it with flame. This is a great secret that our ancestors had but that was lost somewhere along the way."

"You think old Glabadza roasted his meat?"

"Why not, now that I have tasted human cooked meats, I understand very well. It much improves the flavor. Now horse is good even as I used to eat it, with the skin on. It was a treat, like caribou in season, or the aurochs. Aurochs are rare for a good reason. Too tasty to be anything else. But I always looked forward to horse."

"The men regard horses as sacred; they do not allow dragon to eat horse. This they teach us from very early days."

"Taught! Instructed! Manipulated if you ask me. Anything that you want to do, they refuse to allow."

"They feed us well. We fight the great enemy. We retire on this land. Really, there is not choice for battledragon. Cannot survive in the wild, except in the sea, of course, but they keep us away from the sea. Maybe cannot even survive in the sea. Certainly the food would be just as monotonous."

"Just one horse. Already dead horse. We quarter it and take it with us. We not have to kill one later that way."

Bazil sighed, knowing what he was getting into.

"All right, we take one if one killed and we have the time."

The Purple Green bobbed his huge head and clacked his jaws. In his time, the great wild drake had eaten an entire herd of mountain ponies, starting with the stallion and proceeding to the foals. He was looking forward to trying his favorite prey in the human manner, roasted over fire until sizzling.

He caught Manuel looking curiously at him. The dragonboy was always studying him! The Purple Green snapped. "Boy stare too much, he go blind. Get dragon-freeze for good!"

Manuel was undeterred. "You're plotting something, I know it. I know the way you snap your jaws like that. Why won't you let me know what it is?"

"It not concern dragonboy, it only dragon business."

Alsebra, the pale green freemartin, moved closer.

"They are coming, I see them."

Bazil and the Purple Green kept their heads down. The freemartin had the best eyes in the squadron. If she had seen the Baguti, then the Baguti were there.

The Purple Green made sure his legion issue sword was loose in its giant scabbard. He squatted back on his huge haunches and assumed a bipedal position while he worked his shield free of the shoulder straps and slipped it onto his left forelimb. Then he crouched lower and brought out his legion issue sword. Manuel was beside him, fussing with the straps at the back of the joboquin.

Bazil leaned his head close to the wild one. "You do that without thinking now. You are legion dragon, wild friend."

The Purple Green hissed derisively even as Manuel finished tightening the straps.

A group of soldiers scuttled by, bent over, heading down to the river, their spears carried low.

Dragon Leader Turrent appeared out of the reeds.

"We go, after these men. Quietly now."

No one had to tell the dragons to move quietly. Despite their great bulk, they were able to slide through the reeds with hardly a sound. In places, they went down on all fours. At muddy wallows, they wriggled across and lifted dragonboys over the worst places. By the time they reached the edge of the trail, they were covered in mud and so were their joboquins.

Then they were close enough to smell the enemy horses. A few steps closer and those with sensitive noses could smell the Baguti. They accelerated, huge feet digging into the soft ground, and now they could see their target. They surged forward the last few feet and erupted out of the reeds and onto the Baguti.

For the nomads, it was a complete surprise. The reeds parted, and a swarm of great armored Gazaki came lurching toward them. Horses panicked, reared, screamed in terror. Men were thrown, Baguti riders were tossed off their horses, an unheard of thing. The rest fought to subdue their mounts and draw their bows.

Arrows from dragonboy crossbows were already dropping riders, and then the dragons were on them.

Ecator flashed high and came around in a roundhouse chop, and the first Baguti was decapitated in an instant. The riderless horse bolted away.

A Baguti horse, riderless, fell into the river. Others were riding their mounts out into the stream to try and swim them out of range of those terrible swords. Alsebra was in the water among them, however, and "Undaunt" whirled about her claiming heads, bisecting men freely.

The Purple Green had slain two Baguti and a horse, his sword killing it instantly, almost removing the head and the neck in a single blow.

It was not the only horse down. Vlok had killed one Baguti with a clumsy overhand. The sword had cut the rider in half and bit deep into the horse's spine.

Vlok stared down stupidly at the poor beast until Alsebra splashed ashore and took the horse's head with Undaunt.

"Put the animal out of its misery next time, Vlok," she hissed.

The Baguti were gone, riding hard back down the trail, their cries swelling with grief and rage. There were damnable Gazaki, great green and brown Gazaki in the reeds. They most disliked this aspect of the campaign. It was unnerving to men who had spent their lives as ruthless raiders from the steppes. It was they who struck terror in others, who killed at will and took slaves. But against Gazak, no man could stand and thus they rode back in shame.

"Send up the thrice-damned trolls," they called. Then they wept the savage tears of barbarians for their dead.

The enemy column convulsed and a party of trolls thirty strong was sent lumbering up the trail. Two hundred imps went with them. But the ambush party was already moving rapidly away through the reeds to another, secret trail, and

Bazil and the Purple Green were each carrying half of one of the small Baguti horses.

Dragon Leader Turrent said nothing, although he did not like it. Technically it was not against any known regulation. Dragons, in fact, were allowed to eat the corpses of trolls and other wild animals that came their way while on active service. Troll was incredibly tough, of course, and dragons were not overly fond of it. Although once it was cooked thoroughly, it was reasonable and had something of the flavor of mutton.

Turrent decided to remain silent. If the dragons wanted to carry half a dead horse apiece around the country, they could—although it was making a shocking mess of their already muddy joboquins. He would expect everything cleaned to perfection by the next parade.

CHAPTER FORTY-ONE

They marched along hidden trails across the reed plain and eventually up into a forest of aspens and birch where they came upon a campsite set up by some of the Talion cavalry troopers. A big fire was going, and there were a half-dozen cooks at work.

It was announced they were to rest while some food was boiled up. They would probably stay at this camp for the night and move on in the morning.

Captain Eads was out with another ambush party, on a bold effort to scatter the head of the enemy's main column where the trail passed between two areas thick with quicksand. Eads hoped to gain a few more precious hours delay for the column of terrified refugees a few miles ahead, stumbling desperately eastward, toward the mountains.

Bazil, Vlok, and Alsebra were all near exhaustion after the ambush and a twelve-mile march. After peeling off filthy joboquins, they lay down among some tumbled boulders and went straight to sleep. The Purple Green had other concerns, however. He took his sword and went out into the nearby trees. He returned after a while with several huge bundles of wood, which he persuaded a soldier to light for him, he having no skill in the making of a fire.

Eventually he had a blaze, and while it burned down to a pile of hot embers, the Purple Green hacked the two halves of the horse into legs, ribs, and butts, and slid his sword through a leg and set it over the heat. Soon it smoked and sizzled, and the smell of roasting flesh wafted over the temporary camp.

Almost instantly the dragons awoke. One by one their nostrils twitched a moment, and then their great predatory eyes snapped open, their heads stirred, and they licked the air a few times, tasting the strange, sweet-smelling meat smoke.

Dragonboys stirred next, disturbed by the smell and the sudden movements of huge bodies.

Very quickly, the Purple Green found himself with an audience of three wyverns who stared at the roasting leg of horse with fascinated eyes.

The Purple Green merely grunted in reply.

"That smell very good. You will share some with us?" said Vlok.

"I carried this meat all afternoon. Now you want me to feed you. Are you fresh from the egg and in need of feeding? Where is your mother then?"

Vlok was puzzled by this response.

"I am Vlok, you know me."

The Purple Green nodded.

"But it is horse, is it not?" Alsebra spoke up.

"Yes, it is the horse we carried."

"I was raised to care for horses," she said. "I will not eat them."

The Purple Green nodded as if he had expected this response from her.

"They are boiling noodles," he said with a clack of the jaws.

And it was true, there were four great cauldrons boiling on the campfires.

"I would like to eat some," said Vlok.

"But you did not carry it all the way from the ambush in the plain of reeds."

Vlok fell silent. He had not. In fact, if anything he had scorned them for bothering.

Bazil leaned forward with tingling nostrils.

The boy was suddenly at his side.

"Alsebra's right, Baz, you shouldn't eat horse. Men don't do it, unless they're starving."

"That is because men ride on horses. Men have a different relationship to this animal. To dragon it is good meat. Besides, it was already dead, and if we had left it then the trolls would have had it."

The Purple Green tore the haunch apart and handed Bazil half. Relkin moved away in disgust. Behind him he heard dragon jaws chomping and grinding while Vlok licked the air and muttered to himself.

Relkin went over to the cook pit where noodles were boiling and some flat bread had been baked.

Alsebra was already there, and Bryon had filled her helmet with noodles and akh.

"It's horrible what those two are doing," said Bryon.

"I tried," Relkin shrugged.

"Vlok is just slavering for some."

"You know, I think Swane is also."

Bryon made a face. "It seems wrong to me."

"It is not logical," said Alsebra towering above them.

"Why do you say that?" said Relkin.

"Men eat some animals but not others. Dragons eat all animals without exception."

"Even bears?" said Relkin.

"Even bears, even whales. But dragons like to eat some animals more than others. Men like to eat some animals more than others, too. The difference is that men have made more rules about this. Dragons have no rules. Men make rules, and with those rules men organize the whole world."

Relkin was already aware that Alsebra was at the opposite end of the spectrum of intelligence from poor old Vlok.

"But Alsebra does not eat horse," said Bryon.

"But I am not a wild dragon. I grew up from the egg in a place with many horses. I found them beautiful. I would not eat one anymore than you would eat a cat or a dog."

"Ugh," said Bryon.

"You see. But it is not logical."

"They are enjoying it," said Relkin, after a hurried look over his shoulder.

"It does smell delicious, but . . ." Bryon made a face and bent to his noodles.

The Purple Green continued to ignore Vlok. At last, after a nudge or two from Bazil, the Purple Green stopped tormenting poor Vlok and gave him some ribs. Then they ate in silence for a few minutes. By then there was nothing left except a few of the largest bones.

The Purple Green was satisfied.

"That was good. This dragon approves of the way men burn food to make it taste. Much stronger flavor than the old way."

"A lot more work, though," said Vlok, who while not bright was capable of understanding that much.

"But when one eats such good things only occasionally, then it is worth it, no?"

"Yes," said Vlok, without hesitation, "it is worth the trouble. This is an important discovery for Vlok."

"Vlok did not discover this, I discover this," said the Purple Green.

"No, I mean yes. What I meant was that for me, personally, this was a discovery. A new thing. I had not thought about it before."

The Purple Green was going to say something unkind, when he felt a nudge from the Broketail. Vlok was Vlok, and there was no point in ragging his scales.

There was a silence for a while before the Purple Green returned to his new and abiding interest in gastronomic experience.

"What would bear be like if we roast it?"

"Bear? Have you ever eaten bear?" said Vlok.

"Of course," said the Purple Green. "I have eaten the brown bears and the white bear. I have not eaten the small black bear, however. They are not common where I used to hunt. Bear is strong meat."

"Do you think putting it over heat would improve the flavor?" said Bazil, aroused to interest again. That horse had tasted good. Still, there was a vague sense of guilt, thanks to the boy and the damned human superstition, trying to spoil everything.

"I think it would be good to try it," said the Purple Green.

These ruminations about ursine cookery were interrupted by the arrival of a horseman, a messenger from the ambush site a few miles away. Something had happened, it was obvious from the speed with which the fellow rode up to the command post. A few seconds later, Dragon Leader Turrent came running at full pelt.

"On your feet, everyone, we've got to move. There's been an upset, and the enemy is coming on very fast."

"How bad is it, Dragon Leader?" said Swane.

"Captain Eads has been wounded, but not badly. There have been casualties."

"Dragon casualties?"

"Anther is wounded. But he still walks. Now, get going, Dragoneer, we don't have time to chat."

There was a scramble of activity as joboquins and equipment were taken up again. Packs went back on their backs, and then they were marching east away from the enemy, with roast horse now but a memory.

CHAPTER FORTY-TWO

Cuica crossed the Ice Mountains on favorable winds, threading his way westward through the mighty peaks, skimming across vast glaciers, and finally reaching the inner Hazog, a high plateau, bare and cold, that stretched away into the interior of the great continent.

The eagle was late. The small passengers it carried were possessed of a colossal anxiety that communicated itself even to the eagle. Time was precious, but even time would have to wait while the eagle fed to renew its strength.

Cuica, a full-grown wulfeagle, was capable of covering hundreds of miles in a day with favorable winds, but after crossing the High Gan, he had run into a powerful storm tracking eastward from the outer Hazog. All day and all night the eagle and the two small animals it carried, waited in a cranny high up on the White Bones Mountains as the storm howled past. To stay alive, the mouse and the bird fed on the precious store of grain carried in a tiny satchel strapped to the eagle's leg. For Cuica, there was nothing to eat. And so, when at last the storm had passed on, the eagle had dropped from the cliff to hunt.

An elderly rabbit out upon an alpine meadow was sighted almost at once, and Cuica silently stooped from the sky and struck cleanly. He took the rabbit and beat his way upward to the distant cranny, driven by an obscure urge to feed the small beings that were up there.

Lagdalen had established an understanding of the eagle and a method for cohabiting in the eagle mind. The difficult part was learning to relax and let the eagle go about its business. Lagdalen only interfered when the eagle decided to turn about and head for better hunting grounds to the east and south. The farther they proceeded into the west, the stronger and more frequent were these urges. At such times Lagdalen felt the bird's thought, felt its desire to turn, to find lusher slopes where there would be more rabbits, perhaps even rock hyraxes, ground squirrels, and other tasty small creatures. At such times Lagdalen overrode the eagle's mind and kept the great wings fixed, and the bird headed steadily west. Cuica was largely unaware of her presence except on these occasions, when he felt a shadow in the back of his thought. For the most part he ignored it. Feeling vaguely dissatisfied, he continued on the strange westward course into lands that were unfamiliar to him.

Back on the high ledge, the mouse and the bird awaited the eagle with gathering impatience.

Cuica landed, settled, and tore up the rabbit with swift, certain strokes of beak and talon. He seized a morsel, bent over the mouse, and tried to engage it for feeding.

The mouse was not an eaglet, however, and it scurried back to a place of safety, emitting a most un-mouse-like stream of angry, high-pitched language.

The small bird fluttered up to the eagle's shoulder. Cuica almost snapped it up in his beak, but a sound in his ear interrupted his thought and his head swung away and back to the rabbit.

The preferred eagle method of ingestion, rapid gulps of the largest possible pieces was something Lagdalen tried not to participate in, but to no avail, her mind was intermingled with the fierce, implacable eagle mind. It ate, and she ate with it.

The wulfeagle was oblivious to all this. He was ravenously hungry, having sufficed on less than a rabbit a day for three days while covering an immense distance. He ripped, tore, and gobbled.

When he had finished, the mouse and the little bird resumed their positions, and Cuica launched once more into the cloudless sky above the Hazog. Moving west, they crossed the Ice Mountains and found themselves floating smoothly across the sere surface of the Inner Hazog. The terrain was flat, stark, covered only in skeleton weed and lichen. Not even the Hazogi tribes, who roamed the outer Hazog, came here unless summoned.

And yet there was evidence that a great many men came and went from this empty land. Beneath the eagle's wings now they saw roads, dead straight, arrowing into the west.

And then they glimpsed another line of dark, jagged mountains rising ahead of them, smaller peaks than those of the Ice range, dark, jagged: the Black Mountains. In the center of this range stood the horn of the Kakalon, the Dugush Vaal, and to this they flew until they crested above the horns of stone and flew down into the wedge-shaped valley of Padmasa.

In the center of the valley, dominating all, stood the massive block of the Square. As they drew closer Lagdalen became aware of an enormous presence, a palpable mentality emerging from that huge block of stone. It sought to detect intruders with a hunger that was frightening. Deep below that block lurked the great power. This was the center, the apex, the azimuth of its dark, hideous strength.

The eagle flew past the Square and then on, down the valley, past camel trains and staging areas for travelers. Feed trains, great teams of mules and horses, filled other roads as tribute from the western nations flowed to Padmasa.

Farther down there was a small crag some six hundred feet high. To this there flew the eagle, lodging on an inaccessible ledge about a hundred feet below the top.

The mouse and the bird fed once more, stuffing themselves while conferring in rapid little bursts of squeaks and chirps. The lack of space in the tiny animal minds was made up for by an enormous acceleration in the pace of their thought. In each squeak and chirp were condensed the patterns of human language.

Only witches with the power of these two could communicate effectively from such tiny animantic familiars. None on Ryetelth were more skilled at animancy than Lessis of Valmes, unless it were Ribela of Defwode. Still, it required an immense effort to make the tiny brains of mouse and wren serve as communication nodes.

They discussed the options ahead of them and went over their plans for various contingencies.

The eagle flew off to hunt in the setting sun and found only some carrion, the remains of a camel. It chased off some vultures and pecked over the remains.

At dusk it returned to the ledge, unhappy and ready to return to its hunting grounds in Marneri. Lagdalen steadied the bird. Night fell, the moon rose. It grew cold there on the ledge. Cuica was used to cold, but he was hungry.

Then something caught the eagle's attention. Lagdalen saw with those magnificent eyes and glimpsed a speck flying across the moon. With a start, she realized it was miles away, and therefore very big indeed.

A memory from Ourdh came back, and she recalled the batrukh that had circled over Dzu on that terrible day a year before. The night passed slowly thereafter, and the eagle did not seem to sleep.

In the first light of dawn, the eagle lifted away and carried the two smaller animals down into the valley where it deposited them, not far from one of the paved staging areas that ringed the Square. Leaving the two tiny spies behind, Cuica skimmed away, staying low until he found an early thermal where he rose into the higher sky. Through the eagle's eyes, Lagdalen had a last glimpse of them, two tiny dots lost in the immensity of the wide valley.

CHAPTER FORTY-THREE

The staging area was a rectangular space, like a parade ground, paved and inset with drains. In the center stood a squat single-story structure with a flat roof. A pair of imps patrolled the roof.

The mouse hid itself among loose rocks at the very edge of the pavement. The wren darted around the surrounding terrain, for perhaps a quarter of a mile in each direction, seeking information on approaching the Square of Padmasa.

The wren returned to the staging area and carefully worked her way to the mound of loose rock where the mouse hid. As she drew closer, she only moved when she was sure the imps were looking elsewhere. Even a small bird might be reported in such a place. The Masters of Padmasa were aware of the power of the witchly magic.

At length they were together crouching in the dark, two tiny embers of hope set against the dark mass of the city of the Masters.

They did not have long to wait. Soon they heard the rumble of approaching traffic. A train of wagons came first, laden with sacks of grain and hauled by teams of a dozen mules apiece. Kassimi mule skinners, dressed in furs and red turbans, sat atop. Behind them came a caravan from distant Czardha, two dozen or more camels, laden with the skilled manufactures of the Trucial States and Gelf.

From within the stone structure came a team of imps and a couple of men in the black uniform of Padmasa.

The wagons pulled up in a long row for inspection. The mule skinners clambered down and formed a group to one side, where they swigged from flasks and muttered together. No one liked this part of the journey. Being around imps was bad enough, they hated the squat, monstrous creatures, but here the damned imps were empowered to do what they liked to any man. You had to bow and scrape to them. Sometimes they would pick on a fellow, and there was nothing anyone could do about it.

The imps inspected the cargoes of each wagon and every camel. They searched for contraband, and they made certain that no spies could slip by and get into the Square. However, they never noticed a solitary grey mouse that streaked over the cobblestones to the side of the fourth wagon in the line. The mouse leaped to the axle, then the top of the wheel, and vanished between the sacks of grain.

When they'd finished, the imps haughtily waved to the drovers. The men spat and shoved out their chests. An angry mumble began. The imps spat back and adjusted their swords. The men saw the movement. This was Padmasa. The men climbed back on their wagons and cracked their whips loudly to stir their mules.

The wagons rumbled back up the road. As they went, a tiny bird flitted onto the fourth wagon and found a perch on a high strut. No one noticed.

On they went over the last miles to the great gate of the Square. The land was utterly bare, almost featureless, a smooth upward slope of perhaps ten degrees to the structure standing on the crest.

As the eye approached the Square, so the sheer, colossal bulk of this single, brutal building became overpowering. It was intended to intimidate and succeeded. Even the eye of Lessis of Valmes was awed. She had seen many amazing things on this world, but never anything so harsh and yet so mighty. The labor to construct this architectural monstrosity— almost incalculable—Lessis marveled. Ribela was not so impressed.

"It is but a tiny reproduction of the Heptagon of Haddish. But it shows the scale of the ambition of our enemy. Their knowledge of the higher worlds is great already."

"Haddish?"

"One of the worlds of the Sauronlord Waakzaam."

"I have not heard of it."

"The Heptagon is the largest single structure built anywhere upon the sphere board of destiny." Ribela always knew these sort of things.

The wagon rumbled through the gate which was fifty yards wide and twice as tall. The gates were open but guarded by a regiment of imps, drawn up in squads to either side. Great pale-skinned trolls stood just inside the gates as a final line of defense.

It was a city as well as a fortress, a city of halls, tunnels, passages, and secret adits, a city with the desperate life and energy of a place of great wealth and repression.

The halls were great public places, with vast murals on two-hundred-foot high walls. The pavements were teeming with people from all over the world. The predominant color of dress was black, the uniform of one service or another of the power here. But there were also visitors from Czardha in their wools and tweeds, and there were Kassimi in colorful silks, and there were dark-skinned folk from the southern continent Eigo who wore white and ocher djellabas. There were even some exotic South Sea islanders, with their elaborate headdress and talking birds. Here and there carriages paused to discharge wealthy men and women clad in furs and silk, slave traders from every part of the world. Only they were allowed to wear furs within the Halls of Padmasa.

The wagon train rumbled down the center of the main entrance avenue. The sides were lined with shops where the products and services of the entire world were on sale.

Piercing the sides of the avenue were the entrances to commercial courtyards, where firms engaged in a single trade congregated. From one came the din of metalworking. From another the hum of business as gold and jewelry were bought and sold. The wagon train turned into a dark tunnel beneath a carved sheaf of wheat, gilt and gleaming, hanging over the entrance.

They entered a courtyard of granaries and stables. Great bins were groaning with sorghum and maize, which would be fed to meat animals in the outer reaches of the Tetralobe. Racks and lofts were stuffed with wheat, oats, rice, barley.

While teamsters worked their wagons into place, squads of human slaves unloaded grain and shifted it into the warehouse systems.

Their wagon came to a halt in a passage inside a warehouse. The mouse dropped to the cobbles and sneaked along the sidewall of the passage to a drain with a broken grate. In a moment the mouse was safe inside. It reconnoitered and then briefly showed itself.

A moment later the wren flew into the drain.

For a moment they paused. Wren looked to mouse. They were inside the Square.

CHAPTER FORTY-FOUR

Three thousand miles eastward of Padmasa, in the Tower of Swallows in Andiquant, the Imperial Council met to hear a new report on the situation in the Argonath.

Emperor Pascal Iturgio Densen Asturi had aged in the days and weeks since the news of the invasion had come. His hair had gone almost white. He had lost weight. There was a haggard look in his eyes. He worked without pause, doing everything he could to accelerate the Imperial response to the invasion of the Argonath.

Valembre had repeatedly begged the emperor to rest. His health was more important to the empire at this moment than any amount of planning after the fact. There was a response mounting to the invasion. Things had moved smoothly, in fact. The weather had been cooperative, allowing for rapid movements of troops.

Even Master Garsk of the bureaucracy had been encouraged to perform prodigies of organization and efficiency.

Still, the emperor cursed himself for his blindness. He had wanted so much to launch the great mission to Czardha, he had discounted the likelihood of such an enormous invasion host.

When all were present, with Irene, the Queen of Oceans, sitting in for Lessis of Valmes, the emperor called on General Hektor.

Hektor had a long face. The situation in the Argonath was daily growing more dangerous.

"First, I will tell you the worst. We expect an invasion of Arneis to be imminent. The town of Cujac will be the first to fall."

"Have we lost hope of holding the High Pass?" said Sausann.

"When you consider the size of the enormous force the enemy brought to bear and the relatively tiny band of defenders, we can only expect the worst. They might have held for a few days, but once the enemy brought his strength to bear, he would surely have prevailed."

"Ah, surely not," said Sausann. "I have no appetite for this endless tale of mistakes and tragedies. First Fort Redor, then the High Pass."

"The garrison there has been downgraded over the years of peace. We never dreamed that an assault could reach the pass so swiftly. In consequence, we were unable to reinforce the garrison there quickly enough. We have been a half step behind the enemy at every stroke."

"We have always been so well served with intelligence in the past." Sausann looked across the table to the seat where Lessis normally sat.

Irene of Alaf colored in anger.

"No one should cast aspersions upon the Office of Unusual Insight. The office has performed prodigies in providing information about our enemies. It was not the Office of Insight that reduced the level of readiness in Kenor or allowed Kadein to stand down its Second Legion."

Now Sausann flushed, too honest not to. She had pushed the emperor's plan. She had seen it as a way of somehow fulfilling her career, of turning the tide against the great enemy and thus opening her way to a graceful retirement into the mystic. She had fought to find the funds for it from the legion budget.

They were all silent. There had been plenty of failures, enough to go around. But the thought of the Office of Unusual Insight inevitably brought their thoughts to the two absent witches from the council.

The emperor compressed his lips for a moment.

"We are all thinking the same thing, I know it. Where are they? Are they safe? Can they possibly succeed?"

Everyone agreed, and for a moment their thoughts turned to the far west. Lessis and Ribela had gone into the very heart of the enemy's strength. With them went their hopes.

The emperor lifted his head.

"All I can say is what I tell myself ten times a day. It seems like an impossible task, but with those two, anything is possible."

General Hektor coughed politely.

"If I might continue, I will explain our present force dispositions. There has been significant progress in the past twenty-four hours.

"In Kadein we have the First Kadein and now the Cunfshon Legion of the Red Rose. On its way and due to arrive shortly is a mixed legion of reservists from Marneri, Bea, and Pennar. The Vo Legion is now mustered and on its way. A volunteer half legion is being raised in Minuend and Kadein. The Cunfshon White Rose will join them inside the week. Soon we will have seven legions ready to take the field."

"In the meantime, the enemy will be raping Arneis," sobbed Sausann.

Valembre stretched out a hand to comfort the Lady Sausann. "As long as the people are saved, we can recover. Fortunately, our folk were warned well in advance and most have fled to safety."

Sausann was not mollified. "How long will it be before we can meet the enemy on the field and destroy this pestilential invasion?"

Hektor sighed. "Lady Sausann must understand the need for caution. We need to adjust the battlefield to our advantage." He gestured toward the map on the table, a large scale map of central Arneis. "We expect the enemy to come straight down the main road to Kadein. The town of Cujac should be empty by now. Certainly we cannot hold the place. The walls came down a half century ago.

"We hope to block the enemy in front of Fitou and concentrate our force there. Eventually we will have thirty to thirty-five thousand troops there, sufficient to take the offensive."

"Yet the enemy has such a huge force," said Sausann.

"Imps can only be disciplined to a certain point. After that they fight in a disorganized mob. With seven legions, we can go on the offensive. But we will have to be careful. General Felix has assumed command of the army, and we can trust to his judgment. He is a sound man with a long career behind him."

"Indeed, we know that the enemy fears him," said Irene. "They made an attempt on his life three days ago. They failed."

Sausann looked into the steely glitter of Irene's eyes and felt once more that it was past time for her to retire from the world. She was no longer capable of such strength.

CHAPTER FORTY-FIVE

It was over. The gate was smashed, the walls overrun by imps. The garrison either lay where they had fallen or were driven ahead in disordered flight, to be harried by the Baguti cavalry.

The mists were reforming, sliding the dark face of the mountains into obscurity.

Thrembode the magician climbed back into the saddle. Damn Lukash, he'd done it again. Thrembode was torn between rage at the fool and glee, for here was another opportunity to call down the wrath of the Masters on the general's head.

Thrembode spurred across to where General Lukash sat his horse, in front of a cluster of aides.

"General, I have inspected the fortifications, and there are no living defenders here. The imps killed everyone. There is no one left to interrogate."

Lukash shrugged.

"We go on. We take the pass, and now we go on."

"You don't understand do you?" Thrembode spoke in anger. "Did you learn nothing from what happened before?"

In the massacre at Fort Redor, even the senior officers had been slaughtered, and Lukash had done nothing to prevent it. Some of them had even been tortured to death, roasted slowly over low-banked fires. In vain Thrembode had pleaded with the general to preserve the officers. They would be wanted in Padmasa for lengthy interrogations. Lukash had laughed at him and swigged whiskey from a silver flask.

Thrembode had immediately written to Administrator Gru-Dzek, sending the scroll west by the batrukh that visited for the day's news at dusk. A reprimand had come the next night. Lukash had read that scroll and paled. THEY were unhappy about the loss of the senior officers. This was not to happen again.

Lukash made a face.

"Magician, you think you can restrain these imps? Think again. They are not like men. They are more like vicious dogs except more intelligent."

"General, you are in command of these forces. It is up to you to keep some prisoners so we can learn about what may lie ahead. These would have been especially valuable. We might have learned much about the dispositions of the enemy forces on the other side of the mountains."

"It does not matter. We are too quick. We shall strike through to the coast. You'll have plenty of men to interrogate then."

"General, I have learned that it is best not to underestimate our enemies. I have also learned that it is wisest to obey the commands of the Great Ones. You have gone against their expressed wishes."

Lukash squeezed his eyes shut. What did they know of controlling one hundred thousand imps?

"I told them to keep a few alive, but the thrice-damned imps got out of control. When they scent blood like that, they go mad."

Thrembode heard some growling behind him and looked over his shoulder. A knot of trolls was fighting over a couple of men's corpses. They snarled and swung at each other with heavy fists and tore apart the bodies. Thrembode felt a primal disgust.

"You should stop that. It is wrong to let the trolls eat men."

Lukash was a misanthrope of somewhat extreme views. Abused in childhood by father and mother, he had been taking revenge on the world ever since.

"Let them eat what they want. We need trolls to feel content. They will fight better that way."

"It damages the morale of our men. You forget that we depend on men to keep this zoo of an army together."

Lukash set his face in stone. Thrembode knew the signal well. Lukash would be impervious to argument.

"General," said Thrembode in a quiet voice, "the batrukh flies tonight."

Another scroll would go back to Padmasa. THEY would be unhappy with their servant Lukash. The next night the batrukh might be ordered to take Lukash back to Padmasa. Such things had happened before. The threat was implicit.

Lukash growled in his throat from the strong urge he had to simply slay this stupid magician, but he overcame it, turned, and controlling himself with a great effort snapped orders to his aides.

Within a minute there were troll wardens down there herding the huge monsters away from the pile of enemy dead. Horses were being roasted for the trolls; they were to come and feast. They had fought well and were to be rewarded. With grumbles and snarls of disappointment, the trolls slunk away.

Thrembode watched them go. They were necessary, he understood that, but he disliked them.

Lukash was looking at him with half-lidded eyes. Given the chance, Lukash would have Thrembode thrown to the trolls for lunch.

"The batrukh is a mighty beast, is it not, General?"

Lukash chuckled greasily.

"Magician, you will be very powerful after we conquer the Argonath."

"I will remain a humble servant of the High Ones."

Lukash nodded. A weird smile split his face of boiled leather.

"Everything goes well, does it not? We have cut through to their heart. Now we shall kill them."

"Everything goes very well, General, but we still must have better intelligence about what lies ahead."

"They cannot stand against us! We shall crush them and pile their skulls high beneath the sun!"

Thrembode nodded somberly. The general was obsessed with this image. Thrembode detected an increasing arrogance, and suspected that Lukash might even be thinking that he could take control of the Argonath littoral for himself and hoist himself to great power. It would be the act of an insane man. THEY would act immediately. Yet Lukash dreamed. He dallied on the rim of insanity. He might yet tip over the edge.

Still mulling these thoughts, Thrembode rode to his wagon, which had been set up on an elevated rock worn smooth by the winds. The mist had closed in now. The world was lost in the white haze. Inside the wagon, he prepared a scroll for the batrukh. It had to be very special, for much depended on this scroll. Perhaps even the life of a certain magician.

CHAPTER FORTY-SIX

They were not alone. Swarms of small birds and mammals lived in the granaries. Flocks of sparrows flitted between the bins while rats and mice infested the walls.

Hundreds of cats roamed the premises to keep them all in check. Teams of imps equipped with rat-killing dogs would sweep through every so often. For sparrows, they limed perching places and sent slave boys climbing the walls with rackets in hand.

A lean black queen cat was slinking along the side of the cobbled way, ducking through the piles of discarded sacks and barrels. She would surely investigate this drain.

The mouse smelled trouble sooner than that, however. Rats were nearby, not far down the drain. To such rats, they would present nothing but a quick meal.

Above the drain, about three feet up from the cobble-stones, there was an opening in the brick wall of the warehouse. The wren cocked her head with a chirp. The mouse saw the space at once, slipped out of the drain, and climbed the broken wall. Fortunately, the bricks were crumbly, and the mouse had no difficulty in scaling it. She reached the aperture and ducked inside. The wren joined her in a moment.

But they had been seen. The cat accelerated in a streak of black fur. The wren gave a shriek of command and both small creatures plunged into the darkness for their lives. A feline paw slammed into the hole and claws slashed through the very space the mouse had occupied a split second before. The cat did not give up easily, her claws scraped along the bricks again and again as she fished in the hole for that tasty-looking mouse. Her intended prey was safe, however, moving down a narrow gap produced by a sag in the brick course of the outer wall. The inner wall was slabstone, and the passage broadened out in a space between the inner and outer walls.

They paused. There was smell, a very strong one.

The mouse sniffed, hesitated. Feelings of primeval social fear went through the little female mouse. They were on someone's territory.

A moment later, there was a loud challenging squeak, and a large dark-furred mouse appeared out of the dark. It was a male mouse, a mighty male mouse in his prime.

Ribela's mouse submitted to the alpha while Ribela sought desperately to cast a spell. He bit the female mouse and mounted her and then bit her some more to compel obedience and submission. He was pleased, however, she was a pleasant addition to his current harem.

Ribela gritted her teeth through this performance. She could have opted for a big male mouse like this one for her animant, but that would have meant endless fighting with other alpha males. So she had taken a female. The things she had endured for the cause! She deserved a statue, someday, in the main square of Andiquant.

When, at last, there came a momentary relaxation in his grip, she twisted her mouse free. He sniffed, and his eyes glowed in anger. She struck him with a stream of high frequency syllables, a spell so fast that it froze him in place. It broke after a moment because it had been set so quickly, but by then another had been concocted and delivered. This one took, and the male mouse slowed down to a crawl. It could barely move. Ribela's mouse came closer and began a longer spell casting, face-to-face with the big alpha male.

Meanwhile, the wren's eyes were adjusting to the darkness. She darted forward, exploring the space, keeping her distance from the big male mouse, who would be dangerous until Ribela had completed her work.

In the back of her mind, Lessis blessed Ribela. Casting a spell through an animantic familiar was an incredibly difficult task. It required a perfection of skill. Ribela's mind had to use the extremely limited mental power of the mouse brain to not only keep the mouse going, but also to hold up its corner of the animantic spell, which was a constant effort to maintain. On top of this came the difficulties of speaking a spell through the mouse vocal equipment. Proper voluminates were impossible. It was like writing music without half notes. Fortunately, Ribela was note perfect. Within three minutes, she had woven a spell about the big alpha mouse.

By then other mice, the females of this big alpha and a few youngsters, were showing themselves. The larger females edged closer, intent on attacking the stranger. They were puzzled by the subdued appearance of the alpha male and slightly hesitant, which was a good thing for the witch animants.

Ribela relaxed her grip, and the alpha male came awake with an almost audible snap. He sprang about stiff-legged and chivvied the other females back into their holes.

The wren was ahead, her beady eyes peering into the murk.

They had a long way to go, and little time.

The alpha male was ready, he would lead. Their strange little procession began at once, and they headed off down the dark, irregular passage.

Along the way they soon entered the territories of other alpha mice. The first male would then either fight the male or submit to it, if it was even larger than himself. Either way, Ribela would set an immobilizing spell on it, hypnotizing it if it was in its prime.

In this way their numbers increased to sixteen large male mice by the time they encountered rats.

Four of the mice were lost in the first encounter before Ribela was able to control the first buck rat.

After that, it became a little easier. Soon she had a pack of rats, and the male mice were released.

The mouse and the wren now progressed with twelve buck rats in front of them and ten behind. They killed a weasel, drove off a cat from its sleeping space behind a wall of hay in the granary horse barn, and convinced a young stable lad who glimpsed the whole party as it ventured across an open stretch of stable, that he was having a religious vision. The boy was still kneeling there mumbling prayers to great Aten, for he was a boy from far off Kassim, when he was found by the stable boss who knouted him to the bunks with curses.

Eventually they reached the central region of the Square, a great empty space open to the sky. In the middle were the statues of the five titans, the Masters themselves, carved in heroic mode with stern, handsome faces. They were clearly meant to be gods. Heruta Skash Gzug was in the center holding up a rod with a glowing star upon its end. Gzug-Therva, the Vanua Omega of their cultic hierarchy, stood beside Heruta shoulder to shoulder. Prad Azoz, Gshtunga, and Prad Datse stood a little farther back.

The pack of small animals clustered inside an open drain at one side of the great piazza of statutes. There were only four ways down into the underground city, four staircased ramps that went down many turns, all cut through solid rock. At the end of the stairs and ramps lay the Nexus Halls and the four labyrinths of the Tetralobe.

Lessis stared for a moment at the enormous statues. They meant to generate a sense of pride and strength, to uplift the servants of their power. Instead, she saw only brutality and massive egoism. How could they not see the wrongness in what they did? Their intelligence was plain to see, terrifying, in fact, but how could they misuse it as they did? Lessis had fought this enemy for centuries, but she had never understood its deep motivation. The gigantic statues did not unlock the secret for her. Such minds remained incomprehensible to Lessis of Valmes.

Ribela had dismissed most of the rats. From here they could take only a handful. Their best chance of descending lay with the carts taking food and supplies below to the underground city.

At the entrance to the downward ramps were squads of imps under the command of dour men who examined everything passing with a keen eye.

Darkness fell and the light coming in through the ceiling apertures of the Square faded, but the traffic to the Tetralobe continued unabated. They waited patiently until it was dark and a wagon, laden with fresh scrolls, quills, and ink pads, halted beside their hiding place. The mouse and the three rats scrambled aboard and hid themselves from view.

A moment later the wren flitted aboard.

They entered the Tetralobe.

CHAPTER FORTY-SEVEN

The wagon descended to the Nexus Hall of the Third Level, a vast enclosure set beneath a ceiling covered in glittering purple glass. Light was let in through shafts set in the ceiling. Traffic of all kinds thronged here, at the nexus of the Tetralobe. The Nexus Halls connected the four separate systems of passages, avenues, halls, cells, which swelled out into the natural cave systems below.

The wagon of scrolls joined the traffic and slowed. At no more than a shuffle, they crossed the Nexus Hall and entered a wide avenue space. Now the high ceiling was simply bare grey rock, into which were set glowing globes every one hundred feet. To either side were the facades of commercial enterprises, intermixed with those of bureaus of the administration systems. Men and women, all wearing the grey or black clothing that seemed all but universal in Padmasa, strode the pavements busily.

Alleys ran down breaks in the ranks of these building facades, and their wagon turned into one and came to a halt outside a worn-looking entryway. Frayed wooden doors crashed open, and three old slaves emerged. They were the remains of men, spirits crushed long ago. They wore grey loinclothes, black slippers, and little else. Their pale skin was wrinkled with age. They began to unload the cargo.

The mouse and the rats slipped off the side of the cart and darted inside the open door. Within, they found deserted hallways and empty offices. The mouse, escorted by the rats, slipped along the corridor, investigating each office. The wren darted ahead.

On the wall in one office was a chart, a map of the Tetralobe for messenger use. While the rats explored the office, the mouse and the wren examined the map. Both were fluent in the tongue of Padmasa, a special language designed from the beginning by the Masters to emphasize their power.

They discovered that they were in the North Lobe, on Level Three. They memorized the map's important features.

They moved on and came to a busy area. Men were at work in the cubicles, processing scrolls. In other places small groups of men gathered to talk. Occasionally there was a woman among them, but this was primarily a world of men.

It was difficult to move around in these areas until they discovered a way to get into the system of ventilation ducts. Set into both floor and walls, with vertical shafts connecting every fifty feet, this system gave complete access to all parts of the office complex. Air was constantly driven through the passages by some unknown means. In every room there were vents, covered by grilles of metal, that exchanged the air constantly. It made for a great warren. They smelled native rats several times and took care to go around them. There were also predators: a species of miniature cats that roamed these narrow passages. They had a close call at one point with one of these, but distracted by the wren diving at his eyes and uncomfortable with two large buck rats at once, the cat backed off and slunk away into the dark.

For a long time they roamed through the endless passages. Thousands of people were employed here to drive the empire of the Masters. There was a constant babble of voices in some sections, and complete, austere silence in others. Once they crossed an enormous room, a scribery, with long benches and desks stretched across it on which sat row after row of scribes. Slaves were constantly busy fetching paper and ink and fresh quill for this army of writers. Other men, clad in black, removed the completed writing.

They explored farther and found themselves moving through the ceiling above the administrative offices. In one room there was an argument in progress. They heard a robust drover arguing with a fat man sitting behind a table.

"Down to Deep Five? Not again! You're killing me with this. You know how bad the traffic is down there. It'll take me hours. Whatever they're growing down there, it eats more than it ought to. Smells horrible, too. I've been down there three times today already. Whole load of mangel-wurzels, and then whole corn and then whole oats. My horse is worn. You should send Dizmo."

"Dizmo is on another errand."

"Hah. You and I both know what Dizmo is doing; he's sucking up to the administrater again."

"That does not concern us. The delivery has been requested, and you will make it."

"The horse is worn-out."

"Get a new horse at the depot later. Your horse is old. It is time for it to be fed to the trolls."

"Fine, requisition a fresh horse for me. You think I'll get one? I tell you at the depot, they're thieves. They make off with half the horses that get shipped in here. Probably sell them straight to the troll masters."

The fat man vented an explosive oath. "Get out of here and make the shipment, or I really will report you."

With a few ritual grumbles, the drover finally left the office.

Above his head the mouse and the tiny bird conversed together, and then followed the drover through the air ducts.

He headed down the corridor, trotted down some steps, and went out through a pair of wide double doors, guarded by a squad of six imps, with guard dogs at their side.

Above him followed a procession of small animals frantically running through the ventilation system, trying to keep up. At the outer wall of the office complex, they found the ventilation duct sealed with steel mesh.

Hurriedly they hunted along the wall, running back to the mid-room ceiling junction and then back to the wall again to another well-sealed duct.

Below, they could peer through the openings and see the drover being held up by the imps at the door who inspected for stolen items. The drovers were used to this kind of treatment, and this one leaned against the wall passively as the imps prodded and probed.

They ran back to the wall, and this time found the grate had not been properly nailed down in one corner. They pried it up and leaped down twelve feet to the cobblestones of the outer passage.

They were in a wide street passage, along which there came occasional rikshas but not much else. A small horse was set between the shafts of a large wagon.

The drover clambered aboard and cracked his whip. As he did so, several small rodents sprang desperately across the cobblestones and launched themselves at the running board of the little cart, which was old and worn and offered hiding places.

The cart rolled away down to the depot where it picked up a mountainous mass of dried corn plants, complete with ears and tassles, loaded by sweating slaves. With the cart groaning beneath the load, the horse was whipped up, and very slowly they gained momentum and eventually trundled slowly forward. The pace picked up when they descended on a vast ramp with a very gradual incline that spiraled downward for what seemed like miles. The air at once grew much colder. They were leaving the Tetralobe and entering the upper Deeps.

At last the cart came to a halt by a loading bay. Slaves with pitchforks emerged to unload the whole corn, their breath frosting in the cold air.

The rats and the mouse abandoned the load and sped across the flagstoned floor toward an open drain. They were halfway to safety when a heavyset grey terrier sprang forward and snatched up the hindmost rat and tore it in half.

The other rodents reached the drain but with the terrier right behind. The dog's claws skittered on the stone above the drain while it growled horribly down at the terrified rats running along below. The only thing that saved them was that the drain was partly closed off, and the dog could not insert its jaws through the narrow upper aperture. Then to complete the peril, the first dog was joined by a second and both continued to pursue them.

The wren flew above and behind. The dogs had attracted attention, a couple of imps with long poles in their hands were coming over.

The drain snaked rightward and came to an end over a vertical drop into a pit of nothingness from which came a strong animal smell.

The wren dove down and hurled herself at the eyes of the first terrier. With a yelp of dismay, it jerked aside and paused and looked around for the strange attacker. The other dog plowed on barking furiously. The imps with poles were close.

The wren dove again, and this time the dog saw her and his jaws snapped shut far too close. Indeed, one wing feather had been punched like a ticket by his teeth. The wren flew to the edge of the pan and shrieked a warning. The imps with rat-killing poles were coming.

There was nothing for it, the mouse, followed by the rats, hurled itself straight over the edge. The terriers pulled up just short and were barking as the rats fell, spiraling down eighty feet onto a great pile of whole cornstalks.

The wren flew down to join them. They moved at once off to the side of the pile and hid within the corn, which they ate as they hid.

The air was pungent in the extreme. They were in the midst of a herd of cows penned up. A team of sweating slaves were shoveling manure at one end of the space. At the other was a barred entrance. They made their way through the bars, passed down a flagstoned passage, and entered a space broken up into stalls. In every stall was a pregnant cow.

Alas, these poor cows were not with calf. Instead, the malign magic of the Masters had induced them to bear trolls. Every one of these poor brown cows would die in childbirth. Already many of them were in agony from bearing the monstrous, overlarge things that grew in their wombs.

Deep, mournful cries rose up from the stalls of this horrifying place, and Lessis felt her spirit assailed. It was this misuse of the means of reproduction that most fired her rage at the Masters, fueling her lifelong struggle to defeat them. To witness such pain and misery roused the gentle Lessis to a state of hatred.

They entered an experimental area where cows in various stages of experimental pregnancies were trapped in special stalls. A dead cow, her entrails torn out in the birthing process, was being dragged away by slaves with a handcart.

An enormous cry of pain split the air, followed by more, huge trumpeting bellows protesting some terrible agony. There was a silence while they looked to each other. Then came long sobbing wails that shook the timbers in the stalls. This volume of sound was beyond that of mere cows.

They moved toward the source, dodging along the walls, slipping behind the bales of hay. At one point they slipped through a crack in a wall and found themselves in a gruesome storage place for failed experiments. The room was long and lined with racks of cages, where creatures large and small languished. Many were dead, others gibbered in pools of their own wastes. Lessis felt her strength of purpose harden another degree.

They came at length to a broad passage and a gate

guarded by imps with spiked steel collars, beyond which came the terrible cries of pain.

The mouse, followed as ever by the two remaining buck rats, darted swiftly across the passage in the lee of a ricksha bearing an officer. The wren slipped aboard the ricksha, underneath, and rode through the gate.

The mouse and the rats found their way in through a drainage pan in an empty stall. The wren found them shortly.

They moved, working carefully through the straw, pausing to nibble on corn when they found it. When they had to, they climbed the walls. The wren brought them warnings in good time of cats.

And then at last they found it. In a stall almost too small for her, a great she mammoth was giving birth to a creature almost twice the size of one of her own babies. Her trunk stood out rigid as she screamed her pain. She was dying.

The medical officer, dressed in black with a scarlet patch on his right shoulder, placed an instrument against her heaving side and listened.

She gave another great trumpeting wail, and her ears flapped wildly.

The man stepped back and snapped his fingers. Three imps bearing long flensing knives on poles came forward. Quickly they cut the mammoth open, slicing her belly from rib cage to anus. Her bowels tumbled out along with her final scream. Imps with crowbars came forward to pry forth the obscene thing she had given life to. It came free at last in a gush of blood and fluids. Now the imps pried the limbs open and used rubber hammers to straighten them. One imp jabbed the newborn thing with a sharp spike. It jerked and heaved. Another bent over its face with a clipper and punched a hole in its nose. Another imp threaded a brass ring through the hole. A chain was attached.

The imps tugged, and the thing jerked again and then pawed the air and let forth a hoarse bellow. It came upright and then to its feet. It took unsteady steps while the imps guided it by the chain to the ring in its nose.

Lessis felt a horrified sort of awe as she comprehended this newborn monster's dimensions. It was easily fifteen feet tall, a gigantic troll, or at least there were similarities, as between a black bear and a giant brown bear. The legs were massive, the head like that of some obscene giant ape, dominated by a hedge of teeth in a huge mouth. The nose was thick, splayed like a bull's. The eyes were small and close set. The thing tapered somewhat from the huge legs, and yet it had to weigh two tons, she estimated. The great jaws opened, and it roared in pain and shock at being alive.

Slaves were already sinking big hooks into the mammoth's hide while the imps with the flensing blades cut up her body into manageable sections that could be dragged away by the slaves and used for troll feed. Blood flowed freely across the flagstoned floor.

Ribela's mouse conferred briefly with the wren.

"I estimate they weigh two tons apiece. Stand fifteen feet high."

"As big as dragons. Can they fight, though?"

"We need to know more. What is their strategy?"

"They are close. I can feel them. Such weight upon the psychic plane."

"And their Mesomasters, too. Do you perceive them?"

"Not so well as you."

"They are below us. The Mesomasters search constantly for any intruding presence."

"They will be in the Prime Abyss, where they make the Dooms. Afterward they take nourishment. Nectars, honey, and fruit will be set out for them in a small chamber."

"Do we know where?"

"No, alas, we have never had an informant with such secrets."

"We must find the Prime Abyss. That is where they will be."

CHAPTER FORTY-EIGHT

They had turned back and were retracing their path through the heavily guarded mammoth pens when they were spotted by keen-eyed imps. Ratting terriers were released, and they fled for their lives. By staying in small places, behind stacked bales of hay or within a gap between two joists, they evaded the terriers, but sooner or later they would find themselves trapped.

When that moment came, they were caught inside a stack of hay bales formed into a rough cube. The dogs were on all sides, and now the imps were taking apart the stack, bale by bale.

Hidden above on a high beam, the wren could only watch helplessly. The imps would soon reach the center of the pile.

Then the wren noticed that one of the glow globes hung from the ceiling almost directly above the scene. She flew to perch on the fixture above it, which was very loose. The wire holding the chain to the ceiling plate was old, but even so the wren was not strong enough to bend such wire. Lessis concentrated and made a supreme effort to summon a spell of destruction. Working from within, the wren was akin to threading a single needle with ten thousand threads. The only way it could work was to use the speed with which the wren's mind operated and compose the spell at a rate many times faster than normal.

Lessis of Valmes bore down hard. Perhaps only one other person alive could have done it as well. It was a wrenching effort, the faultless, high-speed delivery of a thousand lines, but it came off perfectly. The wire decayed to dust, the fixture gave a groan and slipped, and then gave way, and the glowing globe fell free, dropping twenty feet to the floor and exploding with a dull boom.

Both imps and dogs screamed at the sudden shock and gathered around the fallen light globe. It was a magical light globe, manufactured in the faraway city of Monjon. Such globes contained water that had been invigorated by a strange jinni that resided in Monjon. The water from the broken globe still glowed, but its glow was fading as it ran through the cobbles and was lost in the drains.

The mouse and the rats were streaking down the passage, close to the wall, desperately seeking a crack of some kind, a broken drain, anything. Alas, everything was in good repair, no gaps appeared that even a mouse could squeeze through.

The imps were roused by the sudden departure of the terriers, which had seen the rats run and took off with a chorus of joyful barks. The imps followed, carrying rat poles and clubs.

The wren darted down and into the path of the dogs. They ignored her as they bore down on the rats. She flew up again and ahead.

And then the rats found a chink in a gate of immense wooden timbers, and they were through it in a moment. The dogs slid to a halt on the other side, and pawed and whined.

The mouse took stock of the place, a square pen, covered in straw and littered with enormous dung. Then a huge shape detached itself from the darkness in one corner and approached. It stood over them. The rats fled to the walls. The mouse stared directly up, into those big brown eyes.

The bull mammoth cocked his huge ears. If he'd still had his tusks, he would have rubbed them on the ground in amazement. Unfortunately, his captors had cut off his tusks early on and so he had nothing with which to rub the ground or pry apart the walls of this hated place. This tiny mouse, now, this was very interesting. The first interesting thing to happen in a long time. He refrained from crushing the little animal. There was definitely more here than met the eye, for normally mice fled his approach as those rats had.

He was a full-grown bull, with seventeen summers behind him. He was in his prime, young and fit and very, very strong, and he was hearing odd little sounds from this mouse, and parts of his mind thrilled at them, leaving him confused and intrigued.

In curiosity, his trunk curled down. The mouse clambered onto the tip of the trunk, which curled up and bore the mouse close for examination. The mouse never stopped making the interesting sounds.

In the meantime, the poor wren was trapped outside the mammoth's pen. There was no gap wide enough to admit a wren, except that one on the ground level used by the rats but which was now occupied by the dogs.

Then the imps arrived. They opened the great door and let the dogs inside, and the wren took her opportunity.

The rats chose the mammoth over the dogs and ran tight to the wall around the giant pachyderm and behind him. He took no notice of them. His eyes were focused on the tiny mouse on the tip of his trunk.

He was a wise bull of seventeen summers who had fathered many, many calves. He felt good about being himself for once. Normally he felt sad. Now he felt quite bullish. This was good, because it had been a long time since he had felt good, or bullish. He had been confined here for what seemed a lifetime. All that was good here was that he was required to mount females constantly. Everything else was bad. Confinement, monotonous food, nothing but stone and walls around him. He longed to stride the world again, as he had for sixteen long, wonderful years.

The terriers were uneasy about being this close to the bull. He was chained, but only by one leg. He could move about the pen. Still the terriers were obsessed with those two rats. They itched to kill them.

After a few seconds, the urge to kill overwhelmed the more sensible fear of the bull. They darted in at the rats.

The bull noticed and shifted around with remarkable speed. A huge front foot came down on one terrier and extinguished it with hardly more than a stifled squeal. The other one veered away and fled barking in terror.

The imps stood back, alarmed. They cried out for the mammoth master. But the bull made no further movement. It stood stock-still, its trunk holding up something in front of its eyes.

The mature bull of seventeen summers continued to listen to the thoughts that popped into his mind as the mouse on the end of his trunk made odd little sounds.

It was extraordinary. It was wonderful. It was like walking through a highland meadow covered in new lush grass. There was this sense of warm euphoria, something he had not felt since he had lost his world of upland meadows and wide forests.

It transpired that he had friends. This was wonderful

news. He had felt friendless since the loss of his freedom and the companionship of other bulls. Now these new friends were going to break the thing that bound his leg. He would stand still, perfectly still. The little animals would do something he could not comprehend; mammoths did not gnaw and knew nothing of the concept. Then later he would "rebel." This concept was new, but he understood it clearly. His anger ran deep and close to the surface.

There was going to be a fight of some kind. Good. The bull was ready. He had been itching to punish them for what they had done to him and would gladly fight. His trunk would hurl them down, and he would trample them, again and again.

The wren fluttered down to alight close beside the mouse. She sensed the intense activity in the mouse. Ribela was working the most tremendous magic, rapid little blurts of mouse sound came every few seconds. Lessis heard and understood. Ribela was the greatest practitioner of the witch's art. Now she was achieving some kind of communication with the mammoth. Lessis wondered what gambit she had chosen. Would it be the Bellan way, with little from the Birrak, a direct shift to post-voluminates, relying on incredibly elaborate credenza to hold everything together? Or would it be the classic way, with some mask effect to replace the lost volumes? There was no way that a mouse could be made to voluminate. Or was it all some unique creation of Ribela's, something beyond the spellbook? If anyone was capable of it, it was the Queen of Mice.

An air of tension rose up about the bull like the gathering oppressiveness before a thundershower on a hot and humid day. It grew and grew, and suddenly it dissipated, without sound or fury and was gone.

It was done. The mouse turned away, their tiny eyes met, and Lessis flinched from the explosive burst of fierce intelligence that glared in victory from those of the mouse. Instantly one was aware that this was not just a mouse. That burst of psychic power flashed away like a lightbulb going off in an empty universe.

Not for the first time, Lessis felt a little fear of the Queen of Mice. Ribela had reached levels that were similar to those of the Masters themselves.

The Mesomasters below would feel that pulse of free energy, she realized. Their alarms would have gone off. But it had been a single flash, leaking from concealment. The Mesomasters would be left with simply a single star burst on the esoteric energy levels. They would not have been able to pinpoint the source.

Still, it was to be regretted, for now at least the enemy had warning that someone had worked great magic, alien magic, within the perimeter of Padmasa. Inquiries would be made, sensitivities would increase.

The bull was standing stock-still, bemused. The two rats, drawn by a compulsion that overmastered their terror, came forward through the dung-strewn straw and applied themselves to gnawing at the heavy leather cuff that secured the bull's hind leg.

The imps and the dogs were outside. The dogs were afraid, and with good reason. The mammoth hated dogs. As much as he hated imps, he hated dogs even more.

The imps edged in, spears in their hands. It seemed they were determined to kill those rats.

But at that very moment, there came a blast on a horn and a thunder of drums. Then came more blasts of the horn, summoning their attention. Drums boomed.

The imps milled uncertainly. Hard-eyed men, who managed the breeding program came out of a door farther down the passage. Something was happening, something very important.

The wren fluttered out the gate to investigate and hid herself on a high beam. A presence was coming, an enormous presence, a Master.

She was aghast at this misfortune. Ribela's powerful spell had been sourced by one of the Masters themselves!

As it came, she felt the power increasing until at last she realized it could only be the one, the greatest of the five, the first and Prime Master of the Vanus void, Heruta Skash Gzug.

Lessis had damped down her own thought projection to almost nothing. The animantic spell was subtle in its use of energy, it would not be detectable above the background clutter on the psychic planes from so many minds in this huge place. Still, she tried not to think.

Ribela, too, was taking precautions, slipping away to hide in the straw. The bull was left to eat quietly in the corner. The rats hid as well.

But now both Lessis and Ribela began to notice hopeful

signs. The tone of the presence they felt did not seem imbued with the passions they would have expected if it was coming to apprehend them.

A few moments later Lessis felt a strong mental image. Heruta's thoughts leaked out every now and then. He was so used to simply projecting the power that he could not turn it off. The most casual thought was expressed with the weight of a pyramid. Images from his thoughts would flash into the minds of those around him. It was difficult for mere men to survive these mental blasts. Often men would keel over or go down on their knees, minds blanked by the aftershock.

He was come, he himself, the greatest of the Five, Master of the Vanus void, come to inspect the mammoth pens and to question the Mammoth Master. There were important questions. The plan developed by Heruta himself was not being adhered to. Why was ogre production still falling below the quota? The Mammoth Master had been chosen by Heruta himself. He still had faith in his choice. But there had to be more ogres. The imps in the gate to the bull mammoth's pen prostrated themselves as the Master was borne past them in his chair by eight powerful slaves who sweated beneath their burden. The Master was encased in shining-steel armor chased with gold. The imps did not rise for half a minute after his chair had passed.

Skipping along the high beams the wren followed the presence as it was borne away.

The chair halted outside an office door as a young man with a powerful physique and long black hair emerged. Immediately he knelt in submission to the Great One.

The chair was lowered smoothly halfway to the ground. The armored figure stepped off the seat and floated slowly down to the floor. Once on the floor it resumed walking, bound to the ground like any ordinary mortal. Try as they might, the Masters remained on the human plane of life energy. They had yet to transcend it despite their terrible strength.

The Mammoth Master rose and accompanied Heruta on a swift inspection of a mammoth pen, then to see a young ogre, freshly born, learning to walk in a small pen. Helping him learn were some bullnecked imps equipped with goads and whips, who tormented the great beast and drove it into a killing rage.

Following, above, skipping from rail to rail, came the wren.

"They must kill soon after birth," said the Mammoth Master in a cold voice. "It must be the first thing they learn. Then they will always want to kill."

The Great One answered him, in a harsh, rasping voice.

"This world teems with life. Pruning is necessary."

An old slave was pushed into the young ogre's pen. The imps withdrew into little safe holes.

The ogre stalked the slave. The man scrambled back and away with little screams of terror. The ogre pursued him and with a sudden roar it lurched forward and grabbed for its prey. The poor man lost control of his bowels and sprang backward, but slipped on his filth and fell, then was grasped by the ankle and lofted and dangled.

He screamed. The ogre tore him limb from limb and stuffed the pieces into its mouth.

"Very, vigorous," said Heruta Skash Gzug.

A special squad of albino trolls, enormously strong, came in to assist the imps in subduing the young ogre. They carried heavy clubs.

"After they have killed the first time, it is vital that we overpower them and render them submissive to our domination."

A net dropped from the ceiling and was yanked tight on control wires held by the imps. The ogre started to break the net, but then the trolls fell on it and clubbed it to the ground and beat it into submission.

"Very good. But production has not met the quota."

The Mammoth Master nodded humbly.

"Indeed, there have been problems."

"Describe them."

The Mammoth Master found his mouth dry.

"The ogres do not take consistently in the wombs of the mammoth. We place the ogre egg as prescribed by the Ogre Development Team. The bull mounts. We know this bull is very fertile. But the ogre egg does not develop past the first week. Then we have the stillbirth problem. One in five we lose like that, and we don't know why. Worse we lose another mammoth cow every time for no purpose, and we are chronically short of cows."

"What do the Ogre Developers say?"

"They blame the cows. They say they are not fed properly. Or that they are infertile. The truth is their process does not work properly."

"So you blame the Ogre Developers, do you?" said the Great One in an ominous tone.

"Well, I can not blame the cows. They are fed whole corn, alfalfa, grain; they do not want for anything."

"I do not like to hear excuses."

The Mammoth Master blanched and struggled not to show the terror he felt. He had enjoyed the favor of the Great One, and he knew that disfavor could be very hard to endure.

At that moment he was saved. Another presence was approaching, a large presence, but small when compared with that of the Master Heruta Skash Gzug. It was a Mesomaster.

All was silent as the Mesomaster climbed down from his high chair and knelt before Heruta Skash Gzug. Quickly it passed along the information that an energy pulse of extraordinary strength had been detected within Padmasa.

An emergency meeting had been called for the Five. It would take place during the evening nectar, which had already been laid out.

Heruta dismissed the Mammoth Master with instructions to do whatever was necessary to increase production of ogres. Then he returned to his chair, summoning the strength to float himself up and into the seat, armor and all.

Let those who saw this feat stare! This was the great power they had unlocked long ago and now rode to hegemony over the world. This was the visible manifestation of a strength that would lead to their complete mastery of the world and their elevation beyond it onto higher realms. Let them all look on the power and tremble, they who were nothing but slaves!

CHAPTER FORTY-NINE

Heruta Skash Gzug was borne away into the Prime Abyss in the utmost deeps, where it was cold, always cold. The air was chilled by being circulated through a cavern filled with ice brought from the far-off Ice Mountains.

The wren followed the chair down, staying low to the ground in open areas and traveling in short little dashes from one point of cover to the next. Occasionally she felt the scanning field generated by the Mesomasters, but the wren's consciousness was so small that it escaped notice.

Heruta was borne to the entrance to the hall of nectars and essences. An orchestra, hidden in the ground just outside, blew on freezing fingers and broke into happy, triumphal music, with a soaring string section and spirited horns. Timpani rumbled. It was designed to improve the Master's mood, and it always did. Heruta floated through the stone portal, and flipped up his visor as he entered.

The entranceway remained open, but the wren hesitated. Lessis was sure that the open doorway could not be crossed without arousing attention. She needed some way of smuggling herself inside.

She heard a slight rumbling sound nearby.

A three-tiered food trolley was being pushed toward the door by a pair of blinded slaves. On the trolley's shelves were plates with wafers and daubs of essence, and other plates with tiny wedges of sweet pastry.

The wren risked all. She flew into the bottom tier of the trolley and hid by the back, behind bottles of sweet essence.

The trolley trundled through the entrance and past the unseen guards. There was a short dark passage, and then the light grew brighter as they entered the Hall of Nectars and Essences.

It was a wide-open master work of style and elegant inlay. The walls, the ceiling, even the floor, were decorated with wondrous detailed mandalas in pastel shades, lavenders, yellows, pale blues, and pinks. The music from the orchestra outside continued to waft in through hidden apertures.

Hanging on the walls, between intricate mandalas of power, were paintings depicting great moments in the lives of the Five Great Masters.

In the center stood a circular table of white marble with beakers of nectar. And rolling in from the kitchens, came the trolley with essence and wafers.

The others had been waiting for Heruta Skash Gzug. They sipped nectar through platinum straws while they floated beside the table, each demonstrating his power of levitation to the others. Prad Azoz was to the right, Gshtunga opposite, with Prad Datse to the left and Gzug-Therva beside him. Heruta said nothing until he had sipped nectar and taken three wafers with essence.

"What has happened?" he said at last.

There was another silence. It lengthened. At last Gzug-Therva spoke.

"Someone performed with magic inside our perimeter."

"Within our perimeter? They grow too bold. We shall have to clean house again. These networks are always starting up among the slaves. Still, I thought we'd scoured them out recently enough."

"We were very successful the last time, but our enemies are resourceful." Prad Datse always supported Heruta Skash Gzug without hesitation.

"It may be a great hag, come to start up a new network. If so, she has overplayed her hand and given away the game. We shall search high and low until she is uncovered."

"We must take her alive," said Prad Azoz. "Such a one could be the final key to ultimate victory."

"We would all enjoy such an interrogation," said Gshtunga.

Heruta Skash Gzug agreed. "I suggest that we take a few moments for a search of our own. Let us conjoin on the esoteric plane and search out this hag."

They nodded, the eyes of black fire did not blink; theirs was the great power.

They all took a sip of nectar and then put themselves into the Nirodha trance state while Gzug-Therva spoke the syllables of dark power. Like a star igniting in the cosmos, their merged intelligence swelled out across the esoteric planes.

As it went, so a wave of terror filled the minds of every living thing in the vast warrens about them. All were suddenly aware that the Great Ones were active, they felt their huge minds sliding past their own, looking in if they wished, seeing their uttermost secret thoughts if they chose to.

Lessis had warning, and she ducked, by blanking the wren's consciousness down to a level below sleep. She prayed that Ribela was not caught out.

The expanding bubble of their gestalt thought grew out to encompass the underground city, even the Square on the surface far above.

Nothing. Again they unleashed the mind quake, and again they found nothing. After probing for a while by shifting suddenly from one mode to another, dropping through the psychic planes to the ethereal, they gave it up. There was nothing detectable on the esoteric plane within Padmasa.

They broke the conjunction.

"Disappointing," said Prad Azoz.

They all sipped nectar and chewed wafers daubed lightly with essence.

Meanwhile throughout Padmasa, men and women went trembling back to their tasks, sweat congealing on their brows and in their armpits. Such quakes were terrifying, but fortunately quite rare.

The wren's brain was brought back to wakefulness with a snap, however. Lessis risked this, to be certain that neither she nor Ribela had been detected. She found the Five already in conversation.

"The Mesomasters will continue their search."

"The Mesomasters reported this so-called witch magic."

"I felt it," said Gshtunga. "Something of the sort happened."

"Of course, Gshtunga. If you detected it, then it happened. But the hag must have left our perimeter."

"Or died of fright," said Prad Datse with a noise that some might understand to be a chuckle while most would think of scratchy chalk squeaking on a teacher's blackboard.

"The Mesomasters will have to intensify their efforts. Nothing could have hidden from our search."

"Perhaps Prad Datse is correct," said Gshtunga, and the group broke into further chuckles.

Heruta Skash Gzug made an emphatic sound that brought a silence.

"Let us turn to the matter of ogre production levels."

The eyes of black fire were all turned to him.

"There is a problem with the quality of the seed produced by the Ogre Developers."

"Difficulties always attend the introduction of something new like this," said Gshtunga. "I warned that this might happen."

"There is no problem, Gshtunga," said Gzug-Therva. "The invasion force is well equipped with ogre-class trolls."

"But how is the invasion proceeding? We have heard nothing for more than a day!"

A silence fell. Then Heruta spoke.

"We approach the critical moment more quickly than we had expected. The enemy is concentrating in a place called Fitou. Our demonstration force will now move out to confront them within three days."

"How great is the enemy force?"

"They have scraped up everything they had, perhaps forty thousand to put in the field."

"Will our demonstration be strong enough?"

"General Lukash assures me that the enemy in Fitou will be fooled, and that our demonstration force will be large enough to hold them in Fitou."

"And our prime host will then move onto Marneri as planned?"

"Exactly, good Prad Datse. We shall find Marneri virtually undefended. We shall take the fabled white city of the Bright Sea. Then we shall move on and take Bea and then Pennar. Three of the enemy's cities in one stroke. We shall build a mountain from their skulls!"

The wren flinched.

"Fetch up the sweets. I have a desire for a pastry with quince essence dripped upon it."

"And I will have honey."

Their conversation moved on to the need for reinforcements. The progress so far had been exemplary, but with the witch empire it was important to carry the thing through all the way. There would be more fighting. The witches would die hard, stabbing back all the time. Eventually, of course, they would have to seize the nettle and build a great fleet to take control of the seas, and then they could at last capture the Isles of Cunfshon and extirpate the witches and their thralls.

Lessis barely heard the final phrases, her thoughts in turmoil. The terrifying thing was that the plan was very likely to succeed. Lessis knew that any Argonath army that held seven legions would be capable of surviving the onslaught of the enemy's whole host in a defensive battle. But how would ogres do in fighting with dragons? And unless the commander of that army realized quickly enough that he was being duped by a demonstration force while another army marched toward Marneri, then complete disaster would overtake the Argonath.

Such an army could live off the country while it cut through the lush provinces of Aubinas, Lucule, North Troat. The legions would be far behind and would have to throw off the demonstration army and march to intercept the enemy's main host. There would be no opportunity to set the field of battle. The demonstration host would be large, perhaps larger than the legion army. It would be a difficult and dangerous task to evade such a force, and light out in pursuit of an even bigger one. To be caught between the two would be tantamount to risking utter destruction.

It was a perfect plan. If the ogres were a complete surprise, as they might well be, then the general in command of the legions might easily become rattled. While compensating for Ogres, he might mistake what was happening elsewhere and be fooled into standing still.

Slaves reached in to pull out bottles of essence with which to drench sweet wafers. The wren dodged the hands, then pecked at the few crumbs of wafer that were left on the plates when they were loaded back into the trolley.

The Five had left. The trolley was trundled out by the slaves. The wren slipped away unseen and flew into the shadows of the Prime Abyss.

CHAPTER FIFTY

The wren returned to the bull mammoth's pen. She had to wait for an hour before imps came to open the gates and bring in fodder and whole corn for the great beast within.

The mammoth fed while the wren pecked at insects and grains of corn. The imps departed. The mouse appeared in the straw.

Lessis passed on what she had heard.

"We have what we came for. We must return at once. Every day is vital."

"Is the bull free?"

"Yes. The sleeve is but a sham, held by a thread, he could break it at any time."

"Good. Then we are ready."

The mature bull of seventeen summers had spent the most interesting hours of his life listening with his whole being to the thought dreams presented by the mouse. He knew it was no ordinary mouse that addressed him.

These ideas had infected him with a deep excitement. In his inner being, he fairly trembled from it. He was promised his chance at revenge. He would go wild.

He remained calm, however, peacefully feeding on whole corn, thinking only about the best times he could remember. The first receptive cow. The days of playfulness as a young mammoth. Even his mother and the family group of his time as a calf.

The mouse had told him that when the time came, the thing that held his heel would break and he would go free. There would be a signal, and he would act.

Once outside the pen, he would be guided by the mouse. It claimed to know the way.

The gates opened once again to admit the dung cart and the slaves that pushed it. They took up their shovels and worked slowly through the pen, moving around the mammoth carefully. He was not normally a bad-tempered mammoth, but you never knew with these huge, dangerous beasts.

The doors opened again, imps leaned in to call on the slaves to hurry up.

Nobody noticed at first, but the placid bull had slipped his chain. He was by the dung cart in the next moment, and he knocked it over onto the trio of imps. He erupted out of the gate the very next moment. Riding on his right ear was a mouse, clinging on for dear life.

Flying up above and behind was a tiny bird.

Running ahead of him was an ever-growing tide of terrified men and imps.

At one junction he caught up with a milling group of imps. He crushed some, hurled others about like rags, and left the rest cowering in abject terror.

He broke into a stall and tore the chains out of the wall to free a young cow.

He broke into another stall but was unable to help the cow there, who was distended by some enormous pregnancy.

He raged along the stalls, smashing them open and liberating two more cows, both were only recently impregnated, still mobile, and just as angry as the bull.

Men with spears came. The mouse told the bull to pull up sections of the wooden stalls and to wield the wood like a branch, to fling it in effect.

The men threw their spears, but from a distance, and scored only a single glancing wound. The sight of entire stable doors flying back through the air at them was too much, and they turned and ran.

The maddened mammoths rumbled on, now bursting out of the mammoth-breeding zone entirely, scattering the guard at the gate and killing a dozen imps who foolishly stood their ground.

The mammoths took wounds, swords, arrows, and spears, but they did not seem to notice. This was a death ride, and in their huge feet and their flailing trunks, they carried a final message from their kind to the oppressors.

The mouse had deduced that a secret entrance to the higher Deeps had been dug recently. The mammoths could not have been brought down through the Tetralobe in secret, so there had to be another way in, and therefore out.

They reached a passage that widened to the left. To the

right it diminished. The doorways were dark, windows shuttered. The mouse spoke into the mammoth's ear. The beast
turned right, and the cows followed.

The mob of fugitives running ahead of them had turned
left. The wren darted ahead. There was a gate ahead,
guarded by a dozen imps and a pair of albino trolls.

The trolls attempted to halt the mammoths. The bull
charged. A troll swung a massive club. The bull jerked to a
halt, dodged the swing, caught the club with his trunk, and
tore it out of the troll's big hands.

He knocked the troll over and trampled it heavily. The
cows did the same for the other, although it managed to crip-
ple one of them with its club. She was slain by imps with
spears who were in turn slain by the bull. Then they went
on, through the gate and up a spiraling passageway that as-
cended to another gate.

There were more guards here, and four trolls. The fight
was longer and quite severe. The bull of seventeen summers
triumphed, however, despite taking some punishing blows.
He was speared, and badly, at the last. Another of the cows
was down, dying with spears in her belly. But the younger
cow was still alive, and she was helping him. The mature
bull of seventeen summers stepped forward, and together
they walked out into the light of day under the sun, into the
cool air of the outer world.

Enemies were coming, a great many enemies. There was
a thunder of horses hooves and the cries of Baguti horse
archers sighting the two mammoths resounded across the
open space. But for a few moments they had succeeded.
They had rebelled and broken their chains and escaped the
Hell imposed on them by the oppressors. Their trunks entwined and remained that way even as the arrows began to
rain down on them.

Two miles away the mouse scrambled across the moss,
with the wren flitting back and forth ahead. The sky was
wide-open and blue, with scarcely a cloud to be seen.

This was a time of terrible danger, the mouse felt more
vulnerable even than when they were inside the Tetralobe.
Hawks could be swinging in at any moment.

A shadow slid over them. They froze, the mouse looked
up and prepared to throw herself to either side. A great eagle
hovered, with wings beating, and then landed with a bounce
on the lichen of the frost meadow.

Cuica had seen the sudden appearance of two great mammoths out of a cave dug into the east face of the height of Padmasa. Such an irruption could only mean one thing.

Now an exhausted mouse climbed onto the eagle's neck and crawled to the leather cup and curled up inside, completely spent. The wren perched beside her.

The eagle lofted away and flapped across the death scene of the young mammoths, surrounded by a circling, ululating horde of blood-crazed Baguti. Rising higher, the bird was seen by the watchers in the Square. A report was made.

In the Hall of Nectars and Essences, the Five conferred.

"Send out the batrukhs, capture that eagle," said Heruta Skash Gzug. "Preferably alive, but dead if necessary."

CHAPTER FIFTY-ONE

Hour after hour, the army of the Masters came over the High Pass. Division upon division of imp, regiments of trolls, brigades of cavalry, endless trains of wagons, in all, a vast river of men, horses, and monsters, pouring through the pass and on down into the lovely lands of the Argonath.

They passed flasks of black drink and chewed strips of dried meat, thousands of drums thundered to keep their feet in motion.

The command post moved in ten-mile shifts before settling again to examine the maps. General Lukash had learned long ago that it was vital to know exactly where one was and where one's forces were deployed. With this army, three times as large as the army he had lead to victory at Barasha, he most feared losing control. To counter the centrifugal tendencies of such a vast host, he had determined to be constantly aware of his dispositions.

One problem was caused by the Baguti. They were good cavalry and able scouts, but had an annoying habit of delaying their reports until after they'd secured any booty that was available. Lukash was always worried that his leading force might crash into an ambush. He knew he wasn't facing some collection of royal armies here. The Legions of Argonath had the reputation of being the best armed force in the history of the world. Lukash respected that reputation.

Lukash was much changed. In just a few days, he had lost his wild ebullience. In fact, Lukash was but a shadow of his former self. Thrembode the New rode beside the general everywhere in a mood that approached pure serenity. A sense of swelling purpose was growing in the magician, a sense of his inevitable destiny. Everything was going perfectly.

The vast army was stretched out from the Upper Alno, back to the bottleneck at the top of the Lis gorge. In Alno, they marched down past burning villages into the plush lands of Arneis. Rolling hills fell away in row upon row to a misted horizon. They passed green fields lush with summer corn, grapes ripening on the vines, and barley ready to mow. Ahead some thirty miles now lay the large town of Cujac. It was walled, but not strongly held. Once they laid some troll-powered rams to the gates and walls, they could quickly take it down.

And just seventy miles beyond lay Kadein, the great city of the Argonath.

Thrembode had to restrain himself from singing for joy. The skies were blue and virtually cloudless, and the countryside was beautiful, a patchwork of little wheat fields and orchards, with neat houses of stone and thatch. All ripe for the looting!

But the prime reason that Thrembode felt like singing was the change in General Lukash. Two nights back, the batrukh had returned unheralded from Padmasa, carrying a passenger, on its back. The passenger was no ordinary presence, but was indeed the Mesomaster Vapul. The Mesomaster had immediately gone to Lukash's tent where he roused the general and drove out everyone else. Those who dared to try and eavesdrop came under a stinging spell that began as a ringing in the ears and then quickly grew louder until it became unbearable. It took half an hour or more to fade.

When Lukash eventually emerged, his leathery visage was visibly pale, his eyes wandered, his voice was flattened, neutral, toneless.

Vapul then summoned Thrembode and informed him that the magician's role in the coming campaign was to be increased. Thrembode was to have the task of monitoring the general and reporting to Vapul. Vapul was now in overall command, but Lukash would continue to run and fight the army. Lukash was a good tactician. But his personality type tended toward the grandiose, he became unstable. It was necessary to choke him off a little every so often. This Vapul would do, while giving affairs an overview.

To control Lukash day by day, Thrembode had been given a little silver whistle. One note and Lukash trembled and shook, and instantly fell silent. Thrembode's suggestions were always acted upon swiftly. Thrembode idly thought it might be amusing to have Lukash clean and polish his boots. It would be good both for Lukash and for Thrembode's lovely Talion riding boots. However, Thrembode also knew that Lukash was extremely busy with the campaign. Later there would be time for the boots, perhaps.

Vapul came and went, riding on the batrukh from some high cold ledge that he had chosen for a resting perch. There, he meditated to achieve the esoteric plane and make contact with the great powers in Padmasa.

Since that moment, Thrembode had found a positive joy to living. The great army moved to the schedule like some colossal clockwork toy. They were cutting into the heartland of the damned Argonathis like a hot knife through butter. They'd be in Cujac on the morrow and in Fitou a couple of days later. Oh, the loot to be had in Fitou! A richer, lovelier little city had never existed. And then after Fitou, it would be Tupin and the lovely land of Pengarden and then on to Kadein itself!

And after they had taken Kadein and reduced the other cities, then he, Thrembode, would be the new ruler in the great city. It was an intoxicating thought.

They dismounted and took up the task of piecing the army's positions together once more. Baguti came in followed by several of the hard-faced mercenary riders who served Padmasa with the terrible skills learned in lives of war in Kassim and Czardha. Several of these men had served in the conquering armies of the Trucial States and had done almost every bestial thing, long before they had even entered the service of Padmasa. Now they brought vital information for Lukash.

Thrembode listened carefully and watched the general make calculations.

Cujac was already besieged and gave signs of being very lightly held. Ample supplies of food were being seized in the farmlands of Epi, Alno, and Fenx. Baguti scouts had penetrated the outskirts of Andelain, where there were signs the enemy's resistance would stiffen. It appeared they intended to fight for Fitou.

Lukash barked orders, and his staff hurriedly wrote them out. Lukash read them and then had them sealed and sent at once. Couriers rode off in all directions. The gigantic host began to enter the crucial maneuvers. Surprises lay in store for all!

CHAPTER FIFTY-TWO

In the swampy midsection of the Kalens Valley, the situation approached complete disaster. Captain Eads had used every trick he could think of to maximize the weight of his little force and slow the onrushing five thousand imps, but the string was running out.

Day after day for weeks now they had marched, the men and dragons crisscrossing the swampy plain before Lake Wattel. Setting ambushes, driving in the enemy's pickets, forcing delays, and then retreating—always retreating.

All, men, dragons, and boys, had passed into a mental state beyond exhaustion. They walked on a grey inner plane toward a distant unfathomable horizon. Their eyes were dead to the light, but they marched and when required to, they fought.

Captain Eads had served them well. He and his officers had performed prodigies of tactical planning and skillful maneuver. They had fought dozens of little engagements, and yet the losses had been minimal, some five Talion troopers, four bowmen, and ten legionaries slain. They had some walking wounded, up ahead with the refugees. Three dragons were wounded and inactive. Two were still marching but not able to fight, although Anther might be able to return shortly. Tenebrak, who was close to death, had been sent in a long boat upstream. But considering how much action they had seen, it was a very slim casualty list. Eads's own wound had come from an arrow, fortunately not poisoned and had responded well to cleaning with Old Sugustus and ten stitches from the surgeon.

Still, all their work had not been enough. The enemy was on their heels, and the refugee column ahead of them was stumbling toward collapse. And now the trails recoalesced into a single road on the south side of Lake Wattel. The enemy was pushing much harder than before, scenting the chance to get among the refugees all bunched together on the trail.

In fact, things couldn't be worse. Eads was running out of room to maneuver just as the refugees were reaching complete exhaustion. Ten days and nights of forced march had killed fifteen percent already. The rest put one foot in front of the other in a slow mechanical way, but the enemy would be on them soon. The terrain was not promising.

The Kalen River moved through soft ground all through its middle course. Lake Wattel was a placid, bean-shaped interruption of the river some twenty miles long and six or seven wide. On the southern side, the lake pressed close to the bottom of the hills of Wattel Bek. Here the road ran between lake and hillside, and here the refugees were jammed together in a slow-moving mass.

Eads rode to confer with the Captain Retiner of the Talion Light Horse. He found Retiner and Troop Leader Croel waiting for him. The troopers were still capable of fighting, but their horses were beat and they themselves were much cut up. Still they were working back and forth across the enemy's front, harassing the Baguti and keeping them off the refugee column.

Eads and Retiner knew they had a disaster looming.

"We will be destroyed if we have to fight them in a line across the trail. They will be able to bring all their numbers against us. The dragons will be worn down, and they will break through."

Eads conceived of a desperate scheme. He called for Dragon Leader Turrent, and when Turrent arrived, he outlined it quickly.

"The dragons are exhausted, sir. I don't know."

"I know they're tired, Dragon Leader. We are all tired. But we will all be dead soon if we cannot slow the enemy's advance."

Turrent nodded. "Yes, sir, of course . . ."

And thus the fittest dragons, Bazil Broketail, Alsebra, Vlok, and the Purple Green, who had feet of iron now and complained far less than he used to, were sent scrambling up the steep slopes of the Bek, through tangled brush at the bottom that hid them from view.

They had become expert at setting ambushes. It brought out the natural predator in their souls. Many times they had managed to throw over the Baguti and get in among the imps, causing general panic and considerable casualties. Once attacked like that, the imps would be balky for the rest of a day.

The enemy had changed his approach, however, and recently there were more trolls up among the vanguard imps. The dragons found themselves in bruising little battles with squads of trolls again and again.

Eads and Retiner planned to engage first, on the road itself, launching fifty Talion troopers in a diversionary charge straight at the Baguti column.

Eads hoped to tempt the Baguti column forward. Then the dragons would swoop down and burst into the fray and drive the Baguti into the lake.

It was a favorite sort of one-two punch for Eads, and he had used it several times. The Baguti had fallen for it before. Had they learned proper caution yet?

The dragons climbed the slopes. Up above the tree canopy there were massive boulders, dropped from the pinnacles that stood out from the main mass of the Bek.

The dragons set themselves amid the boulders, hidden among what cover they could find. Dragonboys watched the scene from vantage points farther down, where they could see through the brush to the trail.

They waited, tense, anxious, tired beneath it all. The sun was high in the sky, the light dappled the great beasts beneath the trees. They were so still that one might almost have taken them for a row of big boulders. Then a long neck turned, and a great dragon's head would swing up and big black eyes would glisten.

"Someday this will be over, and we will drink beer and think back to it, and we will laugh about it," said Bazil Broketail.

"I am not so confident that I will ever want to laugh about this particular experience," replied Alsebra.

"I want to sleep for a week," said Vlok.

"I want to kill imps," said the Purple Green.

"Well, when it comes down to it, so do I," said Alsebra. "I would just like to be able to sleep for a few days before I kill imps again."

"Troll down there," grumbled the purple Green. "I smell them now."

This remark caused the others to sniff the air.

"I don't know," said Bazil. The Purple Green claimed to

have a powerful nose and to disparage the noses of wyvern dragons. Bazil had refused to believe it, but slowly he was coming around.

"By the ancient gods of Dragon Home, I smell nothing, maybe a little horse if I strain."

"Flying dragons have stronger sense of smell than wyverns," said the Purple Green, matter-of-factly. "I can smell horse at great distances. And mammoth, too. Mammoth makes great eating I can tell you. Right now I smell imps and trolls."

"How many trolls?" said Vlok.

"Don't know, could be many."

"Fighting trolls every day is hard work," said Vlok.

"My arms are weary enough," grumbled Alsebra.

"The problem is that we have slowed down to pace of refugees. That means the trolls can catch up."

"Damn trolls, they seem to get tougher every time."

"This is new breed to me," said Vlok.

"This is like sword trolls of Tummuz Orgmeen," said Bazil. "Problem with them is that they move so quick. They clever enough to use a sword, but not clever enough to use it well."

There came a whistle.

"That was Manuel. Time to go."

They shifted in their positions, hefted their swords.

The silvery call of the cornets came from the woods below. The Talion cavalry troopers were making their demonstration charge, generating as much noise as they could.

They heard the charge go past them in the woods below. Heavy brass horns blared from that direction. A huge shout went up. More horns and more shouts, the woods were alive with the enemy.

The Talions blew their cornets for the retreat. Simultaneously Turrent blew his cornet and sent the dragons crashing downhill, stamping through the thickets, swords out and ready.

The troopers were thundering past along the trail. Behind them came a shrieking mass of Baguti, their curved scimitars aloft.

The dragons paused. Would the imps follow the Baguti, blood-crazed by their proximity to the refugee train? This was the crucial moment for Eads's plan.

Suddenly there was a blast from heavy horns and a thunder of drums all along the dragons' left flank. Beneath the horns, they could hear the shrill cries of imps and the roar of trolls.

"Their whole army is coming up, they have outmarched us."

"I smell troll, very close now."

"What do we do?" said Vlok.

"Good question that," commented the Purple Green.

The dragons looked to Dragon Leader Turrent. Turrent was looking off to the left with anxious eyes.

A baying mass of imps was going past on the trail, spear points glittering above their heads. But with a large force coming on their flank, it would be suicidal to attack now.

"Let us go back to where we hid," suggested Relkin. "Those loose boulders. We'll roll them down. That will keep them busy for a while."

The dragons and dragonboys did not wait for Turrent's assent. They turned and scrambled back up the steep slope of the Bek, plunging through the line that separated the lower slope forest of mature trees and the scrub and saplings on the higher level. They were back among the tumbled boulders.

The horns were blasting down below and drums were thundering. Dragonboys darted about the boulders seeking the ones that would be easiest to set rolling down the slope.

"This one's the best," claimed Swane, pointing to a near cylindrical piece of rock, lying on its side atop another similar piece. Each was five feet wide or more.

"For once I agree with you," said Manuel.

Relkin reached the spot. "There's another good one over there. But both of these are ready to go."

The dragons put their forelimbs against the rock, crouched, and flexed huge thews. They heaved as one and the rock rolled, crashing through the trees and hurtled downslope toward the trail.

The booming of the drums ceased like a miracle. A horn blast was cut short. Screams arose, and continued to rise as the boulder rolled on.

The second one was already on its way. The dragons now gathered around the one that Relkin had found.

This was more irregular, six feet in diameter, resting between two flat slabs.

Once again the dragons put their backs into it and heaved

the rock up an inch or two and set it rolling. It fell off the slabs with a crash and then bounced on, skittered down the bare rock slope, and boomed through the thickets and into the downslope woods. More screams erupted at once.

"Over here," called Manuel, "I think I've found a good one here."

CHAPTER FIFTY-THREE

The day wore on. The enemy swarmed up about them, and they were forced to give ground, even before they'd run out of good boulders. The arrows came in so thick and heavy that they had to retreat. As it was, the dragonboys were cutting out dozens from joboquin and dragon hide.

There was nowhere to go but up.

The dragons broke off a section of rock, a triangle thirty feet long, and sent it lurching, sliding, and finally tumbling down into the center of the enemy below. They saw trolls knocked flying. The dragonboys sent up a ragged little cheer. Dragons looked at each other and shrugged. Boys were always finding ways to be noisy; it was their nature.

Arrows shot overhead suddenly. A heavy horn was blaring on their left. The damned imps had gotten up on their flanks again. It kept happening. They had to move.

Behind them, the slope of the Wattel Bek was broken open in a narrow canyon that zigzagged up steeply between a pair of pinnacles, crazy juts that had separated from the main mass of the Bek. Up this the dragons trudged while dragonboys kept up a constant rain of arrows from their quick firing Cunfshon crossbows.

The dragons reached the top and called down. The boys ran up, ahead of the yelling imps that flooded in, driven on by the men who commanded them.

The dragons found two good-sized boulders and had them in position by the time the boys reached the top. The first boulder crushed a dozen imps. The sight of the second one being positioned at the top of the cliff sent the rest of the imps running back to the bottom as fast as they could scramble. In vain their masters lashed at them with whips, even swords. The imps were panicked and could not be checked.

Manuel, who had proven himself to be good with the Cunfshon bow, loosed a long shot and struck down one of the imp officers. The others retreated, cursing loudly while the dragonboys cheered again.

The enemy had cleared back to the bottom of the steep little canyon. They would have to go wide on either side to get up the steep face of the Bek; it was virtually a cliff in this section and the one above it. It would be hours before they managed that.

Meanwhile, the Purple Green had rolled up another good-sized hunk of rock, and Bazil and Alsebra were prying out a few smaller, but handier pieces of stone. They could keep them at bay for now.

The only problem was that there was no obvious way to go anywhere else, except down. The cliff was twenty to thirty feet high all around them, leaving them at the bottom of a kind of cup in the rock. Flies were bothering them, and the dragons realized they were trapped and their spirits sank somewhat.

"We cannot go down."

"Damn, I'm hungry already."

"We get too hungry then we just go down there and eat troll."

"Foolish wild one," snorted Alsebra. "We go down there and troll will eat us. There's a hundred of them down there."

"Not after that big rock we pushed down. We got a few then."

"Look, you go ahead, while they're eating you, we'll think of a way to get out of here."

Dragon Leader Turrent felt the need to try and cheer everyone up. He strode among the dragons, murmuring to each.

"Don't worry. We'll work it out."

When he had passed and gone off to sit by himself and try and think of a way out, the dragons murmured together.

"Looks like we're done for . . ."

"By the ancient gods of Dragon Home, I never thought I'd end up like this."

"I don't know, maybe we can climb this cliff," said Alsebra.

"I don't think so," said Vlok.

Bazil Broketail perked up at Alsebra's words, and he immediately turned and studied the cliff above them. It was not that high, a mere twenty feet in places, but it was steep, virtually sheer. Nor did there seem to be any obvious handholds big enough for a dragon.

"No," he concluded, "I don't think so."

Alsebra shrugged. "Maybe you're right," she agreed.

Not for the first time, the Purple Green lamented his decision to join the legions. Bazil didn't have the heart to argue with him about it.

Turrent stood up and turned to the dragonboys.

"Who are our best climbers?"

They looked down, some glanced at Relkin.

"Relkin, who else?" said Bryon.

"All right, Relkin, you're for the mission. Who else?"

"Swane's good enough," said Relkin.

Swane swelled a bit, proud to be named like that. For all his swagger, Swane was sensitive to Relkin's opinion of him.

"All right, get rid of both my problems at the same time. Both of you, get up this cliff and find out if there's any way out of here."

"Yes, sir," said Swane. Relkin nodded.

They looked along the cliff. It was rock and rock-hard dirt, but there were handholds and a few good deep lateral cracks. For Relkin, who had lived on the crags of Blue Stone as a child, it was not a difficult cliff. For Swane, who'd climbed the fells of Seant all his life, it was equally easy. They were soon up on the ledge above. This was as constrained as the one below on which the dragons stood. However, there were clefts in the cliff face here, and one of them provided a neat chimney that they could climb easily using shoulders and feet on opposite walls. They went up like this for thirty feet and then rolled out onto a larger, flat place, a natural step back for the hill.

More steep cliff wall loomed above them.

Relkin turned to look along the ledge and found himself face-to-face with two young, and strikingly attractive, women.

The girls were as surprised to see them as they were to see the girls. Both girls wore leggings of deer hide, moccasins, and stiff leather shirts. They carried weapons. Their skins were burnished by sun and sky, and their hair was blond, sun-bleached, and blown wild behind them.

"By the breath," muttered Swane.

The one on the left, the slender one, quickly notched an arrow to her hunting bow.

"Who are ye?" she said in strongly accented Verio. The other girl had unsheathed a small sword. They were plainly used to their weapons.

Swane made to pull up his bow, dangling from his wrist down in the chimney. The girl's bow shifted, and she prepared to release.

"Freeze, Swane, not a muscle unless you want to die here."

Swane turned a truculent face to the girl, but did not move. Relkin was right. For a long second they all hesitated. The arrow did not come.

Relkin turned to the girl.

"Dragoneers Relkin and Swane of the 109th Marneri Dragons at your service, young lady." He saluted and stopped himself from asking them what young women of evident fertility were doing leaving themselves this close to a host of enemy imps.

"I thought the refugees were up ahead of us, Relkin," said Swane.

"They are, Swane. I don't think these are refugees."

"Then who the hell are they?"

"And who the hell are ye talking about?" snapped the one with the bow.

"Begging your pardon, young miss, but yourself," said Relkin. The arrow swung to cover him. It was a hunter's arrow, long, sharp blades of steel, at this range it would probably go right through his body. He hoped she didn't release.

The other girl, the heavier of the two, approached, still holding that sword at the ready.

She gave them a long look. "They are dragonboys!" she announced. "I recognize the uniform."

"That's all very well, Silva, but what are they doing here?"

"Why are you here?" said the girl with sword.

Relkin let out a breath. "Perhaps you don't know this, miss, but there's an enemy army just down there in the valley."

"That's right, young ladies," said Swane. "Five thousand imps or more. Maybe a hundred trolls. They be coming up this way, too. You don't want to be here then."

"Of course we won't be here. I am Eilsa Ranardaughter.

This is my friend Silva Geisga. We have been scouting the enemy for days now."

"You're scouts?" said Relkin, still incredulous that women would be so risked around forces of the great enemy.

"Well," for the first time the girl behind the bow seemed something less than imperious. "Not officially."

"Then what are you doing here? That enemy army down there is an army of imps and trolls. They will take you for the breeding pens."

Relkin had seen such things and worse, in Tummuz Orgmeen.

"They will never catch Eilsa Ranardaughter," snorted the girl, as she put down her bow and unknocked the arrow.

The other girl put away her sword.

"Ye are dragonboys?"

"Yes, miss."

"Where are the dragons, then?"

"Down below. We came up a narrow little switchback and found ourselves trapped. There's no way the dragons can climb the cliff, and the enemy is down the bottom of the switchback gulley we came up."

"The dragons cannot climb the cliff?"

"They're too big, too heavy."

"I see." Silva stood up and walked over to Eilsa, who shook her head violently.

"Pardon my asking, miss, but who are you scouting for?" said Relkin.

Eilsa Ranardaughter sniffed. "Clan Wattel, of course. Ye are on our land."

The other girl broke in, trying to soften Eilsa's arrogance. "Clan Wattel holds all the land on this side of the river, from the lake to the heights at Fire Rock."

All Relkin knew about Clan Wattel was what he'd heard through the scuttlebutt. Another highland clan, only a big one. They'd lived up here since the beginning of time.

Swane spoke up. "Don't take this wrong, miss, but I'm gonna pull my bow up now if you don't mind. It's hanging down the well on a strap, if you see what I mean."

Eilsa nodded, impatiently. "Bring it up, but set it down where I can see it."

Swane did so and then got to his feet.

Relkin had a hunch.

"So you know this place well, then?"

"Very well."

"So if there was a way for our dragons to get out, you'd know of it."

The girl seemed to waver. Relkin pressed.

"We have to find a way to get them out of there, or they'll die. We've got thousands of refugees, lots of women among them, just ahead of us. Without those dragons, they're done for."

The girls looked at each other.

"Silence, Silva. By clan law I command thee."

"Eilsa, 'tis not right."

Relkin recalled the girl's confidence that they would be able to escape any imps that managed to make it up here. These girls had come here somehow. There must be a secret way out.

"Well, Eilsa Ranardaughter, perhaps you could tell me how you were going to climb out of here. We have to find some way out for our dragons."

"I cannot do that. It is a clan secret."

Silva was impatient. "You must tell them, Eilsa. Think of the dragons."

Eilsa was torn. "My father will never forgive me."

"The chief will understand the need. We saw the refugees. The enemy will take them. We cannot allow that to happen. Your father would not let it happen."

"To give up a clan secret is to give up one's own life."

"Eilsa, ye have no choice. Ye cannot let all those people die. They will eat the children and the men. The women they will take to one of their hellholes. Ye know their ways."

Eilsa struggled with herself. Relkin could see that she was a young woman of enormous principle, clearly a chief's daughter and proud of that fact.

She gave a big sigh and shrugged her shoulders.

"All right, may the ancestors forgive me. There is a way. We can show ye. The ancient stair."

"The what?"

"The stairway of Veronath," said Silva. "We will show you."

"A stairway? Big enough for dragons?"

"Oh, yes, big enough for many dragons. We will show you."

CHAPTER FIFTY-FOUR

And so Silva and Eilsa lead them through the pinnacles to a flat wall of rock hidden in deep shadow. Eilsa stood close to the rock and put her palm to it and said the word "peace" in an antique form of Verio.

The wall suddenly shimmered with lines of gold running through the rock. An outline of a gate appeared. At the top was the crown of the king, on either side were stonemason signs, a hammer and anvil, a compass and ruler, and written in the ancient Verio script was a blessing from an ancient king.

" 'Written in the 13th year of the reign of his august majesty King Kuskuld the Second,' " Relkin read in the first lines. "Enter here if ye abideth by the king's peace. They that abideth by the peace shall prosper and live long. Their children shall be many and so unto the many generations.' "

"We abideth by the king's peace," said Eilsa clearly.

The gate in the stone rolled back silently on hidden hinges. A dark opening lay ahead of them.

The girls swung back to look at the dragonboys. Swane was stunned. His knees actually trembled.

"What?" was all he was able to get out.

Relkin, however, simply walked in, through the gate, seemingly unconcerned. Eilsa's eyes snapped fire.

"Ye take this for a small thing, Dragonboy?"

He turned to her. "No, lady, I do not. 'Tis of ancient Veronath, is it not?"

" 'Tis a great magic from the ancient ones, and ye should not be speaking their name. Ye are not worthy."

Relkin bridled, but bit off an angry retort.

"In Marneri we make less reverence of the old kings of Veronath than perhaps you do in the hills. We have new kings of our own, and we have the emperors in Cunfshon."

"Hmmmf!" Eilsa turned away from him. She and Silva found more satisfaction in Swane's evident awe.

He ran his hands up and down the edge of the great gate. "This is very great magic. Hey Quoshite, what about this? I never seen anything like."

Relkin had seen far too much magic, especially terrifying great magics that could blind thousands of men, or charm armies of rats to do one's will. He felt no threat in this gate, and he recognized it for what it must once have been. An entrance to one of the great hidden palaces of the kings of Veronath. This was awe inspiring no doubt, but Relkin Orphanboy of Quosh was an old hand when it came to awesome magics, and while his interest was aroused, his knees did not set to knock.

"Yes, friend Swane, it is a powerful magic. A hidden door, and it leads to the stair?"

"Yes," said Silva.

"And the stair leads to the king's palace?"

"No longer, dragonboy. The king's palace was burned by the demon of Dugguth. Long ago in the dark time."

Eilsa clearly knew the history of that time well.

They went on inside. The door swung shut on its own accord when they were safely within. A row of dim illuminations swelled along the ceiling. When standing beneath them, Relkin saw patterns of stars picked out in the rock above and guessed that these were "secret" constellations known only to the ancient kings.

By this light they made out a landing, with walls decorated with enormous bas-reliefs, portraits of the ancient great King Kuskuld, all done in the smooth, realistic style of the middle-Veronath period.

In the center was the stair, a winding circular staircase cut in the rock, following the line of an ancient fault. It was certainly wide enough to accommodate a dragon.

"Where will the stair take us?" said Relkin.

"To the top of the north cliff, where the palace once stood."

"The enemy never found this stair?"

"The secret died with the king. They roasted him over slow fires for days but could not get it from him."

"Great magic, I have seen great magic." Swane was still mumbling to himself in awe. Suddenly he stopped. "We still have a problem. How will we get the dragons up here so they can use this stair?"

Eilsa blinked a moment. "The stairs wind down as well as up, see," she pointed. Swane almost capered on the spot.

"There are three doors to the stairs; this is the middle door," said Silva. "There was once a road that ran from the cliff to the lake."

"One last question," said Swane. "Can we open it from the inside?"

Eilsa Ranardaughter led them down the stair. "Of course, Dragonboy."

When cracks in the rock face suddenly emitted golden light, Vlok jumped up with an oath, scrambled back, and would have fallen down the notch if the Purple Green hadn't seized him by the tail.

Then a piece of the rock wall silently swung inward to reveal a dark cavity out of which stepped Relkin and Swane. Behind them came two wild-haired young women, clad in the deerskins of the hill folk.

The young women put their hands to their mouths when they saw the dragons looming over them. Both went into dragon-freeze and were unable to speak or move. The Purple Green leaned over them and examined them closely for a moment, which only intensified the freeze.

The other dragons were still staring at Relkin and Swane and the hole in the ground they'd emerged from.

Digal Turrent came alive with a jerk.

"What the hell?"

Relkin noticed the dragon-frozen state of the girls, and he reached over to close their eyelids manually. It was the only way to break the freeze when it was this strong.

"Dragoneer Relkin, stand to attention and report!"

Relkin stiffened. "Dragoneer Relkin, reporting, sir!"

Turrent strode forward to inspect the hidden gate.

"If I hadn't seen it with my own eyes, I never would have believed it possible."

"It is a great magic, sir," said Swane proudly, as if he had discovered it himself.

"A great magic, what the hell is that?"

"It was wrought by the ancient ones, the old kings from before the fall of Veronath."

"Oh, that nonsense. Well, I don't belive it for a minute. There must be some rational explanation."

But as Digal Turrent contemplated the work of the ancient Mage-King Kuskuld II, his confidence in that statement began to fade.

The doorway had just opened in the rock. He had seen nothing. It had not been there. Then just "poof" and it was. And this stone was cut perfectly smooth. He shivered at the thought of it.

Meanwhile the young ladies had emerged from dragon-freeze. Slowly their minds unlocked. They opened their eyes again and gasped at the sight of the dragons. Relkin seized their attention. "Don't freeze again. Remember, they're like people in their own way; they talk. It's hard to understand them sometimes at first. Their vocal chords are different from ours, but you can catch it after a bit. They won't harm you."

"All my life," whispered Eilsa Ranardaughter, "all my life I have been wanting to see such dragons. They are wonderful."

"They are," said her friend, "I did not realize they were all so different."

And different they were, from the huge wild dragon, purple on the upper surfaces and black where his wings were folded, and green below, to the leather-colored ones and the dark green one. Each was different. One had an oddly kinked tail, the last few feet were set at an angle and seemed almost as if they belonged on some other beast.

"Come, I will introduce you," said Relkin.

"Correction, Dragoneer," said Turrent, "I will do that job. You will see to your dragon."

Relkin seethed, but he did as ordered.

Turrent took the girls over to introduce them to the dragons.

Relkin had ascertained that apart from being extremely hungry and extremely thirsty, his dragon was not suffering too much from any of the multitude of cuts and abrasions he had suffered. Then Turrent was there, with Silva and Eilsa, whose eye had softened into something lovely to observe, a true beauty.

"And this is our famous broketail dragon, Bazil.'"

Eilsa introduced herself and Silva to the dragon, beating Relkin to it. Bazil thanked her for opening the lower gate to the stair. At the utterance of Verio by this huge beast, Eilsa almost went into dragon-freeze again. Until then, she had somehow not connected it all up. It was as if she'd been addressing a clever horse or something. But it spoke like a person! Even if the sound was different from that of a human throat. If it spoke like a person, then it had a mind like that of a person!

A glance at Silva showed her that Silva Geisga was similarly affected.

Dragon Leader Turrent watched with an odd cacophony of emotions running through him. Overarching was his relief at having a route of escape open to them. Still, he felt a definite chagrin at having Relkin as the hero in all this. And working away within that was a growing admiration for the kid. There was just something about this boy's affinity for the magical that went well beyond the normal.

The dragons climbed the stair on all fours, but there was plenty of room, the ancient masons of King Kuskuld had built on a generous scale.

Turrent led, with Eilsa Ranardaughter beside him. She would not accept anything else, saying that this stair was a "clan secret and she was daughter of the clan chief."

Then came dragons and dragonboys. At the rear, Silva walked up with Swane, behind the swaying bulk of Vlok, his great sword "Katzbalger" visible on his shoulder.

As they went, Silva asked questions. She was alive with curiosity about the dragonboys and their immense charges. Swane was pleased to tell her anything he could.

When she asked him about Relkin, he hesitated, then honestly got the better of him.

"He's sort of a legend in his own time. The elves have marked him out. He's been with the witches and seen things. We've all seen things, actually."

Silva's eyes lit up most satisfactorily when he said this. "Yeah, it was just last summer, we were in Ourdh on this expedition. Our unit, the 109th was attached to the Second Legion from Marneri . . ."

CHAPTER FIFTY-FIVE

The stair spiraled past endless bas-reliefs, depicting great moments in the reign of King Kuskuld II. The work was intricate, carved by skilled craftsmen. The light came solely from the star patterns set in the ceiling.

At last, under a domed ceiling, they reached the top. Eilsa spoke the antique Verio word for "peace" to a blank wall, and it lit up with golden lines, twinkling in the rock. Again she spoke the command phrase and the door swung inward, smooth and silent on unseen hinges.

The light of the day flooded in. They stepped out onto a broad flat space, bare rock that gave way to heather and grass and a view beyond of the rest of the Bek, a series of rolling downs, with strips of forest in the valley bottoms and grass and heather on the rest.

The door they had emerged from stood open in a wall of natural rock standing edge on to the main cliff. When the last dragon was through, the doors slid shut again. The golden lines faded away, and no one would ever have known what was concealed there.

Digal Turrent lay down on the ground and kissed it.

Relkin strolled over to investigate a few jagged ruins, the remains of a wall, and a set of steps. Farther away some broken slabs stood up amid the heather, all that was left of the great palace that had stood here in the days of ancient Veronath.

Relkin shivered in the warm breeze, feeling a haunting sense of presence. The view was magnificent wherever you looked. Beyond the hidden dome of the stair lay the wide lake, spread out below the Bek, and in the distance the dim green of Feutoborg Forest. Relkin felt echoes of the older world here in these quiet ruins. In that older world, ruled by the old gods like Caymo and Asgah, he sometimes felt, he might have been happier. It was an absurd thought. He would have had no dragon! With a shrug, he dismissed it all. He had stopped worrying about "destiny" sometime during the past week, too tired and too frightened to be wasting any energy on worrying about the future. Whatever would be, would be. His destiny had been to be born in this era, when Veronath was naught but ruins and the dusty names of long-dead Kings.

He found Eilsa and Silva standing beside him. He hadn't noticed their approach. Eilsa pointed to the east.

"If you pass down the royal road there, you'll come on the Clove Road. Just follow that, and you will emerge on the northeastern edge of the Bek. Perhaps you will find your captain there."

The side of the Bek fragmented here, and a deep clove valley cut down between two projections of the massif. It was at least five miles distant, he estimated.

"And where will you be going, Miss Eilsa Ranardaughter?"

Her eyes flashed in the old imperious way, but she softened after a moment. "We will march to rejoin my father and the host of Clan Wattel."

A shadow fell over them.

"This was a magnificent thing that you did," said Bazil. "I thank you, Eilsa Dragonfriend."

Eilsa glowed. "I am proud to be so called, Sir Bazil."

The dragon showed a line of wicked-looking fangs. Digal Turrent had recovered himself and taken stock of the situation. Turrent looked off to the east down the clove valley, sinking between the outlying arms of the Bek. Turrent was on the point of giving the order to send them marching east when there was a halloa from their right. Two tall young men stepped out of the heather beyond the ruins and loped toward them.

With a cry of welcome, Eilsa waved to them, and when they drew close, both she and Silva clasped hands briefly with both.

Relkin was struck by how much alike all the young Wattels were, with strong features, full lips, blue eyes, and sun-bleached hair. Both young men stared at Bazil and the other dragons with awe and wonder in their faces.

The four spoke among themselves briefly in their antique, accented Verio and then Eilsa introduced them to Relkin.

"These are two warriors of the Fird of Wattel, this is

Flembard," the taller, "and this is Seegric," the broader, more heavily built one.

"Greetings," said Flembard. "We welcome ye to the land of Clan Wattel and are come to escort ye to the camp of Clan Chief Ranard."

"The chief awaits your presence," added Seegric. "He has flown his battle flag since this dawn. The farthings have been summoned to the muster. The entire fird will be in place soon."

Turrent stepped forward. "I thank you for your greeting. I am Dragon Leader Turrent. This is a detachment from the 109th Marneri Dragons. We're trying to get back to the rest of our unit. Down the lakeshore, yonder," he pointed eastward. "This is the way to go, I understand."

Flembard digested this and looked carefully over the assembled dragons, three of them in the two to two-and-a-half-ton range, ten-foot tall, with massive limbs and heavy tails, and one in the four-and-a-half-ton range, who in addition had great wings folded behind him.

"It is a wonder to see such great beasts," he said.

"Hrrrmph," rumbled the broketail dragon. "We are dragons, man, not beasts."

At the sound of language from the dragon, the two young warriors went into dragon-freeze and had to be pinched back to life by Eilsa and Silva.

"The dragons speak, Flembard, they are like people."

"I . . ." Flembard and Seegric were lost for words.

"'Where is your chief camped?" said Turrent.

Flembard let out a deep breath.

"I beg thy pardon, Sir Dragon, I have never met one of your illustrious kind before. Dragon Leader, our camp lies close by, beside the lake of Shamrocks."

"Then, let us go there at once. We have little time and must rejoin Captain Eads."

They set out at once and reached the shores of the lovely little lake of the Shamrocks within a few minutes.

They found a cluster of tents around a flagpole flying a banner of scarlet and gold. Hundreds of men, all clad in the tunics and leggings of the uplands, were gathered there. They were the Fird, the feudal army of the clan. As the dragons approached, the men rose up and began to applaud. The commotion grew as more and more clansmen emerged from the tents. They wore the horned helmet and chain mail of ancient Verio, and carried round shields and long, straight-sided swords.

Clan Chief Ranard was not one to wait about passively in such a situation. He moved to see what was happening. His big blond head towering above most of the others as he strode along.

And thus he came upon the extraordinary sight of four great battledragons treading forward through the ranks of his men. Over their shoulders were hung great swords and shields. On their heads they wore steel helmets. Dragonboys bounced along at their side, and a young man in the armor of a legionary strode at their head.

Clan Chief Ranard took all this in and then observed his daughter Eilsa, marching with the dragonboys. He connected all these things in a moment's thought. He realized what must have happened. Then he indicated to them with a brusque sweep of his mailed fist and ordered them brought to him.

When his daughter stood in front of him, he fixed her with his fiercest eye.

"What hath thee done, Eilsa, daughter of mine?"

Eilsa confessed that she had brought the dragons up the stair of Veronath. Ranard gritted his teeth and fought down his first reaction, which was one of horror. He mastered himself in a moment. Eilsa could feel his confusion.

"By the breath, it is hard sometimes, but I understand. I would have done the same thing in your place. They could not be left to die. I wish to welcome the great dragons to our lands. If there is anything we can do for them, let us hear it."

Digal Turrent spoke up at once.

"The dragons are starving."

"I am afraid I lack supplies of meat."

"They usually eat grain."

"Good, for grain we have. We carry oats and flour." Ranard turned to his daughter. "Daughter Eilsa, find the cooks and order them to work up some stirabout for these dragons."

Eilsa departed at once on her mission, with Silva Geisga accompanying her.

Turrent then introduced the chief to each dragon and dragonboy, at the chief's request. For their part the dragons did their best to avoid giving the clansmen dragon-freeze.

Clan Chief Ranard found that even he had to fight down

the fear as he met each of these monsters face-to-face. Something in the flatness of the reptilian stare brought up primordial fears. Ranard found his own heart beating considerably harder when it was over. His hands were balled tight at his sides.

The dragons stood, murmuring quietly to one another. Dragonboys went to work on equipment and dragon hide and were soon surrounded by an eager throng of questioners. They did their best to come up with answers despite the difficulty of understanding the clansmen.

Dragon Leader Turrent and the clan chief were still in conversation when Eilsa and Silva returned to announce that the cooks had prepared hot oat mush. Unfortunately they had no akh to flavor it with.

The dragons were downcast.

"The least you might expect," groused the Purple Green.

"They cannot grow those kind of things here in these hills, my wild friend," said Alsebra.

"Doesn't look like they can grow anything but heather," commented Manuel.

"Why do not dragonboys carry akh?"

"Because with the way you eat, it's too heavy."

"Bah, lazy dragonboys, always it is the same."

A lively discussion grew up at once on this topic with sharply opposing opinions from dragon and dragonboy. An audience of clansmen tried to follow what was going on with expressions of awe. It was still sputtering when they reached the cook fire, and under the gaze of the entire host, the dragons and dragonboys ate all the oatmeal the poor cooks could stir up in their potchoon cauldrons.

"Do dragons eat that much all the time?" said Silva to Relkin, gazing in awe at the Purple Green finishing a third potchoon of mush.

"They get hungry fast. They burn hot, do dragons."

Manuel had drifted over. "In fact, they are hotter than even men, so they taught me in the academy."

"You must have to carry a lot of food with you," said Silva.

"We march with a supply wagon or two, I'll grant you that," said Relkin.

He felt Eilsa's gaze upon him and looked up.

"I heard that you are wed to a princess in the great city of Ourdh," she said suddenly.

Relkin flushed with mingled embarrassment and anger. This was Swane's fault.

"I would discount such rumors. I am not wed. I cannot, until I have served ten years."

"Oh?" Eilsa gave him a saucy grin. "And how long have you served already?"

"This is our third year of service."

"Our?"

"My dragon and me," he nodded to the leatherback sitting down with a fourth potchoon.

"By the breath of the Mother, I think they will eat all our supplies before they are sated."

"It's certainly possible."

Vlok trod by on his way to another potchoon.

Eilsa looked back to Relkin with an odd look of calculation on her face. Silva giggled, Eilsa flashed her a look of admonition, then broke into a giggle herself.

A scout rode in on an exhausted hill pony, riding straight up to the clan chief before dismounting and bending the knee to report.

Clan Chief Ranard listened and grimaced. It was bad news, the very worst. The enemy had closed to within a couple of miles of the refugees. The defenders were on the point of collapse.

Ranard of Wattel did not mull it over for long. He had long since thought of this and what he would have to do. He ordered the trumpets blown and called for his horse.

"Dragon Leader," he said, "I expect that Captain Eads will need our assistance. Clan Wattel now goes to war."

CHAPTER FIFTY-SIX

With full stomachs the dragons felt both refreshed and somewhat sleepy. They shrugged off their fatigue. The march was
downhill on a level path, and they fell silent and loped along
at an easy pace.

Relkin marched with his head full of thoughts of Eilsa
Ranardaughter. On the one hand dismay that she should have
heard wild tales of the expedition to Ourdh from Swane, and
on the other a passionate interest in her opinion of a certain
dragoneer first class from Quosh. There had been that gleam
in her eye when they'd last spoken. His heart had not
stopped thumping yet.

Everything about her fascinated him, from her eyes to her
accent. All these Wattels sounded as if they had stepped out
of history, but it was Eilsa's voice in particular that gripped
his attention. And there were her looks. She was an uncomplicated beauty, slim but wide-shouldered, with a jut of the
chin and a nose a little too big for the classical taste. Her
eyes were dark blue, a furious blue that burned easily like
blue stars in the night. Certainly she was all a young man
like Relkin of Quosh could have desired.

It was only when Manuel fell in beside him and asked
him how he felt about the upcoming fight that he even recalled just where he was and what he was going into.

"Has it occurred to you that we might, none of us, survive? They outnumber us so heavily."

Relkin pursed his lips and shrugged.

"There's more of them, but I reckon these Wattels are
going to give them a hell of a fight. They're wild as wolves
and a lot fiercer if you ask me."

"I wondered why you weren't praying. Everyone else is."

Relkin shrugged again. "I ain't really a worshiper like
them. I hold to the old gods."

"If they exist, then maybe you should be asking them for their help."

"I don't know about calling on them for help. You take your chances when they help you."

Manuel smiled. "You have been through a lot in these last few months."

"If old Caymo's been helping me, then my luck must have been really terrible."

Manuel's smile was brittle. "So you aren't afraid?"

"This is your first time in a big fight isn't it?"

Manuel's head dropped slightly. "Yes." He was older than Relkin and well educated, but he knew that Relkin had seen more action in his three years of service than most men saw in their entire terms of ten.

"Manuel, anytime you go into a fight, you take the chance you won't come out of it. You know the most common form of serious injury for a dragoneer?"

Manuel looked up, a sudden gleam in his eye, "Of course. Getting stepped on by the dragon."

Relkin nodded. "Right. So you can forget all that stuff about glory and honor they told you in the academy. Fighting is just a state of fear and rage that goes on and on for as long as you can stand it. Fighting is about you and me and the dragons and the rest of the squadron. It's about us, the fighting one hundred and ninth. Just us, we seen a lot of action and lot of tight corners, and we always come back. Nobody can beat us, right?"

"Right."

Relkin knew that Manuel would fight. He was one of them now.

It was also true that Relkin viewed the battle ahead with a certain detachment, tinged with the curious resignation of the military mind. After the battle of Salpalangum, any battle would seem small. After the siege battles in Ourdh, any battle would seem relatively tame.

And besides, he knew he must survive because his "destiny" was waiting for him in Arneis. And Relkin knew that Arneis lay to the east of the mountains.

Moreover, he knew he was right when he sensed a high mood right through the column. Even though the enemy had five times their numbers, they were seething with a confident rage. The dragons, well fed for the first time in days, were boiling with the urge of coming to grips with the enemy.

Then there were the Wattels, who seemed equally eager. They were a clan with a proud history of war, and their spirit was great. These few thousand were the cream of their young men, led by the greatest of the old warriors.

Even as they marched, riders on little hill ponies were crisscrossing the farthings of Wattel, summoning every able-bodied man over the age of fifteen to serve in the Fird of Wattel.

Manuel fell back, beside the Purple Green. Relkin returned to thoughts of Eilsa Ranardaughter, but the mood was broken somehow. An annoying little voice began breaking into his dreams. It was the voice of reality, and it told him he was a fool to even think that a clan chief's daughter would seek out an orphan dragonboy either for her lover or her husband.

And this train of thought led him to think of Miranswa Zudeina all over again. This would end just as that had with his heart broken and his feelings crushed for months.

If, and the ifs piled up enormously, if only he could speak to her alone. There had been that look in her eye. She could not fake that.

Or could she? Girls were capable of the most astonishing deceptions.

But he had seen that look in her eye. She was interested in him. Perhaps all that boasting from Swane had caused it? She thought he was some kind of hero. Once she found out the truth, would that be the end of it?

It was all ifs; ifs piled on ifs. He shook his head to dispel these thoughts and looked around him, focusing for the first time in miles.

The path moved down a steep track here, with a grassy bank above on their right and a widening canyon filled with rocks and splashing water on their left.

The dragons stalked along, great killing beings, their swords over their shoulders, the hilts rising up like strange crests. Their shields were hung there, too, giving them a carapaced look, as if they were some hybrid of land animal and giant turtle. Relkin shrugged, whatever would be would be, and he was destined for somewhere else, Eilsa Ranardaughter or not.

They marched, swinging along the clove valley path at a

good pace. They cut down by the Whistling Pool and crossed the little river Niss in the boulder-strewn canyon and passed on down until they entered a forest of oak and pine.

At about the same time, they began to hear faint noises. They progressed, moving through ferns and vines on the forest floor. Ahead the noise grew louder. They discerned the elements of a great din. Horns were blaring, and drums were thrubbing underneath, and there was a continual roar of voices.

Clan Chief Ranard had already made his decision. "Broaden the front, one hundred men in each line. Then we go forward, as silently as possible."

They broadened their front and moved out, springing quickly through the undergrowth toward the sounds of battle.

Dragonboys were positioning their quivers for battle use and taking up the first shaft for their cunning little bows. The Wattels had their spears ready and their shields deployed. Only the dragons waited to draw steel, and on they went, treading quietly toward the battle.

As they approached, they heard clearly the clash of steel, the screams of men and animals, and a dull roaring sound that those who knew it knew too well, the raging of trolls in battle.

They pressed on, filtering through the trees in a line one hundred long with the dragons in the center, and ten deep. Soon they could clearly perceive the extent of the fighting ahead. A crude barricade of felled trees and boulders blocked the road at a narrow point where the out-thrust arm of the Bek from the right side of the Clove Valley came within a hundred meters of the lake shore.

In front of the barrier, the woods teemed with a great mass of imps and men. Drums thundered in their midst, a constant booming roar. Horns blared, and harsh shouts drove the imps forward to rush the barricade and go up and engage the exhausted defenders. Among the imps stalked teams of great trolls who engaged dragons at the top of the barricade. The dragons were outnumbered greatly and hard-pressed.

In a forest glade, not two hundred yards distant from the fray, Chief Ranard called his daughter to him. Briefly he clasped her hands.

"Eilsa, I would beg thee to retire. This battle is not for a young woman."

"I will not, Father. My place is with the clan, and I can fight with the rest of them."

"Think of your mother."

"My mother would say the same that I say. Since I am here, and we need every sword arm, then I should fight."

Ranard sighed. He'd known this fiery daughter of his would choose as she had.

"My daughter, if we do not meet again, be it known that I love thee and find thee perfect and goodly and fit to be mine heir."

For a moment they held this way and then they donned helm and loosened sword and made ready for a most desperate stroke.

And now Ranard gave the order for the host of Clan Wattel to charge. They stepped out and ran through the trees, silent, coming in directly on the rear and flank of the enemy. Only when they were within a hundred feet were they even seen. At that moment the Wattel pipes burst into life and sent their eerie ringing cry wavering through the trees to bring a sudden silence to the battlefield.

Then out of the trees and straight into a startled mass of imps burst the Wattels, with dragons among them and those terrible swords awhirling.

A grim slaughter took place in a matter of moments and hundreds of imps fell beneath their blades. Imps and trolls turned back from the barricade, but already the heart was out of the mass of imps as they were taken in the rear by what seemed like a great army of fierce warriors driven on by an insane whirling sound that was like nothing they had ever heard.

As the mass of the imp army began to break down, so its human commanders rode about in panic, laying on with their cat-o'-nine-tails and then their swords, but then arrows from the enemy were whistling through the position and then men were toppling from their horses.

The first trolls turned and met the onrushing fury of Bazil Broketail and the Purple Green. Ecator whistled in a series of tremendous chops and sweeps and a sword troll was bowled over and then sundered in twain with a swinging overhand.

The Purple Green struck into more black-purple ax trolls, crushed heads with his shield, and lopped off limbs, heads, and entire torsos with his good old service blade.

Relkin darted past Wattels engaged in pulling down an enemy trooper from his horse. They cut his throat and took his steel.

Alsebra got in among a great gang of imps, flowing back

from the fight at the barricade, and her sword Undaunt flew among them with terrible effect.

Now the exhausted men and dragons on the barricades had risen and impelled by the legion cornets, they were pouring down over the barricade and pitching into the rearmost imps and trolls.

This completed the rout, the imps panicked, burst into flight and lost all cohesion and sense of purpose. Their officers were forced to ride for their lives, and the trolls, left without handlers, lost heart and ran, too.

They were slow runners, however, and dragons soon caught up with them and cut them down. The dragons pursued the trolls for more than a mile in this way and scattered a dozen or more troll heads among the roots and rocks.

Then, exhausted, they slowed and tramped back to rejoin the rest.

Captain Eads rode up to Clan Chief Renard.

"I thank you, sir, on my own behalf and on behalf of my men and dragons. Your coming could not have been more timely, for had they come at us for much longer we would have given way. I confess we are very much at the end of our strength."

"You have fought well, Captain, I congratulate you on what you have achieved. Your people will be safe now."

Eads's haunted eyes showed that he did not believe this.

"The enemy will regroup, sir. He will come back. They cannot leave the women now."

Chief Ranard nodded. "I expected as much. I have summoned the Fird. We will have a shield wall of three thousand in addition to the host. With your men, we will have four and a half thousand, plus the dragons to hold back the trolls."

Eads gave a big sigh. "That is good news. But the people are very weak. My men need to rest. And they are hungry. It has been days since much food could be prepared."

"We will withdraw at once up the Clove Valley. We shall make them fight us at the head of the valley, where it is narrowest and most easily held. Then we shall see if the strength of Wattel steel is still what it used to be. Either we shall be valiant and triumphant over these shadows of the dark enemy or we will go down to defeat, and the days of our clan will at last be ended on these Beks."

CHAPTER FIFTY-SEVEN

The disorganization caused by the Wattels' sudden charge into the enemy's right flank and rear was severe enough to remove any threat beyond that of the Baguti cavalry for the next two days. For their part the Baguti were tentative, disliking the narrowness of the Clove Valley and the close presence of numerous great Gazaki from whom they had suffered so much.

Then it began to rain in torrents as a storm billowed up from distant Ourdh and brought a virtual monsoon effect to the Kenor side of the Malgun Mountains. The downpour went on all night, well into the following day and effectively hindered the enemy's pursuit, slowing the imps in torrential streams and mudflows, cooling the blood of trolls, and leaving them sluggish and ill-tempered.

During this valuable time, the Wattel muster continued as the men of the farthings came in and presented themselves for duty in the Fird. In addition, they brought extra weapons, which were eagerly taken up by some of the refugees. Quite a few had recovered their strength following two days and nights of rest and good food. They had slept in caves and tents and been adequately protected from the elements for the first time since they'd fled their homes weeks before.

Eads had at first been unsure whether to accept these arms. There were some women among the settlers who wanted to take up sword and shield. Eads did not think it was a good idea. The very presence of human women tended to arouse imps to a blood lust. Nor did he think the legionaries would view it favorably. Only men served in the legion as line soldiers.

A deputation came from the settlers. It was lead by Hopper Reabody and Farmer Besson. The arrogant Tursturan Genvers was noticeably absent. Reabody's green leather suit was now scuffed and worn. His boots were about worn-out.

Besson had lost much of his fat, and his body had hardened to the condition of its youth. Both carried sword and dagger.

They represented one hundred and eleven male farmers who wished to take a place in the shield wall, or to serve in any way useful. Twenty-five of them were legion veterans and had their own weapons, all but for heavy spears. In addition, there were nine women settlers, from all walks of life it seemed, and they, too, demanded a space in the line.

Eads was stumped. This was an unexpected problem. He took their message under advisement and promised them an answer within the hour.

He sounded out his captains. Deft and Retiner were against it. It would unsettle the men. Dragon Leader Turrent was also against it. Women should not be in the line, that was all he had to say on the subject.

Then Bowchief Starter appeared. The Bowchief was nonplussed for but a moment before he made an excellent suggestion.

"Accept their service, use them as messengers."

"Of course!" exclaimed Eads. "Why didn't I think of that?"

Bowchief Starter chuckled. "Perhaps because you haven't slept properly in ten days or more. A man gets worn down by constant fighting."

"Perhaps you are right. Unfortunately we have more fighting in store for us."

"Have you had any word from Fort Dalhousie?"

"No messages have reached me. I conclude the worst. The enemy has broken through the High Pass. He has entered Arneis and will have to be defeated there."

Eads handed out the weapons to the settlers, including the nine women, who took light swords, spears, and knives plus bows for three who were especially good shots. Eads ordered them to elect two of their members as corporals and to organize themselves into a messenger group. They would be required to move rapidly along the front that was being developed along the crest line of the Clove Valley.

Trees had been felled and rocks piled up to form an effective barrier, and raised positions had been created for archers.

The 109th Dragons were set out in line along the barricade next to the 66th. Each dragon had built for himself a platform of tree trunks set along the rear of the barricade.

These gave the dragons the elevation to reach over the barricade and hew down at anyone coming up the other side.

Between the dragons, set out in groups of ten, were the men of the Wattel Fird, armed with sword, spear, and shield. Set back of them were the Kenor bowmen. Beside the dragons were the dragonboys. Behind this line were the regular soldiers, ready to reinforce wherever needed. Behind them were the rest of the Fird.

The dragons were in a strange mood. They were rested and well fed, and still there was a feyness in the air, the gestalt of giant carnivorous reptiles. They were unresponsive, and unusually quiet. Then at night the red star Zebulpator rode high above the moon, and this position was known to be unlucky, indeed quite ominous. All the wyverns were affected, and while the Purple Green had resisted it at first, he had succumbed after the red star rose. They stood stock-still in moody silence, listening to the sounds of the enemy host down below in the Clove Valley.

Dragonboys were infected with the same superstitious dread, but it hardly checked their tongues.

"I've heard that it's the evil time, when the red star rides high over the moon," said Swane to the younger boys. Little Jak quickly became a bundle of nerves. Turrent had already landed on him for absentmindedly leaving loose a retaining strap from Rusp's scabbard.

Relkin was busy reflecting a fresh supply of arrow shafts he'd received from the Wattels. They were good shafts, but the quills needed to be reset farther up the shaft for his Cunfshon bow. While he worked occasionally splitting a new quill and expertly tying it into place in the higher slot, Relkin mumbled a few ill-remembered prayers to old Caymo, the god of luck and good times.

Whether Caymo heard him or not, he could not tell. And he was increasingly concerned with this apparent futility behind prayers in general. Even if they won this battle and survived to a ripe old age, how could one know for sure that it was due to a god's interference with the run of things? There were so many moments, where chance must operate, it could not be planned. It was like tossing a die constantly inside a basket. It could never land, never show a number. Could even the gods read the future? How could they alter the outcome of a battle with all its myriad components?

The absurdity of it came to him suddenly. If they won the

battle ahead, would he really put it down to Caymo's intervention? Caymo was the very personification of luck. Could luck be so pervasive? How could it affect his destiny? If he was destined to be in Arneis, then how could this battle be anything but foretold as a victory?

Did luck work separately from destiny? Could they be in conflict? Were the old gods battling the Great Mother over this?

Relkin's head spun.

He looked up and saw the two Wattel girls, their bright yellow hair quite unmistakable, coming along the line, squired by two lieutenants from the 322s, Apteno and Boxen.

He forgot his concerns about luck, Caymo, destiny, high elves, and all the rest of it, and did his best not to simply stare at Eilsa Ranardaughter like a witless calf. He felt a strange self-consciousness all over him like a cloaking shroud. To move a muscle seemed out of the question, in case she should be looking at him and think he was aware of her and showing off. This degree of anxiety was new to Relkin of Quosh. It took him a moment to remember how to breathe. He looked away, tried to concentrate on the quill he was inserting into the freshly cut groove on the side of the shaft. It wouldn't slide in. He could do this in his sleep, but right now his hands were all thumbs.

For a moment he wavered, then instinct took over and it went in, and he spun a line of thread about it, pulled a little glue across it from his glue pot, set beside his elbow, and tightened it down and knotted it away, all in a matter of seconds.

He breathed a sigh of relief. At least his muscles seemed to know what to do even if his brain had gone off on some wild tangent of its own.

He heard a sound, looked up. They were right there, beside him where he worked, leaning over a fallen tree trunk.

Eilsa and Silva had a look of eagerness about them. Swane managed to slip across from his position by the silent Vlok, and Silva turned to him with a smile. They conversed happily.

Relkin, for once, found himself speechless. Too struck by self-consciousness to think, let alone speak. He noticed, as if in a dream, that the Lieutenants Apteno and Boxen were not amused.

Eilsa seemed to be ignoring them, and was simply smiling at Relkin, expecting him to say something.

His tongue felt as if it were glued in place. Manuel had joined the conversation with Swane and Silva. The Purple Green cast a baleful eye behind himself, then snorted and shifted his wings.

"Hello, Dragoneer Relkin," said Eilsa, "the cat got your tongue?"

Relkin swallowed, recovered himself.

"Welcome, uh, welcome to the line, Eilsa Ranardaughter," he replied.

"My greetings to your dragon, too." The leatherback standing in front of them, looking out across the barricade, made no response to this, or to any human noises behind him. He listened only to the sounds below, of the enemy.

Relkin shrugged, "I'm afraid he won't hear us. The red star rides high; the moon passed beneath it last night. The dragons have been withdrawn ever since. It happens every year, but they regard it as an omen for death."

"Is is truly such a thing?"

"By dragon lore it is."

"Do you believe it is a bad sign?"

"I do not know. I think that I was born under a bad sign myself when I was not born in Clan Wattel."

She cocked her head. "Why do you say that?"

"If I was in Clan Wattel, I might attain to the honor of courting Eilsa Ranardaughter. If I wasn't an orphan, of course. A lot of ifs, I guess," he shrugged.

She laughed, a light sound, genuinely pleased, then sobered.

"I beg your pardon, I do not laugh at your orphan status, believe me."

Lieutenant Apteno coughed. Eilsa blinked, no more.

"What are you doing?" She pointed to the arrows.

"I'm shifting the flights so they'll fit my bow."

"You do it well," she said admiringly.

Relkin was recovering fast. Eilsa was genuinely friendly.

Eilsa showed no sign of wanting to move. Nor did she seem to pay much attention to Lieutenant Apteno, despite his attempts to catch her eye.

Apeno was growing irritable.

"Perhaps we should carry on; there are other positions to inspect."

Eilsa looked up. Her forehead creased in a tiny frown. Relkin saw Apteno flick him a glare. Trouble brewed on that quarter. Having a lieutenant out to get one could be unpleasant, but it was inconceivable that he would do anything but try to keep Eilsa there, for as long as humanly possible.

Apteno was on the point of another outburst when suddenly a powerful voice broke in in greeting, with the strong Wattel accent lifting the words. Clan Chief Ranard strode into the position, with Captain Eads and Sergeant Quertin right behind.

The lieutenants snapped to attention, as did Relkin and Swane. Ranard lifted a clenched right fist in return, then turned to Eads.

"Captain Eads, may I present my daughter, Eilsa. She will be seventeen this year."

Eads was stunned by the girl's wild, highland beauty.

"An honor to meet you," he said. "I must thank you, and your friends here on behalf of all my men and the refugees. Your people came in the nick of time."

Eads's gaze turned to Relkin.

"I should have known, once more it is the redoubtable Dragoneer Relkin. I must offer my congratulations. Through your action and diplomatic skill," Eads beamed, "you helped save the day."

"Dragoneer Swane was there, too, sir."

Eads nodded to Swane, who swelled visibly.

Eads then formally introduced Relkin and Swane to the clan chief and mentioned that Relkin had fought in the winter campaign against the Teetol.

Clan Wattel had grim memories of raids by the Teetol. Ranard's eyebrows shot up.

"Ye have fought them, the savages, eh?"

"Yes, sir, our first campaign. We were at Elgoma's Lodge."

"Aye, we heard of that fight. In deep winter. It was a successful campaign."

"Yes, sir."

"And ye fought in Ourdh last summer, the both of ye."

"Sir."

"Such experience will stand ye in good stead I reckon in this coming trial." Ranard half turned to Eilsa.

"And ye have met my daughter, and she you, I see," he pursed his lips. His daughter avoided his eye, and for a tiny moment he seemed amused, then it was gone and a peculiarly penetrating eye fell on Relkin Orphanboy.

Relkin held that gaze. It was a strong one, as strong in its way as that of Ribela, the Queen of Mice, but he did not quail. He had nothing to hide, not even his open infatuation with Eilsa.

"An experienced young rogue, an orphan with no family but that of a dragon." Ranard smiled broadly as he said this. "And I give ye credit, I like you." The clan chief clasped hands with Relkin and then with Swane.

Captain Eads had meanwhile corralled the lieutenants. "Come, sirs, I want to go over the scheduling of reliefs for the 322s."

The lieutenants were dragged away, with brief apologies to Eilsa, who nodded absently.

Ranard released Relkin from the penetrating gaze. A comely youth, with something hard about him, which he knew came from battle experience. And his daughter was much taken with him, that much was as plain as the light of day. And, he observed with some wonderment, he did not mind overmuch. Eilsa was her mother's daughter and would do what she willed and pay little heed to others at this point in her life. Fortunately, she was a gifted and sensible child most of the time. As for the boy, well, Ranard had been expecting something of this kind to happen sometime soon. This dragonboy was an orphan who belonged to the legions. And as was very well-known, mortality among dragonboys was exceedingly high.

After a few more remarks, Ranard proceeded down the line, meeting the troops and examining positions.

Relkin shook his head in near disbelief. The happiest of outcomes had arrived. He and Swane were left alone with Eilsa and Silva.

There was a momentary awkwardness before Eilsa mentioned that this was her first battle.

Relkin was horrified.

"You do not mean to fight, do you?"

"I am here. I will fight with my clan." Her firm little jaw jutted slightly.

"The imps will be frothing at the mouth. You know what they will do to you if they capture you!"

"They will not capture Eilsa Ranardaughter!"

Relkin sensed a growing resistance to his pleas. He pulled back.

"I beg pardon, I presume too much. But I would give my life to keep you from harm. Eilsa Ranardaughter, already I know this."

She smiled. "I did not know that dragonboys were so quick at romance. We have barely been introduced, and you are ready to die for me. Not even the clan youths are so forward."

He felt himself blushing again. To cover his confusion, he asked the first thing that came into his mind.

"What do you think your life will be like, Miss Eilsa, providing we live through the battle?"

Her face clouded over.

"I will be married one day, probably to one of the sons of the leading family of one of the Farthings, probably to Edon Norwat."

Plainly, she was not happy with this prospect. He was shocked once more.

"You will be married against your will?"

"Aye, it will be so. My wishes are unimportant in such a matter. It will be done to cement the clan together."

Relkin was aghast. "Is that not beyond the Weal of Cunfshon?"

Her eyes flashed bitterly. "Your Weal does not apply to Clan Wattel. The Wattel line goes back to long before the witches came to Argonath. Our laws are older than theirs, so it has been explained to me many times."

"Still, Clan Wattel is within the empire?"

"Yes, but we cling to our ancient ways."

"Forgive me, but I believe you are unhappy with that thought."

She had a most bitter little smile.

"Of course I am happy, what do you think?" She changed the subject. "And pray, tell me what you expect from the future, Dragonboy."

"Fighting again, a lot of it." He looked up. "However, I have been told that my destiny is to stand in a rose garden in Arneis. So I think we must win this fight."

She cocked her head, something she did in a way that made his heart stand still, or so it seemed.

"Who told you that you would go to Arneis?" she asked.

"Two elves."

"Elves?"

"It's a long story."

She laughed, a sound that thrilled him. "You seem to possess a lot of long stories, Dragoneer Relkin."

He grinned. "You might say that."

"I find you are the strangest boy, but I like you. More than Lieutenant Apteno, that's for certain."

Relkin felt his heart leap in his chest. "Well," he said, "if we get as far as Arneis, then maybe Baz and I will survive to the end of our terms and retire."

"When will that be?"

"In about seven years."

"A long time . . ."

"Yes, but then we'll be pensioned, and we'll get a grant of land and we'll set up to be farmers."

"You and the dragon will stay together."

"Have to. Until one or other of us dies; that's the way it is for dragonboys. Dragons and men work well as a farming unit. To get started you see. Once you're going then you buy the horses you need for the heavy labor. But to clear land, dig up stumps, a dragon is the best there is. And where a dragon can't reach, or where the work is delicate, then you need a man."

Eilsa shot him a coy look. "And where might a woman fit into this picture of bliss?"

Relkin flashed serious. "She would work beside him, live in the house they built together, and bear the children they would bring into the world."

She looked at the mighty dragon standing silent, as if carved in stone. She recalled how it had looked at her, with those bright, interested eyes, so uncanny and unsettling. How it had spoken, with that odd, inhuman tone and cast to the words, but words, human speech.

To be the woman of a dragoneer would mean accepting one of these monsters into her life. Learning to accept their strange sounding speech, adjusting to an intelligent animal of two tons or more.

For a moment she envied their life, uncomplicated by the demands of heraldry and family lineage. Vagabonds of war, blown here and there about the world on campaign after campaign. A boy and his dragon, the ultimate fighting machine.

Eilsa had once loved a pony, but Pippin could not speak

except in lowly horse, and in fact, was wholeheartedly stupid, if the truth be known. Dragons ate ponies, she thought suddenly.

And she still liked this boy, who was not really a boy anymore, despite his youth.

Before she could say anything further, there was a scream from legion cornets, and Captain Senshon of the 322s went galloping past.

Sergeant Quertin came running by in the opposite direction.

He whistled up Dragon Leader Turrent, who had been discussing archery tactics with Bowchief Starter.

"Enemy's moving, expect attack within the minute."

Turrent lifted the cornet and blew the blast to bring everyone in the unit to attention. They were already up and peering over the barricade.

The dragons had still not moved a muscle.

A skirmishing line of a dozen or so Kenor bowmen was scrambling back up the valley. Behind them came a sudden charge of Baguti, trying to run them down before they could reach the security of arrow range from the barricade.

Waiting for them were two dozen legionaries who rose up from hiding and scattered Wattel-made caltrops across the grass. The caltrops had four sharp points so that one was always sticking up. The steel points glittered on the grass. Behind this screen they retired with the bowmen.

The Baguti slowed when they reached the line of steel points. They milled about and exchanged arrows with the retreating bowmen. One legionary was hit, two Baguti tumbled from their saddles.

Now the drumming began to thunder into the valley and with an almighty great blare of those heavy horns, the enemy assault began.

CHAPTER FIFTY-EIGHT

The enemy came straight on, a hammer-blow charge. There were five thousand or more imps, a thousand fell men, and ninety trolls, formed up in three platoons. All were drunk on a shipment of black drink that had been brought up the river in the past two days. Under the influence of the dark spirit made in Padmasa, they feared nothing and in their eyes blazed a red rage against life itself. They wished only to sink their blades into the defenders of Argonath.

Now the dragons stirred suddenly, moving as one, their heads coming up and their tongues flicking out to taste the air.

As the enemy came within range, arrows flicked out from the barricade, first the long shafts of the Kenor bowmen, then the shorter ones from Cunfshon crossbows. Imps fell here and there, an officer toppled from his horse, arrows sprouted on the armor of trolls, but on they came. The horns snarling and the drums rolling like a peal of thunder. Up the barricade they came and fell under a volley of timbers and rocks, hurled by the no-longer motionless dragons.

Dozens of imps went down, crushed beneath these missiles. Several trolls were felled and some of these did not get up again. But they came on, up the great mass of trees, brush and rock, like a great ocean wave, curling high, throwing imps and trolls to the fore, axes high.

Dragons rose to meet them, dragonboys crouched and ready at their sides. Legionaries and clansmen stood up in the spaces between the dragons. Steel rang up and down the line of the barricade and punctured the roaring of the trolls and the thunder of the drums. Soon there came the counterpoint of war, the scream of wounded men, the shrieks of dying imps, and the occasional sharp hiss of rage from the great wyverns. The smells of fear, blood, and reeking sweat rose to the heavens.

Three trolls came up the barricade to converge on Bazil Broketail. The leader was a purple-hued brute of great girth in the lower limbs who stepped up smartly and swung with surprising speed. The great ax whistled down and would have taken Bazil's shield arm off at the shoulder, but the leatherback twitched aside at the last moment and the axblade buried itself in the tree below.

Ecator shivered with a living spirit as it flashed forth in answer. The troll barely got its shield up, and a section was riven by the white steel blade. The troll could not get its ax free. Baz put one foot up on the troll's midriff and shoved it away, freeing Ecator just in time to deflect an ocher sword troll's thrust from the right.

The sword troll was quick, whipping its blade back in a well-rehearsed reverse, and Bazil was forced to dodge and hold it off with his shield. His tail mace rapped hard on the troll's helmet, but it still forced him back a step with a heave and mounted the barricade.

Then Ecator came over in a forehand slice. The troll glimpsed the flash of the steel and shrunk aside, and the sword sank into the wood.

The sword troll gave a greasy gasp of joy and hewed at the dragon, who took the blows on the shield until his tail mace struck the troll in the face, and it wobbled backward with a moan.

Frantically Bazil heaved on Ecator, but the blade was buried deep in the green cut wood, and it would not release. Bazil gave a mighty groan as he hauled on it.

A second sword troll came in from the left. It came too confidently, and looked down to see where to put its feet, and in that moment Bazil smashed it in the face with his shield and knocked it to its knees.

The first sword troll was recovering, but now the black-purple troll pulled free its mighty ax, and with a shriek it came straight for Baz.

Relkin darted in front, and his arrow struck just below the monster's eye. It hissed but merely shook its head and came on, lashing out at him with an enormous foot that he evaded by a hairsbreadth. His sword slashed at the thick troll hide protecting its Achilles tendon as it tried to hammer him with its shield.

As he jumped, he caromed off the dragon's thigh and

landed on all fours. His sword had fallen into a chink between two trees, and he struggled to free it.

The troll tried to stamp on him but was knocked back by the dragon. It swung its ax in a cut that whistled low over Relkin's flattened form, while Bazil danced back.

Then three legionaries from the 322s surged forward in the nick of time, their spears thudding home into the ax troll's hide. It gave ground with a sneering roar and broke off the spears, tearing them out of its mute, fibrous flesh.

A sudden move and it cuffed a legionary who'd ventured too close, trying to strike with the sword. He went down on his back, and the troll bawled in triumph and hewed him in twain from neck to crotch.

His friends screamed with rage, hurled themselves at the troll, and were batted back with its shield. It prepared to slay them for their rashness and would have but for an interruption from the left. Leaning over from his own position, the Purple Green thrust in at the troll and forced it to dodge back, an ungainly effort that caused it to miss its footing. It sat down hard and then slid down the outside of the barricade, crushing an imp beneath it.

The Purple Green returned his attentions to a sword troll on his own front.

With a tremendous hiss of effort, Bazil finally pulled Ecator free and swung to engage the sword troll as he closed. Blades rang, striking blue sparks from the steel. Bazil drove in with his shoulder and pushed the troll off balance; as it stepped back, he cut down with the blade and took off its arm at the elbow. The troll's scream was cut off by a thwack from the tail mace, and as it toppled backward, a fountain of black blood arced out and away.

Baz turned to face the next ocher sword troll, aware that two more ax trolls were already climbing the outside of the barrier. Relkin dodged in front of it, firing an arrow that bounced off its helmet and then slashing with his sword.

The troll swung at the boy but missed. He spun away, and Bazil thrust in with Ecator. The troll barely deflected the thrust with its shield and then struck with an overhand that the leatherback took on the shield. They struck again, sparking and clashing. The ax trolls were almost on them, and behind them came more. Imps were coming, too, sensing the dragon's desperation.

Bazil swung, Ecator struck down the troll's sword but did not go home. There was no time for this!

And then the sword troll stopped dead in its tracks, and Bazil looked on in puzzlement for a moment before he saw the arrow jutting from its eye. Silently it toppled backward and fell off the barricade and knocked the ax trolls over and sent them rolling back.

"By the ancient gods of Dragon Home, sometimes a dragonboy is a useful thing!" he said over his shoulder. Relkin was too busy rewinding the bow, which with its cunning box of gears, could be done far more quickly than any normal crossbow.

A swarm of imps, their eyes inflamed by the black drink, came up the barricade, over the fallen trolls and ran in with their swords ready to cut a dragon's hamstrings and leave him helpless.

Bazil stepped back smartly and swung his shield arm out to batter aside the first three imps. Ecator sang a moment later and sent the skulls of two more flying into the air. Another imp sagged to his knees, coughing over Relkin's arrow, lodged firmly in his chest.

Meanwhile the first ax troll had recovered its feet again and was starting back up the barricade. Relkin's arrows sprouted from the troll's head and shoulders, but these were protected by thick leather armor and thick troll hide. Certainly they did not seem to stop the troll.

Other trolls were either arriving at the scene or were getting back on their feet. Men in the black gladiatorial costume of the mercenaries of Padmasa were there, rallying the imps and urging them up the slope. With a scream of rage they came, a thick column of them.

A line of clansmen met them shield to shield and engaged with spear and sword. The Clan Wattel did not fight with the precision of the Argonath legions, and though the legionaries did their best to maintain the pure line, the clansmen found the discipline difficult. Yet they drew on the ancient well of pure fury that was the mark of their kind. Their swords rained down on the imps in a hail of steel, and from their eyes spoke death.

The imps kept coming, climbing up the mound of bodies that built up along the outer side of the barricade. And now and then a member of the clan staggered back with a mortal wound and fell and rolled to the bottom of the inside. The battle raged on, sustained by the enemy's numbers and the terrible energy unleashed by the black drink.

At one point trolls broke through the line between Alsebra and Cham. They got to the top of the heap of bodies and crashed through the line of clansmen, trampling any that got in their way. The trolls started sliding down the inside of the wall. There they were delayed by ten legionaries from the 322s, but it was plain that they would soon be through, and behind them came a mass of imps seeking to exploit the break. The legionaries jabbed with their spears and gave ground. The trolls came on.

The men of the Fird were summoned by the clan pipers, and the Fird hurled themselves forward into the gap, swarming around the giant trolls, hacking at their legs and chests.

The imps were hurled back, but the trolls were hard for men on their own to kill. Alsebra from the left and Cham from the right did their best to help, but each was constantly engaged by other trolls from their fronts. The Fird were forced to engage the trolls and close the gap, a bloody, horrifying task. Men were smashed, trampled, pulped, and even torn asunder by the trolls before they succumbed. Spears sank deep into them at last, penetrating leather armor and troll hide, but not before they did murderous work upon the Fird.

Among the trolls there were men, grim warriors, mercenaries brought from all over the world to serve the dark power of Padmasa. Taller and stronger than the imps, they wielded sword and spear freelance, seeking any opportunity to break the line and get the imps through. To them, the men of the Argonath showed no mercy.

One of these, clad in black leather and steel, sprang past Bazil as he held at bay two sword trolls.

A legionary from the 182s engaged, their swords rang. Relkin released, set an arrow into an imp that was about to thrust home into the legionary's back.

Relkin drew sword and hewed down another imp that sprang toward him. It tumbled, and he looked up just in time to see the legionary fall, blood gushing from his mouth. The man in the black leather pulled free his sword and swung to confront Relkin.

No time to notch an arrow, Relkin attacked, sword to sword. The man was a giant, a head taller than Relkin, and powerful to match. After three strokes, Relkin felt his arm turning numb. The man smashed him back, shield to shield, and he almost tumbled.

Manuel leaned over and fired point blank, but his arrow caromed off the nose piece of the man's helmet. The mercenary snarled and slashed sideways, and Manuel tumbled away, cut slightly on the right leg. This attack opened his side, however, and Relkin's blade was there in the same second. The man gaped, screamed in rage at the sight of his blood running down his side. He lashed his shield hard into Relkin's, again throwing the lighter youth back on his heels. He was wounded, but he was hardly affected. This was a common effect of the black drink. Men felt little pain and fought like maniacs, but they often neglected their defense.

The man's sword whirled down, and Relkin barely deflected it with an arm that felt leaden. The mercenary was too strong, and too quick. Relkin knew he could not match the next blow. And then a legionary leaned in from the side, his spear sank home, and the mercenary slid backward with a final groan. Imps climbed over his body. The battle raged on. With a huge groan, a troll was picked up bodily by the Purple Green and thrown with both hands. One of its legs knocked a line of imps flying, and the troll bounced and crashed into the butt end of a sawn-off tree trunk.

"Ah, I see you have lost your temper again!" hissed Bazil to the Purple Green.

The wild one gave his battle roar, the cry of the Dragon Lord of Hook Mountain. Trolls and men cowered back from him at that moment.

Bazil roared a salute to the wild one, and Ecator sang through the air, sundered a sword troll's helmet, and toppled the brute back onto a solid mass of imps and men.

The enemy still came on, but the defenders held the crest of the barricade, the Fird mixed in with the rest, and everyone cheering and screaming their defiance as they swung swords with arms that were beyond weariness and struck down the enemy like heroes on some ancient painting dedicated to the gods of war.

Relkin was struck on the helmet, kneed in the groin, cut along one shoulder, and punched hard in the mouth by sundry imps during the next hectic half an hour. It was an exceedingly rough fight, he had to admit.

Swane went down, hammered by an imp from behind, but he was saved by the intervention of several men from the

Fird, who were now pressed up with them, bolstering the tiring men of the Host and the legionaries. Swane was soon back on his feet and back in the fight beside Vlok.

Rusp was badly wounded. Vlok was wounded, but not badly. Cham and Anther and Chektor had all received slight wounds. The Purple Green had damaged his fist where he'd punched through a troll's faceplate. Bazil's strange tail had been trod on by another troll and bitten by yet another. All the dragons had innumerable arrows sticking out of their joboquins and their hides. Yet they remained indomitable.

And now the force in the battle ebbed somewhat for the first time. The fury of the black drink began to fade, and the imps grew weary.

The imps had taken terrible casualties, at least one-tenth of their number were strewn across the ground, and almost a fifth of the trolls were down, mostly dead. The fire no longer glowed, but merely flickered in their eyes.

The enemy wavered.

In the midst of the struggle, Clan Chief Ranard had received light wounds and some bruises, but he was awake to the moment and sensed that the tide of battle was changing. He called for the Fird to go over to the offensive and charge.

At that very second there came a blast from Eads's silver cornet, and it was taken up by other cornets. The command rang out for the charge, and the legionaries, the dragons, and the dragonboys went over the top, with Clan Wattel at their heels, and pitched into the retiring mass of imps.

The dragons struck home hard and heavy. Four more trolls bit the dust. One of the enemy commanders was caught up in the ruckus, his horse surrounded by maddened imps. Alsebra's blade, Undaunt, looped in and took the man's head. Men from the Fird ran in, alongside men from Bur Lake and men with the Kohon Yeomanry and they knocked imps, horses, and even a troll down the barricade and tumbling in chaos.

Suddenly the imps began to run, their spirits abruptly quailed and the black drink ebbing from their blood. Arrows and spears followed them and then the men of Clan Wattel sent up their ululation of triumph and rushed on. They completed the rout and drove the enemy in a terrified mass down the Clove Valley, slaying them by the hundreds as they ran. Snarling trolls, too tired to run, stood their ground here and there, and died by the score as they were speared or cut down by dragonsword.

CHAPTER FIFTY-NINE

The rest of that day was an eerie, tormented time. The sun appeared fitfully through high clouds. A strange silence replaced the din of war. Captain Eads roused himself to ensure the victory. The fittest of the Talion troopers mounted up and harried the fleeing enemy with support from squads of legionaries and bowmen who shrugged off battle fatigue and carried the pursuit as far as the southern end of Lake Wattel.

They found that the enemy force had virtually disintegrated and could be left to flee in terror down the Kalens Valley. A few prisoners were taken and brought back for interrogation.

Meanwhile at the battle site, around the barricade, the sad work of burying the dead and tending the wounded went on through the afternoon and into the night.

Hundreds of homes across the Wattel lands would never see their men again. More than four hundred graves were dug for men of the Fird and the Host combined. Hundreds more were wounded, many seriously. Then, of the one hundred and eleven men of Bur Lake, fully forty had perished on the field. Of the nine women who had been impressed as messengers, two had been slain, found with enemy arrows jutting from their backs.

There were other casualties. In the 109th Dragons, Rusp had bled to death from a terrible sword thrust in the belly. Little Jak was left to sob over the hulk of his dragon. In the 66th Dragons, the nimble leatherback Oast had been slain by troll ax. In addition, there were three dead dragonboys, Jin and Tunu of the 66th, and Bryon of the 109th, stabbed through the heart by an imp. Alsebra was now without her dragonboy. Then in the late hour of the afternoon, the 66th lost their commander when Dragoneer Mescual succumbed to his wounds.

A score of legionaries, yeomen, and bowmen were also to

be buried and among them were Captain Senshon of the 322s, Lieutenant Grass of the Talion Light Horse, Sergeant Quertin and Sergeant Jist.

Almost everyone bore wounds to some degree. Bowchief Starter had been stabbed in the hand, cut on the back, the legs, and the arms, but remained on his legs, sporting a lot of bandages and keeping his cheerful presence among the men, lifting spirits wherever he went.

Dragon Leader Turrent had a face almost flayed of skin and a suspected broken arm. He had been trampled slightly in the crush, but whether by troll or dragon no one could say. He complained of a ringing in the ears after being struck down with the butt end of a troll ax. For once, the dragon leader was incapable of enforcing his demands for polished steel and brass on all equipment. In truth, he scarcely even thought of such things. The pain in his arm was dramatic.

Relkin had a bandage around his forehead, which had been laid open sometime during the victory charge, he thought by the dragon's tail tip or possibly an arrow. He also had bandages on two cuts on his left leg and a poultice on a big bruise on his right arm above the elbow.

All the dragonboys were cut up and swathed in bandages. All were downcast over the fate of Rusp and Bryon.

Huge funeral pyres were lit for Rusp and Oast, and the remaining dragons stood in a loose circle about the blazing fires. There was no beer, but the dragons still sang their dirge to the dead, and their voices carried away far into the night and brought wonder to those who heard them.

Clan Chief Ranard heard the sound in his tent, where his wounds were tended by his daughter Eilsa. He looked up in wonder at the sound, for the voices were good and great and inhuman and like nothing he had ever heard before. Eilsa went out for a moment and returned with her eyes widened in wonder.

" 'Tis not so astonishing, daughter," he said. "Think of a wolf that's lost its mate, or a member of the pack. Wolves mourn their losses. The dragons are predators, too, and more intelligent than wolves."

Ranard lay back on the cot. In truth, he was feeling his years. He had a nasty stab wound in the upper arm and a slicing cut along the side of his neck. But what really affected him were the two cracked ribs on his right side and the deadness he felt in his legs. He didn't think he could walk a mile.

He had never seen such a fight. He was sure the memories would haunt him for the rest of his days. He had seen horrors as should never be allowed under the sun.

In his heart there was a great weight, for the dead of the Fird and the Host. Many had fallen, more than in any single battle in clan history. It would take a generation or more for the clan to recover. But the honor of the name Wattel had been burnished for all time. Ranard felt a glow of pride in that. But there were so many mothers and wives and sons that he would have to visit. They would weep and their eyes would accuse him, and he would have to live with it. Such was the responsibility of a war chief, to explain to the grieving that there was no other option, that they had to defeat the enemy or there would be no Clan Wattel.

His gaze fell on his daughter's face, so stern, so beautiful, so focused on the bandages she was cutting. Something had been taken from her forever by the battle. Something fey and silvery and young was gone and replaced by something of iron and steel and hard ground.

She said little, changing the dressings on his wounds. Fortunately the bleeding from the neck had stopped, there was no need for surgery there.

Eilsa herself had been in the fight on two occasions, and had struck furious blows against the rough, square shields of the imps that had sought to take her during a break in the line of the Fird.

She had lopped off the hand of one who had seized her leg, and she remembered her sense of horror at that moment. Yet to be captured and taken away by those imps would have been a horror far greater and of endless duration.

There were cook fires lit and cauldrons of wheat noodles were boiled and served with leeks roasted in the embers and some Livolese wine that had been brought up from the cellars of Castle Wattel.

The dragons had finished their chant, and the great majority of men were fast asleep when Captain Eads returned from the pursuit. He ate a quick meal and then went at once to Ranard's tent.

Ranard roused himself and sat up. Eilsa brought the captain inside and showed him a seat on a folding stool across from Ranard's cot.

"The name Wattel will always live in my heart," he said. "Truly did your people fight valiantly today. My men and I owe them a great debt."

"I thank you, Captain, for such pretty speech. The Clan Wattel stood firm, despite the cost."

Eads nodded grimly. "Well do I know that. And it has cost my men as well, not to forget the dragons. A hard fight, indeed."

"Never have I seen a harder."

"I am afraid that for my men it will not be the last fight in this campaign. We must go on, as quickly as possible."

Ranard's wits had not been dulled by his wounds. "You speak of Arneis?"

"I do. I must get my men and dragons there as quickly as I can. I head for the Kohon Pass in the morning. I ask your leave to abandon the refugees to your care. They will only slow us up."

"You plan to join the legion Host on the other side?"

"If I can. Every sword arm will be needed there. I fear the very worst has happened. The enemy will have to be stopped there, the odds will be great."

Ranard fought down his first response. In agony he suppressed what he wanted to say, and merely mumbled platitudes and hopes for the safety of Eads and his men and dragons.

"We will take in the refugees, of course. May the Great Mother protect you and bring you victory."

Eads went out soon after, and Ranard was left with a peculiar agony burning in his heart. To get to Arneis there were several ways, and the shortest of all was known to Ranard, and only two other living men of the clan. It was the greatest of the clan's secrets from the ancient times. Ranard could not bring himself to give it up, although he deeply wished to help Eads and his men. The hidden entrance to the Dark Stair was but five leagues away, and down below, in the deeps, it opened on the underground river, Eferni, which flowed to the Danding Pool in Arneis, on the other side of massive Mt. Livol. But to tell of this to a living soul, other than to his successor, was a crime too great to be borne, and Ranard quailed at it.

CHAPTER SIXTY

In the morning, Captain Eads made a quick inspection of the men and the dragons. Despite his deep desire to move on as quickly as possible, he realized that a day of rest was absolutely essential. Everyone was too worn, too sore, too battered, to march that day.

They were perhaps forty miles from the Kohon Pass, and from the pass it would be another forty miles before they came down into the vale of Dandelin in Upper Arneis. Eads retired to his own tent to examine a map of the route and plan for the march.

Relkin rose late, fed the dragon, and hauled water despite a great number of aches and pains. His sword arm was sore, and the bruise above his elbow was already purple. He pressed a pad soaked in Old Sugustus to the cuts on his leg and sucked in a breath at the sting. When he was finished with his own wounds, he turned to Bazil's and changed a dozen big bandages on the dragon's hide. Despite leather joboquin, chain mail, breastplate, vambraces, cuisses, and elbow guards the dragon had still taken a lot of punishment. In particular, there were nasty bite wounds on the tail, and Relkin packed them with honey after a thorough cleansing with Old Sugustus. Throughout, Bazil remained calm, although Relkin could sense that the leatherback was preoccupied. "Big fight" was all he would say, though.

When it was over, he took up his great sword Ecator and a whet stone and began to work over the blade. Ecator had come through in perfect shape. Relkin marveled again at how Ecator came through fight after fight with nary a notch in that gleaming swathe of white steel. Truly the sword was inhabited by a wild and perfect spirit.

Elsewhere there was nothing but damage. Both their shields were much cut about. His own sword was notched, and one of Bazil's tail maces had broken just below the head. There was a dent in Bazil's helmet.

Relkin piled it up before taking it down to the smithy for repairs.

"I liked Rusp," Baz suddenly murmured. Relkin looked back to the dragon, and their eyes met for a moment and then he went on.

The camp was quiet. Even the great Purple Green was subdued, submitting to the ministrations of Manuel concerning a nasty cut on the lower back.

"So, Relkin," said Manuel a little later while they were filling water jugs. "You still believe in your old gods?"

"Yes, why not?"

"You think old Asgah is now delivering the souls of our comrades to Gongo in the caverns of the dead?"

Manuel was surprisingly well-informed. All that book learning, thought Relkin wistfully. Relkin had never had much time for books after this third season in the village school. He'd learned to read and count, and that was about it.

"Yes, I suppose so. Where else do you think they would go?"

Manuel smiled. "Into the arms of the Great Mother, of course."

Relkin turned away. Did old Gongo really exist? A monster with eight heads and thirty-seven arms? Who lived in a cavern beneath the world and ruled the souls of the dead unless they were specifically taken up by one of the gods of the upper world?

There was no way to know if Gongo was really down there, below the dwarf kingdoms, deeper than the lurkers. Relkin felt uncomfortable. Compared to the Great Mother, old Gongo suddenly seemed barbaric and even bizarre. How could there really be something like old Gongo down there below the ground?

" 'The Mother runs through all of us, forever and forever.' " The litany ran through his mind.

Relkin thought of old Caymo, his own favorite god. Had Caymo intervened in the fighting? It didn't seem so. It had been a hell of a fight and a long one, and at the end they had strode over the barricade and put the imps to flight. They had done it themselves. Old Caymo hadn't done a thing. Or at least, if he had, he'd allowed a lot of men to die needlessly. Relkin had seen the graves being dug, hundreds and hundreds of them. If Caymo had responded to his worshipers, then why had he let ol' Rusp die, or Bryon for that matter.

It seemed senseless to Relkin. He was angry with the god and with himself for his stubborn clinging to these old-fashioned beliefs.

He borrowed a barrow to carry shield and helmet to the smithy, and when he'd seen they were stacked up in line for the smiths' attentions, he took up his bow and went out onto the heath to hunt and to be by himself for a while.

He moved slowly, his legs felt weak and quite ill-used. On the heath he saw rabbits. Unfortunately, they saw him, too, and disappeared into their warrens as soon as he got close enough for a shot.

He located a spot at the crest of a mound topped by heather where he could command a semicircle of ten rabbit holes. He hid in the heather and waited.

The rabbits were cautious but they were also hungry, and after a while nervous heads popped out for a moment and then withdrew. After a few tentative sallies, the entire rabbit appeared and roved over the grass at the bottom of the sandy bank. Eventually one came within range. Relkin waited. He didn't want to miss, and he didn't want to have a wounded rabbit running back to its hole to die underground.

The rabbit came closer, but he was still not absolutely certain of a kill. At last the rabbit took that final hop. He aimed and would have released, but the rabbit gave a sudden jerk, squealed and died, pinned to the ground by another's arrow.

A figure in clansman's leather leggings and top came out of the heather and scooped up the rabbit and pulled the arrow through.

Relkin stood up in the heather, indignant and angry and about to curse the fellow when he saw that it was Eilsa Ranardaughter.

"Oh, by the ancient prophets," she said in surprise, "you startled me." Then she took in the bow in his hands. "You were aiming at this one, too?"

His complaints had suddenly evaporated.

"It's that kind of a day, I suppose. We used up our luck yesterday."

"We won a great victory. Why does it feel so bad, Relkin?"

So she had reached that point already. A grim inner smile flickered. She had been ready for a fight before. She just hadn't ever seen so many die.

"Always does when you take a lot of casualties. Makes it all seem pointless. When everyone's dead, what does it matter who wins a battle? But after a bit that wears off, and you remember that you were protecting a lot of innocent people, who the enemy wants to use to breed imps. And you remember all the things you've ever seen of the enemy, and you know you had to fight, even if it cost every single one of your friends' lives. Even if it costs your own."

She was silent for a moment.

"I think ye are correct, Relkin. I feel sorrow for the losses, but also a terrible satisfaction that we destroyed that swarm of horrible imps and those demonic trolls."

"Not just trolls and imps," said Relkin with anger in his voice. "There are plenty of men who fight for the enemy. Captain Eads and the troopers captured some of the mercenaries. They're being interrogated. Later they'll be hanged."

Eilsa's eyes flashed fire. "I'd burn them at the stake."

Relkin nodded. This was the old Eilsa. "No one loves the men who fight for the enemy. But hanging's the clean way. That's the way they do it in the legion."

She sniffed. "In Clan Wattel we only execute proven murderers. But we do not hang them. They kneel and put their heads on the block in Castle Green, and the headsmen cuts off their heads with an ax."

Relkin felt more emanations of old Gongo. These Wattels were from the old time, from the age of Veronath. You heard it in their speech all the time.

"Do you need the rabbit?" said Eilsa suddenly. "Perhaps we should try and take another."

Relkin looked back to the dark holes in the sandy bank. "No, I don't need it. There'll be beef for dinner tonight. I saw them bringing out some steers from your clan herds."

"Yes," she said proudly, "my father had ordered a feasting tonight. I wanted a rabbit to make a pie for my father; he loves a good rabbit pie. And at the feasting, I know we would be honored to receive you, if ye wouldst come."

Relkin was taken aback, unused to such an invitation.

"I would be honored, indeed, to be received at your fire. But, are you sure that it would be taken well by others? Your father for instance. I am only a dragoneer. Would he not prefer lieutenants from good families, with land in Aubinas, to seek you out, Eilsa Ranardaughter?"

She laughed. "I do not care for the lieutenants. And I particularly do not care for Lieutenant Apteno and all his land in Aubinas. My father is a wise man, Relkin, and he will always welcome a warrior as brave as yourself."

They walked together through the heather and down a dry, steep-walled gulley. As they went, they discussed the world and how they hoped to live in it when they were "free." For Relkin, this freedom was a very palpable thing, visible just seven years away. For Eilsa, it was far more nebulous and hard to imagine, although she desired it just as strongly.

The gulley opened out into a circular depression with a dull dark pond in the center, gummed with weed, yet home to an assortment of voluble frogs. On the far side they saw some more rabbits, but they made no effort in their direction, being happier to just sit on some hummocks of bunch grass and chew grass stems and talk.

Eilsa Ranardaughter liked talking to this dragonboy. She felt that there were no barriers between them. Furthermore, she was intrigued by his mention of "destiny."

"You were right, Relkin. You said we would survive, and we did. And now you will go on to Arneis and find your destiny."

He laughed. "For all I know, it is simply to stand in a field in Arneis and die there. Sometimes I think all this is just foolishness."

"Do not say that you will die so soon," she said. Relkin saw that she cared for him, and his heart soared. Meanwhile, Eilsa was stricken with sudden horror at losing him all so soon. He would march to the east on the morrow and leave her behind. And in a few days he might well be dead on a battlefield, and she knew she would be devastated. She would never love anyone again.

She shocked herself. She was daughter of the clan chief, she could not have a love marriage, a "make your own mistake" marriage, as the old joke went.

They walked through the sand and the heather under bright sunshine, and Eilsa put her fears out of her mind for the while and tried to simply enjoy this moment. As they went, they talked about their lives, and she described as well as she could, the life of a princess of the Wattels. They laughed together at her descriptions of her teachers in Castle

Wattel, old Rimmeer the mathematician and Miss Gimbrel, who taught them language and deportment. And she told him about her wicked but wonderful maternal grandmother, who always got tipsy at winter feast and told rude jokes. And even went further than that if you were to believe everything you heard.

Then she talked about her friends, like Silva, who had always been there since she was a little girl. And old Rufus the woodchopper, who had whittled things for her since she could remember. And then she told him a joke she had heard concerning Edon Norwat, the callow youth to whom she expected she would be wed, sometime in the next two years.

This thought left both of them quietened, saddened by the realization that theirs was an impossible love.

Eilsa knew that even if she really loved this youth, she could not have a life with him. He was already wed, to the legions for seven more years, and to his dragon for the rest of their days. Dragons could live up to forty years.

No, it was not possible.

She wondered to herself for a moment if that was why Ranard had been so casual about this acquaintance, because he knew that Relkin would go over the mountains and probably never return. Ranard was a crafty man, how well she knew that! And he knew his daughter's nature. Had he calculated that this would be how it would end?

Relkin was telling her about the cities of Ourdh that he had seen, how they teemed with people, how there were great avenues that ran for miles and miles and were choked with wagon traffic. How the rivers swarmed with small craft. And above it all, how there loomed the pyramidical ziggurats of the innumerable ancient religions that had held sway over the masses of the Fedd. For a few moments Eilsa forgot everything and imagined these huge ziggurats. She had heard of them many times, they were the largest man-built structures in the world.

Quite suddenly this idyll was shattered by a peculiar harsh scream that sounded right behind their ears, and they spun apart and crouched as an eagle flew low overhead and veered right across the pond and then turned back again, very low and headed toward them. Relkin's bow was wound and the arrow notched. He lifted it but did not aim.

He had barely had time to notice that there was something not quite right about this eagle when a much larger bird, or flying thing, swooped over the crest beyond the pond and flew straight at him. Wings the size of ship's sails beat loudly, and a great ratlike face swung toward them, dominated by red eyes that glowed like fiery coals.

"Batrukh!" Relkin screamed, and shoved Eilsa out of the way, before taking careful aim and planting his arrow in the thing's breast as it swooped by just overhead.

It gave a chilling shriek of rage and pain, then veered away and flapped up, gaining altitude over the pond and turning to come back at them. Relkin had a second arrow notched, and the bow wound and ready. But then at the highest point of its climb the Batrukh's wings folded, and it plummeted directly into the pond and disappeared with a tremendous splash.

A moment later the eagle returned and landed close by, wings beating slowly above its head. Relkin saw that its tail feathers and some of the wing feathers were damaged. It had been attacked in the air by the batrukh.

Relkin also saw the most curious thing. The eagle wore a leather pouch on its neck. There came a flicker of movement, and he could have sworn he saw a small bird, a sparrow perhaps, detach itself from the eagle and flit across the ground.

The eagle remained still and silent, wings folded, regarding Relkin and Eilsa quite calmly from twenty-five feet away. Relkin had never seen one of these great birds so close, and the leather cup had sparked many questions in his mind.

"What was that thing?" said Eilsa, pointing in the direction of the downed batrukh. Waves were lapping around the shore of the pond.

"A batrukh, a thing of the enemy. I saw one once in Ourdh, just after we left the city of Dzu."

This boy had seen far too many weird things for his years, thought Eilsa Ranardaughter. The world outside of the Beks where she had lived all her life suddenly seemed terribly threatening.

"That was a great shot, Relkin."

Relkin shrugged. "Nay, Eilsa Ranardaughter, I'd say it was a tolerably easy shot. It flew straight overhead, not fifty feet away, and never changed course. You could have done it just as well. I saw you shoot that rabbit."

"Still, you found a killing spot."

"Maybe the old gods are looking out for me, after all."

"This eagle is behaving so strangely."

"I think it is hurt."

"What is that leather thing on its neck?"

They approached the eagle very cautiously, but it remained utterly still.

The small bird had returned. It hopped across the ground for a moment then perched in the heather, where it regarded Relkin with a very intent gaze from tiny, dark eyes.

It was a wren, quite unmistakable. Now it flew past him just inches from his nose. He ducked. He'd heard of aggressive wrens before, but never one that would attack a man.

The wren settled on the heather close by and stared at him. It emitted a high-speed burst of sound that was not at all like normal wren song. Relkin stared and the hair on his neck rose as a mouse came out of the heather and stood up on its hind legs and fixed him with another pair of tiny, beady eyes.

Eilsa was transfixed.

"What are they, Relkin?" she said with a tremulous, near giggle. "Are they friends of yours?"

He felt his eyes bulge. The two tiny animals came together. They spoke to each other with the strange bursts of sound that were unlike either birdsong or the squeaking of mice.

"Weirds they are, they can be nothing else," Eilsa backed away a step.

The mouse came toward them, quite confidently, pausing only when it was right in front of him. It sat back and looked up at him.

There was something about those eyes, some power in them that was irresistible. Relkin bent down and picked up the mouse.

"Nay, Relkin, do not touch it. It be a weird of some kind. Unholy work, the things of the enemy."

"I do not think so, Eilsa. I have a feeling that I know this mouse."

Eilsa stared at him. He could only mean witchcraft. He'd mentioned elves and witches before this, but she hadn't really credited any of that with being more than dragonboy tales. Not things to be taken seriously.

He knew the mouse. How? From where? Questions multiplied in her mind. The wren flew up to his shoulder and perched there quite content.

"I know them, Eilsa, I feel it in my bones."

He looked down into the eyes of the mouse. Such brilliant little eyes. They glowed like glossy pearls of black, swimming with hidden motions that seemed to hint at meanings. There was something here he needed to learn. He groped for it, staring more intently than ever. Things were moving in circles, and he felt his thoughts emptying out of his head as if he were falling asleep, except that this was no sleep state.

And then, faint but unmistakable, crossing the divides between them, he understood a "voice" speaking in his mind. It was small and distant, as if a child were shouting from the far end of the street. But he understood it and knew that it was the Queen of Mice herself.

CHAPTER SIXTY-ONE

Relkin emerged into normal consciousness quite suddenly. He had expected it, forewarned by the voices, but to Eilsa it was a pleasant surprise. She had grown increasingly concerned with his silence, with the fact that he and the mouse appeared to be in a mutual trance, their heads locked but a few inches apart.

"Eilsa," he said, staggering, and put out a hand to her. She took his and felt a slight shock at the touch. The mouse stood silent on his other hand. The wren had gone off in pursuit of insects, never going very far, however, and returning occasionally to feed the mouse, a sight that caused Eilsa to shiver at the weirdness.

"You have been silent for an hour or more Relkin. Are ye well?"

"I am well Eilsa, very well, and I was right. I do know these creatures. They are animants of my friends the Great Witches Lessis and Ribela."

"And the eagle?" She nodded toward the great raptor that had taken the opportunity to hunt and had returned with its own rabbit, which it was tearing up ravenously.

" 'Tis an extraordinary feat. The eagle is an animant as well, of another friend of mine, a young lady that once I loved, before she was wed that is." His face grew concerned. "Now I love only you, Eilsa Ranardaughter."

"I know, Relkin, and I love thee. But our love is doomed before it can begin."

"And destiny is a matter of likelihoods. Some things are more likely than others. Some can be glimpsed in the future if the seeker knows how. Some can be glimpsed by the Sinni."

"Destiny, likelihoods, the Sinni. I'm not sure I understand you, Relkin."

"I'm not sure I understand it all myself, but I do know

that we have to find Captain Eads. There is something very
important that I must tell only him."

Holding hands, blissful in the moment, they ran for the
camp, both small animals riding on Relkin's shoulders.

Upon reaching the camp, Relkin went to Eads's tent and
requested permission to speak to the captain.

There was a guard, a legionary from the 322s, who looked
askance at the mouse and the wren, then took in the beautiful golden-haired young lady, and then swung back to
Relkin.

He heaved a sigh. "All right. This looks like something
weird. It better be important. If the captain comes down on
me, Dragonboy, then I'll come looking for you, got that?"

"Understood."

They were ushered into Eads's tent.

"Speak, Dragoneer," said Eads, with an uneasy glance in
Eilsa's direction. If Relkin had gone and compromised the
young lady, there might be hell to pay. These stiff-necked
upland clans could be very tricky about their women folk.
Eads felt a strong annoyance at the boy. This one was always getting into trouble. What the devil was wrong with
him?

Then he realized that there were small animals riding on
the boy's shoulders and his annoyance turned to anger. His
cheeks reddened. Before he exploded, Relkin said, "Sir, I
have to report something so strange that I would scarcely believe it possible except that I've seen this kind of thing before. Too much, sir, far too much, I agree. I know what
you're thinking, sir. I am not crazy. Eilsa Ranardaughter is
here to confirm some of what I have to tell you."

Eads was still close to an explosion; it had been delayed
a few seconds, no more. If this dragonboy thought he could
get away with this sort of impertinence, then he was going
to find out that he was wrong, terribly wrong. He'd be running extra work details for three months, perhaps six, perhaps a full year.

Relkin launched into a long, halting explanation of how
he had seen the eagle, slain the batrukh, and discovered the
small animals.

Eads's eyebrows rose, rose higher, and rose almost into
his hairline as he listened to all this.

"If you are angling for a dismissal from the legions,
young man, then you are going about it in the right way.

However, before I have you drummed out, you will receive a week of field punishment. Am I understood?"

"Yes, sir. May I continue, sir, it is vital that you hear me out, please believe me. Ask Eilsa Ranardaughter if what I have just told you is true."

Eads swallowed heavily and looked to the girl. She was the clan chief's daughter and was said to be strong-willed but level-headed.

The questions were many for Captain Rorker Eads.

Was the boy utterly mad? Was he spouting nonsense? Was he angling for a dismissal from the service so he could pursue the beautiful young heiress of Clan Wattel?

Then speaking clearly and unhurriedly, Eilsa confirmed Relkin's story, that they were not ordinary animals, not at all, she concluded.

Eads nodded slowly. It was too deep for him. Both of these children had gone off their heads. Perhaps they'd eaten some funny mushrooms or been snakebit. He would have to call in the surgeon, perhaps the good doctor would be able to prescribe a tonic.

Relkin could see that Eads had not accepted their story; he wasn't taking it seriously. Too strange. In desperation he stepped forward and put the mouse on the table beside Captain Eads.

The mouse sat there quite still, looking directly up at the captain.

Eads looked down. The mouse was behaving just as strangely as the children. This was getting decidedly beyond a joke. He raised his head to call for the surgeon, but the mouse eyes seemed to say "no" to him.

The black eyes were so bright, so beady, so lustrous, and filled with swirling motions. Eads felt the hair on his arms and neck rise, and sweat started from his brow.

"May the Mother preserve me," he whispered.

"She will," said a tiny, precise voice in his brain.

Eads stared down at the mouse with horror. It was speaking to him. A damned mouse was speaking to him!

"This is not a mouse speaking to you," said the voice in his mind quite clearly. "I am Ribela of Defwode. I fight in the service of the Empire of the Rose."

Horror turned to amazement in Eads's face.

"What is this?"

"You need to reach Arneis. We go there as well, but ahead of you, once our eagle has recovered his strength."

"Eagle?"

"The boy told you. The girl told you. They speak truth."

"By the breath this is amazing."

"I would agree with you. It is the product of exceptional effort, of that you can be certain."

Eads shook his head. It did not change a thing. He still heard the voice. He looked up at Relkin and Eilsa with horror and amazement, struggling for control.

"I'm sorry, Captain," said Relkin, "I could think of no other way of making you understand. You do understand, don't you?"

Eads swallowed.

"You do," said the voice in his head.

"I do. I . . ." But he fell silent and turned to look back to the mouse on the table, and there he stayed, with his mouth part open.

The bird flew down to the floor and seized a fat spider and ate it. Then flew up to Relkin's shoulder again.

Eads shook his head. He had known that witchcraft was one of the empire's great strengths, but he had seen only the ceremonies to give strength to walls on Fundament Day. He had never even dreamed that such a thing could happen. But two witches were here, in the persons of these tiny animals. And one of them was talking to him.

And what she told him was electrifying. "There is a secret stair. Not five leagues from here it lies. The great stair of Veronath it was called once. It has lain hidden here for centuries, unused except by occasional agents of the Office of Unusual Insight.

"The stair was built by the Emperors Fedosius and Chalx in the Vapasid dynasty of Veronath. There are twenty-three turns in the stair, and it connects to the underground cavern in which runs the Eferni River to the Danding Pool, and beyond the pool lies Dandelin and Arneis."

"Arneis," breathed Eads.

"You must get to Arneis, Captain. Every man and every dragon will be needed."

"You're right. By all the—I just don't know, I mean, I . . ." Eads fell silent, stunned by this latest revelation.

"It is the Dark Stair," said the voice. "The Wattels are the ancient keepers of this region. They keep the secret of the Dark Stair."

"They did not tell me."

"They have dwindled into goatherds and lost much of the knowledge of their forebears. They view all outsiders with suspicion. The clan chief only thought of his clan's interest. But you must forgive him. The Wattels must march. We will need their Fird in the battle line in Arneis."

"How," he began uncertainly, "how can we persuade him to undertake this mission?"

"You will take me to him."

As these words came into Eads's mind, popping out of nowhere, like his own thoughts except not, he saw the wren flit back and proffer a tasty big beetle to the mouse. The mouse ate the beetle while the wren sped away, out the tent through a side flap.

Eads rose, and with Relkin and Eilsa accompanying him, he headed for the tent of Clan Chief Ranard.

CHAPTER SIXTY-TWO

It was a harrowing moment for Clan Chief Ranard. All his clan's secrets were exposed it seemed. Weirds, like things out of ancient myth, had appeared and rode on Captain Eads's shoulders. His deception exposed, Ranard flushed with shame and could not meet Eads's eyes.

Shaken by the experience, the clan chief called together the leaders of the Fird. Mastering a tremor in his voice, he informed them that he had received a summons to the Imperial Mustering, which was being held in Arneis. Every able man was required to present himself.

He told them that it was time for him to reveal to the world the greatest clan secret of all. He spoke of a Great Stair to an underworld river not five leagues distant. The stair had been built in the latter days of the king emperors of Veronath, and Clan Wattel had originally served by guarding it. It was still hidden by great magic, and had been built as an escape route under the mountains. For in those days, the power in Padmasa had first arisen.

They were to take the Dark Stair and the underworld river to Danding Pool on the far side of Mt. Livol. From there they would march to the mustering, wherever in Arneis the standard had been set up.

The Clan greeted this with a roar of approval. They had fought and been bloodied, and they knew very well that if the great battle in Arneis were lost because of their absence, then they would die accursed. For die they would, under the iron foot of the great enemy, which would surely stamp them down, even here in their ancient remote fastness.

As Ranard told them, this assault was the greatest ever made by the enemy, greater even than the Hosts of dread Dugguth that had poured forth to overrun Veronath in the ancient days.

The word went through the Host and the Fird in a matter

of minutes. The response was swift and echoed that of their leaders. They streamed over to form a dense mass surrounding Ranard's tent, and loudly pledged themselves to the fight in Arneis.

Ranard sent them back to their tents to rest, for they would march the following day.

The clan chief was left alone with his daughter. There was still a haunted look in his eyes. What Eads had told him had been the greatest shock of his life. He had almost fainted when he realized that Eads was talking of the Dark Stair, the great secret that his clan had guarded for centuries. And Ranard's deception was exposed to his everlasting shame.

He had never imagined such things coming to him in his life, but they had and there was no getting out of what had to be done. It was their fight now. He knew that in his bones and had ever since the battle of Clove Valley. Those abominable things would come back eventually, to take all the Wattel women and to slay all the men.

In the end Clan Wattel could not remain above the call of the empire. It was just as Ranard's father had predicted. And now Ranard wondered if the old man's prediction of complete doom and destruction would also come about.

Eilsa brought him a cup of a bitter herb infusion, and she insisted he drink it. As he did so, she checked the bandages. The wounds had been cleaned, but in some places they were deep, and she worried about corruption in them. She had already suggested that Ranard visit the medic in Eads's force. He had refused. Her concern had grown so that she had broached it to Relkin. Relkin had given her some Old Sugustus disinfectant at once.

She treated a swab of shredded boiled cloth with the foul-smelling liquid in the little bottle and pressed it to the wounds.

Her father jerked suddenly as the liquid soaked in.

"By the breath!" he whistled. "That stings something sharp!"

"It shows that there is corruption in the wound, Father. It is a thing of the empire, a cleaning thing that kills the corruption and prevents death from small wounds."

Ranard stared at the swab and the small bottle. "So my own daughter betrays me and uses dragon liniment on her father," he teased.

"I did not betray us, Father. The weirds knew everything."

"Aye, so they did."

"Father, there is a tide to these events, do you not see? The dragonboy says his destiny has been foretold and that he must stand in a field in Arneis. We must all go there. That seems so clear to me now."

Ranard gave a slight nod, he hissed again as Old Sugustus sank into another pocket of corruption. "Perhaps you are right, child. Perhaps we shall all die in Arneis, and the name of Clan Wattel will wither and go out like a lamp that has finally run out of fuel."

"I cannot say to that, Father. The dragonboy says his destiny was foretold him by elves. Can you imagine that? I really don't know whether to believe that dragonboy sometimes."

"Ye are much taken with the youth, I think. And he is a comely one and intelligent, I'd say."

"Oh, he is, Father. He is amazingly learned about the world. He has seen a great deal of it for his years."

"Ye may be taken with the boy, my child, but ye will be careful, will ye not? There are passions that can run wild and lead to unfortunate predicaments."

She blushed. "Oh, Father, we love each other but we know that our love is doomed. He is written to the legions for seven more years. How can I wait that long to be wed, especially when the delightful Edon Norwat is there to hand?"

Ranard grunted. He knew his daughter's true views on Edon Norwat.

"My child, if you wish to make your own mistakes, you may do so, but then ye'll not beget any heir to Ranard Clan Chief."

She sighed. The biological imperative of inheritance.

"I understand, Father."

Ranard was silent as she bound up the wounds again with clean linen bandages. His thoughts circling the future and the doom it seemed to hold for all he held dear.

On the far side of the camp, in the line of big tents that housed the 109th Marneri Dragons, Relkin sat with little Jak. The younger boy had learned to stifle the sobbing and the tears. His dragon was gone, and there was nothing to be done about it. Rusp had been burned to ashes, as was the proper thing. But Jak was still alive, and sometimes he had begun to think this was not right. He should die and join the dragon in the shades.

Suicides were common among dragonboys who lost their dragons and everyone, including Dragon Leader Turrent for once, had been very concerned. Turrent felt that he could hardly hope to convince young Jak of anything. He had been hard on Jak for weeks. Turrent was forced to ask Relkin to speak to Jak.

Jak, while not crying or sniffling, was morosely silent. Relkin waited a long while, trying to choose his words carefully. Jak sat, lost in misery.

"Jak, listen to me. You have lost Rusp, and for that we all grieve with you. Everyone liked old Rusp. We don't expect you to forget him in a day or two, but look, Jak, you have a job to do. Bryon is gone, too. We buried him today."

"I know, I was there."

"That means Alsebra doesn't have a dragonboy. Mono looked after her wounds, but she needs someone full-time. Take her on, Jak. We're counting on you."

Relkin sighed inwardly with relief when he saw that Jak was not inherently against the idea. However, the younger boy was not sure it would work.

"I like Alsebra," he said. "But she is a snappish one. She's not like my Rusp. And I don't think she likes me."

"Alsebra's an uncommon smart dragon, Jak. We all know that. You can count on it that she won't make things difficult for you. She knows she needs a dragonboy. What do you think she feels? She and Bryon grew up together. She is very sad, just like you."

"Truly?" Jak searched Relkin's face for any trace of deception.

"Why have I always felt that she didn't like me?"

"Perhaps she didn't at first. She's like that. As you said, she's not easily pleased. She was hard on Bryon, too. He was always complaining about it. But she's so handy with a sword that she's a joy to watch in a fight."

"That is true, I have seen her pull off things that only a man with a small sword could do."

Relkin nodded. Both he and Baz had commented on Alsebra's skill with a sword.

"Of course, Undaunt is small for a dragonsword," Jak went on. "All her kit is smaller than Rusp's. I won't be able to use any of the old stuff."

"They will give Rusp's equipment to another brass, Jak.
You know that."

Jak looked at Relkin.

"You really think I can do this, Relkin?"

"Of course. Ask her."

After a few minutes to get up the courage, young Jak
upped and went into Alsebra's tent. The green freemartin
was awake, sharpening Undaunt with a whetstone.

Relkin glanced in through the tent flap a few minutes
later. Jak was up on the freemartin's back, inspecting her
bandages and the wounds beneath them. They were talking
together, the usual back and forth between dragon and
dragonboy. Relkin slipped away and returned to his own
agenda. They marched in the morning, and there was a lot to
do.

All night a forest of smithy fires blazed on the site of the
ancient palace of the kings of Veronath. As weapons and
shields were repaired, so figures passed the fires laden with
swords and shields or pushing barrows filled with dragon armor and helmets. In the morning the smithies were still at
work and eventually had to be left, with wagons to bring up
the weapons as they were repaired, for the camp was struck
immediately after breakfast and they marched, legionaries,
clansmen, farmers from Bur Lake, dragons, and dragonboys.

The pace was brisk but the dragons accepted it without
comment. They were used to such marching now, every day.
They were lean and very much hardened by the experience
of the past few weeks. In addition, there'd been precious little beer since they'd left Dalhousie months ago.

The deaths of Rusp and Oast had changed the inner mood
as well. Zebulpator still rode high in the sky at night, but the
dragons were no longer so concerned. The ancient cycles
continued. The dragons had known that death was coming,
and it had come. They had bid farewell to their comrades.
Now they returned to the here and now. Slowly their normal
good cheer began to surface.

Dragonboys in both squadrons noted the change at once,
and the word flashed around. It was good to have the dragons free of their preoccupation with the red star and the
Moon and death and fire.

In fact, it was a beautiful day, with clear skies but for the
occasional white fluffy cloud. The land was still drying from
the previous few days' downpour, but the rainfall had

brought out the wildflowers on the hillsides. They were ablaze with poppies and asters and white daisies of a hundred different kinds.

The march took them through the heart of the Wattel lands. They passed small villages built of white stone with slate roofs. Women in brown tweeds and white blouses came out of the houses. Blond-headed children scampered past, squealing with excitement at seeing the Fird and the Host march to war and even more by seeing the grim-looking legionaries and the wondrous dragons, which they had never seen the like of.

Down narrow lanes, muddy from the rains of the previous few days, and on through a patchwork of small, square fields of green, surrounded by stone walls and hillsides of grass crowned with heather on the ridgelines. Sheep dotted the green hills, and the small streams were home to a champion race of trout.

When they halted, the folk brought them food, loaves of rye bread and great steaming potchoons of oatmeal and stirabout for dragons and legionaries alike. Unfortunately there was a shortage of akh. The dragons grumbled. On the bright side, however, there was a small amount of beer, a peculiarly dark and bitter brew that the dragons found to their liking. Those who had served in the Ourdh campaign found a certain resemblance to some of the beers they'd enjoyed in the far-off land of pyramids and palms. Alas, there wasn't that much, and it was soon gone. It was barely enough to get the dragons singing, but not enough to keep them at it.

For some, this was not entirely a bad thing.

The sky remained clear and calm, and they made good time and reached the site of the ancient stair by late afternoon.

They faced into a great bowl-shaped corrie, cut into the hillside by ice in ancient times when all this land had felt the breath of glaciers. Grass covered the lower slope of the corrie, but farther up there was nothing but bare rock.

The mouse and the bird escorted Ranard and the Clan Wizard Unoa to a certain expanse of bare rock. The mouse riding on Ranard's shoulder. The wren riding on Unoa's.

Unoa gave the commands for the ancient spell, and the golden outline of the door shimmered into view.

The men of the Fird gasped at the sight. All their lives

they had lived with the memories of mighty magic from yesteryear, but never had they seen any of it, until now.

At another command, the rock opened inward silently, and after a moment's hesitation, they marched in.

Here they came to a halt. Ranard had neglected to tell Eads that though Clan Wattel had retained the secret of the stair and the spell required to open it, they had lost the secret spell that turned on the interior lamps. This spell had not been lost among the Great Witches of Cunfshon, however, and Ribela had communicated the details to Unoa. Now the clan wizard repeated the words, slightly nervous, but without a mistake. In a moment a glow began in the ceiling and soon dozens of lights erupted to brilliance all along the ceiling and down the walls.

Before them was stretched a sample of the ancient glories of Veronath. The sweep of white marble, the gleaming inlay of gold, and then above on all the ceilings were the panels of paintings, great sweeping paintings in a triumphalist style, protected by great magic from the ravages of time and thus still as fresh and bright and lively as the day they were completed, in the long-ago reign of Emperor Chalx the Great.

Ranard sighed inwardly at the beauty and sheer magnificence of all this. The Dark Stair was dark no more.

Overhead were paintings of the Seven Wonders of Veronath, including the Magic Cairn of Seagloss, the water gardens of Veron, the Tame Dragons of the Kings, wyverns like those who marched beneath the paintings.

Now their march became a fantastic descent on the great curving stair that wound down into the rock of the mountain's foothills. The ceilings were lit up and scenes from the history of Veronath went on, one after the other, as they marched downward.

On they went down the twenty-three turns of the stair until at last they emerged in the caverns of the river Eferni.

And there in the shadows, bobbing silently beside the docks, were the gondolas of Veronath.

In awe they stared at the enchanted fleet as it stirred under the spell saying of Unoa. One after the other, the swan-like boats glided up to the dock and accepted a heavy load of men and horses, and even a dragon apiece in the larger ones.

The boats were made of wood and should have fallen to pieces long ago except that they were maintained by a spell

of such masterful, intricate magic, that it had held them together for a thousand years or more.

And now they slipped on under their own magical power
down the secret river Eferni, through the very roots of Mt.
Livol and into darkness. Beyond the darkness lay Dandelin,
in Arneis.

CHAPTER SIXTY-THREE

Thrembode the Magician sat his horse on a hillock over-looking the river Alno just outside Cujac. On this side of the river Alno ran the north road to Rundel, to Bel Awl, and eventually to Aubinas and Marneri. On the far side was the east road, straight down the Alno to Fitou and eventually to Kadein.

Both roads were jammed with a constant-moving mass of war. Imps by the thousands in marching regiments under the dark banners of Axoxo. Trolls in great platoons of fifty at a time, marching with their axes on their shoulders; men on horseback, wagons by the thousand, a veritable avalanche of war making.

Thrembode felt a strong apprehension when he looked across the river. He had never studied war in any formal way. His path had always lain through the schools of magic, trickery, and the arts of deception. But he had absorbed the great military maxim that it was a bad idea to divide one's strength in the face of the enemy.

But this was the strategy commanded by Vapul, and Vapul got his orders directly from the Masters themselves. This was their plan.

As had been expected, the Argonathi resistance outside the town of Fitou had strengthened. A force of around thirty thousand legionaries had arrived quite suddenly two or three days earlier, delivered by skillfully handled river craft that brought them up in an endless stream of sails. Works and fortifications around Fitou had been built up quickly since then and now offered a formidable obstacle. It was also known that another legion and a half was about to join this force, ferrying up from Kadein. And that would put almost forty thousand legion troops in the field. With such a force and with a competent, bluff, direct general in command, which Felix of Brutz certainly was, one could take on the world.

Thrembode the Magician had seen what these legions could do. Just two of them had routed the huge but disorganized army of the Sephisti at Salpalangum. It was another military maxim that thirty thousand Argonath legionaries tipped with dragons were unbeatable, especially if they had adequate cavalry, and the force in Fitou had not only some legion cavalry squadrons, but thousands of horsemen who had come in from the countryside to the muster. These were the squires, the prosperous farmers of the bountiful lands of Arneis. Most had some legion experience, all were born in the saddle, and all knew this land, from Bel Awl to Fenx, like the back of their hands. They had made it hot for the Baguti cavalry. The Baguti had become somewhat timid, even nervous as a result, and the quality of their reports had suffered.

It was also a blow that General Felix had survived the assassination attempt made in Kadein at the beginning of the campaign. Yet survive it he clearly had. General Rastonel Felix was a hard man, an able, authoritarian commander with a long career in the frontier legions behind him. Thrembode feared what such a commander might do with seven or eight legions at his disposal.

So far, however, the Argonathi had remained on the defensive, and thus the gamble could be taken. Forty thousand imps, driving south on a broad front, with five thousand Baguti to screen them and create confusion, could likely fool the Argonathi into staying down there at Fitou for a day or two more.

The Argonathi were now standing in a fortified position that would cost an opponent fifty thousand lives to take if it could be taken at all, precisely the sort of position against which a vast Host might dash itself to pieces. General Felix would surely be loathe to leave it. Furthermore, he would be sure to imagine that the object of the invasion was Kadein, the greatest city of the Ennead of Argonath, the fat plum just seventy miles away.

To get to Kadein, an enemy would have to go through Fitou, or else detour painfully around through farm lanes and dense woods. A Host like this vast agglomeration from Axoxo could easily become unmanageable if it spread out over miles of country lanes. The main roads were essential to the success of the Masters' plans. The Argonathi knew all this perfectly well, and so they waited at Fitou.

In the meantime the greater half of the Host, more than sixty thousand imps, six hundred trolls, and thousands of men, was marching on the woodland road through Rundel, heading for the river crossings at Waldrach and Rusma. Beyond Rusma was the Bel Awl gap and the road into Setter and Seant. Beyond Seant lay Aubinas, Marneri, Bea, and Pennar, the four rich provinces of the central Ennead.

Once they were over the bridges at Rusma, they would be unstoppable. The Argonathi had emptied their land of men and concentrated them at Fitou to await the onrush to Kadein. Beyond Rusma there was nothing, no defensive forces at all, except scattered militias of old men and boys.

They would break through to Aubinas and Marneri, and there they would deploy the secret weapon to break the city gates.

Thrembode understood now. He had seen the ogres. Not even the magics of the witches would hold the gate from them.

If there was anything in this ambitious plan to still give Thrembode immense confidence, it was these secret monsters. He had seen them several times now. They were still awesome. Kept hidden in the very heart of the marching horde, kept away from imps, for they had a habit of snatching them up and eating them directly. Kept away from trolls and men, too. Kept secret until now; they offered a sure way to break gates and shatter dragon lines.

All they had to do was to cross the counties of Rundel and Lennink, bridging the river Walda at Waldrach and the Finger River at Rusma, and then push through the gap of Bel Awl, and they were home. There would be nothing to stop them from storming through fat province after fat province until they reached Marneri. And when they sacked the white city, they would pile the skulls of their people to the sky.

Such a blow to the Argonath would be mortal. The Masters well knew that it was Marneri, not the great Kadein, that was the heart and soul of the Ennead and the Empire of the Rose. If Marneri was taken and burned, and along with it perhaps Bea and Pennar, then the remainder could be isolated and reduced one by one until even mighty Kadein surrendered itself to the power of Padmasa.

But they had still to march across the hostile countryside

of the counties of Rundel and Andelain, and then of Kilrush and Dondee. And if by some miracle the enemy did catch up to them, then the fight would be between a mere sixty thousand imps and forty thousand legionaries, and even the secret weapons might not save them in such a case.

Lukash emerged from the brush behind Thrembode. He rode his horse up beside the magician's. His eyes had a peculiar luster.

"You have come to report, General?"

Thrembode toyed with the little silver whistle.

"I have come to report." Lukash spoke humbly. Since his deflation by Vapul, he was a changed man. Thrembode understood. Lukash was one of those who either lorded it over you or else licked your boots.

"Go ahead, General."

"I have heard from outriders on the north road. There is a small opposition force gathering in Waldrach. It consists of local men, reservists, some youngsters. Hardly more than a thousand or so, nothing for us to be concerned about. The way is clear for us to march all the way to Marneri."

"We will burn the white city, General. Your name will go down in the histories as the man who torched the city of white stone by the Bright Sea strand."

Thrembode was amused by this rather slight poetic image, he chuckled indulgently. Lukash smiled. His madness was growing steadily. Someday, he promised himself, he would avenge this moment and all the other petty humiliations put upon him by this popinjay magician. For now, he must submit. But someday, ah, he would kill this one slowly.

"And now, what are the reports from Fitou?"

Lukash roused himself from his dream of revenge.

"The enemy continues to stay on the defensive. Main forces remain within the perimeter down there in Fitou. He has aggressive cavalry patrols working through the woods of south Andelain. There have been clashes all the way along that stretch of the road between Conjona and Andelain town. I have sent the Baguti to push them back."

"And what do you think is passing through General Felix's mind right now, Lukash?"

"He is watching carefully to see what we do. He fears we may try to come down on the north bank of the river. There is a good road between Conjona and Andelain. He has already thrown up breastworks and forts on the north shore in

Andelain so we can be certain that this is something he fears. He hopes we will come straight down the main road on the south side of the river and hurl ourselves at his main lines outside Fitou. Then he would fight a defensive battle within his fortifications and let us wear ourselves down."

"I believe I have the gist of it, General. I will report to the Mesomaster this evening. I will say that you have responded very well to his attentions and that you are doing a splendid job."

Lukash smiled again, a weird thing to see since it masked such complex emotions.

"Thank you, Magician."

"You're welcome, General Lukash." Thrembode fought down the urge to make Lukash get off his horse and kiss his boots. For some reason he had a strong urge to humiliate the general, in revenge for Lukash's unbridled arrogance. For a moment he toyed again with the little whistle and then let it go.

"You are dismissed, General."

Without a word, his face an impassive mask, Lukash rode back into the screen of leaves.

CHAPTER SIXTY-FOUR

Under the mountain, floating on the chill flood of Eferni, Relkin slept uneasily. He was bone tired. The march, the recent battle, the weird excitement of walking down that enormous stair, under the magical paintings, all had taken a toll on his strength. He slept, and beside him the dragon slept, enormous rib cage rising and falling steadily as the magic ship bore them along the river. Asleep in the same boat were the Purple Green and Alsebra, with Manuel and Jak, and wedged in among them were a dozen or so soldiers and a party of clansmen. Every boat was jammed tight with men and dragons, and their equipment piled up around them.

Men with torches stood in the stern of each vessel. The fleet could be seen as a line of torchlights, dimming in the distance until lost by a curve in the course of the river, winding through the caverns of the enormous cave system here below Mt. Livol.

Twice they floated through great caverns, each with forests of stalagmites and stalactites. Frills and fans of lime had formed in places with a strong drip, and by the light of the torches they could see this forest of strange limestone excrescences stretching away all around them. And yet the magical craft of ancient Veronath glided smoothly through with nary a hitch.

But Relkin saw none of this beauty. Deep sleep had claimed him early in the voyage. Bazil had gone to sleep even earlier. The whole boat was asleep by the time they floated through the first of the caverns.

Relkin dreamed that he was in his first room, back in Quosh. A narrow cubicle, six feet wide and ten feet long. Just enough room for a bunk, a table, and a stool. There was a slit window that never let in light and a door with a lock. And it was his. His own place, the first he'd ever had.

Someone was calling to him, but he couldn't understand

what they were saying. He turned and found himself in front of a doorway that opened into the gymnasium where the village women were doing their exercises. He passed through the women, who seemed not to see him at all. A powerfully built man was standing to one side, lifting a heavy barbell to his chest and then pressing it above his head.

Someone was still calling, probably the dragon. How he loved that young leatherback dragon. He was a beauty, and so fast for a dragon. Relkin thought that Baz could outduel even a good swordsman; not with his strength but his speed. So he would run outside. He and the dragon were the best friends in the whole world. In all Relkin's short life, there had been nothing so good as being partnered with the dragon.

The village women wore grey tunics and black woolen tights, and they stretched and jumped and went through the steps of the Lausann, a dance from the ancient days. They took no notice of him as he went out the door.

He woke up. He was adrift in the dark, hearing only water slap at ship's side and dragons snoring loudly on all sides. He recalled where he was. It had been a strange dream but at least it had not involved either dwarves or demon serpents. He'd had all he wanted of either of those in his dreams of late.

There was a sudden voice in his head.

"Relkin of Quosh," it said. "Greetings."

He looked around wildly.

"What is this? Is this just another dream?"

"This is not a dream," said the little voice which was somehow familiar.

Then out of the corner of his eye, he saw something small dart along the side of the vessel. It came to a stop nearby, perched on Bazil's helmet. His eyes focused intently on the bird.

"I should be getting used to this I suppose. You are there, in the wren?"

"Yes. This is an animant, a form in which I am projected. Right now my body is sitting in a room in the Tower of Guard in Marneri. Ribela is sitting there, too. So is Lagdalen."

"Lagdalen is an eagle now."

"She is not an eagle; she cohabits in an eagle's mind. The eagle is still there."

"This is so strange."

"Correct. The amount of effort required to do this aston-
ishes me. Fortunately, I have a gift for it."

"I wrote you a letter, Lady."

"I received it, Relkin. You are concerned with destiny and
the influence of the Sinni."

"Yes, Lady."

"The Sinni are a complex concept. They are not of our
time and space, they are of another level of existence entirely. Can you understand this?"

"I think so. They are like gods; they live elsewhere."

"Yes, they live elsewhere. One of their greatest arts is in
the foretelling of the future. Sometimes they glimpse the set
of the gathering threads of destiny; they see through the
chaos of the ever and constant 'now' to places where the
flowing threads run tightly together. These are places where
great events in our world are often indicated."

"Sort of a tightness in the cloth, then? The cloth of the
world."

"Yes, Relkin, you understand it well. And in such a wrinkle, the Sinni have seen you, and they have intervened in our
world to ensure that you reach Arneis."

"Why do the Sinni do this?"

"They work to help all of us in the less energetic worlds,
like Ryetelth. The struggle continues across the sphere board
of destiny. Even in the higher realms, there are conflicts.
Natural alliances spring up."

"The sphere board again. Ribela told me of that."

"The Great Mother must have had some plan in mind
when she brought you into the world, Relkin. You have been
the instrument for great changes. I have seen it in Tummuz
Orgmeen. Ribela saw it in the serpent's pit. We are convinced She has some plan for you. So you must get to
Arneis."

"You are going to Arneis, too?"

"We are. We ride the cavern craft to the Danding Pool.
The eagle is resting. He was wounded slightly during the
pursuit by the batrukh. It was a close-run thing at the end.
Your arrow was true and straight, young Relkin. It was perhaps another example of the peculiar destiny you are living
out."

"Thank you, Lady."

"When we reach the Danding Pool, then we will take to

the skies again. We must find the Argonathi army, and find a way to communicate with its commander."

"And what will we be doing?"

"That is Captain Eads's responsibility, child. But I expect he'll be seeking to join with the force already in place, which I would expect to be of at least six legions, perhaps seven. I would also expect those legions to be in one of the Alno River towns, perhaps in Pengarden, perhaps as far up as Fitou. I hope it is Fitou."

"How far is that?"

"About fifty miles south and east of Dandelin, which we will see shortly after we leave the grotto of the Eferni and enter the Danding Pool."

"Lady, how is it I can hear you speak in my mind, although you make no sound?"

She was amused. "If you really wanted to know that, my child, you should have spent your formative years in the magic school. You would have memorized the Birrak by now and about forty tomes of spellsay. Let us just say that it takes an enormous effort of concentration combined with great powers of memory. You will notice the aftereffect in a moment. Good-bye, Relkin. I pray that we will meet again."

The wren flew away. Relkin stared off after it. He realized that his pulse was racing, and his breath was coming in fast and deep. It was as if he had been sprinting hard for a long distance. He was suddenly very tired once again.

He knew only that the destiny laid out for him lay close ahead. And he wondered where Eilsa was. He knew she was on the voyage, aboard a boat with her father and his closest followers. Was she a part of his destiny, too?

He was asleep again in moments and did not awake until they were not only in the Danding Pool but emerging into sight of Dandelin, outlined on the farther shore by a few dim lights. Ahead stretched a row of vessels, each with a torch sputtering at its stern, heading for the ancient landing steps at Dandelin.

The steps were much diminished now, for the glories of Dandelin in the Veronath Era had long been replaced by a different kind of life, that of a farming center and a market town. Thus, among tumbled remains of the huge structures of yore, stood the solid houses of yeomen farmers.

Each magical gondola came to the dock and unloaded its

passengers and then moved on again, passing on out onto the pool before circling and heading back to the Eferni grotto.

Awestruck, Relkin watched them go. Such had been the glories of the old world ... great stairs and enormous palaces ... paintings so rich and lustrous, they seemed more real than life ... and magic so powerful, it lived on long after the demise of the kingdom of Veronath.

He reveled in all the wonders he had seen in his short life, which might be reaching its end. Was he to die in Arneis? Was that to be his destiny?

Then he heard Dragon Leader Turrent coming and switched his attention back to his dragon. Bazil was upright, but still half-asleep.

Relkin jumped up and ran lightly up the dragon's back.

"Aargh!" said the dragon, or something closely related. "You are no boy anymore to jump on an old, tired dragon. You put on weight in this life. It is sure that this dragon does not put on weight."

"You're fitter than you've been in years," said Relkin calmly, as he adjusted the collar of the joboquin.

"Where do we go now?"

The Purple Green leaned over. "I already asked that. Nobody knows."

Relkin knew. "We go to a field somewhere in Arneis."

"Fool boy, there are thousands of fields in Arneis. It is covered in them."

"That's for sure, but there's one that will be our place. I know it."

CHAPTER SIXTY-FIVE

Carrying the mouse and bird, the eagle flew away at dawn, soaring off beyond the roofs of Dandelin town, over the ridge and into Arneis.

Captain Eads and Chief Ranard put their force on the road to Fitou as soon as they could feed their men. The townsfolk of Dandelin turned out magnificently with hot water, firewood, and food straight from their own kitchens.

Eads hurried their breakfast, however. Knowing now that the huge enemy army might have split in two in Arneis, he knew that he had to move his men toward Fitou as quickly as possible.

Between Captain Eads and Chief Ranard there existed now a strange vacuum. The shock of uncovering Ranard's deliberate deception concerning the Dark Stair had deeply disconcerted Eads. He was unsure what to think. Indeed, the good relations forged in the heat of the battle of Clove Valley were gone. And yet they were in the middle of a campaign march. This was not the time to settle anything. They had to cooperate if they were to be effective.

Thus when Ranard approached him at the campfire, Eads made the effort to be cordial and welcomed the chief and took some hot kalut with him.

In front of the captain, Ranard was downcast at first, guilty and remorseful, even ashamed of the weakness he had shown. Disunity in the face of the enemy in Padmasa had brought down all of its victims. The chief knew what Eads must think of him. As he sipped kalut, however, Ranard realized that Eads was trying hard not to show any sign of his true feelings concerning the stair. Ranard forced himself to rise to the occasion.

Eads carefully laid out the plan of action for the day.

"We go southeast directly. It's about fifty miles to Fitou. We must get there tomorrow. I know that my men can keep up that pace, now that they've been rested and fed. I expect that the clansmen of Wattel can keep up that pace, too."

Ranard nodded, the clansmen spent their lives pursuing sheep across the moors.

"The only problem is the dragons. Their feet get sore. But we have to have them, as you know."

Ranard understood. He'd seen dragons in action at Clove Valley. Men alone could not stand against trolls. The disparity in strength was too great. The dragons were like enormous swordsmen, armed with a prehensile tail tip.

"So we march as quickly as the dragons can march."

"That about sums it up."

"And when we reach Fitou?"

"I very much hope we will also reach the Argonathi army."

"And then the last battle."

Eads shrugged. "Only the last battle if we are defeated, Clan Chief. If we win, then there'll be others."

Ranard finished his kalut and spoke somberly. "And if we are defeated there, then it will be the end of all that is fair and lovely in the world. The iron foot of the great enemy will crush us in our own land. We of Clan Wattel understand this."

They marched, the men setting out with vigor, the dragons a little less enthusiastically. Within an hour they reached the hamlet of Satchen and turned southeast on the main Fitou road. Quite a few houses were already shuttered up. The remaining folk watched uneasily as the small army of mixed clansmen, settler militia, and legionaries tramped past. The sight of war dragons, with those huge sword hilts rising from the scabbards on their backs, turned unease to outright fear.

After a century of peace, the threat of war had come once again to this lovely land of vine and wheat.

It was a beautiful day, warm and sunny with a few white clouds passing overhead, slow sailors across the azure vault. They marched at a good pace, in the shade of the great oaks that lined the road.

By noon they were lunching on the village green of Hay. The remaining inhabitants of Hay brought out grain and bread and cheese in plenty, with wine and even winter ale to wash it down.

They ate prodigiously, dragonboys slathering fresh loaves

of bread with soft cheeses, one after the other, while the wyverns poured ale by the pail down their gullets to wash down the bread.

Then they turned their attention to potchoons of stirabout enriched with milk and honey. And to finish if off, they each took a bucket of fresh boiled noodles slathered in akh.

Full, for once, they heaved themselves to their feet with a few deep groans and hisses, and resumed the march.

As they went the dragons complained mildly about their feet, which always took a pounding on any march beneath so many tons of dragon. In truth, the great reptilian feet had been hardened by the campaign they'd fought up the Kalens Valley. So far they were merely sore and not blistered at all.

Now they moved out of the wheat fields about the village of Laleet and climbed up onto the gentle northern slope of the long Sprian Scarp. The south face was much steeper, forming a bluff perhaps two hundred feet at the highest point near the town of Lennink. The scarp ran on for thirty miles or more, trending east of south. The road to Fitou went along the top of the ridge for most of that distance before coming down off the slope to the town of Consorza.

The broad, gentle slope on the northern side was given over to fields of hops, vegetables, and flowers. Bees were at work in vast numbers over clover and alfalfa crops.

The south face of the ridge presented an altogether different picture. Here there were woodlots on the steepest parts. Elsewhere there was a long smooth slope of poor soil over calcareous limestone where lay some of the greatest vineyards in the world. They grew the black pearl grape, known locally as the "micoste" and from it made the wines of Spriani known and loved across the world. Each legendary vineyard was separated from the next by a stone wall or a narrow lane. Solidly built farmhouses stood at every road junction along the ridge section of the road. The villages of Sprian and Lennink were built of stone and encompassed a flourishing wine-making industry.

It was a prosperous land, and marching under the beaming sun, the men and the dragons kept up a good, league-consuming pace. Morale was high.

In the villages, the people came out to stare at the dragons. Wyverns were unknown here, and war had become nothing but a set of legends from the past.

Captain Eads had the Talion troopers working out on the

front, scouting the ridge down to Lennink, where the Fitou road crossed the royal road to Bel Awl and points north to Marneri.

The heat of the day had arrived, and a hush enveloped the land broken only by the hum of bees and the song of the lark.

In one way, the hush was ominous. The bells of the temples in Sprian and Lennink should have begun ringing for the early afternoon services.

Then, from way off to the north, they heard the big bell of the temple in Waldrach, but it was not calling for the afternoon services. It was ringing wildly, broadcasting alarm.

They looked off to the south, down through the walled vineyards to the woodlots. Beyond the ring of woods lay fields of wheat, more vineyards, then the dark mass of the Rundel Forest where they grew the oak for the barrels that aged the wines of Spriani.

The bell clanging away in the distance could be heard clearly, though faintly. The men looked off in that direction, but saw nothing but lines of trees and the bright green of hop fields.

Eads confided to Ranard that he wouldn't feel confident of anything until they'd reached Consorza. By then he expected to have some intelligence as to where the enemy armies were. All he knew for sure was that Cujac had fallen to the enemy two days previously and that the enemy intended to make a lunge for Marneri.

Eads's earlier forebodings had been borne out. This made it even more important to get to Fitou as quickly as possible. The great battle could come at any time.

They had to reach Fitou! Eads prayed that the army was still there and not driven farther back. He prayed even harder that the enemy was not between him and the Argonathi army. To get around a vast enemy army, with clouds of Baguti cavalry surrounding it might be impossible.

Where was that eagle? The witches had promised they would return with information about what he was marching into. But they were not yet in sight.

Eads reassured himself that once they reached Consorza, they'd have only fifteen more miles to cover to get to Fitou.

They were now crossing the highest part of the long ridge. Ahead stood Sprian itself and then Lennink, a crossroads town, where the Fitou road met the main road to

Waldrach and points north and east. Eads pulled up his horse to one side of the road and studied the terrain ahead carefully. The ridge rippled its way due south, rising and dipping as it followed the line of the hard sandstone that formed it. To the south the dark mass of Rundel Forest filled out the horizon. To his immediate right lay the entranceway to the Vineyard of Kepeche.

He climbed the wall of the vineyard and used his spyglass to examine the land to the south. Empty wheat fields and vineyards sparkled under the sun. Stone houses stood at every crossroads. He saw three Talion troopers riding up a farm road about two miles ahead. They were unhurried. Gave no sign of any alarm.

He pulled down the telescope and scanned the sky for any sign of the eagle. Nothing but a couple of white clouds interrupted the vault of blue.

The streets of Sprian village were nearly empty. Only a handful of residents remained, and these were hurriedly packing belongings in their donkey carts.

He sent a patrol through the town. Obviously the people here had heard something that the Talion troopers had not yet picked up.

In short order, he learned that a small party of Baguti had ridden up toward Lennink just a couple of hours before. They had been driven off by determined archery from a handful of good bowmen in the village.

Their appearance had started an immediate panic. Everyone in Lennink had packed and left. A couple of Sprian men, in Lennink for business, brought the news to Sprian, which emptied right afterward. Many folk were already packed, nervous since they'd heard of the fall of Cujac.

Eads pondered this news. It was stronger than a rumor, and recent. He rode ahead and climbed another wall, this time the crumbling brick wall surrounding the vineyard Etek.

He saw a dragonboy already sitting on the corner pillar of the wall. The boy had a bandage around his head.

Eads scanned the Rundel Forest. Some hidden sense, perhaps the whisper of the Great Mother Herself, told him that he was not far distant from a great army.

A minute later, two dusty, sweat-stained troopers rode up to report that Lennink was deserted.

Eads pondered the situation. He had no accurate map of

the region. His campaign maps were all of central Kohon.
He called over Troop Leader Croel, who was posted nearby.

"Where does the Lennink road go to?" he asked.

"To Waldrach."

"And beyond Waldrach?"

"To Rusma. Bel Awl."

"And past those lies Lucule and Seant, Troat and Aubinas."

"Correct, sir."

"Thank you, Troop Leader."

Eads reconsidered the road to Rundel and the dark forest.
It seemed the enemy had done as the witches had foretold.
They had split their force and sent an army marching up this
very road.

The Argonath army was sitting down in Fitou, twenty
miles away. The enemy's screening force was large enough
to convince the Argonathi that they faced the whole enemy
Host, while another force, probably just as large, was sent
marching away through the Bel Awl gap and into the helpless provinces of Marneri.

Eads realized with a somber kind of helplessness that his
small force, allied to Clan Wattel, was probably all that
stood between the foul enemy Host coming up that road and
Marneri itself.

Suddenly there was a shout. A dragonboy, the one with
the bandage around his forehead, came running up from the
vineyard.

"Baguti, sir, I see Baguti, down in the forest there."

Eads spun around. "Keen eyes there, that man," he said
clearly, and noted to himself that it was Relkin of the 109th.
His glass came up to his eye, and he studied the forest.

At first there was nothing but trees and shadows, and then
he saw them, the legs of horses in motion in the shadows,
their hooves quite distinct. And then out from under the
eaves appeared a Baguti riding a chestnut pony. Only for a
moment did he appear, and then he was hidden again. He
and his fellows were riding toward the Lennink-Cujac road,
which divided the forest of Rundel.

Eads came to a decision.

"Quick march to Lennink," he ordered. "We will set up a
blocking position there. The enemy comes up that road. We
will hold him up."

He sent a trooper riding for the south with a message for
General Felix describing the situation as Eads saw it.

CHAPTER SIXTY-SIX

They found the town of Lennink empty and immediately set about fortifying the southern approaches. There was still no sign of the enemy, not even of the Baguti they'd seen riding on the forest's edge.

Fortunately, their task was made simpler by the fact that the town boasted a multitude of walled enclosures. There were the vineyard walls on the southern side, and then within the town proper there were more walls surrounding gardens and yards. The houses were large, built of stone, and exceptionally sturdy.

Poplars and lindens grew along the main street, and Eads ordered them cut down to build a barricade across the main road to Waldrach at the southern edge of the town.

The trees were laid in a V with the point aimed to the north so as to provide a killing zone inside the V for any attacker. In addition to the trees, they wedged in whatever they could find in the nearby buildings, a rich haul of old wine presses, barrels, crates, and several metal-wheeled wagons sturdy enough to provide fighting platforms even for dragons.

The evidence of the hasty departure of the citizenry was widely visible. A torn bolt of cloth trailing through the street, a door banging somewhere, a child's doll lying on the pavement in the center of the town.

Through the town went the men and dragons working at a feverish pace, hauling heavy materials to the barricade on the main road. Captain Eads oversaw the construction. This was the third such structure they had built, and he had learned something from the previous two. The V formation had suggested itself to him most strongly after the battle of Clove Valley, where they had fought along a line with just a slight curve inward. They had enjoyed a persistent tactical advantage as a result, always having a longer line than the enemy at the contact point and thus having the advantage of numbers where it counted, where swords and shields were in play.

Now Eads deepened that curve to a *V* hoping to increase the advantage. However, this created two vital, and potentially weak points, where the top of the *V* joined the rest of the defensive line.

Within the *V* the enemy would be constrained, and at the point of the *V* he would be so crushed together that it would be hard to wield a sword freely. But at the points where the *V* attached to the rest of the line, there would be two salients: strong points that would have to be held.

For each of these strong points Eads chose massive houses, built of stone with plastered interiors, oak floors, and windows of colored glass, the homes of prosperous vintners. Each house had a surrounding walled garden, and Eads had men throw up earth embankments on the inside of the walls to allow men and dragons to stand and repulse any attempt to climb the walls.

To each of these houses, Eads posted a force of three dragons. Bazil, the Purple Green, and Alsebra were assigned to one, and three dragons from the 66th were assigned to the other.

The rest of the 109th were stretched along one side of the *V*-shaped barricade, and the 66th took up the other side.

Next to the houses at the top of the *V* were other homes and walled gardens that continued to the edge of the village, where they merged into the walled vineyards of the southern slope. Along these walls, in the houses, and other strong points, Eads and Ranard, aided by Bowchief Starter, placed their men.

They were interrupted by a sudden roar of noise from the center of the position, on the road to Waldrach.

Eads ran out of the house where he'd been working on positioning a dozen men, and looked back in alarm. He'd seen no sign of the enemy and could not believe they'd been attacked so soon. But the uproar continued, though he still could see no sign of any enemy column coming up the road from Rundel, which lay open in plain view and quite empty.

With Ranard and Lieutenant Ranousmure he ran back, pulse racing, through the walled gardens and narrow lanes to the main road.

As they drew closer they heard individual voices, high-pitched shouts from dragonboys, whoops from men, and roars from dragons. And then they burst out of a walled-in pathway to witness a minor miracle.

Marching down the road from Waldrach came a column of reinforcements, hundreds of local men armed with small sword and ancient round shields. Then behind them came rank on rank of legionaries, four hundred men from the Kadein First Legion, who'd been shipping around to Fitou, and had missed the fleet at Marneri and chosen to march instead of waiting.

And with them, most blessed of all, were dragons, the entire 33rd Kadein Dragon squadron with the mighty rust-gold, brasshide Burthong at their head.

There came a tremendous roar, and the broketail dragon burst through the cheering men and went up belly to belly with Burthong, the brasshide whom he had fought in the summer games; both great monsters roared and slapped forehands in greeting.

"By the fiery breath of old Glabadza, it is Burthong!"

"Well, well, the broken-tailed one. And the rest of the Marneri 109th."

"And the 66th, they are on the other side of this position."

"Then we are among old friends, and I am glad of it. When do we fight?"

"Soon. We are going to have one hell of a fight, right here."

"It is good to see you, Broketail. Often have I thought of our bout. That was a good contest. You showed me a thing or two."

"By the fires of old Glabadza, you showed me a thing or two. I had never seen a brass move so fast."

"Next time we fight each other, I will show you some new moves, and who knows, maybe this time Burthong will be winner!"

"Here comes Captain Eads," said Relkin, who had been shaking hands with the dragonboys of the Kadein 33rd, most of whom he had met before.

The 33rd were commanded by Dragoneer Bekfor, who came forward with captain Velichek to meet Captain Eads. Eads knew Velichek by reputation only. Velichek was the older man, on the reserve list now and retired to a small estate in the county of Bea.

Velichek made it clear at once that he was quite happy to let Eads assume overall command.

"Thank you, Captain Velichek. Your arrival is little short of miraculous. I believe an enemy army is due to come up that road from Rundel at any moment. We've seen Baguti cavalry in the margins of the woods."

"Through here?"

"The enemy has masked the Argonath army in Fitou with a smaller force. He's put perhaps half his strength on the road to Waldrach. If he gets past us, there's nothing to stop him burning his way to Marneri."

Captain Velichek became pale. "We must make a stand here, then. We will deny him the road to Marneri."

CHAPTER SIXTY-SEVEN

The great eyes of Cuica soon spotted the massive columns of the enemy moving off to the south. An army of some size was in motion along the south bank of the river Alno, marching due east to Fitou. Clouds of cavalry were set out ahead. Another army of considerably greater size was moving northeast through the woodlands of Rundel.

Cuica would normally have paid little heed to any of this. These were not motions that interested the eagle. Instead he would have looked for young hares in the wheat fields under his wing, or in the vineyards along the Sprian ridge.

Cuica was, however, not the only mentality to peer through his great eyes on that morning. Lagdalen of the Tarcho saw those dark columns on the roads and immediately grasped the implications. She knew that the road through Rundel ran north and east and eventually to Aubinas and Marneri. She understood that there was unlikely to be any defensive force gathered on that side of the gap.

The past days had been hard, nightmarish ones for Lagdalen. At times she had thought the eagle would perish from hunger, there was so little game to be had around Padmasa. And then she had felt certain they would be destroyed by the batrukh and all three of them would lose their minds, trapped forever within dead animants. Along the way, however, she had learned how to deftly guide the eagle when it was important. It was not entirely unlike riding a horse, although eagles are much fiercer than horses. Essentially, the great raptor did not understand why it did some of the things it did at these times. It simply wished to hunt. There was distress, and a feeling that something wrong was going on in the back of its mind, but it was unable to put a talon on whatever it actually was, and so it merely obeyed.

Now she pushed, and Cuica turned and spiraled out into the south and west, looping down over Rundel Forest away

from the young hares in the wheat field, away from the vineyards on the ridge.

The two tiny passengers were immediately aware of the
change of flight direction. The wren poked her head out of
the leather cup and glimpsed woodlands below.

Then, on the road through the woods, she glimpsed the
dark mass of an army, an endless column that went back and
back into infinity, a vast snake of men, imps, and monsters,
with a tail of wagons that went on for many, many miles.

The wren pecked the mouse awake. It came out of a fetal
crouch and cautiously peered from the leather cup.

The eagle wheeled in the sky, rode a thermal to a higher
point, and then coasted southward, crossing the river Alno.

And there marched a second army, heading downstream.
Bird and mouse looked to each other, a brief meeting of
beady little black eyes. The Masters' plan was unfolding.

Now the eagle's wings beat steadily as it lofted itself high
above the scene and turned back to the east.

Two enemy armies were in motion. The enemy had under-
taken a bold gamble, but one that, if successful, would mean
almost certain defeat for the Argonath.

None of this vital information was available to one Corporal Henker of the First Regiment in the Bea legion. Off duty,
Henker was fishing in the stream that flowed behind the regiment's position just to the south of Fitou. The stream was
fairly sluggish, but there were trout and perch to be had. He
had already caught a pan-sized brown trout, and he sought a
second to complete a pleasant dinner.

Cooling in the stream was a bottle of white Andelain
wine. He was looking forward to a fine evening. There
would be fighting soon, but Henker was a seasoned soldier
and knew better than to anticipate the worst. Instead he concentrated on a good dinner in the offing.

Corporal Henker dropped his line across the deep pool
again and let the bait trail past that fish he was certain still
lurked there.

There was a sound above him, and he looked up and
glimpsed an eagle in flight, low over the trees. He gaped.
One rarely saw eagles this low. He stood up to watch its
progress, but lost sight of it in the trees.

Then it came back, circling toward him and landed in a
tree not a hundred yards distant.

His cast had returned to him, and he hauled in his line with occasional glances over to where the eagle had landed.

A minute or so later, a small bird flitted past him. He took little notice. Nor did he see it when it perched on a branch above his head and carefully examined him. He heard its wings thereafter when it slipped away back through the trees, a slight rustling sound, no more.

Not very long after that, a mouse strode out of the tall grass behind the corporal and approached him. The bird was back too, nervously flitting from spot to spot.

Henker was first aware that he was not alone when he felt a presence behind him. He turned and saw nothing. Then his eye fell on the mouse. Sitting calmly on the ground beside his fishing satchel, the wee beast looked him straight in the eye.

"By the breath," he murmured. It was the damnedest thing. He stared at it. There was something about those eyes.

A few minutes later Corporal Henker rose from his place by the riverbank, cradling the mouse in one hand while a wren perched on his shoulder.

The lovely, pan-sized trout in his satchel he left for the eagle, which had joined them and tore into the fish with great gusto.

General Felix was in session with his commanders at the time. He had received lots of reports concerning the movement of the enemy army down the road to Conjona. Baguti cavalry were crossing the Tupada and ranging into Andelain. His own cavalry had clashed with them several times.

A sergeant came in with a note. General Felix stared at it for a moment, then hurriedly promised to do something about it in a moment.

A moment was too long, however, and quite suddenly the entrance was jerked open and Commander Sear, of the Bea legion appeared. He had the strangest expression on his face and was wearing a small bird on his shoulder.

CHAPTER SIXTY-EIGHT

The daylight lengthened as the afternoon wore on. Out towards Rundel Forest, nothing stirred except insects and rabbits. Relkin saw a deer browsing along the edge of the farthest wheat field, and remarked that it would be a great day to go hunting.

Bazil grunted that hunting was not that profitable an activity as far as he was concerned. The dragon was a mite snappish, anxious to be in combat and have it over with. Relkin took the hint and brought Bazil an armful of army bread slathered in akh and then a pail of water to wash it down.

The barricade across the main road through Lennink was now a full twelve feet high, a twisted mass of trees, brush, debris, wagons, tables, chairs, and even spinning wheels. A great pile of cobbles had been pried up and stacked to hand for the dragons to throw. Smaller stones had been accumulated for the men and dragonboys.

All along the fortified southern edge of Lennink there were men hidden, lying in wait for the enemy. The dragons of the 33rd Kadein had been placed back of the line to be used as a reserve. Captain Eads had also created a three hundred man special reserve that he would hold back to plug any gap that might develop.

They waited with gathering tension, and stared out over the vineyards to the wheat fields and the distant woods. Was the enemy really coming? Had their glimpse of the Baguti been a freak? Perhaps an outrider patrol, perhaps nothing but looters?

Eilsa Ranardaughter ran messages for her father to the clan captains, dashing back and forth from the clan positions, a vision of energy and beauty with her wild blond hair tucked beneath a square, clan cap of green. Her friend Silva did the same, and they were put to much use that afternoon. Ranard was exceedingly anxious and continually sought to improve and adjust his men's positions. He had watched Eads and his officers at work, had picked up a few things, and now worked at implementing them.

As for Captain Eads, he sat on an easy chair in what had been the bedroom on the second floor of the house on the right side of the V-shaped barricade. Down below him were dragons of the 109th Marneri. From this window he had a perfect view down the road to Rundel, which formed a dark crease through the green murk of the woods. Eads had his spyglass raised, but still saw no sign of the enemy Host he expected. He was tormented by doubts. What if he was wrong? What if he was wasting precious time when he could be marching his men south to Fitou? How long could he stand here in good conscience, on the basis of a hunch and a single sighting of a Baguti patrol? What if the witches had been wrong?

On the garden wall of the same house, sitting with their backs to the stone corner pillars, warmed by the sun in the west, dragonboys passed these minutes in conversation.

Relkin and Manuel sat together there. Little Jak was busy repairing Alsebra's pommel guard: wrapping it with fresh leather and pinning it in place with short tacks. Mono came walking by, vaulted onto the earth bank thrown up below the wall, and then climbed the stones to the top.

"Do you think they're coming?"

Relkin shrugged, "I don't know, Mono. Saw some Baguti. Does that mean the whole enemy army is coming this way? You'd have to ask the Mother."

Mono's eyebrow shot up. "Ho! So now Relkin is invoking the Holy Mother?"

Relkin grinned sourly. "Let's just say my religious beliefs are in flux these days."

"You remember ol' Mumplepeezer, the fortune-teller?" said Mono.

"All that stuff about our 'destiny' on a battlefield?"

"Seems he was right."

Relkin looked around again. "Except for one thing. We're in a garden in Arneis all right, but there's no roses. Supposed to be roses you see."

"Mumplepeezer never mentioned anything about roses."

Relkin laughed darkly, "Mumplepeezer wasn't the only one predicting our destiny."

With that Mono had to content himself because Relkin

would not say anymore. After a few moments' uneasy fidgeting, he went back to his place on the barricade, beside Chektor.

Relkin and Manuel turned back to their previous conversation.

"So, Manuel, what did your father say when you told him you were volunteering for active service as a dragonboy?" Manuel made a face. "Oh, my! Papa was not happy. He even threatened to disinherit me even though I am his only son. The whole house was filled with his anger. I hid at school. I wanted to run away for a while. My mother persuaded me not to."

Like many orphans, Relkin had a wistful fascination for the details of family life. Bazil and the 109th were the only family he had ever really known.

"It must be wonderful to have a mother, and even to have a father who gets angry," he said with disarming openness.

Manuel studied Relkin's face. "You have no idea who your parents were at all?"

"None. I was put out in a basket by the temple door one night. All I remember is this: my first teacher, old Meddee, she told me that I was a farmer's seventh son and that my mother died in childbirth, which was why I was given up. I never asked her who my father was, I never thought to. And when I was old enough to, she had died and nobody I asked knew anything about it."

"I'm sorry." And both orphans could tell that Manuel was genuinely sad for them.

"You see, Manuel, your life was really different from ours." said Relkin.

"Different from all of ours," said Jak. "I grew up in the orphanage in Marneri, down on Dock Street. We always envied the natural children. 'Bastards' they called us. We had plenty of fights with them."

"That's one reason we had a hard time accepting you at first. For us, this is the only career there is, but you could have done anything."

"I always wanted to be a dragoneer and to serve the empire. I kept it a secret from my parents for years, because I knew they would not approve."

"So what happened when you left for the academy?"

"My father cut off all contact. He kept it up for three months, and I thought I would never hear from him again.

Then he came to see me, and we wept on each other's shoulders and yelled at each other. Finally he accepted that this was what I had to do."

"Do you write to your family now?" said Relkin.

"I sent them a note that went in the last messenger's saddlebags, in case we don't make it out of here."

"You'll come through, Manuel. Now that the Purple Green likes you, you're bound to make it."

Manuel laughed with them. The Purple Green was no easy handful, in fact, he was as much work as two wyverns.

"Ssh, don't wake him. He's still sleeping off two big bowls of corn mush."

"Talking about letters, Relkin, did you ever get a reply to that letter you were writing when we were coming up the river to Kohon?"

"Yes," he said. Relkin didn't want to try and tell them about his strange night visit from Lessis's little animant.

"You asked your friend about destiny. What did she say?"

Relkin knew better than to start babbling about the Sinni and wrinkles in the cloth of fate.

"She said there was a reason for us to go to Arneis. We will discover what destiny means for us here."

"What was that about roses?" Manuel pressed.

"Supposed to be a rose garden in our future, that's all."

He left them then to fetch some water for the dragon. Crossing the ruined garden, he almost ran into Eilsa Ranardaughter at a corner. She bore a message for an outlying section of the Fird.

Relkin fell in beside her, all thought of water forgotten for the moment.

"And how are you today, Eilsa Ranardaughter?"

She slackened stride by a hair.

"I am well, Dragoneer, and I carry a message for my father. He has kept me busy all day."

"Do you intend to fight?"

"Of course. In whatever capacity my father orders. Probably I will still be a messenger. He will not let me stand in line with the Fird."

"He is right. You really should go to Waldrach."

"Don't be silly. Messengers have already gone to Waldrach. I am needed here."

"I am serious, Eilsa. I love thee and fear for your safety."

She frowned. "Relkin, I am not the kind of woman that

wants no more than to sit by a fire all my life spinning and tending children. I can fight, and if Clan Wattel is to die this day, then I will die with it in honor."

Relkin saw Dragon Leader Turrent coming around the edge of the house ahead.

"When this is over I shall find you, Eilsa. Count on that."

Their hands met for a moment and then she was gone, with a long backward glance. He turned and sped away in search of water for the dragon.

Clan Chief Ranard was also on the move during this time. Too anxious to stay in one place, he wanted to inspect one of the clan's positions beside the wall to the vineyard Exelo. As he moved along the battle line, he spoke to all his men, doing his utmost to boost morale.

He passed the dragons of the 109th, most of them asleep, backs to the earthen embankment they'd thrown up inside the barricade. They snored like volcanoes, he thought. Dragonboys must have a hard and peculiar life. And the way the beasts ate! He'd never seen anything like it in his life.

He turned the corner, and a dragonboy bounced off his front.

"Ah, Dragoneer Relkin . . ."

"Sir!" Relkin felt that intense gaze upon him. Did the chief know about the times he had spent with Eilsa? Relkin held his breath.

"My daughter is, as you know, a person of fiery spirit."

"Yes, sir."

"You are, I believe, an honorable young man. I trust that I am not deceived in this belief."

"You are not, sir."

"Good. We understand each other. But you also know that my daughter will marry within Clan Wattel. She has to do this for the sake of our family."

"I have been told of this, sir."

"Good." Ranard pursed his lips and stroked his beard. "Of course, we have to beat our enemy here before we can marry anyone right?"

"Absolutely right, sir."

"You sound confident, Dragoneer."

"We can hold them, sir. The dragons have their blood up." A huge snore cut through the air. They both smiled.

"They're tired, of course. We've covered a lot of ground these past few days."

"And we fought a great battle."

"True, sir."

"Well, Dragoneer Relkin, if we should not happen to meet again, I would shake thy hand."

The clan chief's grip was hard, the essence of the durability of the Clan Wattel.

Ranard went on. No sooner had he turned the corner than there came a whistle and a shout. Captain Eads came bursting out of the corner house and jumped into his horse's saddle.

There was a shout down the line.

"Eyes front. Enemy in sight."

And out from the eaves of Rundel wood came a skirmishing line, perhaps three hundred imps, set well apart, loping through the wheat field.

Some Baguti horsemen had appeared, too, riding up the road in the middle of the skirmishers. Behind the initial troop of riders came a larger column, and behind that appeared a solid, dense mass of cavalry. Eads knew that he'd been right, and that he and his small army would now be put to the greatest test of their lives.

Behind the barricade the dragons perked up. Huge heads on long necks inclined as they stared at the approaching enemy. And then they hid themselves, crouching down behind the barricade.

The Baguti came on until they were within a few hundred yards of the barricade. At last its presence was observed by a commanding officer. A squad of horsemen rode forward to inspect it.

They rode up on the road between vineyard walls, came to a halt just out of bow shot, and stared at the ungainly pile of tree trunks and debris.

A horn blew peremptory blasts from behind them. The scouts argued among themselves and then one of them rode close, right up to the bottom of the crazy quilt mass of entwined poplar trees, wagons, barrels, beams, and winepresses. He dismounted, climbed up the outside, and peered over the top, right into the face of a monstrous great Gazaki.

Chektor caught him the next moment with a huge hand, and lifted him smoothly and cleanly over the top of the barricade and into cover behind it. The scout was so surprised that he was slow to scream. When he opened his mouth to start, a legionary thrust his sword into the scout's heart, silencing him. Nothing but a momentary squawk had escaped, and silence fell once more across the scene.

The scout's horse cropped grass at the side of the road, and began to wander back toward the others.

The other scouts muttered among themselves and called out to their fellow beyond the barricade. His disappearance had seemed a little abrupt. Something odd was going on. Why did he not reply? Three more edged their horses closer and called again. Still no reply was to be heard.

The horns were blowing madly back in the column. The scouts carefully refrained from looking back, so they missed the furious signals for them to go on and climb the barricade. The scouts cast their eyes instead on the imp skirmish line that was advancing across the vineyards.

The scouts waited until the skirmishers were within bow shot of the barricade and then they turned and rode their mounts furiously back to the column where they gave a voluminous report. One of their number had gone over the pile of trees and failed to return. They pointed to the imps and suggested that the imps be sent to investigate.

The Baguti chieftain was enraged and spent several minutes venting his anger at their miserable performance. Then he sent a messenger across to the imp commander, a dour man with filed teeth and a taste for human flesh.

The imp commander barked with amused contempt and gave the orders. The imps complained, as they usually did, but flasks of black drink were handed around and then their sergeants worked on them with clubs and words, and they were driven forward to climb the barricade. Up they went and reached the top.

On the far side they found nothing, an empty street, a mound of dirt along the inside of the wall, but no sign of any enemy soldiers.

Delighted, the imps called back the news and made rude jokes about the cowardly Baguti. Still hooting with glee, they stepped down inside the barricade and pushed forward into the empty street. There should be some loot in this place. It looked prosperous enough.

Once they were all down inside the barricade, a sudden fusillade of arrows swept through them. Virtually all were struck simultaneously. A handful remained on their feet, and these were immediately felled by spears and further arrows. Their cries were few and far between, and cut off early.

Once more the silence grew long and ominous.

The imp commander swore at his sergeants, and more imps were sent stumbling forward to the grim pile of trees and debris. They clambered to the top and found an empty street. Not even the bodies of their comrades were to be seen.

Baffled, they turned and called and gesticulated. A sergeant ran back with the news. The imp commander called for reinforcements.

More officers rode up, stern men in black, with glittering badges of rank on their breast. They demanded to know what the hold up was about.

The majors were most concerned. General Lukash was riding the army hard. He had already given orders for black drink to be dispensed to the imps. They were to march all night with as much black drink as they wanted, whatever it took to get them into Waldrach by the morning.

The road behind them was jammed with men, imps, trolls, and an immense train of wagons. The majors ordered an assault column of five hundred imps sent forward to clear the barricade.

The imps were formed up. The horns blared, and the sergeants shoved them forward as the imps rose up the outer wall of the barricade with their harsh scream of battle coming from their lips.

CHAPTER SIXTY-NINE

With drums beating and battle flags raised high, the enemy assault column marched forward purposefully.

Captain Eads nodded to Dragon Leader Turrent. They would delay the battle no longer, although Eads was well pleased with the skillful execution of his chosen tactics during the initial phase. Every minute's delay was golden. There was still no word from the south. Somehow his small force would have to hold this position until they could be relieved.

Turrent whistled and waved a hand; the dragons were tensed, waiting expectantly. They heard the tramp of imps on the far side of the barricade, with their drums going and the horns blaring behind them. At the signal they clambered up into position just below the top of the barricade, each dragon standing on a mound of dirt or on a heavy wagon.

The assault column reached the top, and there came a sudden blast of legion cornets and a roar. Great dragons rose up behind the barricade and swung their deadly swords down among the imps.

Blinded by the fumes of the black drink, the imp column pushed on, but the head of the column disintegrated as rapidly as it reached the top of the barricade, like a sausage being fed into a mincer. Dragonboys worked beside the dragons and in concert with teams of legionaries who had training in fighting alongside dragons. A lot of that training had to do with keeping one's head down, a very low profile, to avoid being decapitated by the backward sweeps of dragonsword.

Not a single imp got over the barricade and when half the attacking column had been annihilated, the commanders halted it and let the rest flow back leaving the top of the barricade strewn with their dead.

The staff majors immediately spurred away to report to

General Lukash. The command went back down the line of the immense army for a halt.

Once more there was a silence on the battlefield, but for the hum of bees and the song of larks. Daylight was fading now, and the sun was sinking behind the mountains in the west.

Lukash received the news with consternation and immediate rage. His plan was perfect. How could the road be blocked? What was this blocking force?

The majors reported that it appeared to be of some size, several thousand at the least. The entire southern approach to Lennink had been fortified. There were cavalry patrols working farther out along the ridge.

Lukash's face settled into a grim mask, and he examined the maps.

There was no good way, no quick way, around this obstacle. He dispatched cavalry forces to scout along the southern edge of the ridge to find a place where he might most easily get troops up for a flanking maneuver.

Meanwhile he rapped out orders for a major assault to be launched straight at the barricade. Two side assaults into the southern face of the town on either side of the barricade would also be made.

The drums began pounding as imps, men, and trolls assembled on the wheat fields below the town of Lennink.

The Magician Thrembode had climbed a tree in the Rundel Forest and used a telescope to examine the defenses.

He had seen the barricade on the main road, the reinforced walls protected by stakes and ditches all along the southern side of the town. Argonathis were visible here and there along this line of positions. He saw men moving around, and glimpsed a couple of dragons, too. That meant it was a legion force, although many of the men he'd seen were not wearing legion uniforms and helmets.

The great army would be delayed.

In front of him Lukash assembled an assault column, tipped with trolls, perhaps sixty of the great monsters. Half were of the heavyset, black-purple type: ax trolls; and half were of the ocher-hued type: sword trolls.

It took perhaps half an hour for everything to be made ready. The sun had set farther in the west, dipping well behind the mountains now, leaving a slow-dimming twilight that would last yet for another hour or more.

Then the horns blared and the massed drums began to thunder. The assault force moved off, still swigging from flasks of black drink.

It was an exciting moment, and Thrembode stayed in his perch to watch the fight.

Behind the barricade the dragons waited, suddenly nervous in a way they hadn't been before. They knew trolls were coming. They could smell them. Their cheerful banter took a bizarre turn.

"My only regret is that I have never gained a taste for troll," grumbled the Purple Green.

"I keep telling you that it needs to be fresh, and you have to cook it right through. You always want to eat things too uncooked."

"I like it that way."

"Not troll. Maybe elk, maybe cattle, you eat like that."

"Horse is good, right on the hoof."

"But you liked it roasted, I remember you said that."

"Troll needs to be baked, and seasoned well. Some like it with a lot of akh," said Alsebra, who up to this point had been quiet.

"I have not tried baking. What is the difference between baking and roasting over fire?"

"Baking is when you apply a more even heat. You have to build an oven."

"How?"

"With rocks. It is not so difficult. You dig a pit. Then you build a big fire and throw rocks into fire. When rocks are very hot you lever them into the pit. Then you put in troll and cover with more hot rocks, though not as hot as the first rocks you put in. Then you wait until the rocks cool down, you take them out, and you have perfectly baked troll. It's delicious."

"This sounds interesting," said the Purple Green.

"We will try it later. I'm sure we'll have plenty of trolls on hand," Bazil decided.

"Yes," gloated the Purple Green, "we will try it all three ways, the Broketail will roast his until it's black, I will roast mine just a little, and Alsebra will put hers in a hole with hot rocks. Then we will taste all three and see which is best."

"Hush, they're coming," said Manuel.

"Why hush?" The Purple Green raised big eyebrows.

"With all the noise they're making, they couldn't hear us even if we roared."

But Manuel did not reply, too intent on the oncoming enemy. He crouched behind broken vegetation at the top of the barricade and watched them come. It was hard not to think that he might die this time. They might all die. They were enormously outnumbered.

They came on, a long rank of imps, perhaps one hundred wide with rank after rank behind them and among them trolls, huge monsters eight and nine feet high, striding among the imps.

They reached the outside of the barricade and began to climb.

A cornet blew. Instantly the dragons seized up cobblestones in both big forehands, and then began pitching them over the barricade on nearly vertical trajectories. The stones flew up thirty or forty feet before falling back with stunning force on the trolls that were struggling up the outside face of the barricade. Trolls were never good at climbing, and under a hail of twenty-pound cobblestones, they were even worse.

As the cobbles flew, dragonboys and bowmen opened fire from the top of the barricade and men readied themselves.

The assault column staggered and then came to a halt. A dozen trolls had been laid out by the cobblestones. The imps were wavering under the storm of rocks and arrows.

The drums thundered, and the horns blared louder than before. The imp commanders lashed on their imps, and the troll leaders goaded the trolls while ordering them to raise their shields over their heads to protect themselves.

The column steadied and then came on once more. Even as more trolls and imps fell, they stumbled up the barricade. The cobblestones kept coming, but now they bounced away from shields as often as they hit trolls directly. Caroms off the barricade flew among the imps, but still they came on, the fumes of black drink thick in their nostrils.

Cornets blew thrice to summon up spearsmen, and legionaries sprang to the top of the barricade and hurled javelins into the exposed trolls. The javelins were made with a long, square-sided point made of soft iron. They embedded themselves in troll hide and the leather armor that the sword trolls wore. The iron heads immediately began to bend, and the shafts became impediments to movement.

Another dozen trolls had fallen by this point, most felled

by rocks, but now, at last, the first among them reached the top of the barricade. Battered, feathered with arrows, smarting from spear wounds, the enraged trolls were now met head on by a line of great dragons, who strode onto the embankment and engaged them at the top of the barricade. Huge steel blades rang off one another and crunched into massive shields. Heavy troll axes swung with a fury, dragon tail maces cracked off troll helmets and smashed into troll faces. Troll shields clashed with dragon shields, enormous muscles bunched and strained. Dragons heaved trolls back and hewed down, huge heads flew, gouts of black blood spouted into the air. Gargantuan bodies fell back sundered from life.

And beneath the clash of heavy weapons, dragonboys kept imps at bay or slew them if they dared to rise to the top of the barricade.

For half an hour it continued thus, and then the remaining trolls lost heart, retreated, and would not fight again.

Among the imps the black drink was wearing off, and they, too, were faint of heart. The barricade was now festooned with enormous troll corpses while a pile of dead imps was forming at the bottom.

Slowly, despite the drums and the horns, despite the frantic lashing with whips by the imp commanders, the enemy assault column broke up and streamed back away from the unbreakable barricade.

A cheer went up among the defenders, and then they set to rebuilding supplies of cobblestones and retrieving arrows and spears.

Relkin examined Bazil carefully. The broketail dragon had decapitated one troll and hewed down three others. During that time, Relkin had shot a brace of imps and taken another one on his sword when it went for Bazil's underbelly with its crude sword.

Bazil had a new wound, just under the place where the joboquin fastened beneath the arm. It was a vulnerable place. From the size of the wound, about an inch long and an inch deep, Relkin assumed it had come from an imp arrow that hadn't stuck. He cleaned it quickly with Old Sugustus and applied a bandage that he wrapped around the dragon's chest. Back on went the joboquin and the breastplate. Back on went the helmet, and once more the dragon was ready to fight.

"Well done, everyone." It was Dragon Leader Turrent making his rounds.

Eyebrows rose among dragonboys who had never heard such words from Dragon Leader Turrent before.

"No casualties on our side of the barricade," said Turrent when he paused to congratulate the team in the walled garden.

"No casualties, that's great," said Manuel, who was working on some nicks on the Purple Green's left thigh where an imp had proved troublesome.

The dragons were silent, breathing hot and heavy, resting their weight on their sword hilts. They were still in the terrifying mental state they went into for war.

"It will be dark soon," said Jak.

"Yes, that should end it," said Manuel.

Relkin looked over the garden wall at the dark mass that could be seen bottled up on the road through Rundel Forest, and was not so sure.

CHAPTER SEVENTY

General Lukash received the news badly. He cursed in his native tongue and spat on the ground. The staff majors trembled. Then he dismissed them and turned to the maps again.

Lukash licked his lips nervously. It would soon be dark. Vapul might come at any time, swooping in on that monstrous creature. Vapul would find him bottled up here, hours behind where he ought to be.

There was only one answer. To continue the assault.

He looked up see the damned magician eyeing him speculatively.

"We will make a night assault."

Thrembode had seen the fighting through his telescope. He knew it would be desperately difficult to break through the Argonathi defense line.

"Possibly you should reconsider going around this force. It cannot be that large. Maneuver around it and go on."

Lukash's mouth was dry. Vapul could come at any time.

"No, there is no time for that. We must smash through them and go on at once. The attack was on too narrow a front. We will widen it. I will have torches prepared to light the battlefield."

"What word do you have concerning the Argonathi army?"

"They sit in Fitou. Our diversionary force approaches their lines."

"Can you trust the Baguti on this? It seems they missed this blockage we're up against here."

"Damned Baguti are worthless. Hazogi are worse."

"Yes, I've thought much the same thing myself on occasion." Thrembode smiled. He toyed with the little whistle for a moment while Lukash's face froze. As it happened, he agreed with Lukash. An assault on a wider front would probably do the trick, the damned Argonathi must be thinly spread. And lingering at the back of his thoughts was the image of Vapul. The Mesomaster was still up on his distant crag, but within an hour or two he would mount the batrukh and fly down to visit them as he did every night. It would be better if he found them in the midst of battle, or better yet, marching on through Lennink after a quick victory, rather than stuck here or blundering about in the back country roads.

"Let it be on your neck, General, but go ahead. Smash through this arrogant little band. Let us get on with our march."

Not long afterward the darkness blossomed with torches, hundreds upon hundreds of flames flaring in the night, each torch cut from deadwood in the forest, soaked in pitch and lit by imps tramping forward to the night assault.

The drums rumbled, and there were the bawling commands of officers as ten thousand imps and hundreds of trolls were lined up.

Now the assault line was widened to include most of the southern approaches to Lennink. At the last moment imp commanders passed black drink through the ranks. Even trolls were given some, an often risky procedure since they might attack anyone or anything once intoxicated.

With such a wide assault fine control was impossible, at least with imps as troops. The horns began to blare, and the drumming rose to a thunder. Now the mass began to move forward once more, stamping up to the barricade, heads bowed beneath a rain of rocks and cobbles and arrows and spears.

In the walled garden of the vintner's house, they faced the onslaught in the darkness with the light of the enemy torches reflected off battered steel helmets and shields.

There was considerable confusion in the enemy ranks. The torches knotted and bobbed and formed blots of flame, but with stentorian bellows of rage the imp commanders untangled their troops each time and sent them on with the whips cracking over their heads.

And now they were close enough for the defenders to see the massed imps and trolls clearly through the dark as they strode forward. Battalions of drummers were driving them on, and as they came into range and began to receive the defensive fire of stones and arrows, they moved more quickly, bent under their shields, scrambling up the outside edge of the barricade.

With a great roar edged by the shrill legion cornets, the defenders rose up and met the assault.

To get up the wall, the assault brought forward great masses of brush bound into faggots, which they piled on the outside of the thick wall that surrounded the vintner's garden.

Up onto this mass clambered the trolls. They were uneasy, for the footing was uncertain and the faggots were springy, giving way erratically beneath their massive feet. This put them at a disadvantage. In their favor was their weight of numbers.

The fight was brutal and desperate, and though the dragons, the dragonboys, and the legionaries had learned lessons from previous battles, it was terribly easy to get killed in this kind of chaotic melee.

Right at the start, one of the spearmen on Relkin's right went down with an imp arrow that penetrated his nose into his brain.

Then dame a blizzard of steel, with men and dragons hacking and chopping into the raging mass of attackers who came on with the mad light of the black drink in their eyes.

At one point Bazil Broketail was almost knocked off the embankment by an ax troll who stood over him with ax raised high. The troll might have killed him except that Relkin stepped forward and thrust his sword into the troll's genitals and distracted it entirely.

Bazil recovered, and Ecator came around, quivering like a live thing and decapitated the troll, still screaming from Relkin's thrust. The huge body fell away, spraying great gouts of black blood and tumbled onto the struggling mass seeking to climb the wall.

Alsebra slew a tricky sword troll with a terrible smashing blow of her shield, crushing its head and sending it toppling inside the wall, where it fell on two soldiers and crippled them.

The Purple Green fell prey to an especially quick sword troll and lost his sword. Quick as lightning the wild dragon seized the troll in his big forehands, lifted it up, and then threw it back over the wall like a missile. Where it landed, imps were tossed up like chaff.

All of this was seen in glimpses in the midst of an endless

inferno of noise, drums, screams, horns, and the smashing of steel on steel. It went on through the first hour with scarcely a break. The defenders drew close to complete exhaustion.

Bazil slew a great ax troll with a thrust. Ecator skewered the thing, and it toppled forward into the dragon's arms. The sword wouldn't come free. It had lodged on the creature's ribs. Bazil put a foot on its chest and gave a great shove, sending the thing flying backward. Bazil slipped, however, and fell right off the embankment and landed on a dead troll slain earlier by Alsebra.

For a moment there was a gap in the line. Spearmen came forward to hold it and hold it they did, although another ax troll came up immediately, and they paid the ultimate price. All three were dead when Bazil hauled himself back into place and slew the ax troll.

The assault kept coming. The enemy lapped around the entire southern margin of Lennink now, seeking the flank of Eads's small force.

Eads had readied a riposte. When at last the attackers turned the right side corner, flowing up onto the ridge unopposed, he unleashed a column of two hundred men and five dragons from the 33rd Kadein, who had been waiting in an alley behind the houses at the edge of the town. This force came out of the dark suddenly and hit the exultant trolls and imps like a hammer and drove them back down the slope into the vineyard of Decleve, which was destroyed beneath their huge horny feet.

The fires glittered redly into the distance. The drums kept up their thunder, and the enemy ranks advanced. It seemed it would go on forever. The mound of dead imps and trolls on the outside of the barricade was almost half the height of the barricade itself now. And still they came on, wading through the imps, over the crushed faggots and up onto the walls of the vintner's house.

Dragons reached for the last reserves of energy. Dragonboys ran out of arrows and began to cannibalize the thousands of imp arrows that had landed in the garden.

At one point the enemy got over the barricade in the center where Vlok and Chektor held the line. Vlok was tricked by a wily sword troll and then struck senseless by a troll ax. A sudden shove opened the way and fifty imps poured in through the gap. Eads sent in a plugging force made up of thirty men of the Fird and fifteen veteran legionaries. To replace Vlok he sent in Harapha, a leatherback in the Kadein 33rd, with his dragonboy Dimmi.

Swane and Dimmi fought side by side around Harapha as they forced the imps back and constrained them and swept them back across the barricade.

Poor Vlok was woken up with buckets of cold water and a shot of hot kalut through his numbed jaws. Still shaking the stars out of his head, he grabbed up his "Katzbalger" and shambled back to the fight.

But now, at last, the enemy assault weakened and fell off. Ten thousand imps had been hurled at the defense lines, and their formations had disintegrated. Two thousand were dead along the margins of the town, huge heaps were piled up in front of the barricade. The trolls were downcast, disorganized, fleeing back into Rundel woods.

The moon had risen and threw a dread yellow light across the field of slaughter. Relkin looked up and saw a great shape flit across the moon, a flying form sliding west across the sky, and he felt a sudden cold go through him and a shiver ran down his spine.

CHAPTER SEVENTY-ONE

A lull settled over the battlefield as the two armies stood back like gladiators, dragging down deep breaths of air while sweat and blood ran from their bodies and dripped to the ground.

Captain Eads staggered back to his command post, set up in the parlor of the Rosebush Inn, and collapsed in a chair, his sword arm completely numb. At the end he had been in the thick of the fight on the barricade, seeking to staunch the gap.

Corporal Fox brought him a glass of water, they'd drunk the Rosebush dry of beer already. Eads felt it slake off some of the crusted salt and dust in his throat.

The door was open, and he looked out on a hellish scene as wounded men, some crying out piteously, were carried back to the surgeons. Torches flared and sputtered. Somewhere nearby a smithy had been set up, and men were hammering hot steel as hard and as quickly as they might. There were a great many swords that needed edging.

The terrible questions pounded in his brain. Could they possibly hold out much longer if there was another attack? How could there not be? He understood as well as the enemy commander the nature of the strategic gamble the enemy had taken. They had to break through here before the Argonathi army could come up. Seven legions could rip the guts out of this enemy force if they met it on open ground. So the enemy would attack again and again until they broke through here. They had no more choice about it than he had.

He felt his eyes glazing over. There was a well of fatigue that seemed to run from the top of his head, down his backbone, and then to split down each leg.

They would have to hold the enemy. It would be very hard. He did not want to think it might be impossible.

He felt his thoughts wander. His wife Lernisse, his boy

Axel, his home in Blue Hills. There had been Eads's in the Blue Hills since the earliest days of the Argonath. Mother preserve them all if they failed here and this foul enemy Host got through. Darkness seemed to settle over his soul.

He slept, and his dream was a seething, terrible one, in which the battle was refought, a continual hammer of men and imps and steel with great monsters roaring above and below.

Something pricked at his ear. He put a hand up. In his dream the sun burned through the clouds, and the darkness faded away.

He woke up with a start. Again something pricked at his cheek and then at his ear. He put up a hand and felt something flit away. A small bird perched on the back of an empty chair. The bird looked at him, and he knew, as his hair rose in an involuntary shudder, that it was no ordinary bird.

"You came back!" he whispered. "Thank the Mother. What news do you have? Did you find the army?"

The bird made no response, but a few moments later he saw something small zip across the floor. A mouse was standing there, paws up, staring at him through little beady black eyes.

The mouse came forward. He bent down, ignoring a stab of pain from his side, scooped up the little animal, and held it close to his face.

Out in the walled garden, they ate. At least the dragons ate, heartily, with enormous gusto. Bowls of corn stirabout flavored with akh, some day-old bread found in the baker's shop, and a jug or two of ale, discovered in the cellar of another house.

Relkin had patched and sewn nine separate cuts and nicks on the dragon. Then he turned to his own injuries. His left forearm had a nick from an imp's blade, and there were lots of scratches where he'd fallen or been knocked. Old Sugustus lay to hand, and the familiar sting caused him to squeeze his eyes shut while he counted to ten.

When he opened them, Eilsa Ranardaughter was there, a perfectly stricken look on her face.

"Sir Relkin, I would ask a favor of thee." There was smeared blood on her forehead, but no cut that he could see.

"Ask."

"My father is wounded beyond my powers to heal. Our surgeons are hard at work, there are so many badly wounded men. My father will not go to them, and I fear he will aggravate the wound."

Relkin understood. "Eilsa, I am not a surgeon."

"I know, but you have a great deal of experience with wounds."

He took a deep breath.

"My experience is limited with human patients, but I will try."

In truth, he would try anything for Eilsa Ranardaughter.

They made their way through the crowded street to a stable. Ranard was lying on a thick bale of hay in a well-lit, clean stall.

The wounds were bad. A deep slash on the right thigh and two puncture wounds in the abdomen that Relkin feared would be fatal no matter what he did.

Relkin offered to clean them and sew them.

"It will hurt, sir. I'm not as good with a needle as some of them."

Ranard nodded. "But it's necessary, I believe."

Relkin probed the wounds. The one on the right was deep, more than an inch. He suspected it must have cut into either the intestine or a vital organ. Either way, it would probably be the deathblow.

Still there was Old Sugustus. At the least he could cleanse and sterilize the wound and the area around it. He would then place an absorbing poultice over the wound.

"We need honey," he muttered. His best poultice would have medicinal herbs, a soaking of Old Sugustus, and an ounce or so of honey with which to pack the wound.

"Honey?"

"Yes, the sugar dries out a deep wound and keeps it from corrupting."

"It seems a strange thought."

"It works is all I know. Where can we find some honey. There must be some in this town."

"The building next door was a general food store I believe. Let us look there."

Eads had ordered the shop broken open and looted. Accounts could be settled later, and at that moment his men needed to eat energy-rich foods like sausage and butters and eggs and cream.

Indeed there were cook fires going everywhere with the whole town's supply of bacon sputtering on the end of sticks. A mouthwatering aroma arose over the devastation.

"It seems that if there was any honey, it has been taken."

"What about below. There must be storage cellars."

Relkin found a locked door down a flight of steps and broke the lock with several swings of a heavy ax he found out back. When at length they were through, they found themselves amid a wealth of stores, mostly of olive oil. The smell of olives assailed them at once, and they raised a lantern over long rows of massive barrels of oil, quietly aging in the cellar.

Relkin went on down a narrow, dusty passage and found another cellar, also filled with barrels of oil. He turned back and bumped into Eilsa.

"I found it, Relkin," she said holding up a jar.

Despite smuts and the smeared blood on her face, she looked supremely lovely at that moment. Relkin leaned forward and kissed her. She stared at him in shock, eyebrows contracting dangerously.

"I might never get another chance, Eilsa Ranardaughter, and I would rather die with your kiss on my lips."

There were tears in her eyes; her shock gave way to softer emotions.

"I can't stand to think that we can fail. We have fought so hard . . ."

"We can hold them yet. And with that honey, we may be able to save your father."

Captain Eads had learned much from the mind of the Queen of Mice. He knew, for instance, that the Argonathi army was close now, but that it had some miles to go before it could exert any influence on his battle. He also knew that the enemy would probably deploy a secret weapon, giant trolls known as ogres.

It had been difficult to comprehend what was being described at first. When he finally understood, he felt the sweat cool on his brow. To defeat these monsters would require heroics from his dragons, and he had so few dragons!

However, he responded with characteristic energy. He ordered long lances to be cut and tipped with steel. He ordered the villages to be stripped of any old weapons with long enough shafts. He sent a search party at once to the manor house of the magnate of Waldrach. The magnate was known to have a passion for jousting in antique armor. Any useful lances were to be brought back at once.

He called for his officers to meet at once, and he briefed them on the likelihood of ogres and the defensive measures they would adopt. The spearmen already trained in tactics against trolls, fighting in trios, seeking to thrust home with stabbing spears, or to cut the hamstrings, all these things would be called on, and the men would be equipped with longer spears.

Bowchief Starter met with him to discuss poisons for arrows. The Bowchief was horrified at first. Poisoned weapons were utterly against everything he knew and understood. They were the technique of the enemy. But when he heard of the ogres, his face cooled and his eyes glinted in fury.

"What beasts of the Mother's Hand have they destroyed to make these?"

"I was told that it was mammoths."

"Oh, by the sacred breath, they have done this with the great trunkers of the northlands. How foul how they are in Padmasa!"

Bowchief Starter agreed to investigate the use of poisoned arrows.

Men came running in from the farther end of the village with a supply of seven great pikes brought from the home of a wealthy man who had traveled widely in the southlands and collected military weapons.

Work on creating lances intensified. The night air was thick with the sounds of saws, hammers, and bellows. Eads's fatigue was forgotten.

CHAPTER SEVENTY-TWO

The moon was sinking in the east, falling past the constellation of the dragon. The night was waning.

Three dragons stood ready on the much trampled bank of dirt thrown up behind the battered wall of the vintner's garden.

Around them was a scene of devastation, frosted by the moon's light. The wall had been battered, but the garden that had been the joy of the vintner's heart had been utterly destroyed. The fruit trees had been cut and incorporated into the barricade. The flower beds crushed beneath feet large and small, the rocks and paving stones had been hurled at the enemy.

The three dragons were oblivious to the damage. They had eaten well. Bowls of cornmeal stirabout flavored with akh. Slabs of grilled bacon. Toasted wheat cakes and honey. Fresh baked bread with hot butter, and all of it washed down with wine mixed with water. The enormous quantities of rich food had both softened their mood and renewed their strength. And although they were bone tired and in need of a week's sleep, they felt much better than they had before eating.

They stared at the moon going down and passed around the remains of a butt of young red wine.

"I do not like wine as much as beer," said the Purple Green.

"It is too acidic," said Alsebra.

"Well, well, for once we agree."

Bazil, who found wine even less appetizing but still drank a mouthful or two because it helped him forget how sore he felt, leaned over the wall and looked down at the bodies piled up on the other side.

"We will want some beer to drink when we cook these trolls," he said calmly.

Alsebra was amused. "That's eating your prey before you've caught it, my friend. We will never live to cook these trolls."

"What?" Bazil was shocked. "We beat them before. What can they bring against us that we cannot face?"

"They will keep attacking until we succumb, that is my thinking. They have to drive us away. Your dragonboy explained it well."

"He is a good dragonboy sometimes, that one."

"You have been blessed. But still it means that the enemy has to keep attacking. He has no choice."

The Purple Green was far from defeated, however.

"So, let him come. We will kill all of them if we have to. I am ready."

"I do not doubt that the Purple Green of Hook Mountain will be the last to fall," said Alsebra.

"We have fought our way out of tight places before. We won the battle at Clove Valley."

"The enemy did not outnumber us by ten times or more at Clove Valley."

"All right then, the fight back at the Lion's Roar."

"That was on a very narrow front. We fought sword tip to sword tip there, sometimes closer."

"Yes," said Bazil with a laugh. "I had to duck a few times when my wild friend lost control of his backswing."

The Purple Green was sensitive about his lack of swordskill. In a fight he tended to rely more on his terrific strength rather than well-rehearsed moves like the wyverns.

"It was not just this dragon that lost control in that fight. I remember it well."

"That was a damned close thing, that fight," said Alsebra.

"But we survived," said Bazil. "We can survive this. And then we will have ourselves a feast. We will eat some of these trolls. There are so many different types now. We can try them all."

"By the fiery breath of the ancient ones," said the Purple Green. "We will try each type three different ways."

Alsebra laughed at this, her jaws clacking. She reached down and patted Relkin on the shoulder as he stepped past with a newly repaired tail mace over his shoulder.

"I have an idea," she said. "We can cook all of them at once. We pour oil over them and set fire to the lot. Roast them all on the spot!"

"What are you talking about?" said Relkin.

"All these trolls, we have so many to cook."

"What?"

"For afterward, we plan to have a feast." She nodded to the trolls strewn across the ground in front of the wall.

Relkin's face wrinkled in disgust. "That's disgusting," he said.

"Oh! Disgusting?" Alsebra reared back with an angry eye. "And humans are so fastidious about what you eat? What goes into sausages? You just tell me that."

Relkin stared at her. "There's a difference between a pig and a troll don't you think?"

"Why? They are both animals, both have flesh and bones. They are not poisonous."

"Oh, well, I don't think you understand."

"Alsebra understand."

The Purple Green made the terrible sound of dragon laughter.

Relkin shrugged and looked out over the wall. His eyes roved south, and he let out a cry.

"Look!"

A reddish light was spreading up into the sky on the far horizon.

The dragons stared. Suddenly the Purple Green sniffed the air. "A burning. A human place is burning."

"The city of Fitou lies in that direction," said Manuel, coming over to join Relkin.

"Show me," said little Jak, jumping up from below where he'd been working on Alsebra's damaged joboquin.

"Fitou is burning." Relkin pointed to the southeast.

The group on the wall of the vintner's garden were not the only ones who became aware of the blaze rising in the distance. From the knoll in Rundel Forest, General Lukash examined the distant glare with a spyglass and pondered its meaning with the Magician Thrembode.

Both were aware of the presence of the Mesomaster Vapul, who sat a horse off in the shadows of the glade.

"It might mean we have won, and our troops are burning the town. It is hard to control imps when we have a victory," said Lukash.

"It might also mean the Argonathi were gone when our army arrived, and the imps went berserk anyway and have fired the place. They're capable of anything in such situations."

"We struggle to control them; you know how they are. If we had more men, then we would need to rely on them less."

"If the Argonathi are not there, where would they be?"

"Coming here as quickly as they could."

"Then, we must turn about and face them."

"We will protect our flank. But we must break through this barrier in front of us and go on at once. It would be better not to give battle to seven full legions of Argonathi."

"We have the secret weapon."

"Magician, you were at Salpalangum, I believe."

"Indeed, I was. I know how formidable Argonathi troops can be. But the army of Sephis was deficient at that time. They lacked trolls or anything that could trouble the dragons."

"It would be better for us if we could avoid giving battle on this side of Bel Awl. If we reach Bel Awl gap, then we can probably hold them off indefinitely. Then our force on the river Alno would march on Kadein, which will be defenseless."

"What are you saying, General?"

"That we use the secret weapon now. We break this line and we go through to Waldrach, then destroy the bridge there and slow up the Argonathi army. At Bel Awl we will go on the defensive. They will not be able to dislodge us from Bel Awl gap."

"The secret weapon is not to be divulged without permission."

"Bah, it is no secret anymore. The damned things have marched in our army all this way. Every imp knows about them."

Thrembode almost lost patience. "General, it is not by my orders that they are kept secret. Ask Vapul."

Lukash flashed a look of annoyance, but there was no choice.

"All right," he said, "I will."

CHAPTER SEVENTY-THREE

It was the hour before dawn. The light from the burning of Fitou filled the southeast sky. Eads had scouts out down toward Consorza seeking for the cavalry that would be the first signs of the arrival of the Argonathi army. So far they had seen nothing except parties of Baguti working the open country to the south.

In the meantime, men and dragons worked with whetstone and paste on their blades while dragonboys and bowmen fletched arrows.

The enemy was regrouping for the next attack. In the vintner's garden, the defenders could clearly hear the bellowing of officers and the burst of drumming. A glance over the wall would show thousands of torches in motion, many gradually coalescing into the outline of another assault column.

The drums began to beat steadily, a monstrous thrub-a-thrub that went on and on like the breath of some monster come to devour the last hopes of the world.

"They are coming," said little Jak nervously.

No one else said anything. The spearmen, led by Corporal Deenst, tumbled out of the house where they'd been throwing dice and took up positions. They had been equipped with a rough-and-ready pair of lances, each ten-foot long and tipped with a foot of steel. They had been told they were to face a kind of oversized troll. They had also been told to try and hamstring the brutes, to fight in the way imp infiltrators fought.

Each man faced the prospect with a different degree of concern or equanimity. All had long since realized that they might well die in this place and had come to terms with this thought. They were professional soldiers; it was their lot to fight for the salvation of the Argonath. This was the fight they had trained for since they had joined the legion.

On came the enemy column, the lights coming closer and closer.

Beside each dragon was a pile of cobblestones. Still they waited, the column was not yet in range.

The column widened out, from the river of torches behind it they estimated it was much the same size as the previous assault column. They watched it with grim determination as the imps formed a wide line for the assault, regiment upon regiment of them. Trolls could be seen, moving in packs of six or seven, in the midst of the imps.

For a moment there was a lull. The drums ceased their infernal thunder. The torches blazed and a near silence fell over the vineyards on the slope of Turmegint, south of Lennink.

Then came a massive blast from the dull horns of the enemy, the drumming resumed, and the lines came on at a trot. As they drew closer now, so the keen eyes of the dragons saw the new monsters first.

"There they are," Alsebra pointed to a trio of shapes that towered over imps and trolls.

"By the breath," muttered Manuel. In the glare of the oncoming torches, Relkin saw the older youth's face tighten with dismay. And well might he feel concern. These things that shambled toward them were as much as fifteen feet tall; they would tower over even the Purple Green.

"They have shields, a design I've never seen before. A lot longer than troll shields."

Relkin felt a shiver go through him. Destiny approached.

"Twice the height of a man, must weigh as much as a dragon."

"Yes for sure, but which kind of dragon?"

"Important point. Let's hope they're slow."

"Seem to have axes over their shoulders."

"Good, that means they're slow-witted. Be bad if they could wield a sword."

"I don't think those are axes. Those are hammers."

"Then they're really slow-witted."

"Maybe they were meant for siege work."

On they came, in groups of three, behemoth ogres, monsters torn from the bellies of dying mammoths. They betrayed no trace of their origin in the elephant race, except in the grey and wrinkled texture of their hides. Instead of being mammothlike the heads were a grotesque mockery of those of the great apes, except that they bore even rows of six-inch daggerlike teeth in jaws three feet across. They lurched toward the defenders surrounded by clusters of trolls and regiments of imps.

Dragon Leader Turrent came around to check on them. They pointed to the ogres.

"Ungainly looking things, we will emphasize our speed" was his comment.

Dragonboys shot Turrent incurious looks. They had long since weighed the approaching brutes and reached that same conclusion. Turrent sensed that he was superfluous and bit off any further remarks. Despite his outward calm, he was feeling nervous. The oncoming monsters were terrifying. He was impressed by the placidity of the dragonboys. They had absorbed the phlegmatic battle mood of their great charges. He wished he could be so inwardly relaxed.

After a few moments he left them and jogged back to the rest of the squadron on the barricade.

The enemy came in range, and the air filled with great rocks and paving stones. Gaps appeared in the ranks of imps. Trolls were felled and left behind. A rock bounced off an ogre's shield and even that monstrous hulk was shaken, but only for a few seconds, and then it resumed the forward march.

The rocks were accompanied by a storm of arrows. Bowmen ranged along the wall of the vintner's garden as they took shots at the eyes of trolls and ogres.

The dragonboys waited, holding their fire until it would count. On came the enemy, the drums throbbing through the world and the ranks of imps screaming in battle lust. They tramped over the bodies of the fallen and up to the great mound of faggots and corpses on the other side of the wall. A paving stone from the Purple Green felled a great ax troll even as it set foot on the faggots. Others surged past it as it fell. Imps were thrusting up crude ladders against the wall, and Relkin joined two spearmen in shoving one away. He got a hand on the top of the ladder and pushed sideways. A spearman had the butt of his spear rammed against it, and despite the imps scrambling up, it slid off the wall and fell, taking down the next one with it.

Relkin's elation was short-lived. The next moment he felt a solid impact on the top of his head, his helmet rang, and he ducked down and realized he'd been hit a glancing blow from an arrow. It was only the first of a near avalanche of shafts. The spearmen and dragons crouched, not all of them in time. Relkin heard a cry and turned his head and saw another spearman topple backward with an arrow projecting from his face.

Relkin scrambled for his bow, then leaned over the wall and fired down into the imps that were lifting up the next ladder.

He saw his shaft go home, and an imp fell. Arrows were bouncing off the wall; one skipped an inch from his hand as he ducked back. He reloaded.

Rocks from the dragons continued to fly and to take a toll on the trolls, but now they felt a different tread on the mound of faggots and corpses. Relkin looked up and saw the ogres looming overhead.

Relkin froze, overcome by the primeval fear of carnivorous monsters. The nearest ogre looked down at him with red eyes that seemed to burn in black pits sunk in the huge ape face. The fear was akin to dragon-freeze, and it pinned him in place for what was almost a fatal second.

He darted sideways at the last moment as he glimpsed a hammer falling from high overhead. There was a terrific concussion behind him, and fragments of rock struck him in the legs.

There was a unified roar from the dragons as they rose up to take on these new monsters of the battlefield.

Relkin took aim at the colossus's face, released smoothly, and saw his shaft sprout from its nose. The ogre uttered a wild roar and swung its huge hammer high again.

Then Bazil disposed of a sword troll by cleaving it almost in two, and then swung and stuck his shield hard into the ogre's chest. It barely seemed to react.

Bazil's big eyes popped. There was no doubting the fact that these brutes were strong. Still, strength was one thing, and speed was another.

Baz tried his forehand, and Ecator rang off the monster's shield as it covered itself. The dragon looked up into the insane face of the ogre, it was at least four feet taller than himself! The red eyes burned with malevolence, and Bazil wondered if anything could shift the brute.

The great hammer swung down at him, and he moved, spinning rightward, tail mace flashing in the monster's face until he brought Ecator in at five feet off the ground.

The ogre's shield took the brunt of the blow and deflected it. Then its hammer came down and knocked the dragon backward. Legionaries scrambled to get out of Bazil's way as he careened back.

The leatherback hung onto his sword and shield, but lost his footing and crashed into the garden. Relkin struck down at an imp as it tried to get a leg over the wall. A legionary thrust over with his spear, and the imp fell back.

The next moment the ogre's hammer obliterated the legionary and knocked another chunk out of the wall.

An ax troll was climbing over unopposed. Men of the Fird ran forward with their battle cry. The troll swung its huge ax, and the men flattened themselves. They jumped to their feet and rushed the monster. It kept them at a distance with its shield and the ax swung again and again and the men were forced back, unable to face such might.

Relkin fired at the troll, glimpsed the ogre's hammer coming down again, and dodged. The hammer blow demolished more of the wall. Relkin had another arrow loaded, and he shot an imp as it scrambled onto the top of the wall. Then a sword troll came over the walk, and its huge sword scythed through the air just above Relkin's head.

Bazil was regaining his feet. Relkin spun away from the sword troll's next blow and almost ran onto the blade of an imp that had climbed over in the interim. Two more were coming right behind him.

The imp drew back to slay him and died instead with an arrow in his throat. Relkin looked over his shoulder and saw Jak reloading.

"Thanks!" he yelled.

Jak had no time to reply since another sword troll was coming over on Alsebra's left side. He fired, reloaded, and fired again, giving Alsebra a fraction of a second in which to shift position and engage the troll.

Three Firdsmen came up to reinforce them. More were coming. They were just in time. More than half a dozen imps were over the wall, and the trolls were almost across.

Bazil hurled himself back to the wall and slashed the ax troll; Ecator sundered the haft of its weapon. It stumbled back with an awed roar of surprise.

The sword troll swung, Bazil deflected the blow with his shield, and came back with an overhand that sent the troll back to the wall. Before Bazil could follow up, however, the ogre stepped closer and lashed out with that huge hammer.

Bazil dodged, and the hammer went past and struck the sword troll at the end of its trajectory. The sword troll was knocked back over the wall.

Bazil planted his feet and brought Ecator around at knee height on the ogre. This time Ecator clipped through the bottom corner of the ogre's shield in a great flash of sparks and sank into the monster's leg. It gave a scream of pain and rage, and tried to pound the dragon into the ground. Bazil deflected the blow, although it left his arm numb.

The damage to the ogre's leg had slowed it, and Bazil regained his position in time to cut down an ax troll and then hammer the ogre's shield once more. The troll subsided, but the ogre's hammer broke out another chunk of the wall.

The ogre struck the wall again and a section moved. Two spearmen ran forward with a desperate cry, both holding the shaft of a long lance.

They raised the point and thrust hard for the belly of the ogre. But they were too slow. The ogre deflected the lance with its shield and its great hammer whistled through their position. One man was not quick enough, and his upper body was smashed the next moment.

A clansman from the Fird leapt at the ogre and landed on its chest. With the ancient battle cry of Clan Wattel screaming from his lips, he thrust into it again and again with his sword, working between gaps in the crude leather armor the ogres wore on their chests.

It snarled and tore the man away with its shield hand, but doing so exposed its chest and this time Bazil made sure, Ecator came around over his shoulder and sank fully into the ogre's neck.

The terrible red glare in those eyes faded and went out, and the monster swayed there like a tree in a high wind. When Baz put a foot up and shoved to free the blade, the ogre toppled and fell sideways.

As it fell it caught the edge of the wall, and the weakened section collapsed and opened a breach. Imps were darting through before the dust had cleared. Men and dragonboys were waiting, swords in hand.

Another ogre was climbing over the wall, fending off Alsebra with its shield. She was distracted by a sword troll that was also trying to get a leg over the parapet.

A brave spearman ran in and thrust home into the side of the sword troll. It cut at him and he ducked back, but an imp shot him down from the top of the wall.

There were imps everywhere. Relkin had his hands full with a squat one wearing an outlandish, square helmet and wielding a two-handed sword that was almost too much for Relkin's shield.

More imps were getting over. Out of the corner of his eye, he saw an imp nip in behind Bazil, and with a despairing cry, he launched himself right over the dragon's tail and caromed into the imp before it could hack at Bazil's hamstrings.

He fell with the imp, and they rolled over. The imp was on top of him. He kneed it furiously in the side and knocked it loose. His dirk was in his hand and plunged into the imp's throat in the next moment.

But now the imp with the two-handed sword was swinging at the dragon's back.

Relkin yelled a warning to Bazil and threw his dirk at the imp with the same practiced move that had slain Trader Dook. The big knife sank into the imp's side just below the arm, and his stroke went wild and slid off the joboquin.

Baz felt the blow, though, and was distracted enough to snap his curiously bent tail sideways and flatten the imp's square helmet and the head within.

Relkin bent to retrieve his dirk. As he stood up, he felt something rush past his face, and the hammer of yet another ogre struck the wall beside him and collapsed the whole section.

An enormous leg loomed through the dust. An imp came through, crouched, put an arrow into Bazil's back. Relkin struck it down and then backed away.

The ogre was through the wall.

CHAPTER SEVENTY-FOUR

The ogre was through! The tide of battle swayed under the dark skies before the dawn.

Bazil danced and spun and struck again and again at the ogre with Ecator, but this one was a little quicker than the last, and it matched every blow with its shield. The huge hammer whirled around, and Bazil had to wobble backward out of range.

Imps ran in, arrows flicking from their bows. Trolls were coming through the gap.

Bazil came back with a combination, a forehand and an overhand. The ogre met the first stroke but not the second, and Ecator sundered the monster's leather, padded armor, and drew a gout of thick black blood.

The ogre roared with pain and jerked the hammer inside and jabbed Bazil in the belly. The air whooshed out of the dragon's lungs as he doubled up. The ogre clubbed him with the edge of its shield, and though his helmet took the blow, he was still stunned. He sagged to his knees. The ogre raised its hammer for the killing stroke.

The blow never fell, however. A slim figure jumped onto the dragon's back and then vaulted over the ogre's shield and landed with legs astride its right shoulder.

The huge head swiveled, and Relkin thrust his sword into the right eye. The ogre jerked its head back, his sword came free, and he almost toppled off. The ogre's jaws opened and lunged for him.

Relkin threw himself off the monster's shoulder and toppled down the inside of its arm, bounced off its thigh, and turned a somersault to land on his feet right in front of it.

"Out of way" came a roar behind him, and he darted sideways, as Bazil came back with a rush, slammed into the ogre, and stood it up tall and straight.

It struggled to find the leverage needed to swing the hammer, and in that space Bazil struck hard. Ecator cut off a corner of the ogre's enormous shield and scored again in the creature's side.

Still it came on, seemingly unkillable. The hammer looped back, and Bazil foolishly tried to take the blow on his shield. For his pains, he was bowled over. The shield was heavily dented, and he was lucky not to have his arm broken.

The ogre came on, crushing three men of the Fird beneath its feet and then sweeping another section of the wall to ruin with its giant hammer.

With a deep breath, Bazil got back on his feet.

The ogre snarled at him and set itself ready with shield and hammer. Ecator flashed and sank into the haft of the ogre's hammer. The two giants went shield to shield, and this time Bazil held his ground. Indeed he set his feet and heaved the taller, more slender ogre backward a step.

It clipped him hard with the edge of its shield again, and he saw stars but kept on shoving and thrust his knee into its crotch. This upset the ogre, and it forgot all pretense of battle training, dropped its hammer, and seized Bazil's shoulders while it tried to bite off his head.

Bazil broke the grip with a sideways shake, slammed his shield into the monster's face, and hewed into it with Ecator once more. This time he found its heart, and the brute fell with a crash that made the ground jump.

At the same time Alsebra slew another ax troll, and the Purple Green knocked the legs out from under an ogre, causing it to topple off the wall and roll back over the faggots, crushing imps and trolls beneath it.

Bazil swung Ecator low and fast to reap the imps like grain, and then all three dragons lifted their voices in a roar of triumph.

Men of the Fird came running up with timbers with which to block the breach. A squad of bowmen came behind them and took up positions to rake the imps in front of the wall to the vintner's garden.

Bazil struck down another ax troll, and the Purple Green slew a sword troll. The momentum was suddenly back in their hands and with a brisk spell of sword and shield work, they completely regained the wall.

To their right, however, the fighting continued on the barricade, and they could hear the dragons roaring in counterpoint to the bellowing of trolls and ogres.

Still, around the vintner's garden, there was a lull.

Relkin saw Dragon Leader Turrent stumbling past. Turrent's eyes were glazed with the shock of battle.

"Sir?" said Relkin.

"What is it?" he said in a dull voice.

"Oil, sir. There's a store of oil nearby. We should pour it on the wooden faggots they've piled up against the wall. When they come again, we set it on fire."

"Oil?" Turrent shook his head. Relkin saw that he'd been struck hard across the side of the head; there was a gash and matted blood. The dragon leader's eyes were vague and empty.

"Yes, sir, there's lots of olive oil, I think. Hard to set it alight so we will have to get some spirits and soak rags with them to ignite it. But once it burns, it will blaze."

"Oil?"

Relkin explained again, trying desperately to be patient, aware that every second counted.

Then at last the light of comprehension glowed in Turrent's eyes.

He looked over the wall, the enemy assault had completely stopped around them. Only on the barricade was it still going. And then he saw the attackers ebbing back even from the barricade. The ogres had been stopped.

"Show me the oil."

Within a few minutes, dragons and men were rolling barrels of oil up a ramp, through the alley, and across the garden.

At the wall they were lifted up by the Purple Green, and their contents poured over the wall. The pile of brush tied into faggots, mixed liberally with the corpses of imps and trolls and men, was soon well soaked in the finest olive oil.

Meanwhile Relkin and Jak had torn up the wardrobe of the vintner's wife and soaked it in spirits of petroleum normally used for lamps. They ran back with baskets stuffed with incendiary rags and the rest of the spirits of petroleum.

They were only just in time. The enemy had reformed and was gathering the next wave of the assault. Drums began to thunder.

"They're coming again," said little Jak.

Relkin built a pile of hay, scrap paper snatched from the

vintner's study and some fragments of wood. He sprinkled some of the spirits onto the hay, tore the paper into shreds with shaky hands, and struck sparks over it with his flint and steel.

Twice he obtained a little flare that smoked and went out.

"Hurry," said Manuel, his voice cracking slightly. The enemy ranks were clearly visible now beneath their torches.

Dragon Leader Turrent came up. He had passed on the idea to the others, and they were pouring stores of virgin olive oil over the barricades while men built bonfires in the road behind the barricade and prepared to set alight bales of cloth soaked in oil that they would throw over the barricade. Turrent had recovered his wits somewhat.

The enemy assault ground forward.

"More ogres this time," said Jak.

He could hardly be heard over the thunder of the drums and the blaring of the enemy horns.

The cornets were shrilling, too, and once more the enemy assault column came forward seeking to batter through the thin line of soldiers standing in its way.

At last Relkin got a flame to take, and he fed it more scraps of paper, and then more, and then a handful of hay. Jak contributed quickly and provided them with a furious little fire.

With this ablaze they waited, oiled rags in their hands, their eyes locked on the advancing horde. Ogres swayed over the rest.

"Did you hear?" said Jak.

"Casualties?" It was hardly a question.

"Anther was killed. His wound slowed him up."

"I'm sorry to hear that. Halm must be in a bad way."

"There's more. Tomas Black Eye was killed, and Swane was almost gutted by an imp."

"Tomas is dead? Ah, that is hard." Another veteran of the Ourdh campaign was gone.

"And Swane?"

"Wounded, but he'll live. They sewed him up. He wants to fight, but they won't let him."

"That sounds like Swane."

"I am saddened by the loss of Tomas," said Manuel.

The butcher's bill was already high and likely to rise, thought Relkin. Would any of them survive?

"They're getting close."

They looked at one another and then to Turrent. There was something wrong with the dragon leader. He was shaking his head and muttering.

"Sir," said Manuel.

Turrent did not respond at first. When he did turn his head, he stared at them blankly.

"All right, let's do it," said Relkin quietly.

They lit the rags, and tossed them over the wall. Soon there were dozens of small fires flickering in the brush, faggots heaped against the wall. Some went out, others merely smoked. The enemy ignored the threat.

Now imps were shoving their ladders against the wall once more while trolls came up to engage the dragons. And last there came the ogres, swinging those huge hammers.

Rock cracked and powdered under the blows. A second breach was blown through the wall. Smoke was rising up in several places from new burgeoning fire.

Imps struggled through the gap, and screaming with the rage induced by the black drink, hurled themselves at the defenders.

And then the oil soaking the lower part of the mound of debris caught at last. With a rush and a crackle, a wall of flame shot up above the wall.

Imps screamed, trolls roared, and ogres bellowed as they scrambled for safety. The heat was so intense that dragons and boys stood back at the inner edge of the earth bank inside the wall.

"Look!" screamed little Jak.

Two ogres had caught fire, so covered in the thick cloud of volatiles and flames that their very hides had been ignited. They stumbled backward, moving pillars of flame that stumbled and then fell to the ground where they thrashed and died.

The dragons hurled the remaining rocks and paving stones over the flames and into the midst of the enemy, which wavered at the edge of the wall of fire, and then backtracked, stumbling backward, foot by foot.

More oil was poured over the wall, and the fires grew, swelling higher and hotter.

The enemy fell back farther, and then the spell broke, and despite the black drink and the thunder of the drums, the assault column lost heart and collapsed back on itself and withdrew.

A frenzied cheer went up from the weary line of defenders as a fortune in virgin oil blazed furiously along the southern margin of the town.

In addition to a vast store of oil, the world had lost the great vineyards of Ard and Desoli, utterly destroyed under trolls and ogres. But the thin line of defenders still held Lennink and the road to Waldrach.

CHAPTER SEVENTY-FIVE

The enemy had no thought of giving up. A new, much heavier, assault was immediately put into preparation. Enemy troops poured through the forest of Rundel and lined up in the wheat fields.

General Lukash would waste no more time. He would commit half his army to the assault. They would lap around Lennink and take the defenders from the rear if they could not break through on the front.

In the hour on either side of dawn as the faggots turned to ash, they watched the enemy formations gathering at the margins of the woods. Regiment upon regiment of imps, with troops of trolls and small clusters of mighty ogres formed up on the trampled wheat.

Now they came on, and the drumming and blaring of horns soon made it all but impossible to hear anything less than a shout in the vintner's garden.

They tried to keep the blaze going outside the wall but without wood, the oil smoked rather than burned. The enemy came up over the mound of corpses and through the ash and smoking oil and clapped their ladders against the wall.

Up and down the line of the scarp, the imps surged forward, and on either side of the town, they lapped around the flanks and pushed in along the Fitou road. Eads had small forces to try and block the road, but they were forced back. Baguti cavalry were moving in from the direction of Waldrach. They were completely surrounded now.

In the vintner's garden they roused weary bodies to block the imps and trolls. For a while they held them in a seesaw contest that saw parts of the wall taken twice before being reclaimed. Then ogre hammers smashed down a ten-foot length of the wall, and a tidal wave of imps washed through.

Dragons fought a retreat through the garden, through the

house, completely wrecking it, and out the gate into the street.

The enemy broke through at several other points along the line at about the same time, overwhelming force finally cracking the defense.

Ogres tramped forward, huge hammers ready to pound dragons down. Men and dragons made stand after stand, side by side, and gave up the ground very grudgingly; but gave it up they did.

It was a time of extraordinary feats. Alsebra slew three trolls with consecutive blows of her sword. Relkin saw the Purple Green belly to belly with an ogre, heaving it back. Their arms and shields were entangled, and they could not win free. It snapped at the wild dragon with its gaping jaws, lined with sharklike teeth.

The Purple Green matched its roar with his own while ducking away from its jaws, and then came back with a snakelike dart of his own jaws to fasten on the ogre's throat. He tore, left, right, and then away. The ogre emitted a shriek and fountained dark purple blood.

But the defenders were outmatched, almost overwhelmed. Poor Vlok was felled by an ogre's hammer and was hauled away by Chektor. Felo, a brasshide in the 33rd Kadein was slain by another ogre. Chut, a leatherback in the 66th Marneri, was run through by a sword troll and finished off by a swarm of imps.

Men of the Fird died all along the line, fighting bravely to the last, but they were overwhelmed by the numbers of the imps and the strength of the trolls. And in the end, there was always the power of the hammers of the ogres. Wherever men sought to hold a strong point—the front of a house, the water well in the sutler's yard—the hammers smashed and crushed and broke it to smithereens and drove the men out.

Captain Eads fought with them, in the vintner's garden when the wall had been lost. Then he fought inside the house until he was wounded in the thigh and was forced to stagger away for a tourniquet and a bandage. The Purple Green was hit hard by an ax troll but saved by his armor, which, though cut, did not give way entirely. He was pulled away by Manuel and some spearmen, and collapsed up the road toward the center of Lennink.

Almost unnoticed during the fight in the house, Relkin fell. Right after Bazil and Alsebra had combined to kill a

sword troll and clear the main drawing room. Imps were
pouring in behind them, however, so they backed out the
broken open outer wall and neither noticed that Relkin was
no longer with them.

Outside in the street, Bazil and Alsebra found themselves
fighting in an alley with great Burthong of the 33rd at their
side.

"Good to see you still live, Broketail!" said Burthong as
his sword "Herak" whistled down and sundered an ax troll's
shield.

"So we fight together now," said Bazil, while methodi-
cally defending himself from sword trolls and imps with
long spears.

He cleared his front and looked around. The boy was
gone. Bazil felt something like panic rise in his heart. Where
was boy? The leatherback surged back toward the house, but
was met by three fresh trolls and a dozen imps.

Jak had noticed Relkin's absence by that point, but before
he could bring it up, a section of the alley wall collapsed and
an ogre started forcing its way in behind them. Alsebra
swung over to confront the monster, and they clashed shield
to shield.

Alsebra was forced back a step and then another. With a
squeal of effort, she dug in her heels and swung Undaunt in
beautiful combinations, cutting the ogre's shield to pieces.
The hammer came, and she responded by stepping inside,
forcing her way past the ogre's shield and taking the dim-
witted monster by surprise. Undaunt buried itself in the
ogre's belly. She got her shoulder down and into its chest,
pushed, and the thing toppled backward, falling into the gap
in the wall and crushing a dozen imps in the process.

Many more imps were already loose in the alley, though.
Alsebra felt an imp sword cut into her tail. She whipped
around and beheaded the imp, but another sword slashed her
left leg. Then another imp tried to work a spear through her
joboquin.

Frantically she stamped and shook, and smashed them left
and right. Jak killed one with a sword thrust and was almost
slain in return by another.

Bazil slew one troll and staggered another, but he was surrounded by imps and felt their swords at his back. He lashed
at them with tail mace and shield. Then an imp sword went
home, deep into his thigh. He gave a grunt, knocked the imp

away, and spun back. A troll struck in, and he barely deflected the stroke. He could not get through. An ogre was coming.

"Fall back" came the cry, and they did, abandoning the alley to the enemy and joining the main remnant of Eads's force, which was standing in battle line in front of the Vintner's Guild Hall, a solid building of limestone, three stories tall with a green copper roof.

There they made the last stand, denying the road to Waldrach, and with them hung the fate of the very world. One final ounce of effort, and it would be over. The enemy would march through to Waldrach and the destruction of Marneri.

The drums began to increase their thunder. An assault column was formed up, swords and hammers raised high as they drank the black drink. Then forward they came under a lofting cloud of arrows.

CHAPTER SEVENTY-SIX

Relkin awoke to the sound of two men arguing in furious voices. He opened an eye and saw a white plaster wall and some floor. He opened the other eye to more wall. Dawn had broken, the light was getting stronger. His head throbbed. His last memory was of three imps cornering him and of his killing one of them.

Indeed, a dead imp was lying across his legs. Another lay wedged against his back.

He moved slightly and eased the pressure on his legs. His head throbbed ominously. He felt his helmet at his side where it had rolled. He inclined his head and noticed some blood on the helmet's lower rim.

Cautiously he put a hand up to the back of his head. It'd been laid open, despite his helmet, and there was a heavy crust of drying blood there. They'd struck him down and left him for dead.

Relkin gave thanks to the Mother for the hardness of an orphan's head! Briefly he wondered if he should thank old Caymo, too.

He eased the dead imp off his legs and felt blood rushing back to his feet with a tingle of pins and needles. His head hurt horribly when he moved.

Throughout, the argument had continued without pause. They who argued were much too engrossed to take any notice of him. He shifted a little more and turned his head to survey the room.

The front parlor of the vintner's house had once been a lovely room filled with stuffed leather furniture and oak bookcases. It had been wrecked to the point that one wall was half-broken open. Kindling and shreds of leather were all that were left of the furniture.

The balustrade hung off the stairs, and the front door had

been torn from its hinges. The bodies of imps and men littered the place.

The argument was continuing. Relkin pulled completely free from the encumbrance of the dead imp, got to his knees, and crawled slowly forward while wincing from the savage pins and needles in his legs.

His hand brushed against a sword hilt and instinctively grasped it. He looked at it dully and noted with surprise that it was his own blade.

Lifting it brought on another wave of pain, this time from his hand. He looked down and saw more blood and a huge, purpling bruise across the back of his hand. For a moment he was unable to move. Then, using the wall to hold onto, he hauled himself to his feet. His left leg almost gave way, and he wobbled for a moment.

Something came loose in his mouth; he spat it out and glimpsed a white tooth bounce across the floor. There was one for old Caymo, who was said to come and take your teeth twice in life, once when he brought you a sugar candy in childhood, and once when he took your teeth for good in old age. No sugar candy this time, however. Relkin shrugged inwardly. That was destiny for you.

To see the argument, he had but to lean around the edge of the doorway. The question was whether he could do that without falling over. He steeled himself and put his weight on his right leg, limped a step, and then took a peek.

The door opened onto a walled, hidden garden, built on the southern side of the vintner's house. Rosebushes grew along the walls, and the air was full of their scent.

Two very dissimilar men were standing toe-to-toe while they yelled at each other with the cords standing up in their necks. One was tall and eloquent, the other short and powerful. The short one had the voice of a bull, although he seemed to be restraining himself from full bellow.

From their glossy black uniforms Relkin knew at once that they were important officers of the enemy army. One wore tunic and breeches, the other a cloak and expensive boots.

This man, the taller of the pair, suddenly stood back with a loud oath and gestured with both hands in the air. Relkin saw his face clearly and felt a dull shock of recognition. It was a face he could never forget: the man that had tried to kill him in Marneri, the man he had pursued all the way to Tummuz Orgmeen. It was Thrembode the Magician.

For the first time he actually listened to what they were shouting.

"Whatever plan was agreed with the M'kred Vapul, it doesn't matter now. Conditions have changed." Thrembode spoke with his habitual impatient arrogance.

"I am in command here, not you, Magician!" The short man emphasized this with a jerk of his thumb.

"And I am here to advise you, General, and on occasion to overrule you."

"You damned fop! What do you know of controlling an army of imps?"

"General Lukash, use your wits, you have been warned by the Baguti. You must act at once."

"I am not to deviate from the plan of attack. Vapul has spoken, and Vapul is right."

Thrembode raised his hands in the air again.

"The wise M'kred Vapul would change the plan in an instant if he knew what we know now. The enemy's main army is now on your right flank."

"I will not deviate. We will go on at once. The imps have tasted victory. They will be impossible to control for hours."

"Give the orders to face right and form up to receive the enemy."

"No! We have a skirmishing line on our right, and that will be enough. We push on directly for Waldrach. There I will hold the bridges."

"You idiot." Thrembode brought out a little whistle on a chain around his neck.

The general suddenly became animated and struck at Thrembode, knocking the whistle from his hand. It bounced on the paved walk with a little ringing sound.

"You dare to raise your hand to me?" shrieked the magician.

The general dared, indeed. He pulled a short sword from his scabbard and drove at Thrembode. The magician uttered a wild shriek and darted backward while drawing his own blade. They engaged, steel rang in the garden, and Lukash stamped forward with a will and the technique of a saber fighter with whirling overhands intermingled with side cuts to the throat. Thrembode was forced to the wall and barely escaped. Again he was brought up close and forced back, step by step, and this time wedged into a corner from which there would be no escape.

"This time, Magician, I will split you like a chicken!" brayed the general.

He spoke too soon. Thrembode had worked a hand into a pouch carried within his robe. Now he flicked a handful of glittering dust into the general's face.

Lukash screamed, staggered, and put a hand up to his eyes. Thrembode ran him through the chest, whipped out his crimson sword, and watched the stumpy general collapse to the ground. Then the magician planted his boot on Lukash's chest and looked down into the defeated man's eyes.

"Lukash, you are lucky to die so easily. Believe me, I had other plans for you."

Thrembode pressed his sword to Lukash's throat and then carefully rocked it back and forth to sever windpipe and jugular.

Relkin stepped into the garden, left leg still tingly. He felt a strange sense of awe overcome him. This moment had been foretold. Stacked atop all the other moments of his existence lay this one, in which he had one thing to do before he died.

He took another step, floating along as if in a dream. The sword came up in his hands.

At the last moment Thrembode sensed him and swung around.

The magician's mouth fell open in shock.

"You?" was all he said, recognition blooming wild in his eyes.

Then Relkin's sword struck home, and Thrembode gave a gasp and doubled up. Relkin hewed down again, and the magician fell. The enemy army was now without leadership.

Overcome by the effort, Relkin went down on one knee. He took several deep breaths, pushed himself up again, and staggered back into the ruined parlor. He leaned by the broken window and gasped for air. Imps were marching past outside. He heard cornets shrilling not far away and beneath their cry, the roar of battle.

The dragons were out there somewhere, fighting to the end. His dragon would be among them. He wanted to join them but found that he simply could not move his feet. There was an uncomfortable flush rising up his face. The dizziness increased. He felt the sword slip from his hand and clatter to the floor. Then darkness fell across his eyes, and he knew no more.

CHAPTER SEVENTY-SEVEN

Outside the guild hall of Lennink the survivors of Eads's force, perhaps two thousand men and twenty dragons, stood at bay in the dawn's swelling light.

Surrounded, they fought in the midst of a thicket of spears and swords. Men of the Fird lay heaped in front of them, and trolls and ogres were struggling to reach in and strike. There was little room for maneuver now, and the hammers of the ogres were hard for even dragon shields to deflect.

Eads himself had been stabbed in the chest and lay with his back against the stone of the guild hall, his eyes glazing.

Now it was the fight to the death, and the dragons reached deep for their last reserves of energy and one more time took up their swords and slew their enemies.

Mighty Burthong took down an ogre with a tremendous slice that cut off a giant leg at the knee. He finished the brute with an overhand that clove the monster's skull in a flash of sparks.

Bazil Broketail slew two ax trolls in quick succession and then confronted a towering ogre. Its foul breath washed over him as it roared and swung its huge hammer. For a moment he thought of his wild dragoness and his young ones, far away in the land of caribou. Would they remember him?

He deflected the hammer blow and felt his shield shiver. It was breaking up along the seam of the damage done at the fight at the Lion's Roar. He snapped his tail mace into the monster's face and ducked an ax swinging in from the right. The ogre struck him with its shield and thrust him backward onto his bad leg. There was no room behind him.

With an oath he shifted, ignoring the pain from his thigh, bobbed his head to avoid the second blow of the hammer, and ducked inside the thing's shield where he brought Ecator up in a powerful blow to the ogre's shield arm.

The shield fell from its nerveless grasp, and now Ecator

swung in again and decapitated the monster, sending the enormous, grinning head spinning off into the mass of imps behind it.

With black fluids fountaining, the monster collapsed on him, and Baz was shoved back on his heels for a moment until he pushed it aside. Behind it came more trolls. Behind them came another ogre. There seemed no end to them. Bazil thought to himself that he had had quite a day. Unfortunately, he sensed he would not see its end.

The Purple Green, Vlok, and several other dragons were heaped up against the wall of the guild hall along with dozens of dazed and unconscious men. Bazil had heard that the Purple Green was badly wounded.

On his left fought Carath and Burthong. Carath was limping. As he spun away from an ax troll so he ran right into an ogre's hammer blow. The brasshide dragon's head was knocked sideways in a violent splash of blood. Carath staggered, and though Burthong engaged the ogre, Carath was easy meat for a sword troll who cut his head from his body in the next moment. The dragon fell, crushing his dragonboy as he went.

Bazil could do nothing but get his shield up in time to hold off the next ax troll.

He glimpsed a slender figure appear in the line beside him. Eilsa Ranardaughter had come to take her place at the last. She fought through tears, wielding a man's sword. Her father was dead, as was her friend Silva, spitted on a troll's sword. And now they faced the end, and with her would die the very line of Ranard.

Alsebra unveiled a lovely feint and spun and slew a troll with a shriek of metal as Undaunt cleft its helmet. Its body toppled back over those behind it as she pulled free her blade.

"Nice work, Alsebra," said Bazil.

"You honor me, Broketail. We die together, I think."

Bazil chopped down to break the haft of a troll's great ax. "Long may they sing of Alsebra the Green." The troll hit him with its shield.

"By the breath, I like that thought!" She deflected a sword troll's blow and thrust home with Undaunt.

Ogres heaved through the mass toward them, hammers on high. The legionary on Bazil's right died on an imp's spear. A clansmen fell to his left. He no longer saw Eilsa

Ranardaughter. A spear thudded home into his ruined shield. The ogres came on. The end could not be far off now.

And then, from the south, they heard the cornets, dozens of them, and then more than dozens, hundreds, a great swelling silver cry.

The legions! The legions were coming!

At the sound Captain Eads came awake. Gritting his teeth he forced himself back onto his feet, seized a cornet, and blew a response, again and again. He fell after the fourth, but already someone else had taken it up.

The survivors gave a great cheer, and renewed their battle with a terrible light in their eyes and a grim song in their throats. The army of the Argonath was come at last, in the very nick of time.

Now a spearhead of Talionese heavy cavalry drove into the flank of the enemy mass below the village. While more ancient vineyards were crushed beneath their hooves, they drove the enemy columns into chaos.

Behind them came seven full legions at the trot, moving in the disciplined, open formation they favored for attack.

As the legions came to grips, so the great enemy army convulsed. Most of the trolls and all the ogres were concentrated in a mass, surrounding the surviving defenders of Lennink.

But now seven hundred battledragons fell upon the men and imps marching for Waldrach. The marching columns had already been convulsed by the cavalry charge. Now they disintegrated.

At the command center of the giant army, frantic staff majors squabbled among themselves. The general was dead, the dreaded Mesomaster was absent, and the Magician Thrembode was unconscious, possibly dying. There was nobody in command!

Belatedly, the enemy formations tried to turn to face the oncoming assault. The effort was slow, too slow, and there were not enough ogres to check the dragons. The legions cut into the masses of imps like red hot nails driven into wax.

The disintegration grew. Whole sections flew away in rout toward the Alno, struggling back through the forest of Rundel. Less organized fugitives streamed steadily west and north toward the mountains.

Captain Eads's band of survivors were left standing amid

the ruin and the dead while the cheering men of the Kadein legions went past all around them.

The first officer to reach the encircled band of survivors was Captain Hollein Kesepton. With him came three dragon squadrons, and they smashed aside the remaining trolls and hurled themselves against the ogres.

The ogres fell back before this fury. With fresh arms, the battledragons swung with a will; ogre shields were clipped to pieces and ogres were felled. The remaining ogres turned and tried to flee, moving at a shambling run. In pursuit followed the dragons, assisted by Talion cavalry.

And at last the battle had become a rout, and the field belonged to the Argonath.

CHAPTER SEVENTY-EIGHT

Relkin awoke to find himself lying on a bed in an unfamiliar room. There was a greenish light and the smell of disinfectant. The smell informed him that he was not in heaven.

He gave a hoarse croak as he cleared his throat. A big shape moved in the dark.

"Boy awake now," said a familiar voice.

Relkin put a hand up to his head. The hand was lost inside a ball of bandages. His head was similarly swathed. He was alive. He felt a distinct sense of surprise at this discovery.

"What happened?" he said.

"Ha, that is a good one. What has not happened would be better to ask."

"Are you wounded?"

"Not badly, Manuel took care of it."

"Does the Purple Green live?"

"Yes, but he is still in danger."

"Who else is hurt?"

"Anther dead, you know. Also Cham, with Tomas Black Eye. Chut and Greger in the 66th."

"The Legions came?"

"Just in time, they broke the enemy and swept them away."

Relkin let out a sigh. Victory then, the victory foretold by the Sinni, but victory bought at great cost.

Another figure entered his field of vision, and then Eilsa Ranardaughter was sitting beside his bed. Relkin felt the shadows lift from his heart at the sight of her face. Then he saw the bandage on her arm.

"You were hurt?"

"A slight thing," she smiled. "I was blessed. So many are gone."

"Your father?"

She shook her head. "Imps slew him where he lay."

"Captain Eads is gone," said the dragon.

Relkin felt his throat harden. So many had fallen.

"The emperor came," said Eilsa to change the subject. "With the little bird and the mouse. He sat beside you. I watched from the doorway. There was a crowd."

Relkin's eyes widened. "And I missed it all."

"They found thee lying beside the body of the enemy commander. They wanted to ask you questions."

"Yes, of course. I was there. I struck down the magician, you remember, Baz, Thrembode. The man we chased to Tummuz Orgmeen."

Bazil hissed quietly.

"They fought each other in the rose garden, while I watched. Thrembode killed the general, and I killed Thrembode."

Eilsa put a hand to his cheek. At her touch he felt a tingling warmth.

"The medicine witch detected a pulse when they brought you in, so they stitched you up and put you with the ones they thought would die. We found you there."

"I thank thee."

"They said thy skull was fractured but not badly. They did not know if thee would ever wake up."

"Orphans have to have hard heads," he said.

CHAPTER SEVENTY-NINE

Torches flared on the battlements of the Tower of Guard, flickering in the wind. Thick clouds hid the moon and stars. Armed men tramped to the changing of the guard. The enemy invasion had been turned back, but there was still warfare raging on the frontier. The martial spirit was high, nerves were strung, officers were anxious.

High as the men's spirits were, they received a further manic uplift in the hour before midnight. It came suddenly, a storm on the emotional plane that brought laughter and swollen faces to many in the great tower. It passed just as suddenly, and left everyone staring and astonished. There had been witchcraft practiced within the tower for hundreds of years, but never anything quite like this!

On a certain high floor, the mania passed into another kind of psychic tension which rose and rose and made those who passed the door to a certain apartment clench their teeth, while their skin tingled, their hair rose on end, and the very breath caught in their throats.

Deep magic was woven within that door. Those who could, fled the upper part of the Tower and formed muttering little groups in all the surrounding taverns. Their complaints were muffled, however, by the realization that there was a war in progress and that whatever witchcraft this was that was being practiced, it was connected to the war effort.

A few, who knew what was being attempted in that apartment, kept apart from these little groups. They kept their knowledge to themselves, although it if had been released, it would have stopped the mouths of the complainers in a moment.

The witches were trying to bring back the dead.

Within the suite, in a room filled with the pungent odor of singed hair and wood smoke, a fire blazed in the grate though the room was uncomfortably hot. At the table, Lessis of Valmes prepared small bundles of herbs and twigs, wrapped tight with leaves of freepure. One was of sea holly, wild carrot, and herb paris; the other contained sage, mandrake, and golden tinkerfoil. She bound these bundles with a scarlet silk thread and, as she bound them, she intoned a passage from the Birrak. On the table in front of her lay open a book of ancient Spellsay, and from this she took pointers for the spell she fashioned.

She looked as a presence entered the room, but did not hesitate in her recitation. She knew these sections of the canon better than the back of her hands. The acolytes who waited in the dark by the door bowed to the Queen of Mice, who acknowledged them with brief courtesy and came to sit by Lessis at the massive old table. The air was hot and stagnant. On a pallet set on the blue-stone floor lay Lagdalen of the Tarcho, unconscious. She had never awoken from the spell that was supposed to retrieve her from the mind of the eagle.

The spell had gone awry. It was a complex spell with many declensions and the caster of the spell had been in a state of deep fatigue, beyond exhaustion. Whatever the cause, something had slipped. Perhaps a volume had been misshaped. Perhaps some detail of phrasing had been too slow or too quick.

Lessis blamed herself. It was true enough that they had been close to the point of collapse. Their time spent trapped within those tiny animals had been far too long. A deep fatigue had built up that in the end had forced her to sleep for two entire nights and a day. Even Ribela had been forced to sleep an entire night.

And Lessis knew well that for Lagdalen, a mere girl, the entire experience of animantic possession had been far worse than for the witches. It was her first experience of such terrifying animancy and she was not in control of the spell. To be powerless in such a position was the most terrible feeling. And there was the effect of sharing the brutal, direct thought of the eagle. The thought of the great raptor was strange indeed to the human perspective. It was obsessed with tiny movements at the limits of vision, a vision that spanned the entire countryside, stoking a constant hunger for warm meat that could be torn apart and devoured. The thing's feet itched for prey to smash and rend. There was an erosive effect to such co-existence. Lessis was sure that this had contributed to the difficulty. Somehow it had affected Lagdalen at the end. During the spellsaying to remove her from the animant, she had lingered as if unwilling to leave.

Slowly, painfully slow, she had emerged from the mind of Cuica, the eagle. It was an exhausting process for Lessis. Then, during the final conversions, the thread had snapped and Lagdalen had never woken up.

While the appalled witches had tried to recast the spell with anxious chanting, Cuica had celebrated the removal of the spell with a scream of triumphant relief. He beat his huge wings until someone flung open the door to the balcony and he'd swept out into the night. There he'd circled, screaming defiance for an hour before finally vanishing into the west.

But Lagdalen had not opened her eyes and now it was the third day and she remained lost in limbo. An occasional low moan was all she had uttered during this time.

Ribela eased herself into the chair. Her body was still stiff and painful after all those weeks without movement. Her lower back was occasionally struck by a thunderbolt of pain and so she moved cautiously. Once seated, she waited with her eyes closed and her palms together in her lap until Lessis had finished her work.

The two bundles were ready. Lessis closed her eyes and took a long slow breath. It was best to let the mind down gently after an effort like this. Three thousand lines, six volumes, all produced in perfect timing and voice. It took prodigies of energy.

"I have good news," said Ribela at the precise moment that Lessis opened her eyes.

Lessis completed her breath.

"That is good to hear, Sister."

"Commander Sear has broken through to Cujac. Another large band of imps was rounded up and destroyed in the mountains. General Felix believes he will retake the High Pass within the next week."

"Thanks be to the Mother."

"The news from Kenor is very encouraging. A victory at the crossings of the Oon has broken the resistance above Fort Teot. The relief force will be there within two or three days."

Lessis raised her hands together.

"We have survived, Sister. The Empire of the Rose has withstood our enemy's greatest thrust. Now we must gain the initiative. We must rededicate ourselves to our work. We must find a way to seek vengeance for what they did."

Ribela stared at Lessis briefly. There was something odd about Lessis, an unusual carelessness, even a wildness that she had never detected before.

"You have never lacked dedication, Sister Lessis."

"I thank you, Sister, I only wish my dedication had carried through to better execution of our mission." Lessis's eyes betrayed a terrible guilt. It was inadmissable. Young women like Lagdalen were soldiers of the empire just as much as the young men in the legions. They must accept the risks involved.

"Lessis," Ribela leaned forward, "we have won a great victory. Indeed, I would go further and say that you, personally, have won it."

Lessis smiled, and Ribela did not understand. The small personal concerns—ties of friendship, love—these things were not Ribela's strength. Ribela sensed the criticism and nodded fiercely. "Yes, you are right, Sister."

She glanced over toward Lagdalen's silent form on the pallet in front of the fire.

"No change I take it."

"No change, but I believe I have the answer now."

Ribela glanced at the book laid open in front of Lessis.

"*Simpkins Parasympathia*?" she snorted. "That was old when I was a novice. For how long have you been going to old Simpkins then? A very quirky old fellow. I don't know that I would trust anything he wrote."

"Now, Ribela, you betray your dislike of the masculine sex once again. Simpkins was a little wild, but he was a visionary and he excelled in animancy as few men ever have. It is not widely known now, but his work in reanimancy is the basis for all the best new work in that field."

Ribela sniffed and bit off her first retort concerning the worthiness of reanimancy research.

"I wish you success, Sister."

If Lessis would try some wild spell from the fourth aeon, let it be on her head.

"I thank you, Sister."

They both turned their heads to the door.

Another figure entered, the Abbess Plesenta, come to say

prayers over Lagdalen's silent form. She had done this every night at the same time. She nodded to the witches, pulled off her outer shawl, and sat beside Lagdalen's still form.

During the prayers, Lessis and Ribela remained utterly silent. Lessis gathered her strength and prepared herself for the major work of sorcery she was about to undertake.

At length, the abbess finished and got to her feet. It had been a long day and she was a little unsteady at first. She saw the witches look at her and she felt their condescension. Undying things, she thought, they would long outlive her. How strange must be their thoughts! Lessis looked exactly as she had when the young Plesenta, then a Priestess Minor, had first seen her in the flesh. Somewhere between her mid-thirties and her mid-fifties, flesh firm, eyes still good, hearing keen and powers still potent, and yet Plesenta knew the Grey Lady was hundreds of years old.

"Will she ever wake?" she said to them.

Ribela's dark eyes showed no emotion. As cold as ice, thought Plesenta. Lessis, however, smiled and said "Yes, Abbess, we will awaken her. I think we know now what went wrong."

"Thanks be to the Mother that you've finally figured it out. 'Tis terribly sad to see our Lagdalen lying there lost in limbo, and she with a babe to bring up."

"Yes, Abbess, we grieve for her as well."

Plesenta looked at them carefully for a moment. Could they be capable of grief? After all that they have lived through?

Plesenta suddenly saw something in Lessis's eyes that told her that yes, they could grieve for the shortlived who served them for their brief moments on the stage of the sphereboard of destiny.

Plesenta made her good-byes and left them. Going down the stairs she told herself that it was a good thing she was retiring soon. She was getting too old to be able to stand the waste of young lives in these endless wars. The room she had left was already darkened and ahum with gathering energies.

The only sound now was of Lessis's voice calmly intoning fresh passages of the Birrak. Volumata were built up and released like cracks of gathering thunder. The bundles of herbs were burned in the fire. The smell of freepure rose. The light dimmed further. A thick, reddish smoke spilled out of the fireplace and settled to the floor of the room. It was an astonishing volume of smoke for two insignificant bundles of twigs. The sound of Lessis's voice grew louder. More volumes crackled from her lips.

A second smoke, this time white, rose from the fire. Lessis sucked in a great breath of this smoke and then bent forward, pressed her lips to Lagdalen's and drove the smoke into the girl's body.

Three times she did this, and the body of Lagdalen choked and spluttered briefly each time and then fell back to somnolence. Her eyes never opened.

Lessis returned to chanting. The power was vibrating the room. Ribela had slipped into a trance state to be ready to assist in any way if needed. The Queen of Mice was impressed by the power conjured up. Lessis had the most foolish way of presenting herself to the world, but one had to admit that she had strength.

Lessis's voice grew louder, the final volumes seemed to shake the very flagstones, and the acolytes pressed their hands to their ears and their heads to the floor. A terrible pressure had built up in the atmosphere. The entire Tower of Guard felt as if it were teetering on an edge.

Lagdalen suddenly shook upon the pallet, the first movement from her in weeks.

Ribela felt her heart skip a beat.

Lessis moved into the final declension. The lines rolled forth, the subtexts congealed and the capstone of a vast piece of sorcery was set in place.

Silence filled the room, a silence so thick with expectancy that it nearly induced vomiting in the acolytes on the floor.

Lagdalen did not move.

The silence grew, Ribela sensed an enormous energy trying to prise open a sealed vault. In her estimation the forces were about balanced. Lessis's eyes were closed and there was a line of spittle running from the side of her mouth. Ribela had never seen her so deep in trance.

The struggle went on. At these power levels it was incredibly difficult to maintain consciousness for any length of time. Ribela marveled as this level of power was not normally achievable in the setting of a world like Ryetelth—a cool world of moderate energies. Ribela was not sure she could generate such powerful fields herself, at least in Ryetelth.

And still the girl remained dormant. Yet she had moved the once, so Ribela knew that Lessis had reached her.

Lessis strained. Her spell was in the process of lifting up one corner of the world itself. Her fists were balled and raised beside her shoulders. The spittle running from her mouth had been joined by the tracks of tears, squeezed from her eyes by the sheer effort of what she was attempting.

And Lagdalen gave a sudden jerk.

Ribela almost broke trance from a sudden blast of elation.

Lessis gave a little involuntary moan and tried again.

The effort grew and grew until once again the very walls around them seemed to vibrate. The tension drove the remaining folk out of the ground floor of the Tower, all but for the guard, who were grinding their teeth and twitching in place as they stood on the battlements.

It reached a new excruciating level, painful to endure for more than a few moments, and now blood ran with the spittle from Lessis's mouth.

Then Lagdalen jerked again and her eyes opened and she emitted a long sobbing scream. Her lungs emptied, she sucked in a deep breath, her eyes wide, perilous, her mouth gaping in fear.

Her hand groped toward them.

"Air, light," she gasped, then broke down into coughing. In a moment she recovered. "Alive!" she croaked.

She tried to sit up and failed, her flesh weakened by the long absence of her mind.

Lessis reached out a hand to her. Ribela noted that Lessis was shaking like a leaf.

"Is this real? Can I trust this?"

" 'Tis real girl."

"I can't move."

"You won't be able to for a while, an effect of being out of your body for so long."

"Thanks be . . . Oh, Lady, I was lost, I thought forever, never to see my home again, never to touch my child's face." Tears broke forth on her face. Lessis embraced her.

"It was all my fault."

"No, Lady, it was not. I did not want to let go! I wanted to stay in the skies, flying with the eagle's eyes."

"I know, child, but still I should have brought you out. It shows that you have the power. It is latent, but it is there."

"Hollein?"

"Is well, at the last word we had. He is with General Felix and they are actively driving the enemy back into the mountains. There has been much hard fighting but victory is at hand."

"May the Mother be thanked."

"May She be," said Ribela, who had joined them. They remained there, the girl's hands clasped with those of the witches and Lagdalen's tears ran freely.

The following pages
are an exciting
preview chapter of the
continuing saga
of Bazil Broketail,

Battledragon,

to be published by Roc
in the fall of 1995.

The globe spun beneath the Emperor's fingers until the great tropical continent Eigo was prominent.

"This Path of Power you have mentioned. Tell me more."

"Your Majesty, it is forbidden to be explicit. You understand that this is a glimpse of other worlds, other places on the great sphereboard of destiny, that pearl of possibilities that lies forever in the palm of the Mother."

Her words seemed muffled by the gloom and the luxurious surfaces of the Emperor's private study.

"Humor me, Lady, I beg."

The Lady Lessis, known as the Grey Witch, stood by the window. The pale light of a stormy day illuminated the slender, careworn face of a woman in late middle years. Her clothes were simple and grey, her demeanor was entirely undramatic. It was difficult for those who did not know her to understand her place in history.

"Your Majesty, the Path of Power is one possible path for the world to take. If skills and technology are allowed to develop without control, then our world will take that road. Down it lie weapons more terrible than anything we can imagine."

The Emperor's brows remained lowered, his dark eyes thunderous. This news was not to his taste. She went on.

"What I can tell you is that there are seven dead worlds in the Mother's palm, worlds covered in ash and a dust that never cools under the poisoned clouds. Those worlds took the Path to Power. That road begins with the weapons that are being developed now in the heart of Eigo."

The Emperor pursed his lips and turned the globe with his fingers as he traced out the route from the Argonath to distant Eigo.

"It seems so faraway,"

"It is no farther than Czardha." She lifted an eyebrow.

"The sea voyage alone will take months."

"With favorable winds a fleet could be there in sixty days."

"Winds in midwinter will not be so favorable," the Emperor said.

"Then in ninety days. Once ashore, it will take several months to cross the Ramparts of the Sun and get within range of the enemy. We have a plan. Let me show you. He will know we are coming, of course, but he will not be able to do anything to stop us until we are deep within his guard and have our blade close to his heart. If we are in time, then we shall defeat him and end this threat. If not, then we will fail. But we fail if we do nothing either. This demon we must put back in its bottle."